'TIL ALL THE SEAS RUN DRY

ELEMENTS OF PINING
BOOK 2

ELIZA MACARTHUR

For all of us who have had to go fishing down to rock bottom again.

With just a few friends.

CONTENT WARNINGS

There are certain elements and events of a sensitive nature that I want you to be aware of before you begin, in case reading them would in any way negatively impact your own healing or mental health. Within this book, you will find the following:

- vampirism
- blood
- murder
- explicit sexual content
- vampire suicide/suicidal ideation (not graphic)

Take care, dear reader. Your heart and brain are worth protecting.

O my Luve is like a red, red rose
   That's newly sprung in June;
O my Luve is like the melody
   That's sweetly played in tune.

So fair art thou, my bonnie lass,
   So deep in luve am I;
And I will luve thee still, my dear,
   Till a' the seas gang dry.

Till a' the seas gang dry, my dear,
   And the rocks melt wi' the sun;
I will love thee still, my dear,
   While the sands o' life shall run.

And fare thee weel, my only luve!
   And fare thee weel awhile!
And I will come again, my luve,
   Though it were ten thousand mile.

A Red, Red Rose
by Robert Burns

PROLOGUE

Orkney, 1117

The ocean felt almost thick as she swam in playful circles in the frigid, blue-green water. A school of shimmering, silver fish swarmed past her, and she pressed down powerfully with her fins, slicing through the swarm like a knife, her mouth open, teeth glinting. She swallowed a fish whole before turning sharply and darting through the school a second time.

She let them pass then, her belly full, and her attention turned back to the daggers of sunlight that pierced through the dappled surface of the water. She swam in and out of the beams, lazily making her way up and up before breaking through the veil between sea and sky. Her nostrils flared as she inhaled deeply, filling her lungs with air. Just as she made to dive back to the depths again, something caught her eye on the nearby shore. The surf beat against the beach as she bobbed like a cork on the wild waves and saw... a man.

Since the beginning of humans, her father had seen

sailors and voyagers slip and sink through the icy water into the depths, the remnants of their bones falling to the wilderness of the ocean floor. Throughout her life, she'd watched enough of those bones turn to soft, shifting sand. It was the way of the world, her father told her. Mortal men died, their lives here and gone in a blink.

"Not like you, my treasure," he would say, as they watched the bones fall.

Sometimes, he would swim with her up to the surface, where the light punched through the water, bracketing the fat hulls of ships that sailed upon it. They would watch, eyes barely above the surface, from a distance, while battles raged and men hurled those ships together, their bodies, their weapons, their lives.

And she would cling to her father, breathless, as they watched men fall from the ships and sink beneath. To the dark, velvety depths that waited for them below, past the fish that would pick them clean on the way.

"Igi badbadani u kunib," her father would say. *Put sleep in his open eyes.*

An old saying. An ancient lullaby, sung to children by tired grown-ups, when the world was big and words were pressed into clay with sharp tools.

What would he say to her now, as she watched the unmoving man on the beach? "Igi badbadani u kunib?"

Perhaps.

She and her father had watched the battle raging earlier, the sea boiling between the warships as men screamed and yelled, as they fell into the water. As some of them jumped. Her heart had been in her throat.

"Men love war," her father had said.

What was there to love about it?

This man lay on his back on the sand. His clothes were

torn, and she smelled blood on the wind. The tide was coming in and would soon overtake him. The seabirds circled him, but they had not yet begun to feast. Perhaps he still lived. Before her mind was even made up, she began to swim, darting quickly under the waves and slicing through the water, until the shallow depth forced her to crawl on her belly.

Only then did she reach through herself. Arms stretching from where flippers had been, feet and long, thick legs in place of a tail. Dark, wild, wavy hair clung to her breasts, ochre brown and freckled. Her sealskin, the skin that was home, draped heavily across her back as she crawled on hands and knees from the surf and onto the deserted sand.

The sea birds looked at her, nervous. They knew what she was. They knew *who* she was. The sea god had a thousand daughters, but he knew them all by name, and so, too, did the birds.

She crawled closer, until she could smell the sharp sweat that clung to his clothes beneath the salt water. She had never seen a man this close before. Not a living man, anyway. He was big and broad, with shoulders that seemed to be sculpted from the living rock itself. Long hair, the color of dry sea grass and shot through with just as much light, tangled behind his head, which faced away from her.

His tunic was off, but tucked into the waistband of his trews, stained dark with blood and saltwater. His torso was a ravaged plane of battered skin and wounds. She reached out, her bronze fingers touching his cheek and turning his face toward her. He groaned.

She skittered backwards, ready to race back to the surf, but he was quiet again. She looked down at the rocky sand beneath her knees, seeing his blood seeping in fine tendrils out to the ocean, as if trying to return to the womb of everything.

She had never tried to save a man before. She had never felt like it was her place. She and her family were meant to be spectators, an ancient and eternal audience to the play put on by mortal men in their constant pursuit of more and better.

But something about this man spoke to her, and she found that she didn't want him to die. She didn't want the gulls to pick him down to nothing or to drag him to the water and allow him to sink to the bottom, for his bones to return to shifting, drifting sand.

She crept near again, examining his wounds more closely. A deep stab in his side had caused immense blood loss but likely missed all of his vital organs. His shoulder was clearly dislocated. More stab wounds marred his chest, and she saw another under his ribs. She shook her head. His lung was likely punctured. He might be too far gone to save.

But she wanted to try.

She made a needle out of a sea urchin spine and pulled several of her own long, black hairs for thread. She cleaned his wounds with sea water before she began to carefully close them with quick fingers. Her mother had taught her how to sew and mend, how to make nets. That's how her father had first seen her mother, sitting by the water and making nets for the fishermen in the village.

The man groaned occasionally as she worked, but he did not wake. When all his wounds had been stitched, she sat back and waited. The sun fell to the horizon slowly before slipping beneath it. The stars appeared. She had never spent so long looking at them before. But as she sat next to this man, she looked up and felt almost dizzy from the sight of the millions of stars, so many that it seemed as if she would tumble headlong into the inky depths around them if she weren't careful.

He shivered next to her. She shivered too, cold for the first time. It was unpleasant. She was never cold in her sealskin. But without it, she took the form of a human. She'd only done so a handful of times, having been cautioned by both her mother and father that she was far safer within the confines of her sealskin.

His teeth chattered. He was a mortal man. She was immortal, even in this form, but that did not mean that she could not be uncomfortable. The sealskin would keep her warm. It would keep both of them warm.

She hesitated. "Do not let go of your skin, my love, for any reason," her mother had cautioned her many times. "And above all, do not give your skin to *anyone*."

She was afraid. She'd heard tales of being trapped on land. She did not *want* to share her skin with him. But what if she saved him from his wounds only for him to die of exposure? She could not let him die. Not when she'd worked so hard to save him. And so she slipped her heavy sealskin off of her shoulders and draped it over his body.

He shifted, mumbling incoherently, but still did not wake. She watched the man and the stars, shivering. If she could have taken him to her home, she would have had everything he could possibly need. They would both be warm and safe. But he would not survive it. Men could not breathe in the water the way she could.

She cursed this abandoned beach. She cursed the men who had hurt him, the men who had left him. She cursed the cold. She shifted closer to him and adjusted the skin to cover them both, curling against the side of him that hadn't been stabbed in two different places. She pressed her body against his and breathed warmly against his shoulder. He made a sound that was almost a sigh. Almost a groan. Somewhere in between. He reached out, fumbling with his hand, until he found hers and gripped it tightly in his unconscious delirium. And then he was still. And she was warm.

He didn't wake the next day, or the day after that. But the sun was too bright and his face burned and chapped, and so she took rocks and stacked them to make short pillars and suspended her sealskin over him for shade during the day, dropping it down to blanket them both by night.

She found a stream and used a bladder to bring him fresh water, which she carefully poured between his parched, parted lips. She left him briefly to fish, going at sunset to dive down and fill her belly before returning to warm him.

On the morning of the fourth day, she woke at sunrise. She needed to give him more water. But as she shifted away from him, his hand closed around her arm firmly. He was strong, even after days with a raging fever, and her heart quickened to imagine his strength when he was fed and rested and whole.

She looked up to see his eyes open for the first time. Gray. Like the skin of whales in soft morning light. Gray like the sky on a stormy afternoon.

"Cò thusa?" he rasped.

She knew his language. She knew many languages. One could learn a great deal when they listened, and she was always listening, just below the surface as the ships sailed over the water, hearing songs and conversations. Some of it was magic, no doubt, but she had a knack for it just the same.

He had asked who she was. There was no way to answer that truthfully. *I am the daughter of the sea, of an old god and a mortal woman made immortal.* That would not do. And so she said nothing.

"Cò às a tha mi?" *Where am I?*

She had heard the sailing men refer to these islands as Orkney, though her father had a different name for them. But this man did not speak the language of most of the men she heard nearby.

The man closed his eyes and groaned as he shifted his body. When his eyes opened again, they were wet with tears. He lifted a shaky hand and touched her cheek gently, his rough fingertips barely stroking her skin.

"Tha thu nad aingeal."

She shook her head. She was no angel.

"Tha mi marbh." *I am dead.*

She made a harsh sound in her throat. He nodded. She was afraid. But as the tears streaked down his cheeks, as he dropped his hand from her face and let his arm fall over his face, covering his eyes, she decided that he was no threat to her. Not really. What could one man do to harm the daughter of a god?

"Tha a' Ghàidhlig agam," she said.

I have the Gaelic. I speak Gaelic.

He let his arm drop to his side and looked at her again. She brought the bladder of water to his lips, her hand supporting gently under his head. He did not fight her, but his eyes bored into hers as he drank deeply. She shook her head, a small smile playing on her lips.

The water seemed to invigorate him slightly.

"Dè an t-ainm a th 'ort?" she asked as she wiped at his lips with a scrap of his sun-bleached tunic.

"Callum," he replied, his deep voice a raspy croak.

"Callum," she repeated, liking the way the syllables

sounded as they rolled across her tongue. His name called to mind the image of a dove.

Utnapishtim first sent forth a dove after the great flood. Then a swallow. Then a raven. With no land or place to roost, the dove returned on the first day after the storm. Utnapishtim placed it gently back in its wicker cage. But the raven did not return. Her father liked to tell her that the raven flew far, far away. Across the sea, across the world.

"Callum? A bheil an t-acras ort?" *Are you hungry?*

He nodded slowly. She shifted to rise to her feet, but he reached out, wrapping her wrist in his hand and squeezing, as if to hold her there. She tilted her head toward the nearby driftwood fire, where the fish she had caught before sunrise was roasting on a spit. He released her.

She brought the fish to Callum and fed him with her fingers, flaking off small bites and placing them at his lips. Once or twice, his tongue licked her fingers, and sparkling electricity, like lightning over the sea, raced through her body.

When he had eaten his fill, his eyes grew heavy. But before they closed, he coughed and asked, "Dè an t-ainm a th 'ort?"

She could not answer him immediately. She had been named for the shimmering pearls that brought her mother such delight. The pearls her father had personally woven into the crown her mother wore, glowing softly in her black hair. She knew the ancient word for it, though the language was no longer spoken on land. She knew the Aramaic word for it. Margdnitha. And in Greek, Margaritári. But she did not know it in his Gaelic.

"Margaritári," she whispered.

As his eyes closed, he whispered back, "Marjory."

The syllables trilled from his tongue against his teeth

and the front of his palate, where the name she'd been given by her parents lived more to the back of the throat. They were both beautiful, but the way the r's had rolled from beneath his teeth had thrilled her.

Margaritári, with its soft sounds, felt like the depths, beautiful but muted. The harsh syllables of this *Marjory* gliding from teeth and tongue felt like this world above the water's surface, with its sharp edges and brilliant light and crashing sounds.

She smiled to herself as she stoked the fire and washed her hands in the surf, testing this new name against her own teeth. As she stood to return to Callum's side, her father rose from the water, his dappled skin burnished in the early morning light.

"Come back," he said in the old language.

"I cannot leave him," she replied.

"You saved his life, now leave him to keep it if he can."

But she shook her head, looking back at Callum's sleeping form, his face and torso shaded by her skin, his long, powerful legs sprawled out beyond the reach of the shade.

"You are not responsible for him, daughter," he said, his voice sharp like a knife.

"I am," she replied softly. "Fate brought me to him."

"No," her father insisted. "Your curiosity brought you to him. Your kindness made you stay. But let your wisdom guide you now. Away from him."

"He needs me, Adda."

"Your mother and I need you safe."

"I feel his destiny twines with mine."

"Your destiny is to *live*," he bit out. "That man will bring you nothing but misery. He will hurt you."

"He will not hurt me."

"He *will* hurt you. Mark me, daughter. He will hurt you. He will keep you from us. He will bring about your misery."

The words became prophecy as he repeated it again.

She reached out and placed her hand over her father's heart, where it pulsed violently in his chest, but not with the rhythm of a human heart. It didn't beat with a steady drum pulse like Callum's, but rather with a rush and ebb, like the waves crashing around his feet. The clouds gathered angrily behind him and the sea began to churn. But he was not angry with her. He was frightened, and she knew him well enough to know the difference.

"Adda," she whispered. "I must stay."

Her father clenched his jaw, covering her hand with his own and pressing it against his chest.

"Adda," she said, moving to embrace him, to be folded in his arms and held close, as he had done since she was born of the sea and her mother and his sheer force of will. "What can he do to me? He is a man," she said quietly. "He will live sixty more years at most. When you next blink, I will return to you. To Ama."

But her father shook his head.

"I feel his fate woven with mine, Adda," she whispered again.

"You could cut the thread," he said, his jaw tight, his eyes clenched shut.

It was her turn to shake her head.

"You are the lifeblood of our hearts," he said sadly.

"And I will return to you."

She saw a single tear trickle down his ancient cheek. He hung his head sadly and whispered, "May it be so."

1

Jory jerked awake in the darkness of her bedroom. She could smell the ocean. She reached over and turned off the sound machine on her nightstand, which played white noise because the ocean sounds were such a cheap imitation that it made her heart ache.

She reached for the large, stainless-steel water bottle she kept next to her bed and drained it. Less than ten minutes later, Jory was in her car. The sun lurked in the wings beyond the horizon, casting a dim glow over the world around her without offering any meaningful light. She drove down the empty streets, to the road that led to Cape Flattery on the Makah Reservation.

Before long, her feet were on the trail, the ground soft beneath her boots and the air thick around her. The boots were a special find from a yard sale in Maine a few years back. A woman had bought them to hike the Appalachian Trail with her husband, who passed away suddenly days before their scheduled departure. In her grief, she had kept them in her closet for a few years before purging everything to move to Canada. Jory had paid double what the woman had asked for them—something she never did—and assured her that she would wear them on adventures.

The boots had a story, like all of the treasures Jory collected, but today they felt heavy. Her coat felt like a straitjacket, and her other clothes too tight. They weren't, but she had an itchy feeling that she hadn't felt in a very long time.

Knowing it was too early for tourists to be out on the trail, she took her clothes off, folding them carefully and placing them in a hollowed, fallen tree. She would return for them later. The chilly morning air raised goosebumps on her naked body. The forest floor was soft beneath her feet.

The ravens flew overhead, here at the end of the world to which they had flown. The Quileute called them Báyak. She was still teaching her mouth to say the Makah word for raven, which began with a juicy-feeling click on the inside of the cheek before the sounds shifted and rolled over the tongue and through the lips softly. Nearly a crooning sound.

Jory imagined the ravens enjoyed that crooning, soft name for themselves better than the corvo of Portuguese or kruk of Polish. They seemed their most at home here amongst the towering trees at the edge of a continent. Their glossy black wings flapped overhead as they cried out in the mist.

She came to the trail's end. Cape Flattery was the northwesternmost point of the continental United States, and as she looked over the dizzying height, she saw sea lions on the rocks below and gray whales slipping in and out of the water like needles through a net.

Jory stood at the precipice, breathing in the salt of the air that blew her black hair behind her like a banner. She gripped the handrail with cold fingers, and the memory of her father came back to her.

"He will hurt you. He will keep you from us. He will bring about your misery."

A sob escaped her lips as she listened to water crashing against the cliffs below. The sea lions barked, the whales blew their spray. The gulls cried, and she cried with them, desperately homesick and miserably lonely at the same time.

"Fate brought me to him," she had said. Jory shook her head as she remembered, wiping her nose with the back of her hand.

"Come back," her father had said.

She would. For just a moment. Not home to her family, but home to the sea, to feel the cold surf against her skin, the thick, heavy water surrounding her. It would be cold in a way it never had been with her sealskin, but it was better than nothing.

Sixty years at most, she'd said while her father had looked at her sadly. A blink, she had said. He had wept.

Instead, it had been lifetimes. Lifetimes of struggling and fighting, of fleeing and never knowing how long she'd be able to stay in one place. Never putting down roots. A lifetime of never having a real home, never feeling safe. It had only been in the last fifty years that she'd been able to settle in any kind of comfort or safety.

She had been so sad. So damned sad for so damned long, to the point that sometimes her grief felt like a sealskin in its own right — heavy and thick and slick on her back. She carried her grief where she no longer carried her skin. Because it was gone.

And there was the biggest grief of all. She had lost everything for love. And she *had* loved him. Desperately. Eternally. She had lost him, too. An eternity without him was painful, but to have lost her sealskin along with her love?

Her family? To be trapped immortally in this human body, cut off from home and family? From *safety*? It was unbearable.

Whoever had attacked them was long dead by now. Lifetimes dead. She'd never find them, but it was always possible that her sealskin, the ultimate treasure, would end up in an estate sale someday. Or in a thrift shop. With some family legend about an uncle who hunted seals once upon a time in the cold, northern seas. She never stopped searching for it. What did she have but time?

But sometimes—sometimes the grief was too much to carry. That was when she needed to submerge herself in all that she'd lost. She climbed over the railing, her toes gripping the rocks. The sounds of the forest waking grew louder and the rising light through the clouds made the gray skies look luminous.

Like Callum's eyes.

With a deep breath, Jory closed her eyes, let go of the railing, and leaped into the air, her body angling downward like a blade, plunging toward her target with the sharpness and speed of a thrown dagger. And as she sliced through the shining surface of the water, as the muffled roar of the endless ocean filled her ears, she heard his voice.

"He has hurt you. He has kept you from us. Come back."

She followed the light, her arms and legs kicking strongly and with all the knowledge and muscle memory of millennia. She broke through the surface and looked around, at the sea lions, at the whales, at the gulls.

And she answered her father. "Soon."

2

Callum MacLeod sat behind the immaculate, polished wood desk in a dark office with deep, hunter-green walls and heavy drapery fabrics. He occupied a three-story Greek Revival building on Ellis Square and had paid the historical registry a small fortune to allow what he had paid architects and engineers even more money to execute.

Because Callum had not retained the ornate foyer or drawing room or formal dining room or sitting room or anything at all, really, other than the office where he was currently brooding. Instead, the heavy front door opened to reveal a huge, open space with a large, semi-circular bar flanking the grand staircase in the center, which led up to the open gallery VIP areas on the second floor. The structural engineers had told him he was asking too much. He'd told them that it was his job to tell them what he wanted and their job to figure out how to do it. Money was no object.

The third floor, however, remained sectioned off into rooms as it had been originally. One for his office. Two others merged for a large conference room. A small conference room. He'd imagined the third floor of Sanguine functioning as a safe place for people like him to do business. People who needed to have their meetings in the dark of night. In fact, one such meeting was happening at that very moment between two local vampire businesses hoping to expand their partnership.

He was thirsty, so very thirsty. He hated being thirsty just slightly less than he hated quenching his thirst, and so he sat moodily in his dark office. When *was* the last time he'd eaten? And what time was it now?

Callum looked at his watch, a Vacheron Constantin Tourbillon Chronograph that he remembered his assistant telling him cost $200,000 dollars. But what was money when you'd been making it for almost a thousand years? Sometimes he rubbed elbows with humans who liked to pontificate about "old money." Politicians and socialites mostly. But their slimy talk about "old money" was laughable. His money had its roots in payment he took for fighting a naval battle for some ancient earl nearly a thousand years ago. He'd hoarded it, not spending a penny. Because what need had he had for money when he'd had *her*?

She'd been a miracle, a marvel, a gift to him from the gods. And he had worshipped her. They had lived in a small cottage by the sea, on an island in Scotland where the sheep had outnumbered the people several times over. They had eaten what could be gotten from the land and sea, worn what could be gotten from the sheep, and burned driftwood in their hearth. He'd buried that money and not dug it up until after she'd been gone. When the idea of living in a now-empty cottage by the sea had been unbearable because no matter how many times the tide had washed them away, he would still see her bloodstains on the sand.

And so he'd taken his money and he'd left. Somewhere along the line, he'd invested some of it. And his old money had become more old money. And then half a millennium passed, and his old money became more money than one person could ever spend in a lifetime, spread out across different accounts and businesses. He paid people good new money to track that old money, to grow it into more.

That money had gotten him into ballrooms and throne rooms alike. He had property on every continent but Antarctica. He dressed like a man who could use hundred-dollar bills as kindling. He employed thousands under various aliases in hundreds of businesses, some within the scope of the law and others... well, the others lived in the murky edges of rules that clung to the law like a parasite. Not legal, perhaps, but... useful. *Helpful.*

But none of it meant anything.

Callum spun in his chair to stare out the windows behind his desk. They looked down on the gardens behind the club. Savannah was full of gardens. Gardens were utterly useless to a nightclub and even less useful to people like him, people who couldn't look upon flowers during the day. He maintained the garden so that his employees would have a nice place to go for their breaks, smoking or otherwise. In the spring, he had it on good authority that the azaleas bloomed a wild, nearly neon pink and tumbled over one another in heaps along the brick garden wall.

Several of his associates supervised daytime activities, when Callum was locked away deep under the ground. Always with security camera footage rolling, always with his phone, but shut away. Those associates always complained about how the azalea pollen stuck to their cars, their clothes, the inside of their noses. And yet on the security cameras, he could see them bend to smell the flowers anyway.

The azaleas were so different, foreign creatures entirely, to the Scottish heather and bluebells of his life before. But he was haunted by visions of a black-haired beauty with skin the color of clay and strong, calloused hands bending her nose to the heather, gathering up heaping armfuls of bluebells and putting them in earthen pots around a tiny, seaside cottage.

Of that same woman stuffing a mattress with heather so that whenever he'd rolled over, whenever she'd shifted closer, whenever he'd thrust deeply into her body, into her heat, he'd smelled heather.

She would love the azaleas. She would love the magnolias and camellias and dogwoods. She would love the sticky heat and the way the air always smelled—Spanish moss and flowers and, underneath it all, decay. She would smell everything—things that no one else could smell. He used to tease her that he needn't bother with dogs because she could scent dinner for them. And she'd laughed but would go out and come back with a fat rabbit dangling by the ears just the same.

Once, just after buying the Savannah property, he'd gone to the garden at midnight. Stepping out of the club's back door and into the already warm spring had made his suit feel heavy and tight, but he'd gone anyway, his Ferragamo oxfords scraping against the brick path. He'd approached the azaleas like they could bite him, like he should be afraid of them. He, who feared almost nothing. He'd bent his head, gathering a stem from the bush and bringing it to his nose.

They smelled to him like the distilled, hundred-proof

version of what flowers should smell like. They overpowered him. Too sweet. Too strong. Too... much. He'd felt his chest tighten.

How very like his life. How very fucking like his life. To want the earthy musk of heather and get the cloying perfume of azaleas. To want to live long and be strong for the duration and to be given immortality instead. To find the most perfect love and have it ripped from his hands before he could do a thing to save it.

Callum had crushed the blooms in his hand and gone back inside. He hadn't returned to the garden since. As it was, staring out into the night, Callum couldn't see the bloomless azaleas. He could only make out the shapes of the magnolia trees along the back of the property because of the fairy lights that his assistant had hung up, insisting they were romantic.

As if people needed romance while smoking cigarettes on fifteen-minute breaks. As if his bartenders needed romance while scrolling on their phones absently, taking their shift break outside where it didn't smell like beer and grenadine and the bass didn't reverberate in your ribcage like a second heartbeat. As if his bouncers needed romance while they silently devoured their keto meals or protein bowls or whatever the fuck human men who spent too much time in a gym ate.

That wasn't fair. They weren't all human.

He made it a point to hire as many people as he could who needed a safe place to work where they could get time off for full moons or fairy circles or whatever the hell else was required of people who were... *not quite* human. Savannah was stuffed with otherworldly creatures. Ghost tours were a dime a dozen, and witches made a pretty penny telling fortunes and selling crystals and potions and, if you knew who to ask, spells. Among other things. Less... legal things. Things that lurked in those same murky edges of legality that, while not legitimate, were certainly useful.

Sanguine was like his other nightclubs all over the world. They operated as luxury spaces marketed for human consumption. Delicious drinks, top-tier dance music, and an atmosphere that made a person feel like they were a part of something special, something expensive, whether their mini dress was couture or consignment.

That was the front. But in each of his clubs, he ran a different sort of experience for creatures like himself. He was a networker. He found willing blood donors, people who thought it thrilling to have someone like him feeding at their throats. They were compensated handsomely and only glamoured enough to prevent them from telling anyone where they really went when they left the dance floor.

His clubs were the safest place for humans to feel that electrifying thrill of unsafety. His team employed biometrics that would send shocks through the vampire feeder when the donor's blood volume dropped below a certain point. If the vampire ignored the warning, they would be removed and their membership revoked without question.

Sanguine's feeding salon was blood red, with comfortable settees designed specifically for the comfort of both the donor and recipient. His patrons were welcome to partake in their meal and then relax while his employees took care of the donors. The humans would be taken home, given IV fluids and a meal, and then, if they chose, glamoured again to forget the experience, the memories of their donation replaced by memories of being put in a cab by a caring friend who then made sure they ate before passing out.

The club was packed every night it was open, even during the week, and Callum employed a large staff to keep it running. Housekeeping and hospitality, bartenders and barbacks, bouncers and security, DJs, promoters, management—almost all of them not quite humans. And, in some cases, not at all human. Though never, ever a witch.

Callum did not mess with the witches of Savannah. They had an understanding. He would not interfere with their businesses or income, and they would not interfere with his. They could operate alongside one another, feeding on the pockets of tourists, feeding on the necks of others, and never have to share.

But their livelihoods relied on secrecy. Witches could be out now, as long as they plied their trade with knowing winks and a lighthearted delivery, as if to say, "Don't worry. Magic doesn't *really* exist. This is just a souvenir shop with a good story."

Just like they said, "Don't worry. Tarot is just a party game."

But he had no such luxury. If more humans discovered the truth about vampires, they would hunt them to extinction. And while Callum had long since grown weary of immortality, if he was going to check out of this earthly realm, he wasn't going to do it writhing in agony as the blinding southern sun turned his cells to dust, popping them like bubble wrap while he screamed because the humans wanted to "set him free."

But when Esther MacLaren had tripped into his club one evening with a job application in hand, he hadn't been able to resist hiring her. She was alone, covenless, and utterly disconnected from the establishment.

She was beautiful, funny, and carried herself with a confidence that would drive patrons wild as they tried to gain her attention. Her first night behind the bar, Callum watched as men held up twenty-dollar bills between pinched fingers, waving them overhead like flags, begging for her notice, for her to lean her forearms on the bar in front of them and take their orders for Bud Light or Fireball or Red Bull mixed with Crown Royal, a drink that seemed like a criminal waste of alcohol.

Esther was magnetic because she didn't know she was magnetic at all. She simply moved around the world wholly as herself. Callum could recognize her beauty and her spark, even if neither held any interest for him. She was an asset behind the bar.

But she was most valuable for her elixirs.

Esther cooked up potions that went into signature drinks that existed off-menu. He told her they were like the Starbucks secret menu—official drinks sanctioned by the club, but if you didn't know about them, you wouldn't know about them. That had satisfied her, and she had made gallons each week for the club.

They made the drinker experience a deep, encompassing sense of euphoria, a lightness of being that made everything sound better, taste better, feel better. Dancing felt like sex. Drinking felt like ecstasy. And having a creature latched onto one's neck for dear life, their blood pulsing thickly into that creature's sucking, moaning, worshipful mouth to sustain life for another week of immortality? Transcendent.

The elixirs were so potent that they lived in the blood and gave the vampires that same sense of weightless, lightness of being. Which, after hundreds of years of monotonous existence, could not be priced.

But then Esther had happened upon the salon. She had wandered into the lower level and seen the feedings and gotten it all wrong.

Or perhaps she hadn't gotten it *all* wrong, but she hadn't

gotten it *right* either. She had seen the facts—vampires feeding from the human patrons for whom she'd mixed drinks, human beings carried up the back stairs. But what she hadn't seen was the finesse. The consent. The waivers. The waiting vans with professionals to care for the donors and bring them safely home. She didn't see that those donors were in better, safer hands than if they had called a rideshare and ended up somewhere they didn't intend to be.

This was fact. Because nobody on his payroll would dare to cross him. They wouldn't dare to skim blood off the top or hurt his donors. But Esther couldn't have known that. She only saw the limp, ecstatic poses of the donors, the ravenous growling of his vampire members. And she did exactly what he worried she'd do.

She ran.

What surprised him, however, was the revenge she took. Esther MacLaren made a dupe elixir. One that looked and tasted exactly the same to a human, but when consumed by a vampire would cause horrible sickness. Vomiting. Headache. Chills and aches. They hadn't died—they couldn't die, not like that anyway—but they had, every one, experienced the hell of a superhuman hangover for days.

And then, after rendering his vampire patrons catatonic, she had snuck the humans out the back, split her tips among them, and called them rideshares. She'd finished her shift, cleaned out the till, and run. He should've caught her that night, spoken truth to her and shown her the facts, the finesse, and then glamoured her into forgetting it entirely. But he'd had two dozen violently ill vampires on his hands and a PR nightmare looming. By the time he'd figured out what she'd done, she was gone.

Callum had spent the last six months chasing her across the country—sometimes personally, other times via associates he hired to track her. But she always slipped just out of his reach, sliding between his fingers like water. And now, staring out at the dark garden, at the murky shapes of magnolias and the glinting of fairy lights, he felt tired.

He was so goddamn tired of it all. Tired of chasing Esther MacLaren, a broke, thirty-five-year-old witch with an art degree who was nothing to him but a liability. He was tired of barely missing her. Tired of traveling. Tired of smelling magnolias and azaleas and wishing they were heather. Tired of sinking his teeth into throats that tasted like vanilla sugar body lotion and not the salt of the sea, the earthiness of sweat and *her*.

He was tired of old money and new money and old baggage and older grief. He was tired of missing someone who'd been dead almost as long as he'd been immortal. Tired of wanting her. Tired of trying to fill the gaping hole in his heart with people who might resemble her to an extent but who lacked the bright, watching eyes and almost carnivorous smile.

And he was still hungry, which made it all worse. Because he was going to be forced to taste that body lotion, with its cloying scents of sugar and flowers like azalea and lily and what someone in a lab thought smelled like lavender. Or "Ocean Crush," which actually smelled far more like cough medicine than the actual sea. He would be forced to press his tongue against a throat and taste those cloying, artificial flavors alongside the tang of blood, sucking long and deep and hard to get it over with as fast as possible.

Because he didn't want azaleas, and he never had. He wanted heather and bluebells and to drag his tongue up and down the long column of a throat that tasted like earth and sea.

He pushed the call button for his secretary, who had a desk in a nook just outside his office. "Penny."

"How can I help you, Callum?" Penny asked brightly, her voice coming through the speaker as clearly as if she were sitting next to him.

"I'm hungry," he said wearily.

"Of course. Do you have a preference? Anyone in particular I should call?"

"Nay," he replied. "I dinnae care who it is. Just—Penny?"

"Yes?"

"Can you have them wash their neck before they come? I dinnae want them to put anything on."

"Of course. I'll have someone up in a jiffy."

"Thank you, Penny," he said, thinking about how he should give her a bonus.

She was chipper and helpful and eager to anticipate his needs. And she said things like "in a jiffy," which were wholesome and made no sense to him at all but amused him anyway for reasons he couldn't explain. The way the language was the same but the vernacular so different.

Twenty minutes later, Penny knocked on his office door.

"Callum?" she said, easing it open. "I have your donor here."

"Send them in," he replied, flipping on the lamp on his desk.

Penny stepped aside and made room for a rangy man of medium height to walk through the door. He was built like an MMA fighter, like someone who had honed their body by getting the shit kicked out of them and then jumped up to do it again. He wore low-slung black jeans and a black V-neck T-shirt with black combat boots only laced halfway. Every inch of visible skin from his jaw to his fingernails was covered in vibrant tattoos.

"Hello," Callum said, standing to shake his hand. "I'm Callum MacLeod."

The man extended his hand. "Robbie Cain."

Callum sat back down in his chair, the expensive leather creaking gently. He gestured to the chair in front of his desk. Robbie sat on the edge of the desk instead. Callum arched an eyebrow at him, and Robbie smirked in response.

"How would you like to proceed, Robbie?" Callum asked, leaning back in his chair and tenting his fingers.

"I'm easy." Robbie shrugged, and Callum snorted. "But before we start, I wondered if you were hiring."

"I dinnae hire dedicated blood donors."

"No. I mean, sure if you like what I've got. But I meant for a *job*, job."

Callum tipped his head to the side slightly. "What are your skills, Robbie?"

Robbie reached out to play with the pens in the silver julep cup on Callum's desk. His tattooed fingers were nimble as they slipped over and around the pens, and if Callum's eyes were any slower, any more human, he would have missed the pen that Robbie slipped out of the cup.

"Put that back."

Robbie grinned at him.

"This isnae the best showing, Robbie. Do you think I make it a regular practice to hire thieves?"

"Just a party trick," Robbie said with a bright smile.

As if to further annoy Callum, or maybe further his point, Robbie opened his palm to display a knickknack that Callum knew came from Penny's desk.

"I dinnae care for you messing with my employees," he said sternly, sitting forward in his chair.

Unintimidated, Robbie shrugged. "I'll give it back."

"See that you do."

"But about a job," Robbie began, "I've got a lot of skills."

"Like what? Wreaking sexual havoc in a kitchen by titillating front of the house?"

Robbie snorted a laugh. "Besides that. How'd you know I—"

"Lucky guess. You have that"—Callum waved a hand—"air about you."

"Well, if that's what you're in the market for, sure, but a buddy of mine said that you're looking for someone. And I'm really good at finding things."

"And what do you do when you find them?"

"Whatever you tell me to, boss."

Callum snorted again. The impertinence was almost charming. Almost.

He sat up straighter. "How exactly do you propose to find this...." He let his voice drop off.

"I know people."

"You know people?" Callum sneered. "What kind of people?"

"Don't worry about that. Just believe me when I say that I can find her."

"I never said it was a woman."

"No, but word on the street is that you're looking for a certain witch who almost chucked your operations off a cliff. And I know I can find her."

"You're verra confident," Callum said softly, sitting back again in his chair. "I suppose that I could offer you a trial employment. If you can indeed help me find what I'm looking for, we can discuss longer-term options."

Robbie smiled again. "You won't regret it," he said, a hint of desperation creeping into his voice. Callum liked that. He liked hunger. He liked rough edges. He could hone edges.

The thrill of maybe finding Esther, of having

momentum after so many near misses, was heady. So heady that he almost forgot the hunger that brought Robbie to him in the first place.

But then Robbie stood. "You still want to grab a bite, boss?" he said with a smirk, as if his face couldn't do anything else.

"I do," Callum replied with a sigh.

Robbie walked over to the couch that sat along the wall. Callum stood and followed but he didn't sit next to Robbie. Instead, he yanked the couch away from the wall.

"Jesus, dude, warn me next time!" Robbie shouted.

"Dude?"

"Boss?" Robbie asked.

"Boss works," Callum replied. "Or Callum. I don't give a fuck."

Robbie smiled a full smile, showing all of his teeth. Then he leaned his head back against the back of the couch. Callum saw Robbie's fists clenched at his sides. Callum could smell the adrenaline wafting off of him. For all his easy swagger, Robbie was nervous.

"You seem tense, Robbie. Why?"

"Oh, you know. Virgin neck."

Callum could almost taste the lie.

"Hardly," Callum replied.

"Fine. I don't like pain, alright? I'd appreciate it if you didn't hurt me any more than you have to."

"This from someone who has had needles jammed into their neck millions of times. Literally."

"That's different. It's different when I sign up for pain," Robbie said in a quiet voice.

"You signed up for this."

"It's still different. There's pain, and then there's *pain*. You know? I like pain. I don't like *pain*."

Understanding that distinction more than Robbie knew, Callum sighed. "I'll be careful," he replied, circling around the couch so that he was standing between it and the wall.

Feeding wasn't overtly sexual. Or it didn't have to be. It never was for Callum. Even though he could appreciate the lean lines of Robbie's body and the way his mouth lifted to one side more than the other when he smiled, when he looked at the corded muscle of Robbie's throat, the only thing he felt was thirsty.

Robbie sat up, his fight-or-flight instincts in hyperdrive.

"Relax, Robbie," Callum said, resting a heavy hand on Robbie's shoulder. "You'll know it's coming. I willnae surprise you."

Robbie nodded and slowly rested his head against the couch again. "I've just fed some really careless people."

"I am never careless, Robbie." *Not anymore.*

Callum bent forward and gently pressed Robbie's head to the side to expose more of his neck. Robbie gritted his teeth and clenched his jaw.

"Relax, mo charaid," he said, squeezing Robbie's shoulder.

Robbie looked up into Callum's eyes, and he could see that they were whiskey-colored. He saw the fine lines around them that came from squinting into the sun. Callum had the same lines from his youth.

"Callum?" Robbie asked in a quiet voice.

"Aye?"

"I don't want more scars."

Callum laughed, but as he did, he looked at Robbie's neck, at the beautiful floral design that spanned it, like spring rising from depths of his shirt.

"I willnae disturb your art," he said. He meant it too.

He was careful as he leaned forward and fit his mouth

against Robbie's throat, as he placed his fangs gently against the vein, as he bit down, puncturing precisely.

Robbie gasped.

And then Callum pressed his tongue to Robbie's throat and sucked, tasting the coppery brightness of his blood mingled with salt. It wasn't the salt of the sea. It wasn't the earthy, loamy taste he'd been hunting for. But it wasn't vanilla sugar body lotion. It was sweat. Honest, clean sweat.

Robbie sighed and relaxed back against the couch cushions as Callum loomed behind him, drinking deeply. But piercing through his grief, his ever-present weariness of it all, was the thrill of anticipation.

He would catch Esther MacLaren. And he could put this whole nightmare to bed for good.

3

Esther MacLaren was a witch from Savannah who had crash-landed into Jory's life and was now sitting in Jory's desk chair, her leg bouncing wildly underneath the surface. Esther had a chaotic vibrance about her that had drawn Jory immediately, and they'd become fast friends.

Her new friend had gotten into some trouble when she'd walked in on a vampire feeding scheme where patrons of a nightclub were being drugged and fed upon and then disposed of. It made Jory sick to think of. There had been a momentary flare of panic in Jory's gut when Esther had told her that the vampire was called Callum MacLeod. But then she remembered that it couldn't be *her* Callum MacLeod. He'd been dead for centuries. *Lifetimes.*

Esther was hiding out with Jory for the night until her car was finished at the mechanic. She'd be gone by sunrise the next day, running not only away from *this* Callum MacLeod, but trying to get out of town before Hank Dove could stop her. Jory knew of Hank. It was a small town. Everyone knew *of* everyone. He was a recluse. The strong, hulking, silent type. And Esther had fallen head over heels in love with him.

Jory's earlier itchiness persisted. Not literally, but a phantom itchiness that usually meant something was about to happen.

"Are you okay?" Esther asked, always in tune to the people around her, and Jory nodded.

Esther raised a skeptical eyebrow but didn't push. They sat in silence for a long while, Esther drinking her coffee, Jory sipping her water. *Always so thirsty, lass,* the deep voice of her memories said.

"Do you..." Esther ventured, setting her coffee down on the desk. "Do you want to see a picture of Callum so that you can tell me if you see him sniffing around town?"

It seemed like a good idea. Especially if shit went sideways. Jory nodded. Esther grabbed her phone and began typing with both thumbs.

"Here," she said after a moment before handing her phone to Jory.

Jory sucked in a breath.

Hair the color of dried sea grass. Gray eyes, like the slick backs of whales at dawn. The thick eyebrows, stern jaw. *It cannot be,* her brain screamed. *It is not possible.*

And yet, for a man to look so identical to his ancestor after nearly a thousand years of genetic dilution and distribution was just as impossible. Moreso, perhaps.

Jory felt the fat tears slide down her cheeks as she stared at his picture. He was *alive.* She stroked a gentle fingertip down his cheek, which did nothing but move the image on the phone.

"Jory?" Esther asked hesitantly. "Do you know him?"

Jory bit her lips between her teeth as her eyebrows came together. A tear dripped off her chin and fell to the floor.

Her brain felt like it was spinning wildly in her head, lights and colors blurring in a dizzying whir like a carousel out of control. It came back to her. The attack. Lying by the sea's edge as she bled and bled. Hearing his shout of dismay behind her. She remembered her dress feeling wet and heavy, from blood and seawater, clinging to her skin as Callum hauled her torso into his lap.

"Marjory. Marjory, mo cridhe. Nay, nay, nay, nay. You cannae—I cannae—You cannae leave me alone," he'd whispered against her hair, clutching her against his chest.

There'd been so much blood. It couldn't possibly have all been hers. His sun-bleached shirt had been soaked red with it. He'd been so cold, too cold to live, and she remembered shivering as she closed her eyes, feeling the breeze feathering against her neck, her cheek, the soft shell of her ear.

She was the daughter of a god. Immortal. Eternal. It would take more than a knife to end her life, or whatever had slashed her throat. But her body needed sleep to heal, and so, wrapped in her beloved's arms, she had allowed herself to sink into it, deep and dreamless. But when she had awoken, she'd been alone on the sand. Callum was gone, not even a body left behind. The sun had risen and begun to set; the tide had come and gone.

Jory remembered standing, stroking her fingers along her throat and shoulder, feeling the healed, whole skin beneath them. She crept to their cottage, ears pricked and listening for any danger. But there had been nothing. Not even the sea birds shrieked.

The cottage was dark, their bed empty, and there was no sign of Callum. His sword was gone and with it, her sealskin. From time to time during their years together, she had let him wear it for warmth. So great was her trust.

He'd been so cold holding her. Perhaps he had lived. Perhaps he had followed their attacker. She had waited for him.

But as the days turned into months and he still had not returned, Jory had no choice but to accept that he had died, either from his wounds or at the hands of the enemy, whoever they were. The loss of him had been devastating. The loss of her sealskin equally so. The loss of both at once had nearly broken her.

Jory stared into the gray eyes on the phone screen, eyes she *knew*, once so full of warmth and good humor. They glinted coldly in his harsh face. But if Callum was alive, that meant he hadn't been killed. And if he hadn't been killed, it meant that he had... *abandoned* her.

But he'd taken the skin with him? Did he know? How could he have known?

It had been on the tip of her tongue to tell him for years. She had wanted to tell him what she was, *who* she was. He would never betray her, she swore to herself. But even still every time she tried, she remembered her mother's warning: *"You must never tell a mortal soul. They will take advantage of you. They will steal you."*

He hadn't stolen her, but he'd trapped her all the same.

Jory heard her father's voice. *"He will hurt you. He will keep you from us. He will bring about your misery."* Her body went cold. *"Never,"* she'd said to her father. *"He would never hurt me."*

Jory took a deep, shuddering breath. She handed the phone back to Esther, her fingers lingering just a moment before she released it to her friend's grasp. "I don't know this man."

It was true. Because the man she had loved, the man she thought she'd known, didn't exist. He'd been an apparition.

A falsehood. Whoever Callum MacLeod was now, whoever he'd been then, it didn't matter. Because she'd loved a lie.

Jory stood and turned to leave the office, to return to the stacks of denim and wool that she had so carefully curated for her shop. Her treasures. Before she left, she looked at Esther over her shoulder and said, "But whoever he is, I won't let him hurt you."

She walked out into her shop and stood behind the counter, staring out at the bleak afternoon. She looked down and picked up the mother-of-pearl brooch she'd been polishing, gliding her thumb over the iridescent surface. She felt her grief, heavy and familiar in her chest, but in the silence, she could feel it shift and change.

For hundreds of years, she had mourned the loss of her great love. She had mourned her connection to home and her family as well, but it had been worth it. The great loss of her sealskin, her one ticket home, had been worth it because she'd gotten to taste the kind of love they wrote sagas about, the kind of love people only dreamed of. It hadn't lasted, but she'd had it. She'd *held* it, and so it had all been worth it.

But staring at the trinket in her hands, the grief suddenly felt far less like sadness and far more like rage. Because it *hadn't* been worth it. It had been a lie. All of it. Their life, years together in that cottage by the sea. When he'd stroked his thumbs against her cheeks and told her that she was the beating heart that lived outside of his chest.

It seemed he'd been as talented at acting as he'd been with a sword.

Jory heard a crack and felt a quick snap of pain at the same moment. She looked down and saw the brooch in pieces, crushed in her hands, the jagged edges having sliced her palms and let loose ribbons of deep, red blood. Jory closed her eyes. The brooch had been beautiful, the mother-of-pearl laid over the shape of a gingko leaf. Her regret was sharp at having destroyed such a beautiful piece, forgetting for a moment an inhuman amount of strength that she had become quite adept at masking.

But amidst the pain in her hand and the pain in her chest, dull and ever present, Jory began to feel a spark of something that felt an awful lot like hope. Callum was coming, if he wasn't already here. He would know where to find the sealskin, and she would make him tell her, no matter what it took. He owed her that. *At the very least,* he owed her that.

And she would take what she was owed.

4

Callum's wickedly sharp knife slipped easily between the skin and flesh of the apple in his hands, making a soft *shrrrr* sound. He peeled a thin, continuous ribbon. He sat at Hank Dove's kitchen table, feeling his host's loathing radiating toward him in waves. "Host" was, perhaps, generous seeing as how Callum and his men had broken into Hank's home and were holding him a *bit* hostage until Esther MacLaren arrived.

Which she would. Any moment now. Callum would stake every dime he had on that fact. Because she loved Hank, and people did ridiculous, dangerous, ill-advised things for the people they loved.

"I thought vampires couldn't eat food," Hank growled.

Callum glanced up, surprised by the statement. Hank was a formidable man, as tall as Callum. He had a thick beard that was just on the kept side of ragged and dark hair that was pulled back into a little bun at the crown of his head. Callum looked back at the apple in his hands, at the juicy, white flesh contrasting starkly against the bright, waxy peel.

Callum chuckled. "You thought right. We cannae eat food. But I picked this habit up when I was a human a verra long time ago. It calms my nerves. Helps me think."

"Calms your nerves," Hank repeated, crossing his arms and leaning back in his chair, his eyebrows drawn tightly, angrily, together.

Callum lifted a shoulder in an elegant half shrug. He remembered peeling apples for his Marjory. She would bake the apples into tarts and throw the peels to the sea birds. He remembered thinking how wasteful it was, but how he had also never seen a person so breathtakingly beautiful as Marjory when she was by the sea, the long, red ribbons of apple skin trailing from her fingers as she stood in the face of the wind. The last of the peel dropped from the perfectly smooth, perfectly bare apple. The ribbon Callum had made of it lay in a delicate tangle on the tabletop.

Callum held the apple out for Hank, who shook his head tightly. Callum sighed and tossed the apple into the air. Robbie reached out and caught it, and a sharp snap rent the air as he took a bite. The crunching of the apple between Robbie's teeth was loud in the otherwise silent kitchen. For the first time in a long time, Callum missed food. He could *taste* that apple. He could taste the salty sea air. Salty skin... salty blood.

The door flew open, revealing the witch who had given him nothing but trouble for months. Robbie swept in quickly, grabbing her from behind and holding her against his chest, his hand muffling her scream.

"Easy now," Robbie said, his mountain twang thick as molasses.

"Get your fucking hands off of her," Hank barked, hurtling himself to his feet.

It must have felt like everything happened so fast to all of them. Hank had blinked, and there she was. But to Callum, it was like watching an underwater ballet. The moves slow, the next moves telegraphed. He'd heard the car pull onto the street. Smelled Esther getting out of it. Saw all of the tiny muscles in Hank's face ripple with his anger when he saw her.

Hank took a half step towards Esther and Robbie, toward Callum, and said, "Let her go."

Callum nodded his head, and Robbie released Esther. She stumbled into Hank's waiting arms. He crushed her against his chest and pressed his nose and mouth against the top of her head, inhaling deeply with a slack look of relief.

They whispered to one another, and it made Callum's heart ache. He remembered laying on a mattress stuffed with heather, whispering with his Marjory in the darkest part of the night, brushing her dark curls away from her face with gentle fingertips.

Esther was touching Hank's clenched jaw with a careful hand, whispering softly to him, though Callum heard every word. Callum set his jaw. The sooner he did what needed to be done, the sooner he could be gone from this place, from the painful reminder that true love did exist even if his was long gone from the world.

"You've been verra hard to get a hold of, Esther," he said wearily.

"On purpose," she replied through gritted teeth.

"I've gone to a great deal of trouble and expense to find you, to make sure you're safe, lass."

"You didn't need to find me. I didn't do anything wrong," she snapped at him, and he arched an eyebrow.

"In your opinion, stealing an entire night's worth of

profits isnae wrong? Poisoning two dozen club patrons isnae wrong?"

"I didn't poison them, and you know it," she said.

The lion had a natural distrust of the hyena, the seal a distrust of the bear. And he had a similar but no less a hard-learned distrust of witches.

Esther blurted out, "If you really tracked me this far and this long for a few thousand dollars, I'll pay you back. I'll sell all my shit, and I'll pay you back."

Callum stood slowly from his seat, weary of the entire business. Esther took a step backwards and into Hank's body. Callum closed that distance. Hank tried to push Esther behind him, but she resisted.

"Just take me, alright?" Esther shrieked. "Leave him alone, and I'll go with you!"

"I was hoping you'd say that," Callum replied, a slow smile spreading like honey across his face. "I dinnae care for big scenes."

No doubt she thought he meant to bite her, to kill her. But the truth was that Callum hadn't killed a human in a very, very long time, and he had no desire to do so now. But he did need to glamour her. And for that, he needed to be close and have her eye contact. He loomed over Esther, and she trembled, staring into his eyes with the stunned terror of a deer about to be struck by a car.

He wondered what she saw in his eyes when the door flew open and a husky voice barked, "If you harm one hair on either of their heads, Callum MacLeod, I'll gut you like a fish and then stake you to the floor."

Callum froze.

It was *impossible.* She was *dead.* He'd seen her. He'd held her lifeless body in his arms as the waves lapped at his feet, sliding away from them and taking her blood with them.

But as Callum whipped his head around, as he saw her slide out of Robbie's reach as deftly as if she'd evaporated and reappeared, as he looked into her brilliant, jade-green eyes, he felt as if his heart could *almost* start beating again, pounding in his chest for the first time in nearly a thousand years. Because inexplicably, *impossibly*, she was *here*.

"Marjory. Mo cridhe," Callum whispered as he beheld a ghost. "Is it really you?"

"No thanks to you, you son of a bitch."

5

ORKNEY, 1126

The full moon rose over the ocean, a gleaming mirror in an otherwise black night. Marjory sat on the beach. She should have waited back at the cottage. That's what a normal person would do, whiling away the long hours in the flickering glow of a warm hearth.

But Marjory was not a normal person, which is why she found herself sitting in the damp, cold sand while the wind blew and the waves crashed like thunder over and over. He would be home soon. He'd been gone for more than a month, called away for his weapon of a body and his sword, and she would never, *never* get used to that. She would never grow accustomed to the heavy feeling of worry that sat like a stone in her belly.

It was a fairly new emotion. In her life before him, her life in the sea, she hadn't worried for much. Her father was a god. Her mother was immortal. *She* was immortal. What was there to worry about? Even the battles of men that boiled the sea above her head hadn't truly worried her. Someone would win, more would lose, and sleep would close all of their eyes eventually regardless.

In her old life, worry had been more of a shifting sort of restlessness, something she felt when she couldn't find something she had misplaced or wondered which of her sisters she had annoyed. At the time, it had felt like everything. But now, as she sat on the shore because she could not spend one more moment in that cottage waiting for him with a rigid back and a pounding heart, she realized that this—*this* —was worry.

Because Callum was not immortal. She had been working up the courage to tell him everything, to tell him what she was. But before she did that, she wanted to talk to her father and gain some promises. Her father had fallen in love with her mother, a human, and granted her eternity by his side. Surely he would not deny his favorite daughter the same.

As if she'd summoned him, he stepped from the sea.

She ran to him, leaping into his arms. "Adda," she breathed into his neck as he held her close, as he'd always done, since she was small.

"How I have missed you," he said, setting her down. His weathered face was softened by his smile.

"How is Ama?"

"She misses you too. She finished her tapestry."

Marjory smiled. "I can't wait to see it."

Her father's eyes sparked with joy. "Then you will return with me?"

"I hope to, yes."

"Let us go, then. I never get to surprise her anymore."

Marjory took a step back and her father's brow pinched in confusion.

"Adda, I want to return to you and Ama. But not without him."

Her father scoffed. "He is a man. He cannot go where we go."

"Ama did."

He locked his gaze on hers. In his eyes, she saw millennia. She could see his hope and his anger and his love churning.

His voice was tight when he said, "Your Ama goes where I go because I love her enough to swell the seas and drown the land."

She stood to her full height, drawing her shoulders back, her dark waves billowing and snapping behind her like a flag in a hurricane. "And I love him enough to make the seas run dry."

He was quiet for a long time. Bargaining with himself, no doubt. Preparing to bargain with her.

"And if I refuse?"

She looked up into his face, blinking back sudden, stinging tears. Callum could be wounded or dying at this very moment. He'd been due home a week ago. That's what the message he'd passed along to her had said. He was a week late.

But if he came home—*when* he came home, she said to herself—she could protect him. She could make it so he could not be killed, he could not be taken from her. Her father could give her this gift of his life, and she would never ask him for another thing again.

"If you refuse, I will spend eternity with a broken heart."

She wasn't trying to lay guilt at his feet. It was simply the truth. She would never stop grieving Callum if she lost him. She knew this deep down in her bones, between the marrow and the delicate web of mineral and salt. Her heart would break, and there would be no fixing it. Her father was the god of the sea and storm, not the god of the underworld.

He might make a man immortal, but he could not raise him from the dead.

"Please, Adda," she whispered, her voice crackling and thick. "Please."

He sighed, a long, weary sigh that she felt as much as she heard.

"I cannot deny you anything, it seems. Even when I wish to."

With a bright peal of laughter, she leapt into his arms again.

He patted her back before setting her away from him. "I do not like this. I do not like *him*. But I love you. Your joy is my joy. Your sorrow is my sorrow. I only hope you do not come to regret this."

"I won't," she gasped. "He is so good. You'll see. He would never hurt me."

Her father nodded. "Then I will return in a week. That should give you time to prepare him for his new life. May he come to deserve it."

And with one last kiss to her cheek and a squeeze of her shoulder, he was gone, vanishing into the depths. She paced the beach for a while, too full of energy to sit still, all hope and fear and anticipation. After a while, she sat down once more in the sand, willing her breath to slow and her heart to beat more steadily instead of the battle frenzy it had been tattooing inside of her ribcage for the last week.

He was close. Maybe it seas her magic. Perhaps it was merely their connection. But she could feel him drawing nearer. He would go to the cottage. She could picture him dropping his heavy sword and scabbard on the table with a thud, sitting in the chair to remove his various hidden dirks and daggers. He'd unstrap the ax from his back and hang it on the hooks on the wall. And then he'd come to the shore because he would know that she would be there.

She felt him getting closer still, and her heart pounded ungovernable in her chest again. The moon shone brightly, and she could feel her own joy and hope slicking out of every single pore. All would be well. All would be perfect.

She heard a rustle, the fast thudding of racing feet, too fast to be his, but before she could turn, she felt a shocking slice against her throat, a tearing of muscle and artery and sinew, a sharp, blinding pain that stole her breath. She felt her body slide into shock, her limbs leaden and impossible to move, as she bled onto the beach.

She was immortal. She was stronger than ten men, faster than any of them, and yet the pain was so consuming, so sharp and bright, that she couldn't muster any of her strength or speed. She couldn't even cry out. She felt her lips, thick with tears and pain, shaping around her love's name though no sound came from her ravaged throat, as if she could summon him and his help, his weapon of a body with only a word.

And then, all of a sudden, he was there. She heard his hoarse shout from behind her before he dragged her body into his lap.

"Marjory. Marjory, mo cridhe. Nay, nay, nay, *nay*. You cannae—I didnae—You cannae leave me alone," he'd whispered against her hair, clutching her against his chest.

She wanted to tell him what she was, that she would survive this. She only needed to sleep.

But she couldn't tell him any of that because of her tattered throat. And so she turned her nose into his chest, the movement agonizing, and smelled blood. His shirt was drenched with it, soaked red from collar to hem, and she gripped his arm with her fingers. *No.* It couldn't be. He couldn't be as badly wounded as she was. He would not survive it. He would die. She couldn't live with that. Not when she'd gained so many promises to save him this evening.

Tears streaked down her cheeks as she clung to him. He rocked her, his body feeling so cold compared to how he normally felt at her back. Something had happened to him, something had starved him and wounded him, and now he would die before she ever had a chance to tell him the truth.

She felt her blood pulsing thickly from her neck, smelled it mingling with the salty sea. The wind whipped angrily around them, nearly drowning out the soft sobs that echoed hollowly in his chest. It was so unfair. She wept for the unfairness, her own sobs choking on thick blood. She loved him enough to walk the entire earth to find him, enough to ask a god for a favor, enough to spend eternity with him. And instead, after a mere few years together, he would be ripped from her.

She looked up at him. His face was bloody, his cheek and jaw shining red as he'd no doubt buried his face against her neck. It merged with the blood on his throat, on his chest, his own lifeblood mingling with hers. At least that was a poetic thought, much good poetry would do her when he was dead.

She felt her strength waning. She needed sleep to heal, and the animal of her body was taking over now, chasing rest with a single-minded determination. She reached up with a weak hand and pressed it against his cheek, feeling his stubble against her palm. And before the world went dark around her and she slipped into unconsciousness, she imagined walking into the shadow cave, not stopping until she stood at the feet of the keeper of the underworld, and demanding they return Callum to her.

6

PRESENT

Alive. The improbability—hell, the *impossibility*—was staggering. Marjory had died in his arms. He had held her in the dark on that beach while the moon climbed the sky and her heart shuddered to a stop. And then he'd held her longer, clutching her to his chest until the dawn had threatened. Only then had he gone. But there she'd stood, her black hair like a wild tumble of seaweed around her shoulders and her green eyes flashing in the yellow glow of the kitchen's overhead light. Joy and relief and shock and—godsdamnit, was that hope?—had all swirled in his brain like a cyclone. They were feelings he hadn't felt in a very long time, almost long enough to forget them entirely.

It had been a disaster. Cover to cover. From the moment Esther had flown into Hank's kitchen to the moment Jory stormed out. They'd fought. She'd always been a fighter. Even more than him. He'd been a sword for hire in his human life, his life with her, but he'd always known when to leave the field. Marjory had never once walked away from a fight.

As she'd raged, as he'd tried to make sense of it, tried to place her anger, he had remembered climbing the masts of ships, remembered how it had felt to have rope slip through sweaty hands, to lose his grip and fall briefly before he regained his hold. Close calls. Near misses. He felt it the moment that the rope of his temper slipped out of his hands, and he fell, free and flailing, into the churning of his feelings, all of which rose to consume him.

But she'd been there, just beyond the reach of his trembling fingertips. He had tried to hold her, and she, slippery as water, had kept herself out of reach. She'd called him a liar. She'd called him a murderer. And when he'd explained that he'd only been trying to find Esther so that he could glamour her, to tie up the loose ends, she'd called him a monster.

In the end, after explaining the mechanics of how Sanguine operated, he and Esther had shaken hands. She gave him her word that she was leaving Georgia, that she had no interest in making trouble for him, and he'd believed her. He'd gotten what he'd come for, what he'd been seeking for months, and yet there was no victory. No pleasure in it. He'd left, unable to stand another moment in that kitchen with the snarling creature he'd been longing for for centuries.

Callum stood in the middle of the street for a long time after Marjory left. He watched her taillights as she sped away from him and forced himself not to follow her. He could chase her. Before she blinked, he could be in front of that sleek, black sedan of hers, forcing her to a stop like Superman in front of a runaway bus.

But maybe that wasn't true after all. Because while he could catch the car with ease, there was no guarantee he could catch *her*. Was she like him? A vampire? Or something else entirely? He didn't know, and that not knowing ate at him. After a thousand years of existence, there wasn't all that much he didn't know at least something about. But his Marjory was an entire mystery to him. How was she here? How was she alive? And the question that burned the hottest: why did *she* hate *him* so much? She was the one who had lied.

He couldn't recall ever having been so angry in all his years. His rage had more of a pulse than he'd had in centuries, but it was more than that. Because beneath all of that anger, deep within the empty drum of his chest, rested a petrified heart that had once beat for no other purpose than to love her, that had sat in memorial of that love, had *kept* loving her. Through the years, through the despair, through the wins and losses, he had never stopped. And so the rage hurt. It felt like betrayal. Because she was *here*. She hadn't died. And what did that mean?

Lost in his thoughts, Callum was startled by a throat clearing behind him.

"You gonna stand in the street all night staring after her like the dog she left behind?"

Callum spun slowly on his heel and saw a small woman standing directly under the streetlight. She wore a shiny silver puffer jacket and bright red sneakers. Her purse was covered with sparkles and shimmered, even in the dim yellow glow from above. Her hair was long and straight and gray, hanging over her shoulders.

"May I help you?" Callum asked.

She smirked, looking him up and down from head to toe, and said, "Funny. I was going to ask you the same thing."

As a general rule, Callum didn't like people who spoke

in riddles. He'd met a Sphynx once in Egypt and had found him to be maddening company.

"I beg pardon?"

"Such nice manners, Mr. MacLeod," she cackled. "Good to see you're not just a fancy suit."

It was immediately apparent that she knew more about him than he knew about her—which was nothing. He hated that.

"It seems that I am at a disadvantage," he said, feeling his brogue smooth out and away, leaving behind a neutral, clipped accent that sounded posh and refined. It was a good illusion, a voice that matched the exterior he presented, and it had served him well over the years.

"You met Hank?" she asked, canting her head in the direction of the house Callum had just left.

Callum's jaw popped as he ground his molars together. "I met Officer Dove, yes."

She hooted, slapping her skinny thigh. "Officer Dove. Oh, he hates that, Cal. Don't ever call him that to his face."

"You know O—Mr. Dove?"

"I know everything. Is that your car?" she asked, pointing to the black SUV with dark tinted windows.

Callum lifted an eyebrow. "Do you live on this street, Ms...."

"Magda. Magda Nutter."

Callum suppressed a snort. Nutter was right.

But she knew anyway, snapping, "Very original, Cal," with a smile that gleamed like a knife.

"My apologies. That was rude."

"Oh, stuff that fake accent up your tailpipe, boy-o. What's the point of talking to a big, burly Scotsman if he sounds like Benedict Cumberbatch?"

Callum sighed, raking his hands through his hair. "As you wish, Ms. Nutter. Do you—"

"Magda," she interrupted.

"Magda," he said, wondering how the hell to get on level ground. "Do you live on this street?"

"Not remotely."

"Are you visiting someone?"

"I was waiting to see if I was needed."

"Were you?"

She smirked again. "Well, if our dear Jory hadn't left the field of battle when she did, I might have been."

At the mention of her name, Callum felt his entire body lift. "You mean Marjory? You know Marjory?"

She blinked slowly, owl-like, as if the question had been an obvious one. "Remember? I know everything."

He crossed his arms over his chest, feeling the suit fabric strain against his biceps. "Everything? Do tell."

"I know that you sent your goons back to Seattle in a different car."

He nodded. That much was true but hardly impressive.

"I know that you have about an hour before you have to leave for Seattle too, if you want to miss sunrise."

That made him pause. "Dinnae you mean traffic?"

She smiled a Cheshire Cat smile. "I don't think a traffic jam alone would turn you into burnt toast, would it?"

He let himself move. Really move. At his full speed. In less than a heartbeat, he was looming over her in the circle of the streetlight. She didn't even flinch. She smiled with her whole face, her eyes wide with delight.

"Very impressive, Cal. Very, very impressive."

He glared down at her, so small before him. Nothing about this night made sense. Not finding his Marjory alive.

Not Esther's ready concession. And certainly not Magda Nutter.

"As ye said, I cannae risk traffic. If that's all, I'll be going." He turned and moved toward his vehicle.

"Oh, that's not all, Cal. Not by a long shot."

He looked over his shoulder at her, an eyebrow lifting high on his forehead. "Enlighten me, Magda."

"I know you love her."

He scoffed, turning away again and talking another step.

"And I know you killed her."

He froze.

"Well... almost," she said with a snort.

He forced himself to pause, to take what would have been a deep, calming breath when he was alive but was now just an expanding of his lungs with air, an affectation. He spun slowly around and found her right behind him, both of them standing in the dark now.

"I dinnae ken what ye think ye—"

"Lie to other people all you want, Cal, but you can't lie to me."

He could see her smile in the dark. "What is it you want?"

"I want a ride home."

"A ride home," he repeated slowly.

"Yes."

"Why cannae ye ask Hank to drive you?"

"Because Hank doesn't need my help. You do."

"I dinnae need—"

"You do. You don't even know you do yet. But you do. So unlock that wholly unnecessary dinosaur burner that you're driving, help me climb into it, and we can murder some ozone while you drive me home."

"It's a hybrid," he replied through gritted teeth.

"Oh, well, that changes everything, now doesn't it?"

"I dinnae like ye verra much, Magda."

She smiled and patted him on the chest before breezing past him and approaching the SUV. "You just don't like missing pieces."

He stared at her.

"Come on, Cal," she said brightly. "Night's wasting, and I've got something to show you."

What she had to show him was an A-frame cabin about a mile down a gravel road behind what she had pointed out as her house. As he pulled in front of the cabin, Magda climbed down from the SUV as if she were bouldering.

"You coming?" she hollered, as if he were on top of the boulder instead of across a center console.

Callum sighed and rolled his eyes. "It seems I am."

He turned off the SUV and got out, following Magda as she climbed the steps onto the porch. She flipped a switch, and Callum saw that the inside of the cabin was filled with worn furniture. It smelled like Esther. He caught a faint scent of Hank too, though that was less prominent. It smelled like lemon-pine cleaning solution and bleach and wood smoke. They weren't unpleasant smells, though. It smelled like a home, like a real home.

Magda went to a broom closet and opened it. "Come on, Cal," she said, disappearing inside.

Were he a mortal man, he would have thought, "This is it. This is how I end up the subject of a true crime podcast about a man who was lured to a cabin and murdered by a tiny old woman with boundary issues."

But he wasn't a mortal man. And unless Magda was waiting in that closet with a wooden stake—actually, that didn't matter. She'd have to stake him through his heart to kill him, which would require her to stand on a stepladder.

That thought made him smile, though it was a mirthless one. Of all things. To survive a thousand years of wars, rivals, and existential dread, to be taken out by a hundred-pound senior citizen in a broom closet.

He looked into the closet, which was empty, except for a trap door that opened to reveal a staircase that led down to what appeared to be a basement. He walked down the stairs, ducking his head. He saw a queen-sized bed with an iron frame covered with a red and black quilt. There was a TV, a small refrigerator, an armchair, a desk, and a rolling chair.

"Well, what do you think?" Magda asked, her arms spread wide.

"It's a verra nice panic room."

She snorted. "It's not a panic room. It's a vault. For you."

"For me," he repeated slowly.

"What? You expected to win her back all the way from Seattle? Or, goddess forbid, *Georgia*?"

"Win her back..." Callum felt like he was back in Hank's kitchen, where his brain was moving a half step slower than his life around him.

"Jory. Marjory."

"Ye think I want to win Marjory back?"

"Don't you?"

"She hates me. And I dinnae—"

Magda waved her hand, as if shooing a fly. "Psh. The line between love and hate is razor-thin."

Callum's throat tightened like a vice and his voice seized before he could argue.

"She'll forgive you. With the right incentive."

"What incentive?"

Magda smiled, and for a moment, Callum thought she would answer him directly for the first time all night. But then she breezed past him and through the vault door.

"It's long past my bedtime, Cal," she said with an exaggerated yawn. "We can talk more tomorrow night."

"But I'm going back to Seattle," he protested, moving to follow her.

"Alright," she answered.

"I am."

"You said that."

"I'm leaving now."

"By all means."

He started to. He wanted to. He did. But he hated missing puzzle pieces. She'd been right about that.

"Ye think she'd forgive me?"

Magda smiled, grabbing one of his hands and holding it in both of hers. It was comical-looking, like a child holding an adult baseball mitt.

"Of course she will. You didn't mean to kill her."

He was stunned speechless as he stood in this vault under an A-frame cabin in the middle of the woods behind the house of a woman who was—at the very least—a powerful witch.

"What if I don't want to forgive her?"

She smiled softly. "You come to my house tomorrow night, okay? It's about a split-second walk for you. I'll answer all your questions then."

"Because you've answered them so well tonight," he said drily.

She snorted a laugh. "Tonight was an icebreaker. We're friends now. We can be honest tomorrow." She stood in the doorway for a moment. "The vault door locks from the inside. Nobody can get in from outside unless you unlock it. And nobody can lock you inside from the outside either."

He nodded tightly, appreciating this safety measure.

"Tomorrow night, Cal," she said firmly, her voice taking

on that no-nonsense maternal tone that hadn't been used on him in hundreds of years. He felt an ache behind his ribs.

"Get some sleep. You look like shit," she said as she climbed the stairs and Callum's laugh burst forth from his chest.

He was tired. It was hours until sunrise, but he wanted to sleep now. He wanted to sleep now and all through the day in this vault that locked from the inside behind the house of this woman who, despite what he'd said, he did like. He locked the vault, turning the crank and hearing the heavy steel tumblers slide into place.

He slid into the bed, the quilt providing a pleasant weight over his body, and closed his eyes. Sleep was close, lingering just beyond the jumble of his thoughts, his grief. His guilt. And as he let it wash over him like a fog, he tasted salt.

7

Jory woke to find tears streaming down her cheeks, soaking the pillow and her hair equally. She pressed the heels of her hands against her eyes, relishing the sparking light the action created in her vision. She'd been inches away from him after hundreds of years, and she hadn't been able to decide whether to kiss him or strangle him. Or kiss him, and *then* strangle him. Or— No. None of that.

She couldn't be around him. She was sure that he'd left town last night and that she'd never have to see him again, but something about his parting words before he'd left rattled her. *"We're far from finished."*

She inhaled a deep, shuddering breath before rolling to her side and grabbing her phone.

Esther had texted last night.

You okay?

Jory?

Jory, so help me god, if you do not respond by 8am tomorrow, I will break down your door.

She looked at the clock at the top of the phone screen. It was 7:09 a.m.

I'm fine. No need to break the door.

She saw the three dots that indicated Esther was typing. She was surprised, frankly. She thought for sure that Esther would still be asleep because she knew for sure that Hank, hungover from panic and worry, had been balls-deep in Esther within moments of getting her alone and probably hadn't quit for hours.

You okay? Last night was bananas.

It was fucking bullshit, Esther.

Or that.

Another three dots. Jory sat up and drained her water bottle, feeling less shaky from her nightmare as the water poured down her throat.

Are you sure you're okay? Do you want to talk about it?

Yes. And yes.

But not right now.

While Esther typed her response, Jory clicked over to

her email app and scrolled. Her eyes caught on one from her old friend Rosa.

Jory,

I'm liquidating an estate in Santa Fe this week. The sale opens on Wednesday, but if you could get here tomorrow, I'll give you a private showing. Jewelry. Clothes. Antiques. Frida Kahlo sketches. EVERYTHING. Get your ass here.

Jory didn't even finish the email before she clicked over to her travel app and looked for flights. If she left within the hour, she could make the afternoon flight from Seattle to Albuquerque and then rent a car to drive the remaining hour to Santa Fe. She booked the ticket before clicking back to her texts.

> I love you, Jory.
>
> I'm here for you.
>
> Whatever you need that to look like.

>> I love you too. I'm headed to New Mexico today for an estate sale.
>>
>> Tell that big bear of yours to take care of you while I'm gone.

She tossed her phone onto the bed and walked to her bathroom. She turned on the shower and stepped into the hot spray, feeling it seeping into her hair, into her pores. She turned and opened her mouth, letting the water fall against her tongue. She swallowed it down as it beat against her face and chest.

She hated the desert. Nowhere on earth felt more foreign to her. But at the moment, the idea of a desert felt like heaven. No reminders of the sea that she had lost, the love that she had lost. She would be landlocked. Just like she was landlocked without her sealskin. She might as well make it literal.

Besides, she never dreamed in the desert. It was like her brain needed proximity to water to play. In the desert, her sleep was more like a coma. She welcomed that idea. She would buy treasures. She would drink gallons of water. She would sleep like the dead. And she would forget the memory of Callum MacLeod's tormented face staring at her as if she'd mortally wounded him, as if staring at her alone would keep her with him.

It hadn't then.

It wouldn't now.

8

Callum's eyes flew open and he leapt off the bed, landing beside it in a naked crouch in the pitch darkness. But just because there was no light didn't mean he couldn't see—a small reward for the price he had paid over and over and over for his immortality. It all came back to him quickly. The wrought-iron bed, the quilt, the desk and rolling chair. Magda's cabin. He went to his jacket, which he'd carefully draped over the back of the chair, and saw on his phone that it was six o'clock in the evening. He had slept fourteen hours.

When had he last slept more than a handful of hours at a time? When had he last slept without computer monitors and tablets at the ready, checking on business and keeping track of responsibilities throughout the day when he was meant to be resting? He sat in the armchair. The faux leather squeaked under his naked weight, and he braced his elbows on his knees, hands clasped around his phone as he looked up sunset times.

According to the internet, the sun had set a half hour ago. His email notification showed one hundred and fifty unread. He had sixty-one text messages and eight missed calls. Ordinarily, those little red bolded numbers would have made his skin feel as if it was crawling. He would have felt a sudden burst of adrenaline—or whatever coursed through his veins now—and plunged headfirst into clearing them.

But he didn't.

For the longest time, for as long as he could remember, his mission had been simple: grow the businesses. It had made him a wealthy man, but more importantly, it had kept countless creatures like him off of the necks of unsuspecting Timber dates or people wandering in dark alleys. His clubs, which had started in the Middle Ages, more like brothels than anything, became salons in the seventeenth century and then slowly morphed into speakeasies and then swanky nightclubs.

And the mission still existed. It mattered. But it was a hazy peripheral at this precise moment while his eyes were laser-focused on the vision of a tall ochre-skinned siren with wild black hair.

He opened his text messages and created a new thread for his assistant, Penny, and all of his club and business managers.

> "I'm away on business. You know what to do. Send me a report at the end of the week, but in the meantime, I'll only be taking calls from Penny. If you need me, reach out to her."

There was a flurry of activity as three dots appeared on the screen. No doubt dozens of thumbs were moving in unison all over the country and a few internationally, but he clicked over to his email and set up an out-of-office reply that said mostly the same thing.

Then he thumbed back to his texts and sent one to Penny.

"I'm finally taking your advice. Sorry for the extra work you'll be taking on. Hire an assistant. You're getting a raise, effective immediately. I'll send the number to Davis. And for God's sake, finally listen to me and take that rust bucket of yours into Jacobsen's and pick up the car I bought for you months ago. Don't be an arse. Or at least be a safe arse."

His lips twitched with the beginning of a smile.

"You're a lifesaver, Penny."

With that, Callum put his vibrating phone face down on the desk and reclined back in the chair, relishing the dark coolness of the room. He rested his laced fingers on his belly and stared at the ceiling. Penny had been gently nagging him to take a vacation for years now. He had always brushed her off. Too much to do. He made her take a vacation, though. Multiple, in fact. Last year, he'd sent her and her fiancée, Marisol, on an Alaskan cruise because Penny was fascinated by bears. One of the adventure packages had been a bear-watching excursion, and Penny had come back to work with three hundred pictures and a souvenir T-shirt for Callum, which he had never worn but had carefully folded in one of his drawers just the same.

Penny was the best assistant, and he'd never be able to replace her in a million years. He'd plucked her out of one of his other clubs a few years back. She'd applied for a job as a bar manager because she needed work that was at night, all night, so she could spend her days with her vampire fiancée who was a night shift nurse at the hospital. He'd watched her manage the bar for a solid week before offering her the job as his assistant, and she'd been giving him hell ever since.

His phone rang, and he lifted it to see Penny's name on the screen. He answered, and before he could say hello, Penny was charging ahead.

"First of all, I said you could *recommend* a car. Not that you could buy us a $90,000 SUV. Second of all, I expect pictures."

He smiled. "You said nothing of the sort. Take the car, Penny. Call it an early Christmas gift. You need it for that horse you call a dog." The horse dog in question was a Great Dane named Beast who took his meals at the kitchen table and loved to try to knock Callum over.

"Has anyone told you that you're overbearing?"

"You tell me every day."

"You're overbearing."

"Aye. But ye love me."

"Lord knows why."

But he heard the smile in her voice, and he found himself grinning. Penny liked to fuss over him, and he had been surprised to learn that he liked fussing over her too.

"Be safe," he said. "I'll be in touch."

"Aye, aye, captain," she said, cheerfully.

He put the phone down again and stood, pulling on his pants and shirt and making his way to the steep staircase that led up to the main floor. He was hungry and needed to figure out what to do about it. Robbie had likely left with Marcus and Gus to go back to Savannah. He was far from desperate, but he found himself wishing he'd secured a donor before passing out last night.

He came out of the broom closet just as a door in the hallway opened with a cloud of steam. Robbie stepped out, a white towel wrapped around his narrow hips and another in his hand, with which he roughly scrubbed at his short hair.

"Evening, boss," he said, that crooked smile spreading across his face.

"Robbie," Callum said, stunned. "What are ye doing here?"

He slung the towel around his neck, holding onto the edges, looking like he stepped out of a locker room.

"Nat Jasper dropped me off last night. Said that Magda told him I should stay here. You hungry?"

"Famished," Callum said, deciding to worry about Magda and her plans after he'd eaten.

"Let me go put pants on," Robbie said and disappeared into a room at the end of the short hall.

Callum went to Robbie's backpack on the kitchen island, which was covered with an absolute riot of patches and buttons. He hadn't known Robbie long but he knew that there were packets of electrolyte powder in the front pocket of that backpack. He filled the tallest glass he could find with water and mixed the electrolytes into it. He saw a bunch of bananas on a stand on the counter and pulled one off, peeling it and placing it on a plate next to the drink.

Robbie emerged wearing ripped black jeans, boots, and a black tank top.

"Where do you want me, boss?"

"This first," Callum answered, gesturing at the hydration drink and banana. Robbie smiled and joined him at the counter, eating half of the banana in one astounding bite, cheeks full as he chewed. Callum shook his head.

"Wha?" Robbie asked around a mouthful.

"You're an animal," Callum replied drily, and Robbie snorted.

He finished the banana in another bite and then downed half of the glass in a few swallows. Callum watched Robbie's lean throat move, the flower tattoos across the front of his neck looking like they bobbed in a breeze as he swallowed. Robbie exhaled a satisfied sound and wiped the back of his hand over his mouth.

"I'll drink the other half after," he said.

Callum nodded. "Do you want to lie down?"

"Here's fine," Robbie said, hopping up onto the counter. It put his neck right on level with Callum's mouth.

"If you're certain," he drawled, and Robbie kicked the lower cabinets with his heels as he nodded and grinned.

Callum braced his hands on the laminate countertop on either side of Robbie's thighs. Robbie spread his knees so Callum could step between them.

There was something primal about drinking blood, just as there was something primal about sex. As such, many vampires enjoyed blurring the lines, drinking while fucking or drinking as foreplay, where the sex was the aftercare. But for Callum, the drinking was a necessity whereas the sex no longer was. Sex had become a dull approximation of what it had once been, a perfunctory performance of rehearsed movement. He hadn't bothered in decades.

Callum tended to let his mind go blank while he fed. It was meditative. He would let his focus narrow until the only thing he sensed was his donor's heart rate, paying close attention to the beats and the pressure so that he could ease away before going too far. He never thought about his

Marjory while he fed. It was too painful to remember. He knew what the salt and iron of her blood tasted like sliding across the softness of her skin and into his open mouth.

"We doing this, boss?" Robbie asked, his face close to Callum's ear, and Callum startled, not realizing how deeply he'd fallen into his reverie until he was yanked from it.

"Aye," he rasped, feeling a thickness in his throat.

Robbie leaned back, tipping his head against the upper cabinet and closing his eyes. He took a deep breath, and on the exhale, Callum let his fangs sink in carefully. Always in the exact same place. He'd looked at the beautiful flowers tattooed on Robbie's throat and found dark space between the petals of two different blooms that had been filled in with black ink. His fangs fit perfectly into those black voids, and he was careful to hit the mark every time.

The blood slid across Callum's tongue in a thick flow, viscous and slippery and rich. He held back a sigh as he felt his mind clear.

Ba-dum. Ba-dum. Ba-dum.

Robbie's heart beat steadily now, not like the racing rabbit it had been the first time he'd offered up his throat to Callum's teeth. He gently kicked the rubber heel of his boot against the bottom cabinet like an idle child waiting. When he was sated, Callum drew back, dragging his tongue over Robbie's throat, an enzyme in his saliva causing instant clotting and healing.

His saliva could heal two puncture marks almost instantly, sealing and sterilizing without a mark. But it was not powerful enough to clot a wound caused by a careless, ravaging animal bite. Grief boiled in his belly as he stepped away from Robbie. He handed him the half-full glass of hydration drink, and Robbie took it without comment.

Callum was happy to take care of him, in the same way

he was happy to take care of Penny and all of his other dependents. His nightclubs existed to keep people safe, to provide a mutually sought-after, mutually pleasurable experience. He liked to take care of people. He *needed* to take care of people. He always had.

Except for that night on the beach, when—

"You okay, Callum?"

Callum. Robbie never called him that. He looked up and saw the empty glass sitting on the counter next to Robbie's tattooed hand. His gaze traveled up a tattooed arm to a tattooed neck, perfectly healed and unscarred, to Robbie's concerned face.

"Aye," Callum croaked and stepped back.

"I know that this is... professional," Robbie said hesitantly. "But I have four sisters and a mama who said that I was going to be a good listener if it was the last thing she did. So, if you ever want to talk about anything, I'm... I'm here."

Callum remembered that awful Christmas movie with all the vignettes and couples, the one that started and ended at the airport arrivals. Love... something. He remembered a grizzled rock star Bill Nighy showing up at his manager's house on Christmas Day and saying something like "It's a terrible, terrible mistake, but you turned out to be the fucking love of my life."

Robbie wasn't the love of his life. Robbie was his employee. Just like Penny was his employee. But as he looked at the sincere face staring back at him, as he remembered Penny's sisterly teasing and enthusiasm for him leaving town, it occurred to him that they might be the closest things to friends he had on this earth. And wasn't that fucking sad.

But it was beautiful too. That of all the people he'd

employed over the centuries, of all the people he'd hired and fired and paid and promoted and mentored and made, that Penny and Robbie would find their ways onto his payroll and into his life in the same lifetime. That Robbie would have been the one to find Esther, that Robbie would have been in the room when Marjory had blown in and hurled Callum's carefully understood, carefully blank world completely off its axis.

Callum's eyes stung. He felt a tear leak out and glide down his cheek. Robbie reached out to swipe it with his thumb, and Callum saw a smear of ruby red blood on the pad of Robbie's finger.

"Wow," Robbie breathed, his mountain twang somehow even thicker in a whisper. "Did you know you cry blood?"

"Aye," Callum said, his voice soft. "I dinnae drink water, so I cannae cry water."

"Does it happen often?"

"Nay."

"So why now?" Robbie asked, reaching for a paper towel off the roll that hung from the underside of the upper cabinet and wiping the blood on it, leaving a brilliant streak against the white weave.

"Because fate is vicious," Callum whispered. "Robbie, I cannae—I cannae—"

He hung his head, clenching his fists at his sides and staring at the knots in the pine floorboards.

Robbie hopped off the counter and stepped around him. Callum heard a rustling of clothing. And then the door was open.

"Come on," Robbie said, and Callum looked up. He was wearing a hooded sweatshirt with the hood up over his head and a scuffed and worn bomber jacket over top.

"Where are we going?"

"Magda's," Robbie said matter-of-factly.

"Magda's," Callum repeated slowly.

"Yeah. She told me she'd cook me dinner tonight. She also told me to bring you."

"I dinnae feel much like company, Robbie," Callum said, feeling the tightness in his throat that hadn't eased, the tears still hovering at the corners of his eyes.

"Come on, boss," Robbie said, holding the door open wider. "Magda will fix us both up."

Callum sighed.

"I'm gonna start walking. We both know that you'll catch up to me before I get out of the driveway."

He wasn't wrong. Callum raced in a blur to put on his shoes and shrug into his coat, not because he needed it but because it made him feel put together, like he belonged in this world.

As Callum fell into step beside Robbie not thirty seconds later, Robbie barked a laugh.

"I will never get used to that shit, man."

"Bollocks," Callum replied, the tightness in his chest easing slightly.

"But we're walking my pace, 'kay? I'm down a pint and don't have a gift like yours."

Callum snorted a mirthless laugh. "'Tis hardly a gift, Robbie."

"So you say," Robbie replied.

Twenty minutes later, Callum found himself sitting on a lumpy couch in Magda's living room while Robbie sat cross-legged on the floor rubbing the belly of an ancient basset hound named Mr. Dick Van Dyke. The dog had bayed loudly when they'd knocked but, as soon as Magda had invited them in, had practically melted into the carpet, as if the effort had sapped him of all energy.

The dog was fine, even if he did smell, but while Robbie was petting his long, velvet ears, Callum was fending off a tiny, flying creature that Magda told him was called Walter. He was small, about the size of a dandelion head and covered with long, wispy, canary-yellow fluff. He had little white wings that looked like flower petals and two glossy little black eyes that were occasionally visible when he created enough of a draft to lift the fluff away from them.

Walter was apparently something called a Brightling Beetle, and since arriving, Callum had learned a few key things about Walter. He was highly poisonous but, like a daddy longlegs spider, didn't have a big enough mouth to puncture human skin. He loved Magda and Dick Van Dyke. And he *loathed* Callum.

This was evidenced by the fact that Walter kept attempting to fly directly at Callum's nose at top speed. Eventually, Magda took pity on Callum and called him off.

"Walter! Dick! Come on, my babies. Dinner!"

Walter stopped mid dive at Callum's face and veered off to Magda.

"Dinner!" Robbie said, straightening quickly.

"Come on," she said, though it was unclear whether she was talking to Robbie or the hound, who was jogging toward the kitchen with a speed that Callum would have believed impossible for him after watching his earlier collapse.

When Callum reached the table, Magda was petting Walter's little body with a single, crooked finger. He was roosted atop a large Gerbera daisy and eating something that looked vaguely like brown sugar.

"Sweet little murder boy," she crooned before stepping into the kitchen and ladling stew into a deep bowl, which she handed to Robbie.

"Blood's in the fridge," she said over her shoulder.

Callum opened the refrigerator, where he saw an unmarked six pack of dark amber bottles filled with thick liquid. He pulled one out, and Magda pressed a bottle opener into his hand with a wink before he had a chance to ask for it. He popped the top and immediately smelled the tang of blood.

He took a careful sip and then pulled the bottle away to look at it. It had once been a beer bottle, but the label had been soaked off. It its place was a piece of masking tape that said, "ELK NOVEMBER" in messy permanent marker. He looked at Magda, who was ladling another bowl of stew.

"I got them from Nat. It's good?"

"It's different."

She snorted before moving past him and sitting at the table, where Robbie was already parked and leaning over his bowl, shoveling stew into his mouth like he hadn't been fed in months. He stopped eating as she sat, wiping his mouth quickly with a napkin and sitting up ramrod straight. She waved him off.

"Tuck in, honey. There's plenty more on the stove. But maybe chew, eh?"

Robbie smiled brightly before diving back into his bowl.

"You ever feed him?"

"He's a growing boy," Callum said, lowering his big body into the chair across from Robbie.

Magda snorted again and took a bite of stew. Callum took another sip from his bottle. It was different. And yet not. There was a heartiness that he had never experienced from human blood. The difference between soup and stew.

"This is good," he said, lifting the bottle in Magda's direction.

"I'll have to take your word for it," she said with a chuckle.

"You said it's from Nat Jasper?"

"Yep," Magda said, chewing. "He's a ranger at the big park and hunts to keep the populations managed."

"Isnae hunting illegal in state and federal parks?"

"Well, he's not exactly marching up to declare his kills at Fish and Wildlife, is he?"

"Wouldnae someone notice discarded animal carcasses all over the park?" Callum asked, the bottle poised at his lips.

"Nat would never be so wasteful. No. He drains them for his purposes, and then he has a guy who processes the animals and distributes the meat to shelters and among those in the community who need the protein. And I know sometimes he doesn't kill the animal at all."

A deep respect settled within Callum's chest.

"There's a market for this," he said after another sip.

"Oh?" Magda asked.

"Aye."

"You replacing me, boss?" Robbie asked.

Callum looked at Robbie, at the two black spaces in between the tattooed petals on Robbie's neck.

"I wouldnae replace you as a—" The word "friend" stuck in Callum's throat. It was entirely possible that Robbie didn't see Callum in the same way, that he viewed their relationship as being strictly professional. But he couldn't bring himself to say "employee."

"I wouldnae replace ye," he said with a cough. "But if I didnae have to *hurt* ye..." He trailed off.

Robbie shrugged. "You don't hurt me."

Callum cleared his throat. "I try my best."

"Nat Jasper is only on animals, you know," Magda said.

Callum hadn't known. He knew of Nat from Robbie's reconnaissance and had seen him last night in Hank's kitchen, but they hadn't been formally introduced.

"Aye?"

"Yeah. He told me that he's been off of humans for a few centuries now. Ever since he came this far west. Said he couldn't risk it. It's why he took that job at the national park."

Callum had heard rumors about vampires doing it, living off of animals instead of people. Everyone had heard rumors. But he'd never seen it with his own eyes. Never tasted an alternative. It was... good. More than good. It made him feel hopeful.

Marjory had clearly despised what he'd become. *"You hurt people. You* kill *people,"* she had snarled.

There was no way that she could know the great lengths to which he'd gone over the years for that to not be true, how his entire empire had been built upon not killing or hurting humans, but rather the opposite. But he hadn't had a chance to explain. He'd been too shocked to string two sentences together at all.

But if he could live this way, if Nat Jasper could teach him how, he could leave that behind. He could find a way to actually be Robbie's friend, instead of... whatever they were now. He could—

"Careful, boy-o. You think too much harder, and your brain's gonna start smoking," Magda said.

Robbie was leaning back in his chair, his hand resting on a slightly distended belly, a sleepy, satisfied look on his face. Magda was sipping wine from a stemless glass. He didn't remember her having wine before.

"I apologize. I didnae mean to zone out like that. That was rude."

Magda waved a hand. "You don't have a rude bone in your body, despite what Walter has decided about you."

Callum saw the little yellow puff sitting placidly on Magda's shoulder. There was so much... hair? Whatever it was, he was so completely covered in it that Callum couldn't see his eyes, though he had the distinct impression that Walter was glaring murderously at him.

"Watch your drink, Cal."

"Why?"

"I told you. He's got three talents. Being small. Being adorable." She scratched underneath what might have been a chin. "And poison."

"But he cannae bite me."

"More than one way to skin a cat, Cal. More than one way to kill a man."

"I like you, Magda," Robbie said with a bark of a laugh. "You're spooky."

Magda preened for a moment before fixing her eyes on Callum. "Enough chitchat. What are you gonna do about Jory?"

That was the million-dollar question, wasn't it?

"I dinnae ken. She hates me, remember? And I'm angry with her, too."

Magda leaned on her forearms on the table. "I had this dog when I was a kid. Boots. One day, Boots got lost. Maybe she ran away. Maybe someone stole her from the front yard. She was a beautiful dog. Anyway, one day, she came back. I was sitting on the front porch reading a book, and there was Boots trotting up the front walk like she hadn't been missing for four years."

"I—"

"I'd grieved Boots. I'd buried her toys in the backyard under one of the trees. Made her a little headstone from a rock I painted. And then, suddenly, she was back. But she wasn't the same. She was wary. She bit if you came at her too quickly before she realized you were there. She hated surprises. She gobbled her food and growled if you looked at it."

Callum sighed. "I'm the dog?"

"No," Magda said, taking a long sip. "Don't be ridiculous."

His eyebrows knit tightly together.

"She was dead. Right? You avenged her."

"How do ye ken—"

"Don't worry about how I know things, Cal. Just trust that I do." She sighed. "I buried Boots's things because I couldn't bear to have them around anymore without her. So I put them somewhere where I could go to sit with her memory, but I could also leave and keep living. Jory mourned you. For *centuries*. She had to bury you and how much she loved you deep because if she didn't, how was she supposed to keep going? And then she finds out that you aren't dead. You never were. And she doesn't know you left to avenge her."

"I didnae ken she was alive! If I'd known she—"

Magda held up a hand. "You never would have left her. But you didn't know, and you *did* leave. You left her for dead on a goddamn beach. Which was fine when you were supposed to be dead too. But you weren't. Which means you abandoned her. Didn't bury her. Didn't attempt to give her the courtesy of a good farewell. You just left her in the sand."

"Magda," Callum croaked, feeling the hot dampness in his eyes gathering. He'd be crying blood in a moment, and it would probably scare the shit out of her. Or maybe it wouldn't. Magda knew things. Magda certainly knew a hell of a lot more than he did.

"You wanna know what happened to Boots, Cal?"

He swallowed thickly and nodded.

"Well, it took some time and a lot of patience and a few bitten fingers, but eventually, Boots came back to us. I mean *really* came back. She let us pet her. She slept at the foot of my bed again. She chased our new dog around the backyard and let herself be chased. She wasn't the same as she'd been before. She'd seen too much for that, whatever it was. But she let us love her again."

Callum hung his head, a bright red tear falling and splashing onto the wooden tabletop. Robbie reached out with his napkin and wiped it up before handing the napkin to Callum.

"And she did the damnedest thing too, Cal. She found the little grave that I'd made for her things, and she dug them all up. Every toy. Every ball. She dug them up and shook them out and carried on with them like she'd never been without."

Callum looked at Magda. He felt bleak. Hollow. Hopeless, the anger having almost deflated completely. *Almost.* But Magda was smiling at him, that gentle mother's smile she'd shone on Robbie. She reached out with a sure hand and swiped the bloody tears from under his eyes. She wiped her thumb on her napkin and swiped beneath his other eye. He couldn't take his eyes off of her, unfamiliar with being mothered.

Callum reached out blindly and clasped Magda's hand tightly, feeling the warmth of her skin, a sharp contrast to the coolness of his own. She smiled again and chafed his knuckles with her thumb, leaving a bloody smear.

"I guess what I'm saying is that when Jory starts digging, you best be there to be found."

9

Jory had spent two weeks in the desert. Two long weeks combing through a mansion full of treasures and antiquities and vintage clothing finds to bring back to sell in her shop, including a spectacular Thierry Mugler gold lamé corset from 1978 that had gone directly from the trailer she'd rented to bring everything back and straight into her closet. It wasn't something she would usually wear but the corset fit her like a glove and reminded her of armor. She felt as though she could use a little armor at the moment.

She imagined all of the ways she would style it. Perhaps with loose-fitting, ripped jeans and a pair of stiletto heels that could double as a weapon if a person needed them to. A stake, to be precise.

"How was the trip?" Esther asked from her place on the green velvet couch in Jory's living room.

Esther was propped back against a big pillow and the armrest, a mug of tea cupped in her hands like a baby bird. Jory smiled at her over her own mug.

"Successful."

"I can't wait to see everything you bought. I know you didn't send me pictures of even half of it."

"I didn't send you pictures of even ten percent of it. There's a U-Haul out back with our names on it tomorrow. That is, if you're willing and free."

Esther beamed. "Uh, of course I am! I've loved working in the shop."

Jory was unspeakably grateful for Esther. It had been a terrible time to leave town for two weeks, so close to Christmas. Though she did a steady business year-round in the brick-and-mortar shop, her online orders definitely stacked up around the holidays.

"Was it awful managing the online part by yourself?"

Jory hadn't even considered it when she'd booked the flight to New Mexico, which was completely out of character for her. She was a person who dotted i's and crossed t's. Always. And yet ten minutes breathing the same air as Callum MacLeod had sent her abandoning her business to run away to the desert for half a month. She'd called Esther in a panic from her gate at the Seattle airport and walked her through the entire process over a video call.

"My first day was... intense," Esther said, taking a sip of her tea. "I kept trying to pack up orders as they came and then losing track of what I'd done and what label went where and ended up having to do the whole thing over again."

Jory felt that punch of guilt again.

"But then I took a deep breath and remembered that your system doesn't have to be my system as long as the end result is the same. So I made a little assembly line and checklist for myself. I got everything sorted and put in boxes, and then Hank came and helped me seal them all up and label them."

"Hank?"

Esther smiled brightly. "The assembly line was his idea. I double-checked the packing slips, and then he followed behind me with the tape."

"I owe him a paycheck too."

"He would rip it up. Politely, of course," she added quickly. "But he'd never take it."

"Well, I have to do something for him."

"Get him a gift certificate to the diner."

"Be serious, Esther."

"I am serious. Diner breakfast is his favorite."

"What about a night in a hotel somewhere for the two of you? Or concert tickets? Or—"

"Jory," Esther interrupted. "Diner. Gift. Certificate," she said, enunciating each word. "It's the only thing he'll accept."

Jory sank back against the opposite arm of the couch with a huff. "Very well, then. Diner gift certificate it is."

"Good. He'll love it."

Jory snorted a laugh. "It's the least I can do. Although that man would walk into traffic for you, so I'm not surprised he'd volunteer to tape boxes for you."

"Well, he said that the sooner I finished, the sooner I could come home." Esther blushed over the rim of her mug.

"How is that going? Living together?" Jory asked.

Esther sighed. "We're redecorating. We painted the doors blue as a first project. It makes the house look so different."

"I love a blue door," Jory said.

"Me too! And Hank's going to redo the floors in the

kitchen after Christmas and Yule. Then we'll probably paint in there too."

Jory remembered those floors vividly. She remembered how, though impeccably clean, she'd felt as if her feet had been stuck to them, like a mouse on a glue trap, when she'd seen Callum's face for the first time after so long. She had so many questions about what had happened after she left, but she didn't have the first idea how to ask, nor was she sure she really wanted the answers.

But she'd always been too curious. Wasn't that how she'd ended up in this mess in the first place? Curious about a wounded man on the beach? About why her body felt like it was on fire when she lay next to him? Always, too damn curious.

"What else did I miss while I was away?" Jory found herself asking.

"I honestly don't know. I've been so busy with the shop that I haven't done much else. Hank's been working at the motel, fixing things up for Alice. Magda's stopped by a few times. And Nat's got a new housemate. Niamh. He brought her to dinner at our house one night. You'll like her. She's—oh! That reminds me. I'm having a party next weekend for Yule. Super casual. Just a bonfire in the backyard and some snacks and drinks. Will you come?"

Esther hadn't mentioned Callum—and she would have if he'd still been around. No doubt he'd gone back to Georgia. She'd expected to feel relieved by that information. She knew she should be, but that itchy feeling was back in her brain.

"Who all is coming?" Jory asked absently.

"Me and Hank, obviously. Magda and Jamie, Nat and Niamh. Maybe Buck? I told Buck and Jamie they could bring their kids. And you, I hope. It won't be a big thing, but it should be fun. Hank's building a firepit. I don't know where he's going to find the time, but he says to let him worry about that."

Jory smiled at her friend. Hank would build her a city if she asked for it. She remembered being in love like that. She remembered being *loved* like that. But as soon as that thought crossed her mind, she shut it down. Because she *hadn't* been loved like that. It had all been a lie, hadn't it? Even if it had been true, it had been expendable, just like her. Easily abandoned on a beach in the middle of the night.

"I'll come," Jory said, shaking herself back to the present and reaching for her stainless-steel water bottle. She drained it. *Always so thirsty, lass.*

A week later, Jory found herself wrapped in a wool blanket over her winter coat and sitting in an Adirondack chair next to Niamh and Esther in front of a stone firepit that Hank had, indeed, found time to build. It was beautiful and simple and well-made, and if that wasn't also a description of its maker, Jory didn't know what was.

Esther was talking about her Yule present from Hank, a tiny kitten named Hawkeye who was currently sound asleep in the pocket of Hank's coat. Niamh had found the kittens and their mother in the small barn behind Nat's house and brought them in. Mama had gone straight to the vet to be spayed, and Niamh was trying to find homes for the remaining three kittens. There were five in the litter, but Niamh had decided to keep the mother and a little tan kitten and named them Lucy and Ethel.

"Do you want one, Jory?" Niamh asked in her soft voice.

Jory laughed. "No, thank you. I love to visit cats, but I have no desire to live with one."

Niamh smiled. "Fair enough. Nat isn't a fan either. Says

he doesn't want to scoop the shite of a creature who watches him with disdain all the while he does it."

Jory felt her smile crinkle her eyes and turned to look for Nat to ask him how he liked his new roommates when she saw a hulking form in the shadows, just beyond the glow of the fire. Esther must have seen it too, because she stopped talking and gripped Jory's forearm tightly in her gloved hand. Niamh swiveled to look, and the combination of those actions was enough to catch the attention of Hank and Nat, who ambled over to the dark side of the yard.

Jory watched, her heart beating frantically. Hank stood with a wide stance, his arms crossed over his chest, but Nat slouched comfortably with his hands in his coat pockets. Her pulse hammered in her ears, drowning out the sound of the fire, Magda and Jamie laughing, Jamie's sons' tablets. After what must have been a mere minute or two, Hank turned and walked back toward the fire, trailed by Nat and —her heart lurched—*Callum*.

He looked different than he had in Hank's kitchen weeks before. There, he'd been a brutal man in a dark, expensive suit that made his sharp edges look even sharper. But tonight, he wore jeans and a blue ski jacket. A wool hat covered his blonde hair except for the ends that stuck out the back at his collar. His jaw was relaxed, his walk easy, the long strides familiar as his strong legs brought him ever closer to the fire. To her.

Esther grabbed for her hand, holding it firmly. But Callum didn't actually approach them. Instead, he followed Nat to the other side of the firepit, taking a cautious seat in an Adirondack chair next to the other vampire and accepting an amber bottle from a special cooler that was labeled with a strip of masking tape. He twisted the bottle open and put the metal cap in his coat pocket before clinking bottle necks with Nat, who said, "Sláinte."

Jory glared at him, but if he noticed, he didn't let on. He was too busy looking at Esther, a nervous expression on his face.

"I thought you went back to Georgia," Esther said testily.

"Nay," Callum replied, his voice quiet.

"Aren't you needed at Sanguine?"

Callum took a small sip, his tongue darting out to lick the dark blood from his upper lip. "I dinnae think I'm truly needed anywhere. That's what you get for hiring competent people."

"Have you been here the whole time?"

Another sip. Another sweep of his tongue. Jory swallowed thickly. She knew the contours of that upper lip, knew the way it felt under her own tongue. She gripped her own beer loosely, deliberately so, knowing well that she could crush the glass in her fist if she wasn't careful.

Callum replied, "Aye. Magda has let me use a cabin she owns."

Magda.

Jory shot a glare at the older woman at the same time that Esther whipped her own head around. Magda was sitting in a bag chair next to Jamie. She stuck her tongue out at Esther before winking at Jory.

Through the fog of betrayal, Jory heard Esther ask, "How long will you be here?"

He didn't answer right away. But instead of taking another bloody sip, he stared across the fire, locking his gaze on Jory's with a pained look. Jory looked away, feeling the need to hide from his piercing eyes. She'd never been able to keep anything secret from him.

Well, except that *one* secret.

"As long as I need to be," he finally said.

Esther snorted and Callum turned his intense gaze on her. "Esther, I—" He paused, as if considering the right words. "I want to apologize again for scaring you, for making your life such hell. Sometimes I— Immortality has been... och, it doesnae matter. I forgot myself for a while there. And you suffered for it. And for that, I'm sorry."

A part of Jory wanted Esther to punish him, to make him squirm, or at the very least to withhold her forgiveness until Callum had had more time to stew in his own regret. But Esther was too good, too kind to refuse a sincere apology. "You're forgiven, Callum," she said, and Jory clenched her fist.

For this. He'd been forgiven *for this*.

He nodded, looking relieved. Callum and Nat both took long pulls from their bottles, and Jory watched their powerful throats bob as they swallowed the blood. She didn't want to know where they'd gotten it. It wasn't the blood that disgusted her. Blood was life. She'd bled every month for a thousand years and more. It was the *harvesting* that she couldn't stand. And nothing he could say would make her feel otherwise.

Callum MacLeod used people. It didn't matter that he took care of his victims in the aftermath. It didn't matter that he didn't leave his victims for dead. Because he'd left her for dead, and why hadn't she, the supposed love of his life, deserved that kind of care?

Callum wiped his mouth with the back of his hand and looked at Jory again. She felt her breath catch. His gray eyes glittered in the light of the fire, the sparks shining in them as Hank tossed another log into the pit and stoked it with a long poker.

"He's staying in Magda's cabin," Esther said quietly.

"I heard," Jory whispered.

"He's been here the whole time."

"I know," Jory replied, her voice a bit thicker than it had been just before.

"I heard he made a bag of it following Esther across the country and there was a to-do when he found her, but how do you know him, Jory?" Niamh asked.

Jory looked at Callum, who was deep in conversation with Nat, and murmured, "He was my husband."

10

There was a stunned silence before Niamh asked, "Was?"

"Aye," Jory replied. "A very long time ago."

"Did he leave you?"

"Something like that."

Jory knew Callum heard her. He could probably hear how fast her heart was racing.

"So you're divorced now?" Niamh asked.

"Well, when one's husband leaves them for dead in the middle of the night, that achieves much the same purpose, don't you think?"

Out of the corner of her eye, Jory saw Callum flinch. Niamh whistled through her teeth and muttered, "Gobshite." Esther squeezed Jory's hand.

"Now, now," Magda said from behind them. "Not everything is as black and white as it seems, my darlings."

Jory spun quickly, feeling the hot tears spring to her eyes as she looked at her friend, or who she had believed to be her friend before a few minutes ago. She grabbed Magda's hand and hustled her away from the group.

"Magda, how could you?" she hissed.

"How could I what?" Magda replied, a penciled eyebrow arched high on her forehead in a way that made Jory's pulse pound with fury. The old crone was going to make Jory say it.

"How could you host him? You—" She lowered her voice even more, as if it would make a difference to Callum's ears. "I told you what he did to me. And you gave him a place to stay?"

Jory had been on the run for so long. *For lifetimes.* She'd never been able to stay in one place longer than a decade or so before people began to notice that she never aged, never fell ill. And whatever meager savings she'd been able to accumulate always went to securing a new home, a new identity, a new place to feel safe. Until she'd stumbled upon World's End and Magda fifty years before. Magda, who'd taken her in and given her the money to start her business, who'd promised her that she could be safe there, that she could stay. There were a lot of people like them in World's End, after all. And besides, there were spells that would prevent people from even considering her age.

Magda had been her lifeline. But what was more, Magda *knew*. She knew what had happened to Jory. Magda knew *everything*. Even the things she shouldn't have. The betrayal stung all the more for that simple truth.

She pulled on Jory's hands, drawing her close enough and cupping her cheeks in her palms. Magda's hands were warm despite the cold.

"Cal's on a journey, my lo—"

"Cal?" Jory scoffed. "*Cal?* You really must have taken him under your wing if he's got a pet name."

"He's on a journey," Magda continued, more insistently.

"So are you. And those journeys were meant to intersect. It's a quest now."

"Stop speaking in riddles, Magda," Jory said impatiently.

Magda held her hands up in surrender. "Look, girly. That man is not the man you think he is. He's—"

"He's a faithless piece of shit!" Jory interrupted.

Magda's hand snapped out, and she gripped Jory's wrist in her strong fingers, her nails digging in lightly through Jory's coat. "*He's not the man you think he is.* And he doesn't know who the hell you are either. Too many secrets. Aren't there, Marjory?"

Jory glared mulishly at Magda. "I owe him nothing, Magda."

"You're right, honey," Magda said, but the way her sentence ended made it sound as if it hadn't really ended.

"But?"

"But you owe each other everything at the same time."

"I can't do this," Jory said, turning to walk away.

"You'll never get it back if you don't talk to him," Magda said quietly, stopping Jory in her tracks.

"What?"

"You'll never get it back and you'll never go home again if you don't talk to him."

The air sizzled in the air around her like a prophecy, and Jory felt the truth in Magda's words hanging like snowflakes in the air.

"How do you know that he has it?" Jory whispered.

"Don't worry about how I know, my love. Just trust that I do."

"And let me guess. You want me to forgive him."

"I want you to be well, Jory," Magda said, reaching up to cup Jory's cheek again. "I want you to be *quenched.*"

Jory looked up at the sky above, her teeth clenched tightly. "Goddamnit," she said, and Magda chuckled.

"You could be on a quest with a worse person, you know."

"Oh, really? Worse than a monster?"

Magda squinted at her and tilted her head to the side, as if examining her closely. "Oh, honey. What you don't know could fill the sea."

With that, Magda squeezed her hand and made her way back to her chair by the fire.

Magda and her son Jamie and the kids left not long after that, followed by Buck and his family. Jory had eventually rejoined the circle of chairs around the fire, sitting at an angle to Callum rather than across from him. Music played quietly from a speaker on top of a cooler. She chatted with Nat and Niamh, with Esther occasionally jumping in. Callum and Hank were quiet, watching the fire and listening to the conversation around them. She could feel his gaze on the side of her face, but it was better than avoiding it directly.

Hank's silence was easy, normal; he was always more of a listener than a talker. Rationally, she knew Callum's silence was to be expected as well. But it felt deliberate, as if he were waiting for her to speak to him. He could keep waiting.

She had nothing to say to him. Although that wasn't really true. She had *everything* to say to him. She just had no idea how to say it without striking him or bursting into tears. Or both. Because she didn't know how to articulate how she felt. She was angry, and that was certainly the most tangible emotion. But she would be lying to herself if she said that was all.

She hazarded a glance at him and found him looking at her, the firelight dancing across his eyes. She sucked in a quick breath before glaring down at her watch. It was just after midnight, late enough that she could excuse herself. She needed to leave. *Now*.

Jory pressed her palms against her thighs and stood.

"You're leaving?" Esther said, sitting up.

"Don't get up. It's just past my bedtime," Jory said with a smile for her friend. "Niamh, it was lovely to meet you. Nat," she said, inclining her head. She went and leaned over to kiss Esther on the cheek.

"I'll see you in the morning, Esther." They had dozens of orders to box and ship.

"Magda and I will be there around ten, if that's okay," Esther replied.

She wasn't ready to talk to Magda again. But she also wasn't in any position to refuse willing help, and so she nodded, thanked Hank and Esther again for their hospitality, and stepped outside of the circle of light from the fire.

Jory picked her way through the circle of chairs and across the yard. She felt Callum at her back before she heard him. She didn't want to talk tonight. She didn't really want to talk to him at all. She was too raw, too in shock. And while her heart was broken and her anger fresh and bloody, she could also admit that the relief at him being *alive* was so tangible, so visceral, that she was just as likely to kiss him as she was to shout at him. Or something equally stupid.

She shivered, though not from the cold as she took a sharp turn to the right and into the shadows behind Hank's shed. She spun around, and he was right there, so close that the nylon of her coat brushed against his. His big chest rose and fell with breathing, but no clouds of air puffed from his mouth. He wasn't actually breathing. He was *imitating* breathing. An affectation.

The truth knocked her back. She almost lost her feet.

"You're dead," she croaked.

He stood, watching her, his hands at his sides. His voice was soft when he answered, like he was comforting a scared animal. "In a manner of speaking, I suppose. In another, I'm verra much alive."

"But you're not," she said, feeling strangled by her own tears, sudden and unwanted. "Not really."

Because it was all too much for her brain. She'd known vampires before. Hell, she'd known Nat for years, and the facts of his existence had never sent her into a spiral. But to know that within Callum's broad, strong chest beat... nothing—that was more than she could handle.

He was too close. Too familiar, and yet too foreign. And with that hollow, affective breath, she felt her own chest begin to rise and fall with rapid, necessary, actual breath.

"You owe me an explanation, Marjory," he said quietly.

"You owe me the same," she snapped.

"You first."

"You're dead," she said again, her voice thick with threatening tears.

"But I'm here. I'm right here."

A small sob escaped her, and she found herself instantly surrounded. Her face was pressed into the broad strength of his chest as his arms wrapped tightly around her. And because she was a masochist, she allowed him. She pressed her ear to his chest, remembering so many nights held against him, falling asleep to the steady beat of his heart. But while his body felt the same kind of strong as it always had before, there was silence beneath his coat.

"Oh, gods," she said around another sob.

"Marjory," he whispered against the top of her head. "Look at me."

She couldn't. She couldn't take her ear away from his chest.

But he'd never let her hide from him before. Of course he wouldn't let her hide now. He leaned away from her and tipped her chin up.

"I cannae believe you're here, Marjory," he whispered.

A war raged inside of Jory at that moment. On the one side, her rational, wounded brain was shrieking at her to put as much distance as possible between them. To scream at him and claw at him and make him feel every bit of her pain and loneliness. That side screamed about his empty chest and expensive cologne and bottled blood and how she didn't know a single thing about him anymore and how she was righteously, incandescently *furious* with him.

But on the other side of the battlefield was the part of her that had loved him enough to give up everything for him, who had loved him enough to beg a god for a miracle, to mourn him for a millennium. The side that looked into his stormy gray eyes and couldn't believe that he was here either. Across millennia, across continents, across lifetimes and life spans.

It was that side that had her reaching up with a hesitant hand to stroke the stubble on his cheek, so familiar and yet so strange at the same time. He groaned like a contented animal and leaned into her touch, a sound so embedded in her memories that fresh tears sprang to her eyes.

"Why are you here, Callum?"

He brought his hand up to her cheek, their bodies mirrored. His hand was cold, and she swallowed against the lump in her throat at the feeling of that coolness against her skin. He'd always been so warm. Like a blaze on a summer night. She'd tucked her hands and feet under and all around him in bed while he groused about how cold they were. But he'd let her do it anyway. He'd let her steal his warmth.

But he had none to offer her now. Only cold hands and an empty chest.

She leaned in anyway. Because she liked to torment herself or because she couldn't not, she didn't know. But she leaned into his palm. He brushed a thumb under her eye, sweeping the moisture away. Another familiar gesture. It felt as natural to let him do it as it had to let him hold her.

And so she let him. Just for a minute, she told herself. She let him wipe away her tears and take a half step closer. She let him cradle the back of her head with his other hand. She let him draw her closer to his empty chest.

While that formidable, fighting side of her brain screamed that she should run, she let him lower his head and press his mouth against hers, shivering when he groaned like he'd found an oasis after days in the desert. She wrapped her arms around his neck. And she let herself kiss him back. Just for a minute, she told herself. Just for a moment she would let herself feel like she had before. The emptiness, the anger, the despair would all be there in a minute.

11

Callum wrapped Marjory up in his arms, pulling her flush against his chest, feeling the strong contours of her body against his. She let out a breathy little sigh as she twined her arms around his neck and pressed into his kiss. The slick slide of her tongue against his lips made his knees momentarily weak.

"Marjory," he murmured against her mouth before chasing her tongue with his own.

She pulled back enough to say, "It's Jory now."

Jory. He didn't know what to think of it. Marjory was the most beautiful name he had ever heard in all his life. It was lyrical and lovely and the kind of name that required you to chew it a bit even as it rolled easily over tongue and teeth and lips. It was the name for a queen. For a goddess. Hadn't she been just that to him? His goddess, rising from the sea to save his life, to drag him back to the land of the living the way she'd dragged his half-dead body across that beach so many years ago?

Maybe she *was* a goddess. Maybe she always had been. He had no way of knowing. Because *Jory* had so many secrets. Which, of course, meant that his Marjory had too. He didn't know what to do with that. He didn't know what to do with her, Because this new person, this *Jory*, was a stranger to him. He wanted to hate her. But when had he ever gotten what he'd wanted since—

She bit at his bottom lip, her sharp teeth nipping. He groaned and pulled her tighter against him.

Jory. It was shorter. Without the soft yawn of the *Mar* before it, it slid off the tongue like a blade. Sharp. Honed. Without any attempt at pretense or nonsense. Perhaps it suited her after all. Because the woman in his arms now was sharp like a dagger.

Perhaps that part was his fault. Perhaps he was the stone that had sharpened the blade. Perhaps his abandonment had given her that cutting edge.

"Jory," he whispered, and she pulled herself closer against him again, kissing him with more fervor. Or was it fury? So be it. He was furious too.

She moaned softly into his mouth, and he pivoted their bodies, pressing her back against Hank's shed. He reached behind her, palming above the back of her knees, and lifted her. Her legs wrapped tightly around his waist, and he drove her against the siding.

As he kissed her, he remembered one of his bouncers talking to a bartender about "putting a date through the wall during sex." He smirked, thinking that while his mortal bouncer would have had to work very hard to do that, it would be no trouble at all for Callum to put Jory through the whole goddamn shed and out the other side.

"What's so funny?" Mar— *Jory* snapped at him.

He almost lied. It was on the tip of his tongue to say something about being ticklish—he always had been—but he decided against it. Hadn't there been enough untruths between them?

"I was just thinking about one of my employees bragging about—"

"You're thinking about an employee right now? I can— *oh*."

He ground his hips against hers roughly and set his teeth against her throat. Gently. So very gently. Not enough to hurt or even *hint* at hurt, but enough. Her words died in her mouth with a moan. He felt his hands shake. The last time his teeth had been against her throat, he'd... he couldn't think about it.

But now, he scraped his fangs against her racing pulse before latching on with his lips and sucking gently—a kiss, not a bite.

"I cannae believe it," he whispered against her throat.

Jory swallowed, her throat bobbing against his kissing lips. "Don't," she hissed.

He pictured her snarling. He pictured them both snarling, circling one another in a rage that was nearly a thousand years built, one tear at a time. They kissed like that, all teeth and anger and anguish. It was not a lover's kiss.

Jory dropped her head back, banging it against the metal siding of the shed, and Callum instinctively brought a hand behind it, to cradle it. Because while he knew it would take a hell of a lot more than a shed to break Jory, while he was *furious* with her, he couldn't bear the thought of her being harmed, even by accident.

He rolled his hips gently, finding a rhythm. Jory's breath came in short, sharp gasps. "Do ye remember the day that I came home from being away, and ye missed me so much that you met me at the door naked as the day ye were born and I took you against the open doorframe?"

Her moan sounded like a sob. She grabbed his cheeks between her palms and pulled his face toward hers, kissing him desperately.

"Because I remember, Jory," he said, her name still foreign on his tongue. Why couldn't she have stayed there? Why couldn't there have been a solid door between her and what he'd become? Why couldn't she have told him what she—

"Shut up," she growled. "Just shut up and kiss me. I don't want to talk. I hate you, Callum MacLeod. I hate you so fucking much."

His hand left the back of her head and returned to her thigh, kneading it firmly. But he did as she asked, kissing her like it was the last chance he'd get. Because he knew that it very well might be.

He moaned into her mouth as she ground hard against him, writhing in his arms. Across the yard, on the other side of the shed, Callum heard Esther go into the house. He heard Hank collect empty bottles and then cross the yard to the shed. He heard the recycling bin lid lift, but then there was silence on the other side.

Just then, Jory bit down on his lower lip. Hard.

"Jory," he groaned softly.

"Shut up," she panted.

"Jory," he whispered, his lips skating over her jaw. "Tha mi gad ionndrainn."

It was true. He did miss her. He missed her like he missed the smell of heather and the simplicity of their life before where he'd lived by his sword for short spans of time and then lived for her the rest of his days. Even if he was livid, he could admit it. That longing for what had been, for her, had defined nearly his entire existence.

He heard the recycling bin close, but Hank's steps did not retreat. Jory was oblivious, kissing his neck, dragging her lips across his skin over his collar and whimpering every so often as she did. He squeezed her ass once more before pulling his head back.

In Gaelic, he said, "I should go. I shouldnae have stayed."

She stared at him as if he'd slapped her. And maybe he had. It seemed that all he could do was hurt her without meaning to. He never, ever, *ever* meant to. But that didn't negate anything. Well meaning didn't mean well done.

"I want..." he trailed off, looking into her emerald-green eyes, bright and otherworldly in the darkness. Too bright to be human. They always had been, hadn't they? Why hadn't he noticed that before?

There were so many secrets, and he was angry. He was more than angry. He was *enraged*. But even with that anger boiling just below the surface, he could admit that he loved her. He'd never stopped. *I don't want to talk. I hate you*, she'd said. She'd meant it too.

"I shouldnae have kissed ye. You hate me. It was wrong to... take advantage of old chemistry. I just.... I missed you so goddamn much. I never stopped. But you have a life. Without me. And I should do the gracious thing and let you get back to it. I'll leave tonight."

He heard Hank turn to walk away from the other side of the shed, and he bent at the waist to set Jory down, but she gripped his coat in her strong fingers and levered herself against his chest, her nose touching his as she hissed, "Not until you tell me where it is, you bastard."

12

Jory had had lovers. There had been the Lycan prince she'd met while traveling through the Highlands. The relationship wasn't destined to last, but they'd passed an enjoyable fifty years together before he'd met his fated mate in the middle of a dark forest under a full moon in a turn of events that felt almost overwhelmingly cliché.

She'd lived with an exiled demon on the Isle of Wight for another hundred years or so. Halphas was a munition and weapon supplier for Hell. He'd been exiled to earth for losing a battle and forbidden to do what he did best—wage war—for one hundred years.

They'd both been angry at their circumstances, their losses. It had been enough to bind them. His punishment was peace, and they'd found it together for a century. But on the last day of his hundredth year, he'd wrapped his rangy arms around her, called her his bigliad, his comforter, kissed her forehead, and been swallowed whole by a flash of flame and smoke. He'd liked her well enough to feel guilt for leaving, but not enough to stay.

She hadn't loved either of them, Halphas or the Lycan prince. Not like she'd loved Callum. They'd been... companionable, which is why it hadn't devastated her when they'd gone. But they'd still left. Jory had stood in yet another empty seaside cottage, this one smelling of brimstone and magic. Alone.

There'd been a vampire chimney sweep in London and a witch in Paris and a brief dalliance with a fae couple in Germany that had been as toxic as it had been thrilling. She'd had plenty of lovers. But nobody, mortal or otherwise, had ever made her body feel like she would catch on fire like Callum MacLeod. When he'd kissed her, when he pressed her against the shed, so strong in how he held her, every single nerve in her body had lit up like a wildfire.

As her body slid against Callum's with so much familiarity that it made her ache, she could admit how desperately lonely she'd been. And now he was going to leave. *Again.* So be it. But she'd be damned if she let him leave without telling her where to find the sealskin. For centuries, she had searched, listening for news of it. But she had never found it. And eventually, she'd left Europe and found her way here, to the Pacific Northwest, to a place where the waves crashed loudly against the rocks and the wind whipped the coast and the trees grew lush and green and silent.

But all of it, absolutely all of it, had been in service of going home. Biding her time until she could return to the sea, to her family, to her *real* life. That mission felt all the more essential since she'd learned that the life she'd left all of it for, the life she'd *thought* she had, had been a lie.

Callum MacLeod would not be leaving without telling her where she could find her ticket back.

They were nearly nose to nose now, her breath making

clouds in the cold air, his breath... nonexistent. But that crackling tension sparkled between them like heat lightning, and it would be so easy, so very easy, to close that breath of distance and kiss him again.

She gripped his coat in her fingers, feeling the artificial down compress within her grip.

"What?" he asked, his hold on her strong and steady, his gaze anything but.

"You're not leaving until you tell me where it is."

"Where what is, Mar—Jory? I dinnae ken what you're talking about."

"My sealskin," she said, her teeth bared. "You stole it and it's mine and I want it back."

"Your... sealskin?" he asked.

"Yes. My sealskin. I want it back."

He got a look in his eye. A gleam that was sharp. Just for a moment before it disappeared. If she hadn't been glaring at him, she would have missed it. But it sliced through the forlorn look he'd had all evening.

"Don't even think of lying to me, Callum MacLeod. After all the lying you've done. You can't—"

"All the lying I have done. All the lying *I* have done? I never lied to you a day in our lives. But you? Och, you did a whole lot of lying, aye? *Jory?*"

Her name felt like a weapon in his mouth.

But he wasn't wrong.

"So let's trade honesty, aye?" Callum said, gripping her ass and pushing against her, even closer than they were before. He was angry now. *Good.* They could be angry together. "You tell me your tale, you tell me how many lies you told me. From the beginning. And I'll tell you where it is."

"You're blackmailing me?"

"Nay. I'm offering an even exchange. I'll give ye your sealskin. Though why the fuck you're so concerned about it, I cannae guess."

"Because it's all I have!"

"All you have? *All you have?* I'm here after a thousand years of missing you, *grieving you*, making my life worthy of having had you in it. Lifetimes apart, Jory. *Lifetimes.* And a goddamn animal hide is *all you have?*"

"You left me," she said, clinging to that bit of high ground with her fingertips.

"Aye. I left. To *avenge you!*" Callum barked.

Jory's head was swimming again. He was too close, intoxicatingly close. Avenge her? Against whom? She had no enemies. She never had. The attack on the beach all those years ago had been an act of random, senseless violence. Against the both of them. Hadn't it? Unless...

"What do you know about that night?" she asked.

He froze, his hard, cool body going even more rigid around her.

"I have secrets, Callum. But do not stand here and pretend that you don't have any of your own."

His throat worked, bobbing with a heavy swallow.

"You're not going anywhere, Callum. Not until we have this out. You *owe* me."

He looked as if he would speak, as if he would answer for himself. She waited, the night around them cold and crisp and quiet. But in a flash, she found herself standing on her own two feet, leaning against the shed. Faster than she could blink, he had gently set her down and stepped away from her, standing ten or so feet away.

"I'm sorry, Jory," he whispered.

And then, in a blur of movement, he was gone.

13

At precisely ten o'clock the next morning, Magda and Esther breezed through the door of Jory's shop with Styrofoam cups of to-go coffee and tea, a bag of donuts, and a large bottle of honey. They were an excellent pair as Esther was always ten minutes late to everything and Magda always seemed to be ten minutes early; with their powers combined, they usually arrived exactly on time.

Not that it really mattered. They were packing up and shipping orders since more than half of the stock that Jory had brought back from New Mexico had sold in a frenzy that had surprised and bewildered Jory and Esther. It was Sunday and the store was closed, giving them the whole day to work undisturbed. Unfortunately, that also meant that Esther and Magda would have unlimited, unfettered access to Jory to ask her anything they wanted without any real chance of escape.

"You saucy bitch!" Esther crowed as she squeezed through the door, her arms full.

"Good morning, Esther," Jory said in a monotone.

"Morning, saucy bitch," Magda said with a broad smile.

"Magda," Jory said, rolling her eyes.

"He kissed you!" Esther screeched. "And you liked it!"

Jory felt her cheeks heat with a blush. "How the hell do you know that?"

"Hank," Esther said, beaming.

"Hank?"

"He was taking the empty bottles to the recycling bin by the shed and heard you. Or he heard someone that sounded an awful lot like you. And someone who sounded an awful like Callum wooing the shit out of that person who sounded an awful lot like you."

She raised her shoulders up and down quickly and winked an electric blue eye. Badly. It looked more like a squint than a wink, and Jory couldn't help but snort. Nobody, in all her years of living among humans, had ever made Jory laugh as easily and as freely as Esther MacLaren.

"Knew it," Magda said smugly, removing a little fabric box from her massive purse.

"You knew what, exactly? And that reminds me. I still have a bone to pick with you, Magda. You have some nerve giving him a—what *the hell* is that?" Jory exclaimed as Magda lifted the lid on the small box to reveal something that looked very much like a tiny Cousin It, if Cousin It had been buttercup yellow with tiny iridescent wings and beady black eyes peeking out from a wealth of fluff.

"This is Walter. He just had a haircut," Magda answered matter-of-factly.

"Yes, but what is he?" Jory asked.

"He's a Brightling Beetle," Esther supplied helpfully. "Isn't he adorable? Yes, you are!" Esther crooned at the tiny creature, which flitted out of the box and landed in Esther's open palm, seeming more than content to be there.

"Alright then. Why is he here?"

Magda clucked her tongue. "He doesn't like to be alone. Plus, Mr. Dick Van Dyke needed to rest, and Walter won't let him nap in peace. You won't even know he's here."

Jory narrowed her eyes at the tiny creature, who seemed to narrow his tiny eyes back.

"So..." Esther said.

"So what?" Jory replied, loading more labels into the printer.

"Tell us about the kiss!"

"I'd rather not," Jory said tightly.

Esther rolled her lips between her teeth, practically chewing on her smile.

"Fine," Jory said with a huff, throwing her hands in the air. "I kissed him."

Esther took off her puffy coat and bunched it into a wad, which she stuffed unceremoniously under the desk. "Aaaand?"

"And what?" Jory replied.

"Oh my god, Jory. How was it?"

Jory loved Esther's warm, southern drawl. *Oh mah gawd, Johr-y.*

Magda listened quietly as she poured honey from the large jar into a tea saucer. Walter flitted clumsily through the air, landing on the rim of the saucer and attacking the honey with far more gusto and noise than Jory would have thought possible from so small a creature.

"Well?" Esther prompted when Jory still hadn't answered.

"It was... different," she said quietly, remembering the feel of Callum's lips against hers.

Magda perked up at that. She arched a penciled eyebrow, waiting for Jory to continue. Jory sighed.

"He used to be so... warm. Sometimes almost too warm. And now he's..." she trailed off.

"Dead?" Magda supplied helpfully.

Esther elbowed Magda. "Magda," she hissed.

"What?" the older woman said, elbowing Esther back, just as hard.

"He's not dead," Esther insisted.

"My mistake. *Undead,*" Magda corrected tartly, her gaze returning to Jory.

If Jory didn't know Magda as well as she did, she might have mistaken that sharp look for judgment. But she did know Magda, and so she knew that Magda was simply stating the facts.

"Technically," Jory answered. Because undead did seem the most accurate way to describe Callum, who had proven himself to be very much alive. All except that empty, silent chest beneath her ear.

The two women looked at her expectantly while Walter slurped loudly on the counter between them.

"It was good. I wanted—" She'd wanted everything. All at once. She'd wanted to pull him so close to her that their cells melded at the same time she wanted to push him so far away that he'd never find her again. "He said he wanted to leave me alone. That he couldn't handle me hating him."

"Do you hate him?" Esther asked quietly before taking a long sip from the Styrofoam cup with her name written on the side in sloppy permanent marker.

"I don't know," Jory whispered immediately. "But it doesn't matter. He left."

"No, he didn't," Magda said, stuffing her own coat beneath the counter next to Esther's.

"He didn't?"

"By the time he got back to the cabin and stomped

around, it was too late for him to travel. Too risky. But I wouldn't be surprised if he left tonight."

Tonight.

"What are you going to do?" Esther asked excitedly, leaning her elbows on the counter.

Jory had known Esther for all of thirty seconds before it had become clear that Esther was a romantic. She'd been a begrudging one, too tired and knocked around by her life to have the clarity to admit it, but one didn't fall head over heels for a man in less than two weeks without having a romantic streak buried somewhere.

Jory had recognized it because, once upon a time, she'd been desperately romantic herself. Why else would she have given up immortality for a mere mortal man?

Her throat ached.

"She's going to go talk to him," Magda said with a nod.

"I am?" Jory asked, it now being her turn to raise her brows.

"Yes, you are," Magda said, pointing a painted red fingernail at Jory. "Because you have to tell him the truth. You'll never be able to live with yourself if you don't. And while I don't have experience with it, I imagine that eternity is a hell of a long time to live with that kind of baggage."

Jory set her teeth and glared petulantly at Magda. She didn't want to dig up the past—his or hers—and examine it under the microscope of hindsight. But Magda reached across the counter and laid her small hand on top of Jory's, letting it rest there. She looked deep into Jory's eyes, the way she so often did, like she was actually looking inside of her.

"Jory, my love," Magda said, "you have been so brave and so strong and have accomplished and survived so much. Alone for the most part. Aren't you at all curious? Aren't you at all interested in knowing how, after a hundred lifetimes, he found his way to you?"

"I don't owe him anything," Jory said, tears burning suddenly in her eyes.

Esther sniffed wetly. Without looking at her, Jory whisked a tissue out of the box and handed it over.

Magda squeezed her hand. "You owe it to yourself to find some peace."

Jory remembered lying on her back in a field of grass while the wind whipped and made the clouds race across the sky overhead. Callum coming upon her, blocking out the sun with his body, before laying down beside her and gathering her in his arms, rolling her on top of him. Of falling asleep with the hot sun on her back and his warm, pounding chest beneath her.

It had been the little things she'd missed the most, in the middle of the night when sleep was elusive and her thoughts too fast to catch. Cooking dinner together. Mending nets side by side in the sunshine. Building their home together, taking care of it. Going to sleep in his arms at night and waking each morning when he pulled her close against his chest, the way he mumbled sleepy good morning greetings against her neck, in the wild thicket of her hair.

Esther handed her a tissue, which she gratefully took.

"I don't know that my heart can take it, Magda," she said, tears blurring her vision.

"Are you willing to risk it if you don't? How else will you ever go home?"

Esther stared at Magda with a puzzled look on her face. "Home?" she asked.

"Home," Magda repeated, her eyes locked on Jory's.

"Home," Jory answered. She *had* to go home. It was all

she'd wanted, the only thing that had kept her going through the misery of centuries of struggle.

The store was quiet, the essential oil diffuser sounding far louder than usual in the stillness as the three women exchanged very different looks between them. Jory did not practice magic, but she'd witnessed enough of it. The moment felt like the charged suspension just before a spell was broken, when all of the energy and light and possibility hung in a fraught, delicate balance.

And like a catalyst breaks a spell, so, too, was the tension shattered as Walter emitted a comically loud burp.

Jory and Esther packed boxes, and Magda sat on a stool behind the counter, affixing shipping labels and checking off the list. They drank tea and coffee, ate donuts. Walter fell asleep in a basket of vintage silk scarves. Eventually Hank dropped by with a paper grocery bag of sandwiches he'd made, along with a zip-top bag of grapes and a tin of cookies leftover from the Yule bonfire the night before.

He offered to return later with snacks and more coffee, and when Jory protested, Esther insisted, saying that Jory could let her friends take care of her once in a while. She'd said it with such a pointed, obvious look on her face that Hank had glanced curiously between the two of them. Jory had no doubt that later that night, Hank would hear every single bit of their conversation recounted to him in minute detail with two dozen different sidebars. Esther rose on to her tiptoes and pulled him down for a kiss before shooing him out the door.

It was a pleasurable day, spent in the easy company of friends. But as the afternoon light dimmed and softened into the velvety purple of dusk, Jory felt her anxiety rise higher and higher. Just after sunset, Magda and Esther packed up the trash and coaxed Walter back into his little box.

"Call me if you need anything tonight, Jory," Esther said. "Anything at all. No matter what time it is."

Jory nodded, her smile tight and brittle. Esther was such a good friend. Sometimes it felt like too much, like more than she deserved.

Magda approached, her large purse strap cutting through the puffy down of her jacket and leaving a deep divot on her shoulder. "He'll be up now. I wouldn't wait too long."

After they'd gone, Jory finished tidying the store so that it would be ready for business the next day. She went upstairs to her apartment and changed her clothes, swapping out her leggings and sweatshirt for a pair of worn, soft jeans and an oversized fisherman sweater. She laced her boots and threw on a coat before locking her door and going down to where her car was parked behind the building.

After a drive that felt like it took an eternity and mere moments at the same time, the little A-frame cabin appeared at the end of the drive, snug and welcoming, with the lights shining out the big windows. She didn't see anyone moving around, but a black SUV was parked in front. She pulled in next to it and turned her car off, sitting in the warm silence for a few minutes, gathering herself.

She was going to knock on the door. He would invite her in. She would sit on one of the hard bar stools. He would offer her a drink. She would ask for a water. And then she would come out with it. She'd be blunt and to the point. She wouldn't touch him. She wouldn't even look at him more than was necessary. And she definitely wouldn't let him come close enough to remind her of how it felt to kiss him.

She shook her head. No, she was definitely not going to

think about that. A person needed sturdy knees and dry panties to have a conversation like the one she was about to have. She opened the car door and closed it behind her. She walked up the slick, wooden steps and crossed the deck. Her knock sounded loud in the quiet of the night around her. She heard it echo in the house on the other side. There was no answer. She knocked again harder and heard a banging and shuffling from within the cabin. The deadbolt turned. Then the knob.

Jory had been prepared to see Callum in a suit, as she'd seen him that first night in Hank's kitchen. Or perhaps in an outfit like hers, warm and concealing. She had not, however, been prepared for him to answer the door shirtless in gray sweatpants, with water trailing down his torso in small streams, soaking the waistband a darker gray, drawing her eye down, to where certain places on the front of the sweatpants were also darker. Wetter.

"Fuck me," she hissed before she could stop herself, slapping a hand over her mouth and snapping her gaze back up, where it belonged.

14

His gray eyes locked on hers, his blond hair wet and dripping onto his shoulders. He held a towel, which he'd been using to dry his hair when he answered the door but now hung limp and forgotten in his hand. So much for breezy, queenly composure. So much for having the upper hand. Apparently all it took to completely rattle her was a pair of suspiciously damp sweatpants and a wet, naked torso.

"Marjory," Callum said, as if he couldn't believe she was here. "I wasnae expecting you."

"I can see that. Do you often answer the door like"—she gestured up and down his body but didn't look—"this?"

"I didnae want to answer the door in only a towel."

"And this is better?" Jory choked.

"I *am* wearing pants. Far less chance of a wardrobe mishap in pants than a towel. Magda didnae buy towels with a man my size in mind."

"I wouldn't be so sure of that," Jory muttered under her breath.

Callum smiled wolfishly. "She hasnae ever dropped by

to see me in my birthday suit, if that's what you're implying."

Jory rolled her eyes, her gaze catching on a drop of water that dripped from his hair and sluiced down his neck, following the muscled lines of his chest and disappearing into his chest hair. She didn't allow herself to follow it further, couldn't allow herself to look back down at those obscene, damp sweatpants. She came here to talk to him, and if she let her eyes follow that water drop where it was about to lead, she'd forget about talking and try to climb him like a tree.

Instead, she stared hard at his Adam's apple, at the stubble of beard that dotted his neck. It felt safer than looking up at his piercing eyes or down at... *Stop it, Jory.*

Callum cleared his throat. "Would you like to come in?" He opened the door farther and stood out of her way, giving her space to wordlessly pass into the cabin.

When he had closed the door behind her, he said, "If you'll give me a moment, I'll be right back."

She'd been here before. She'd *lived* here before, and so she was confused when he disappeared into what Jory knew was a closet. She followed him and saw a hatch door that had been cleverly disguised by the planks of the wood floor, which opened to a staircase. She knew she shouldn't follow him. And yet before she could stop herself, she was on the stairs going carefully down.

"I never knew this was down here," she said, her boots sounding heavy on the wooden steps. She reached the bottom of the staircase in time to see the muscled lines of Callum's back as he bent over a suitcase on the floor in the corner. Her mouth went dry. This was a bad idea. No, this was a terrible idea. Hadn't she learned her lesson last night? *Always so thirsty, lass.*

He straightened and pulled a white T-shirt over his

head, his big, tanned hands yanking the hem down.

She crossed her arms tightly over her chest, realizing that she was still wearing her heavy coat. She was too warm. He crossed the room, and her gaze fell to his feet. She'd always marveled at them, at how different they were from her own. He stopped a respectful distance from her and waited, quiet, as if he was afraid to spook her.

She looked at him and saw how tight his jaw was, how wary his eyes looked.

"I came to talk," she said. "I think... I think we need to talk."

"Aye," he replied. "I agree."

They stared at one another for a few spans of breath, in this vault that Magda had never told anyone about. Jory had *lived here*. When she'd first come to World's End. Had the vault been there then? How many other secrets did Magda have? Jory's gaze travelled around the room, to the quilt-topped iron bed frame. To the little sofa and the desk and chair, the rumpled pile of clothes underneath the desk. The laptop and tablet, cell phone, and watch on top. Retail was her business. Designer brands. Vintage. All of it. She knew a Vacheron Constantin Tourbillon Chronograph when she saw one.

"Nice watch," she said.

"Aye. It is."

"Expensive."

He sighed. "Aye."

"Very expensive."

"Aye." He rubbed his neck, as if uncomfortable. "I've made a lot of money," he said flatly. "My assistant told me that a man with as much money as I have should wear a watch to match."

"Do you agree?"

"I dinnae care," he said, his voice tight.

"About what? The watch or the money?"

"Both."

"And yet you bought it anyway."

She was needling him. She knew it, but it felt so good, so familiar in a moment where nothing else did. When they'd lived in the cottage by the sea, she could have packed all of their essential belongings into two rucksacks and all of their earthly possessions in a small cart. Now, he wore a watch that cost more money than some people made in their lifetimes.

"Aye. I bought it anyway. 'Tis a good watch."

"For as much as you paid, it should be."

He dragged a hand through his wet hair. "Did you come here to harangue me about my finances? Should I pull up my accounts? Do you want to see what I'm worth now? I couldnae give you anything before. Maybe I can make up for that now?"

"I don't give a shit about your money," she said.

His jaw was tense. They were getting nowhere like this. Struggling for calm, Jory took a deep breath.

"It has come to my attention," she went on, looking at the floor, at his familiar feet, "that there are quite a few secrets between us. And I"—she swallowed thickly—"I would like to put them all out on the table."

"Why now?"

Jory squeezed her eyes shut tightly, refusing to cry.

"I want to be honest. You deserve my honesty. And I deserve yours. At the very least I think we can give each other that."

He took a prowling step closer. "And I have something you want." His voice was still hard and defensive. But she was too tired to fight.

"You do. But tonight, the only thing I want is the truth."

"An exchange? You'll tell me your secrets in exchange for a worthless animal hide?"

"It isn't worthless," she snarled through her teeth, her vehemence almost startling. She sucked in a breath, collecting herself. "Look. I'll tell you everything. But I want the same promise from you."

He was quiet for a long moment. Long enough for Jory to study the tight set of his shoulders, his clenched fists. She'd never once feared those fists, and she didn't fear them now. He was like a lion, brutal and powerful, but he'd always been *her* lion, eating out of the palm of her hand and rubbing his shaggy head against her palm even as blood dripped from his jaws.

That image felt eerie as it shuddered through her brain, as she pictured blood dripping from his fangs as he pressed his groaning face against her throat now.

"Would ye prefer to go upstairs for this? I can offer you some tea. Or perhaps a whiskey?" he asked, his manners far more refined than they'd been when she'd been his. *Before*, she corrected. Because for all his defensiveness tonight, she had the distinct impression that she was *still* his, that she only had to beckon to him and he'd conquer the entire world to lay it at her feet.

But this room, for all that it was small and sparse and windowless, reminded her of the cottage. It was the same size, with a big bed in the corner. They hadn't had a sofa or a desk. They hadn't had suitcases or tablets or watches. But they'd had a worn wooden table and two chairs, a rocker that he'd built her from driftwood, a hearth, seashells hanging from the rafters and catching the warm light of the fire.

"Can we stay here instead?" she whispered.

"It's a bedroom. I dinnae want to make you uncomfortable," he said gruffly.

"I'm not uncomfortable," she replied. The truth was that this room strangely felt more comforting and familiar than any space she'd created for herself in a long time. Maybe it was the size. More likely it was him.

Callum cleared his throat and gestured to the couch. "Would you like to sit down?"

"Sure," Jory replied but stopped herself as a thought crossed her mind. She couldn't sit next to him on the couch, stiff and distant like strangers while she told him the whole story.

"Actually," she said hesitantly, kicking herself for the question she was about to ask, "I have an odd request."

He waited, his arms crossed over his chest, as if it would protect him from what she was going to ask.

"I don't want you to see my face when I cry, which I will, but I don't really want to cry alone." She took a deep breath, forcing herself to continue. "And I'm so mad at you that I could scream. I might scream. But... can we... lie down? And you could... hold me?"

He sucked in a breath that she knew was an affectation but appreciated so much anyway, a reminder of what he would have done before, of what his instinct was still to do now. It was so very *human* of him.

She expected him to refuse her. She should have known better.

Without a word, Callum crossed to the bed and flipped back the quilt. He climbed in and scooted to the far side, next to the wall, holding the quilt open and looking at her expectantly. Jory unzipped her coat and draped it on the desk chair over his. She unlaced her boots and placed them against the wall next to his. And then she went to the bed and slid in beside him, turning away from him onto her side.

Callum dropped the quilt, and she gripped it in her fists, pulling it up to her chin. He was so close behind her. She felt his body and his bulk, even if she didn't feel his heat.

This was a terrible plan. Jory was about to climb out the way she'd come when Callum's big arm wrapped around her, pulling her back against his chest. He slipped his other arm under her neck, cushioning it, the way he'd always done.

She didn't feel the thudding of his heart at her back or the steady rise and fall of his chest pressing against her shoulders. His skin was cool, but she marveled at how it felt almost soothing, like a damp cloth on a feverish forehead or a toe dipped in a stream on a hot day. His arms were solid and strong, and his body cradled hers as if they'd been made to fit together, all of their angles lining up perfectly.

He pressed the bridge of his nose and forehead against the back of her head, and she felt him breathe in. Tears sprang to her eyes at the familiarity of it all.

"I dinnae ken how it's possible," he whispered.

"What?" she asked, her lips feeling thick from her unshed tears.

"You smell exactly the same. I've searched for this smell for a thousand years." He breathed in deeply again.

"I should have told you the truth from the beginning," Jory said, so softly that she wondered if he'd heard her.

"This is a beginning," he said carefully, pressing his forehead more firmly against her hair. "Tell me now."

"In a minute," she said and closed her eyes.

He huffed what might have been a chuckle and pulled her closer.

"Alright, Jory. In a minute, then."

15

Callum could hardly believe that she was here. In his arms. In his bed. He buried his nose in her hair and smelled deeply. The salt. The earthiness. The heather. For nearly a thousand years, he'd sifted through rosewater baths and heavy perfumes and those goddamn azaleas that surrounded his club to find this, the smell of her.

If he closed his eyes, he could take them back to that heather-stuffed mattress in the little cottage by the sea, with nothing but the sound of her sleeping breath and a crackling fire, the delicate seashells clinking together in the rafters as the wind shook the house. He squeezed her tighter against his chest and let himself live in that memory, his eyes closed, at home in his mind with her in his arms.

Callum didn't know how long they lay there. Hours, at least. It was hard for him to grasp time. When a person was immortal, the difference between minutes and hours felt rather insignificant. He wondered, briefly, if it was the same for her. She seemed perfectly content to lie there. Let the night pass into day. Let the sun rise. Let the world crumble to dust around them. He would lie here with her in his arms until the very sun burned out. And then he'd hold her in the dark.

A fierce stab throbbed in the center of his chest as he imagined telling her the truth. She probably wouldn't let him hold her like this ever again once she knew. He'd be damned if he rushed this then. If he was going to lose her forever, he'd savor every single second of this moment.

But no sooner had that thought crossed his mind, she took a deep breath.

"I wasn't honest with you. Back then."

He waited, holding her close and keeping his nose in her hair, his forehead pressed against the back of her skull.

"I didn't find you on land. I found you from sea."

That confused him. He'd boarded the enemy ship and lost himself in the battle. He had barely noticed the shallow dagger wounds in his chest, the deep stab beneath his ribs. The slicing of a sword against his back. He took it all, inflicting as much if not more damage on his enemies.

And though a fire had broken out, he'd fought till the bitter end, until he was caught grappling with a man and hurled overboard, dislocating his shoulder on the way down. The impact had nearly knocked him unconscious, the saltwater in his many wounds caused blinding pain. But he'd found a bit of wood, and as the ships sank around him, he'd clawed his way through the water, through the dead, through the flotsam and jetsam, to shore. He'd crawled onto the sand and promptly fainted.

He remembered some of his fitful, feverish state. Unconscious for most of it, but he'd *felt* her gentleness, her warmth, her care. And then he'd opened his eyes and seen her. The waves of her wild, dark hair had been speckled with sand and tangled from the relentless wind. Her bright green eyes had seemed so otherworldly, so beautiful. Like an emerald he'd once seen against a fine lady's throat. The sun warming her naked skin made him wonder if she was an angel come to save him.

He remembered her bathing him, spooning fresh water into his parched mouth, shading him with her cloak. She lay down next to him every night, warming him with her own heat when the tremors racked his body.

"What do you mean?" Callum asked. Of course she had found him on land. There had been no women on either ship.

"I am not..." She paused, and Callum could imagine her chewing on her bottom lip, the way she did when she was thinking. "As you might have guessed, I am not human."

"Not anymore."

"Not ever."

He tried to turn her to face him, but she tensed and resisted. "No," she whispered. "Please."

"Tell me," he said and then, because she had, he added, "Please."

"The Norse called us kópakonan. The Irish said merrow."

He'd grown up with the tales. You didn't spend time on or near the sea without hearing them. Stories of strikingly beautiful women who could turn into seals, women who could be bound to human men with simple thievery and cleverness. Selkie brides. The old men would tell stories of them. Someone had an uncle or cousin who had caught and married one. All a man needed to do was to steal their—oh, fucking *hell*.

"Marjory," he whispered, dread and regret filling him. But also anger. So much anger. Because she was immortal, and *she always had been*. If only he'd known. He would never have...

"Why didnae you tell me you're a selkie, Marjory?" he bit out finally, after she'd remained silent.

She sighed. "How does one go about telling someone that? 'Oh, hello. I'm the immortal daughter of an ancient sea god.' How do you expect that to have gone?"

"I would have believed you."

She was quiet for a long moment. She didn't believe him. He didn't really believe himself either.

"My mother warned us to never tell a soul. To keep our skins safe. To keep our identities secret. She said that if a man found out, he would trap us forever. Much good the secret did me. I got trapped anyway."

"With me," he said, hearing the bitterness in his voice. The anger was palpable. "And ye thought I was one of those men? That I would trap ye without a care for your safety or happiness? Ye thought so little of me?"

She sucked in a quick, watery-sounding breath. "I was going to tell you."

"When?" he snapped.

"When you got back."

"Sure," he said and tried to sit up, but she dug her nails into his arm.

"It's the truth! I was going to tell you the moment you returned. But before I could, I—"

He flinched, allowed himself to be pulled back down to the mattress. Because this was the juncture where here untruth met his unforgivable.

She rolled over to face him. Her eyes were wet with tears. "I never felt trapped with you. I *wasn't* trapped with you. I loved our life. I loved—" She blew out a shaky exhale. "But then you left me *for dead* and took my skin with you and... and... where did you go, Callum?" His name was a sob.

Callum swallowed thickly. He wished she'd turn back over. It would be hard enough to tell the truth to the back of her head. It would be devastating to say it to her face, to have to see the hurt and betrayal in her eyes.

"I'd been hired away to fight for an earl, aye?"

"I remember," she said. "I didn't want you to go. I was so afraid for you."

He dared to lean in and place a soft kiss to her forehead. She let him.

"Aye. I ken ye were. On my way back, I was set upon by a witch and his band. He said that he'd been watching the battle and been impressed with me. Told me he had big plans and that he needed a swordsman like me to bring them about. I politely declined his offer."

"What kind of plans?" Jory asked.

"I dinnae ken. I didnae ask. I wasnae interested in delaying my return to you any longer. He told me that if I refused, that he would curse me. I carried on my way. But from behind me, I heard him issue a command. The next thing I knew, I was on the ground with teeth in my throat and a beast above me. I lay in agony in his camp for days, while he told me that it would all be over soon, that I would feel better soon."

Jory looked horrified.

"On the third day, I woke to a nearly full moon. He told me that I'd been bitten by his creature, a vampire, and been cursed to the night, to the blood."

"What did you do then?"

"I ran." Callum swallowed again, an unnecessary gesture unless feeding, but a familiar one nonetheless. "I left them. I buried myself underground during the day. I walked all night to get back to you. I didnae understand the thirst. I didnae understand the full extent of his curse. I—"

Callum closed his eyes tightly but nodded. "I was so tired. So cold. I dinnae ken how to describe it. All I knew is that I only wanted to bury my face in your lap and weep, to feel you stroke your fingers through my hair and tell me all would be well. I stumbled back to our home. You were nae inside. You were at the beach, waiting. I just knew, deep in my bones."

How could he tell the next part? How could he tell her the horrible, devastating truth that had haunted him for centuries?

"Say it," she said, her eyes bright with tears. "I want to hear you say it."

He sighed, ducking his chin to his chest and hanging his head. "I saw you down on the beach. Your hair was blowing in the wind, and you looked like an angel in the moonlight, sitting by the sea. My body *ached* for you. I stumbled down the rise, without a thought in my head but reaching you. But as I got closer, I smelled you. I smelled... your *life*. And the part of me that wanted to fall into your arms lost the battle to this new part of me, this cursed part of me. I'd never been so thirsty in all my life. And you smelled so good. And I —I—"

Jory leapt from the bed. "You attacked me!"

He followed her, coming to stand before her, faster than a blink.

"If I'd been a mortal human, you'd have killed me!"

She was right. His curse had been too new, too strong, and he'd had no control. He'd watched, like a person trapped behind bars, as his body had feasted upon hers, powerless to stop it.

"Marjory," he croaked. "The curse—"

"Fuck the curse! You're a monster!"

She could have said nearly anything else and he would have accepted it. But that word, that horrible word, it caused something to snap inside of him. "And you? You are nae a monster as well? You are nae human, Jory, and if you'd told me that back then, we wouldnae be standing here screaming at each other!"

She scoffed, crossed her arms over her chest and glaring at him. "Oh, really? If I'd told you I was a selkie, it would have stopped you from tearing at my throat like an animal?"

"Nay," he said, his voice dropping to a near whisper. "Nay. It wouldnae have stopped me. But I would never have left if you had. If I had known, I would have stayed by your side. I would have waited for you to heal, to return to me. I wouldnae have left to go destroy that warlock and his entire band. That's all I could think about, Jory. Revenge. I was consumed by it. I—" He broke off suddenly, not sure how much more to say.

"You what?" she seethed. "If you hadn't gone and fought in that foolish war, you wouldn't have encountered that goddamn warlock at all! And I wouldn't be cursed either!"

"Cursed, Jory? But—"

"Cursed to be trapped here on land! Cut off from my home, my family, everything else I loved. You cursed me when you took my sealskin and left me for dead!"

She was screaming now, looking like a vengeful goddess, her eyes flashing dangerously. She was terrifying and beautiful. And she was going to leave him. When she spun on her heel and rushed to the steps, scrambling up the first few, he was there, crowding behind her, his arms wrapped tightly around her legs. She froze.

His face was pressed in the gap between her thighs, just below her thick backside. He couldn't let her leave. Not yet.

She stood as still as if she'd been turned to stone, the only thing giving her away as a living creature being the way her breath heaved in and out of her chest. But he could smell her. Through the denim of her jeans and the cotton of the panties he knew she was wearing beneath them, he smelled her. Another smell he'd chased. Earthy and musky, with a hint of salt and sweet, that had driven him to madness how many nights, when he'd worked tirelessly for hours to drag more of that scent, that essence, from her writhing, pleasure-racked body.

He inhaled deeply, drawing that smell into his lungs, and his fury abruptly died.

"Marjory," he said, his eyes tightly closed, blocking out everything but the feel of her body in his arms and her scent around him. "Jory," he corrected. "That warlock cursed me. But the real curse was living day in and out without you. Knowing I wouldnae ever see you again. Knowing that I was the reason you were gone. That was the curse. To have been so verra happy, so verra loved, and to lose it all by my own hand."

She exhaled a shaky breath. If she'd commanded him to release her, he would have. Without hesitation. If she'd asked him to let her go, to send her the sealskin, and to never speak to her again, he would have agreed. Because her pain was his pain, and any lies she'd told him paled in comparison to what he'd done.

"Then why did you leave me in the first place?" she asked, her voice thick with tears. "Why did you have to go fight that damned battle?"

It was a question he'd asked himself a million times at least—literally—ever since. He'd had more than enough. They'd kept sheep and lived off the sea's bounty, and Jory had woven the finest yarn to trade for the rest. He hadn't needed glory or recognition. But...

"I... I wanted to give you the world. You deserved to live like a queen. I didnae have a castle or a title or even a family. I had my sword and my strength. Men paid a great deal for that. I wanted to give you everything you deserved."

"I only wanted you," she whispered. "I gave up everything up for you."

He dropped his head, the top of his skull pressing into the soft meatiness of her calf beneath the bend of her knee.

"Wasn't that enough?" she asked, and he could smell her tears, heard them drop and splatter onto the wood steps. "Wasn't I enough?"

If he could have clawed his own heart out of his chest and offered it to her, if that would have made a difference, he would have done it. He would have knelt at her feet and let her take from him what she felt she was owed.

"Jory," he said cautiously. "Can I... can I hold you?"

16

She didn't answer as much as she collapsed backwards. He caught her. He always had. He always would, if she let him. He gathered her in his arms and sat on the hard steps, holding her like a groom holds a bride as he carries her across the threshold. As he'd carried her across their threshold so many times.

Her eyes were closed and she wept into his chest, her tears soaking the white cotton of his T-shirt as he held her, stroking her hair softy and murmuring to her in whispered Gaelic. Endearments. Praise. Telling her how brave she was. How strong. How perfect. How much he'd missed her. How much she meant to him. He spoke so fervently and softly that he wasn't sure she even understood him, but it didn't matter. He'd been speaking those truths about her, about his memories of her, into the endless void for centuries. He didn't need her to hear them. He only needed her to keep letting him hold her like this.

Eventually, her sobs eased to sniffles. He dropped his chin to the top of her head, tucking her closer. She let him. He leaned his head to the side to look into her eyes, which were bright and clear, even if the skin around them was red and puffy from her crying.

"I've known vampires. I've heard that the first few months are horrible. That you need... a mentor. Someone to help you be safe. That otherwise, vampires cause too much damage and have to be... dealt with."

"Aye," he replied, because it was true. There was no larger governing body for vampires, just as there was no supreme council of supernatural creatures operating in tandem or opposite of the mortal institutions. But there was an unspoken law among his kind that, if a new vampire wreaked havoc, if they went rogue and put the rest of the community in danger of discovery, they must be dealt with. His entire species depended upon secrecy. Most creatures like him did.

"What did you do then?" she asked, playing with the soft cotton of his shirt, pinching a bit of the fabric and rubbing it between her thumb and forefinger.

That answer was simple.

"Well, when I left you, I went after those men. I dinnae remember it. Have you heard of the Berserkers?"

She shook her head.

"Well, the legends say that the Berserkers were fighters who went into battle in a near trance. They went without armor. They fought with impossible strength and speed and rage. They couldnae be felled by normal means. After the battle, surrounded by the carnage of their felled enemies, they recalled nothing that had transpired."

She waited, still rubbing the T-shirt between her fingers.

"I remember finding them, the dozen of them sitting around a fire, as if nothing could touch them. The next thing I remember is standing in a dark clearing, that full moon shining down, my body soaked with blood. It was in me and on me. And magic. The warlock had been powerful, and the leavings of his magic hung so heavy in the air that I could almost taste it."

His voice sank into the timbre of storytelling, something he'd been raised with, as a way to pass the long nights. He'd told stories to his comrades on ships and in soldiers' camps, and he'd told stories to Jory as he'd held her just like this in front of their little hearth, their driftwood rocking chair creaking beneath their combined weight.

"That sated the thirst for a time. Glutting yourself will do that. And then I wandered. Eventually, I found a woman who was like me. She came upon me when I was unearthing myself after a day beneath the ground. She took me in. We lived in the Highlands for a long time, hunting wayward men up to no good. She helped me learn to control my thirst."

"You were very lucky to have found her," Jory murmured, her body tensing slightly in his arms.

"Aye," he replied, kissing the top of her head. "She taught me to blend in. How to breathe and blink and sigh and yawn at intervals, though I didnae need to. She'd been the daughter of a Highland laird. She'd once been a pawn for a doomed alliance that ended with her entire clan nearly destroyed and her becoming, well..."

"A vampire."

"Aye."

"Where is she now?"

"Dead," Callum said flatly, the pain of that loss still sharp.

"Dead?" Jory asked, looking up at him. "Vampires don't die."

"We can, even if we are verra hard to kill."

"How did she die?"

He felt his eyes go unfocused as the memory swept in. "She said that she wanted to feel the warm grass beneath her toes. That she wanted to be with her family. She walked out of her crypt into a beautiful spring morning when the flowers were blooming."

"Oh," Jory said, an involuntary, shocked sort of sound.

He had been shocked too. He'd watched from the shadows as she'd stepped out into the sun, as she'd disintegrated into millions of sparkling, shimmering particles and blown away on that gentle spring breeze, leaving no trace. As if she'd never been there at all.

Callum cleared his throat, feeling it growing thick with his own tears. He had no desire to weep blood on Jory. He didn't think she'd be able to handle another shock for the day.

"It sounds like you loved her," Jory said. He could smell her jealousy. He felt it in the rigidness of her body in his hold.

"Aye," he said. "Elspeth saved my life. I wouldnae be here without her."

She tried to remove herself from his arms.

"Jory, stop."

"I don't want to hear about a woman you fell in love with days after killing me."

She flung herself off his lap.

"Would you listen?" he said. "I didnae love her like that! I have never loved anyone the way I loved you!" *The way I still love you!* his brain screamed, the words on the tip of his tongue. He bit them back.

"But you loved her enough!" she spat.

"Aye," he said, feeling those tears rising again. But this time, he did nothing to stop them. He felt one slip past his eyes and slide down his cheek. Jory gasped. "I did love her.

Elspeth was the closest thing to a mother I'd ever known. She was old when she'd been cursed. She had watched her entire family fall to ruin. Her children. Her husband. And then she'd been turned into this." He gestured to his torso.

Jory blinked at him, biting her lips as if she, too, might cry from how tragic it all sounded. And it was tragic as all hell. So many wounds, self-inflicted and otherwise.

"She said I reminded her of her oldest son," he said quietly. "So, aye, I loved her verra much."

Jory stood a few feet away from him, and they were both silent, staring into the blank middle space where memories lived.

"She taught me how to survive. And if I hadnae met her, I dinnae think I would have. And if I hadnae survived, if I hadnae learned to live in this world as... what I am, I wouldnae be sitting here, begging you to stop hating me just long enough to hear me." He stifled a sob. "I cannae bear your hatred, Jory. I cannae bear it."

Callum hung his head. She didn't move. The heat kicked off, and the room felt suddenly silent. Eventually, she stepped between his bent knees and raked a timid hand through his hair, sifting her fingers through the now-dry locks and gently pulling, lifting his head. She stepped closer still, until his cheek rested against the warmth of her torso, the bloody tears soaking into the wool.

He pulled away quickly.

"Your sweater. The blood. I—"

"Fuck the sweater," she whispered, gently tugging his hair until he collapsed against her, his face pressed against the soft, worn wool. He closed his eyes and breathed her in, breathed in her smell, as he'd done since she arrived. In some ways, he felt as if he were filling up a bank with it, so that if she left, *when* she left, he would have it stored in his memory, enough to get him through another thousand years. And then, who knew? Maybe she'd finally forgive him.

But he knew what he had to do. Though he'd been entirely ignorant of it, she'd been held hostage by him for too long.

"What will you do when ye have your sealskin back?" he asked, though he was terrified of her answer.

She was quiet for a moment before she whispered, "I'm going to go home."

"Home?"

"Yes. To my mother. My father. My sisters. Home."

"Will I see you again?" Callum asked, because he was a masochist.

She didn't answer. Which was an answer by itself. She wouldn't be returning. He wouldn't get another chance in a hundred years or a thousand years. He would never see her again.

Jory kept stroking his hair absently. He almost groaned from how good it felt. He craved her touch. He wanted to kiss her again. When he'd been behind her on the stairs, he'd wanted to tear her jeans away and bury his face in her heat. He wanted to devour her. And now he might lose her. Forever.

There would be no second chances. If he couldn't win her now, if he couldn't convince her to stay, to remind her of what they had shared, of the way it had been once, he'd never get the opportunity again.

He pulled away far enough to look up at her, his hands wrapped behind her legs, his palms cupping the muscle of her calves. "I have some conditions. For bringing you the skin."

She set her mouth in a hard line. "You think you have any right to place conditions on this?"

"Nay," he admitted, stroking up and down the long line of her calves. "I dinnae have any right. But if you are going to leave and never return, if I am to face an eternity where I never see you again, what do I have to lose?"

She sighed, a gusty, frustrated exhale that he felt in his hair. She didn't agree. But she didn't disagree either, which was almost as good. His mind raced as he tried to plan an attack. No, not an attack. *A seduction*. Not of her body. Well, not *only* of her body. But of her mind and heart as well.

"One month," he blurted out. Entirely uncollected. So very unlike himself.

"One month," she repeated slowly.

"I get to see you eight times. Twice a week. And then I'll go to Scotland and fetch the skin for you."

"Twice," she said, her hands leaving his hair, arms crossing over her chest. "I'll agree to seeing you twice."

"Marjory, seeing me eight times isnae so much to ask in the face of eternity, is it?"

"It's Jory," she snapped. "And two is my final offer."

"Four," he said. "Once per week."

She glared at him, her eyes narrow and cat-like. "Fine," she agreed after a long pause. "Once a week. And I'm coming to Scotland with you."

"You dinnae trust me?" Callum asked, aiming for light-hearted but realizing his misstep the moment the words had left his mouth.

She lifted an eyebrow high, as if to say, "What do you think?"

"Verra well," he said, his despair shifting into determination. "I see you once a week, and I'll take you to Scotland."

He stood and went to wrap his arms around her, but she stepped back, her palm out to push him away.

"But they're not dates. They're... meetings. As friends."

Now it was his turn to raise an eyebrow. "Friends."

"Yes. And as we're just friends. No more kissing. Definitely no sex."

"But—"

"No sex," she repeated. "You can be my friend, or you'll be nothing."

The businessman in him, the person who had negotiated countless difficult deals, wanted to remind her that she had no real collateral to bargain with or against either. She'd never find the skin without him. She needed him. But that was the businessman. The man who had loved her for nearly a thousand years, who had just pondered carving out his own heart for her, knew that he could never deny her anything.

And so with a slow nod, he stuck out his hand. She took it, and they shook.

"Verra well, Jory. Friends."

17

Jory couldn't help the tiny smile that tugged, unbidden, at her mouth. Callum returned it with a twitch of his own mouth that wanted to be a smile—would have been a smile—if he'd let it.

"What time is it?" she asked.

Callum crossed to the desk and picked up the watch. "Seven thirty."

"Shit," she hissed between her teeth. How had she been there all night? "I've got to go! I've got to open the store."

Callum stood staring at her, his arms down by his sides. Jory could hear the subtle, barely audible ticking of the watch in his hand. She did need to leave now if she wanted time to grab a shower and eat breakfast, perhaps drink a cup of coffee before opening the store. And she *had* to change her clothes. Her sweater was smeared with Callum's bloody tears. But she found herself struggling to make herself pick up her purse and coat, to climb out of the vault.

"I wish you didnae have to go, Jory," he said quietly.

She didn't really want to go either. But she had a business to run. More to the point, he was dangerous. She'd been so confident a few moments before, when she'd forbidden kissing. But the truth was, she knew that if she stayed in this small, cozy space any longer, she was likely to throw all of her own rules out the window.

Besides, he had a ragged, weary look on his face.

"You look tired, Callum."

"I am tired."

"So sleep."

He looked at the floor, as if thinking. Then he murmured, "I dinnae expect I'll sleep much today."

"Why not?"

He looked up at her. "Because I'll be remembering everything that happened tonight. I dinnae want you to leave without a plan to see you next."

It was all too much. His focus, his attention, *him*. She spun around and reached for her coat, sliding her arms into the sleeves before bending to retrieve her purse. She put it on her shoulder and turned, gasping loudly when she nearly ran into him. He'd moved directly behind her, and she hadn't heard.

"Easy," he said, his big hands holding her upper arms to steady her.

"What the fuck, Callum?" she said, slapping his chest. "You almost gave me a heart attack!"

He released her arm and pressed a palm against her furious heartbeat. "Dinnae joke about such things."

"I—"

"Please, Jory. I cannae bear to even hear the joke."

"Friends. We said friends," she blurted out because she needed the reminder, because she couldn't breathe with his hand there.

He dropped both hands as quickly as if she'd burned

him, but he still stood so close that if she had shifted her weight onto her toes, her chest would have touched his.

"When can I see you again, *friend*?" he asked, the "friend" trapped somewhere between a purr and a growl.

"Friday?"

"It's Monday. I dinnae want to wait until then to see you."

She had to get out of there. If she didn't, she would probably do something decidedly un-friendlike.

"Friday," she repeated.

She needed that time. She needed the space of four days to sort out her brain and her feelings where Callum was concerned. She was still angry with him. Wasn't she? Her head still felt like it was spinning from everything she'd learned that night.

He looked like he would argue, and she knew that he was more than capable of it. They were both stubborn. But she hoped he wouldn't. She needed this. She needed him to grant her that space willingly. She didn't want to have to fight for it. She was so tired of fighting.

Jory wondered if Callum could read minds because he took a step back, putting enough distance between them that she felt as if she could finally breathe properly.

"Verra well. Friday. I'll pick you up at six."

"Seven."

"Six thirty."

Jory snorted a laugh. "Are you just arguing for the sake of arguing?"

His mouth twisted again, that would-be smile. "Perhaps. Are you?"

She huffed a sigh. "Fine. Six thirty. What should I wear?"

He thought about that for a minute. "I'll call you."

"You don't have my number."

Without taking his eyes off of her, Callum reached over and snatched his phone off the desk, unlocked it quickly, and handed it to her. She added her contact information quickly and gave it back.

Jory adjusted her purse strap. "Okay then. I guess I'll get out of your hair."

"Aye," he replied, and she ducked around him. But as her shoulder brushed his, he said, "Jory."

She froze, feeling the strength of his arm against hers, his tension radiating off of him in waves.

"Yes?"

"Do friends hug?"

Jory felt as if she had somehow inched her way into the middle of a frozen pond, the ice new and blue and unstable. One wrong move, and she'd be doomed. She could have kept walking. She *should* have kept walking. That would have been the safest way to prevent the ice from shattering and swallowing her whole. But Jory wasn't good at doing the things she *should*, at least not where Callum was concerned.

She heard herself say, "Friends can hug."

Carefully, he wrapped his arms around her, pulling her close. She rested her cheek against his chest, loving the way he set his chin against the top of her head. There was silence beneath her ear, but it didn't fill her with despair like it had behind Hank's shed. With or without a heartbeat, he was very much alive. She knew this now. She felt herself sinking into him. Just for a moment, she told herself.

Jory left him standing there, his hands at his side with a look on his face that was, at once, determined and despondent, and climbed the steps to the main level, saying a goodbye at the top before she opened the vault door. Someone had closed the closet door so no sunlight streamed into the vault when she opened the hatch. Callum must have done it while she'd been sleeping. Or maybe she forgot closing it herself the night before.

She'd gotten very little sleep and was dehydrated and hungry. She needed to go home and get water, breakfast, and coffee before she started shaking. Jory opened the closet door absentmindedly, shutting it quietly behind her and turning for the front door.

"Good morning," a voice said, and she shrieked.

It was him. The menacing, heavily tattooed man that Callum had hired to track Esther, the one that had come with Callum to Hank's house. He stood in the cabin's kitchen wearing black soccer shorts and nothing else. His chest and arms were fully covered with brightly colored ink, and his feet were bare. He held a skillet in one hand and a spatula in the other.

The phone on the island started vibrating. The man put down the skillet and picked up the phone.

"What's up, boss?" he asked, and Jory could hear the rasp in his voice of a man who had smoked too many cigarettes once upon a time.

Jory couldn't make out who was on the other line, but it sounded like they were shouting. Robbie smirked and put the phone down on the counter, pressing a button.

"You're on speaker, boss."

"Jory, mo cridhe, I heard you scream. Are you alright?"

Jory squeezed her eyes tightly shut. She had exactly four days to figure out how to be friends with this man and he had to call her "his sweetheart."

"I'm fine. I was just startled to see..." she trailed off, and the man helpfully replied, "Robbie," around a mouthful of scrambled eggs, which he ate directly from the skillet.

"Robbie," she repeated. "I'm fine, Callum."

"See? She's fine. Go to bed, boss."

"Robbie," Callum growled through the phone's speaker.

Robbie sighed dramatically. "Fine. *Please,* go to bed, boss."

Jory could almost hear Callum grinding his teeth through the phone.

Robbie swallowed the enormous bite he was chewing. "You need breakfast before you sleep?"

It was on the tip of Jory's tongue to snark that she didn't have time to go back to sleep right then when she realized that he was looking at the phone and directing the question at Callum. Something clutched at her. Surely it wasn't... jealousy? No. It couldn't be that. Jory had absolutely no interest in being food. And yet...

"Nay," Callum replied softly. "I am fine."

"Alrighty then. We'll see you tonight."

Robbie hung up without a goodbye, returning his attention to forking another huge bite of eggs into his mouth. With that mouth still full, he said, "I'm sorry about the other week. I promise I'm harmless."

"I don't believe that for a second, Robbie."

He smiled brightly, revealing slightly crooked teeth. "That's fair. How about this? I'm harmless to you."

He stood over the skillet, thoroughly unbothered, eating with easy efficiency. He was about her height, five foot nine or so, but had the rangy, muscular build of a fighter.

Sinewy, she thought, which then led to a momentary appreciation of the word and how satisfying it felt to say.

Every visible bit of skin was covered in vibrant tattoos, from his neck to his knuckles. Beautiful botanicals and vibrant flowers decorated his neck and chest, and from behind the leaves, just over his heart, two golden eyes peeked out, like a panther in the jungle. Or a wolf.

He had script and symbols and more flowers and a lunar

cycle up his forearm. Robbie's tattoos reminded her of a collage she'd seen once in a local gallery, where a woman had taken magazine clippings and made a technicolor wonderland that took up nearly an entire wall. It had been the sort of piece that would never look the same twice because you would forever notice different things.

Weeks ago, when she'd seen Robbie from her car in the cold, gray light, he'd seemed dangerous. He'd seemed even more dangerous in Hank's kitchen, like he could use his knife to peel a peach and then, while still chewing, plunge that same blade into your gut.

But here, in the warmth of the cabin's kitchen, Jory couldn't help but remember the teenage boys she'd encountered over the years. Always hungry. Full of a boisterous energy that was barely restrained. Robbie was fully grown, but the energy, the puppy-like hunger and play was much the same. She wondered if the danger was a persona he put on like a coat and took off when the day was done.

When the eggs were gone, he straightened, stretching his arms long over his head before he locked eyes on her and startled.

"Oh, fuck," he said, "I didn't ask if you wanted any. Shit. I'm sorry."

"It's fine."

"No, it isn't. I don't hang out with many other humans anymore. I usually only have to worry about feeding myself. But that was rude of me. My mama would make me go cut my own damn switch if she knew."

There was something endearing about him—the colorful tattoos, the mountain twang, the way he seemed completely at home in his own skin—and Jory couldn't help herself. She smiled. "You're a little old to be cutting your own switch."

He smirked, his eyes bright and teasing. "Don't tell her that. Can I make you some eggs?"

Jory hesitated. She needed to go home and change clothes, to drink coffee in her silent kitchen where she could begin sifting and sorting through her tangle of thoughts. But at the same time, she didn't really want to be alone.

"Is that bacon?" she asked, noticing the plate next to the stove.

"Hell yeah it is," he said, smiling widely again, flashing a better look at those slightly crooked teeth, the way one crossed a bit in front of the other.

She sat on a stool at the island while Robbie went to the fridge and took out eggs, tossing them into the air and catching them before cracking them into a bowl.

"Coffee's over there," he said, tipping his head to the coffeemaker in the corner.

Jory poured herself a cup before returning to her seat, watching as Robbie reheated the skillet and swirled butter around it. He poured the eggs in and scrambled them with a silicone spatula before expertly turning them out onto a plate. Robbie added two strips of bacon and set the plate in front of her with a flourish, wiping a spot of butter off the rim with a towel.

"Such service," she teased, and he shrugged.

"Just taking care of Boss's lady."

"I'm not his lady," she said, swallowing a mouthful of eggs.

He lifted an eyebrow.

"I'm not," she protested again before shoveling in another bite.

Jory ate while Robbie cleaned the skillet, wiping it out and setting it back on the stove.

"Doesn't Boss ever feed you?" Robbie teased, turning

around and seeing her nearly empty plate. He swiped the plate of bacon off the opposite counter and held it out to her. She selected another piece and took a bite.

"We, uh, haven't spent much time together in a long time."

Robbie nodded thoughtfully. "Well, I have to feed myself, obviously, when Magda doesn't, so I'll just start making enough for two."

Magda. *Again.* Jory wasn't at all surprised that Magda would be here feeding this golden retriever of a man, but she wouldn't be joining him.

"You don't have to do that. I won't be here often."

That clearly surprised him. "Why not?"

She had to think about it for a moment. "We're just friends. Friends don't spend every free moment at each other's houses. Friends don't eat all their meals together. Friends don't hang out all the time."

"Sure they do," he replied.

"Friends have their own lives."

"Sometimes," Robbie allowed. "But y'all aren't *really* friends."

"We're certainly not more than friends," she snapped defensively. "Not anymore."

He held his hands up in surrender. In that thick accent, the words slow and syrupy coming out of his mouth, he said, "I reckon y'all are in the in-between. You used to be way more than friends, and now you're... not."

"How do you know Callum, Robbie?" Jory asked, changing the subject without any attempt at grace.

"Through the blood donor program."

"I'm sorry?"

Robbie rubbed the back of his neck. "Boss started a database for humans who are willing to be blood donors for vampires. Kind of like a dating service, I guess? Or a match-maker? I dunno. Anyway, I was on the registry, and his assistant called me one day and asked me in. That was"—he paused, looking up at the ceiling as if counting backwards—"three months ago?"

"And you also run errands for him? Stalk women?"

She couldn't help it. It bothered her. She'd *almost* forgotten about that part, that Callum had sent this man to follow Esther. It more than bothered her, actually. It made her mad.

He sighed heavily. "I've always been good at finding things. People too. And I've been a donor since I was eighteen. I've lived in twenty-three states and worked every job from bartender to line cook to road construction to exotic dancer and about a dozen other things. I know a lot of people. And people talk. So when one of my contacts told me that Esther was here, Boss sent me to check it out."

"Were you ever going to threaten her?"

"I was never going to talk to her at all. My job was to watch her."

"Stalk her."

He shrugged. "I guess you could call it that." Robbie looked at his feet and sighed. "Look, Jory, I know how it looked. And if it were anyone else, I wouldn't believe me either. I'd-a told you to call the cops. Or whatever. But Boss wasn't never gonna hurt her."

"You couldn't have known that," Jory protested, wondering why she had agreed to eat breakfast here anyway, the eggs suddenly sitting like a rock in her stomach.

He looked up at Jory. "I did know that. I don't know what you've told yourself about him, but it isn't true."

Jory snorted and shook her head, but Robbie wasn't about to let that go.

"You don't know him, Jory."

"I do know him, Robbie."

"Not anymore," was his simple, gutting reply.

It stopped Jory in her tracks. Because godsdamnit, he was right. She didn't know Callum anymore. She only knew what had led him to what he had become. She knew absolutely nothing about what had come after that. She didn't know how he'd spent his centuries, what he'd done with his immortality.

Once, she could have drawn his body from memory. Every mole. Every scar. She knew his tastes, his likes, his dislikes, his moods. She had known him so well that she could feel a fight coming days ahead, could soothe him with dizzying efficiency. It had been a point of pride for her. But now?

"He takes real good care of his people, Jory. Even people who never even heard of him. Who never will hear of him."

She leaned in, waiting. Damn the time. Damn the store. Damn changing her clothes. "Enlighten me."

"Well, take the nightclubs."

"You mean his blood trafficking operation?" Jory muttered.

"Is that what you think?" Robbie asked, reeling back, his face twisted in horror.

"Aren't they? He coerces people to the club to become food for his members."

"Let me ask you a question, Jory. How do you think most vampires feed?"

"How the hell would I know?"

"Because you do know. How do they feed?"

She took a deep breath and said, "They find humans, take them by surprise, and drain them."

"And do the humans usually survive?"

Her silence was an answer.

"Right," Robbie said, his eyebrows pinched. So serious. All evidence of playfulness gone. "What do your friends do when they go on a date?"

"What does that have to do with the clubs?"

"Just answer the question. What do your friends do when they go on a date?"

"I don't know. I don't really have many friends."

"I'll tell you. They send an 'in case I get murdered' text to the group, with the location of the date, their date's name and picture, and anything else that might give the cops a lead if they disappear. It's the same for blood donation. But I can text my buddies and tell them where I'm going and give them as much info on the vampire as I can, but what's to stop that vampire from bleeding me dry? You think my buddies can call the cops on a vampire? You think they'd take that any kind of serious?"

"Surely there's someone—"

"Some global vampire task force? Come on, friend."

Jory sighed. "What does any of that have to do with Callum?"

Robbie leaned his forearms on the counter. "Okay. So here's the deal. Sanguine, and his other clubs, work with the blood donor database. People who have signed up for blood donation. When you go to Sanguine as a donor, you get hooked up to a biometric device that monitors your blood pressure and blood volume, and it sounds an alarm if either gets too low. Then, an employee steps in. If the vampire doesn't stop feeding, they are forcibly removed and get booted from the club. If they do it twice, they get banned for life. But that doesn't usually happen. What happens is the vampire feeds, and then the donor gets driven home and given electrolytes and IV fluids and whatever they want to eat. Then they're monitored remotely for twenty-four hours after the donation."

"Wow. That's... quite an operation."

Robbie nodded. "He's saved thousands of lives, Jory. And he gives those biometric monitors away to anyone who applies. Free. He's... Fuck, Jory, he's the best guy I know."

Jory was silent.

Robbie scratched his shoulder with hot pink painted nails. "But you already knew that, right, Jory? He's the best guy you know, too."

Jory found herself nodding, remembering Callum being the first to show up to help and the last to leave when the helping was done. How selfless he'd been. How good.

But it didn't really matter, did it? Because *even if* he were the best guy, even if he spent his nights rescuing orphans from burning buildings and helping elderly nuns cross the street, even if he was out to save the world one vampire feeding at a time, it didn't change anything.

He had still trapped her here. With his damned impatience, his revenge. He had still left her to fend for herself, to *struggle* for almost a thousand years. Besides, no matter how good he was or how much she had found comfort in his arms, the same comfort she had so many years before, she was going home.

She would do well to remember that.

Of all the things Jory had been in her eternal life, of all the iterations of improvised, imitated humanity, the one thing she had always been was reliable. Which is why she felt completely unmoored when she sent a text to Esther from the parking area outside Callum's cabin and asked her if she would be able to open the store that morning.

> Something came up. Can you cover for me?

> I'll buy your coffee for a month.

You already buy all my coffee, weirdo.

> Okay, well, I'll let you take whatever you want from the store.

I'm on my way now. You don't have to give me anything.

1. Last I checked I work for you

2. Even if I didn't we're friends and I will always help you

But you can keep buying me coffee, sugar mama

Jory smiled and pressed her head back against the headrest and closed her eyes, remembering the way Callum's arms had wrapped around her, how familiar it had felt, how safe. She was not a small woman. In fact, in most situations, she was guaranteed to be the tallest woman in the room. But Callum made her feel small. He always had. There had always been something irresistible about that, especially for someone who was immortal and eternal. The feeling of smallness, even if only physical, had been comforting in a way it hadn't been since the last time he'd held her.

She'd felt small other times—when she'd run through a moonlit marsh with only the most important things she could carry tied in a sack slung over her shoulder as she raced to escape an angry mob who had found her to be an easy scapegoat for the recent crop failure. She usually settled on the fringe of a settlement or town, close enough to have the security of numbers and the access to resources, but far enough away that people didn't want to befriend her. But this was the third time in a row that that plan had failed.

A witch, they'd called her, and accused her of bringing the plague last time, of causing the local lord's daughter to bear no sons before that. This time, they said she had withered the crops in the devil's name. She'd seen them coming, a long line of torches moving in a blazing stream from the village to her home. She'd raced into the marsh, the mud sucking hungry and thick at her ankles, swallowing her shoes and weighing down her skirts. She'd wept silently, racing through the night toward the road that led to the port, praying with all her might that there would be a ship, that she would have enough coin to tempt them to take her. She didn't care where.

There had been a ship. There had been a captain who agreed to take her to the Americas if she would stay in his cabin and warm his bed on the journey. He'd been a bit lonely, and she'd been so *desperately* lonely that she'd agreed. He was kind enough and, she learned later that afternoon, a lynx shifter who loathed water but had needed a career with ever-changing personnel so that no one would discover the fact that he never seemed to age either.

Jory had loved the ship. It had made her feel closer to Callum, and as she'd stood on deck and watched the men climbing in the rigging, she imagined him high on the main mast, staring at the distant horizon. It had been a comforting thought. She'd gotten on well enough with the captain and thought that, perhaps, she could stay with him for a while, that she could be *safe* with him for a while.

But just before arriving in the Americas, he told her that

he had a wife in the colony and a wife in England and that he didn't have room for more commitments in between.

Jory drove down the gravel drive and remembered standing on the beach, apart from the activity unloading the ship. The people of the colony stared at her with disdain. She had been a lone woman on a ship. No chaperone. No companion. No one to pronounce her virtuous. And she hadn't been virtuous, had she? Though what good had virtue ever done anyone? She saw their condemnation and knew that it would only be a matter of time before another line of torches and pitchforks wound its way to her doorstep in the dark of night. So she ran. The running was almost more familiar than the staying.

The parking lot at La Push was empty, the weather too cold and gray for tourists and the waves all wrong for surfing. Jory locked her car and made her way to the shore. She bent down to loosen her boots and stepped out of them onto the cold sand. She was a masochist, she knew. She could have moved any number of other places and been near the sea. Somewhere tropical and warm, wholly unlike the Orkney Islands. But there had been something about the cold water and the fact that it also rained half the year. She felt the cold sand shifting beneath her feet and sat on a large tree trunk that had been carried out to sea with a storm and then washed back onto shore.

She didn't have to wait long. Moments later, the air went still and the sea birds went silent as her father emerged from the sea, striding easily through the shallows. She smiled. She saw him often now, making up for the five hundred years that she avoided him after Callum had di— *left*.

In that immediate aftermath, she'd been ashamed and embarrassed and devastated. Heartbroken. She had known that a single look from her father, one hint at him saying that he had warned her and that every warning had come to pass, would have broken her.

"Daughter," he said with a smile that crinkled around his eyes.

"Adda," she said, standing to hug him.

He held her close, resting his chin on the top of her head. "How we have missed you."

"How is Ama?" Jory asked, feeling her throat get tight. It always did when she thought about the fact that she hadn't seen her mother in almost a thousand years. It was nothing in the scheme of eternity, a long day, but until Callum came back, it had been a torturous eternity without any notion of ever seeing her again. But things were different now.

"She is well. And you? You look tired."

"I am tired," Jory said, swallowing against that tightness.

"You need to sleep more," he chided, and she couldn't help but smile.

"You're right. I do."

They were quiet, sitting together on the driftwood, watching the sea birds dive at the water. The silence was full of anticipation, but her father had always been patient. He clasped his hands in his lap and waited.

"He's back."

She didn't need to say who. He made a single sound in his throat.

"He has my sealskin."

At that, her father turned to her, an eyebrow arched high on his forehead. "And yet you sit here with me?"

Jory stared at her feet, curling and flexing her toes in the sand.

"Has he refused to return it to you?"

"No," she answered quietly.

"I do not understand. Why do you not go and retrieve it? Or send this man to do so? No. Don't send him. You must go, lest he disappear again. Faithless, feckless fool. He cannot—"

"Adda," she whispered, and he fell silent immediately.

He cleared his throat. "Will you retrieve it soon?"

"In a month." She felt his gaze on the side of her face.

"A month," he repeated.

"He wants to... see me."

"He has forfeited the right to see you. He saw you, and he *left* you. He cannot possibly believe himself worthy of a single second of—"

"*Adda,*" she hissed, and he was silent once more, though his silence was more mulish this time.

After a long handful of breaths, she said, "He is very different now. And yet he's exactly the same."

"Bah," her father said, waving a hand.

She sucked in a shuddering breath. "I loved him, Adda. I loved him then, and I loved him ever after."

"And now?"

She didn't need to answer. You didn't *just* stop loving someone because they hurt you. She couldn't, anyway. The question wasn't whether she loved him; she'd love him until the world ceased to be, be it with a bang or a sigh. But that didn't mean she could stay.

"I see," her father said. "You will remain here with him then?'

"No," Jory answered, the word strong and easy. "No, I will not stay with him. I love him. But I don't trust him. I can't forgive him for—"

She was torn. On the one hand, she wanted to tell her father what Callum had done, what he had *become*. But she another part of her was protective of him, of his *guilt*.

"I know what he did," her father said.

"What?" Jory gasped. "You knew? And you never said anything? You didn't try to stop him?"

It was her father's turn to sigh. "I was not there. I had business in another sea. And when I returned to check on you, you were gone. But there are eyes everywhere, and they told me. They told me what he'd done. They told me that you'd gone."

"Why didn't you tell me?"

"I thought you knew."

"How the hell would I know?"

Her father leaned forward, his head in his hands and his elbows on his knees, a shockingly *human* posture. "You disappeared for five hundred years! And when you returned, you deliberately never spoke of that night. You never spoke of *him*. I assumed you wanted to forget him after such a betrayal."

Hot tears scalded as they gathered in her eyes.

"You struggled for so long, my darling. For centuries. Running from these foolish humans. Scrapping and barely getting by. And still you never even *mentioned* him. I thought —well, it doesn't matter what I thought. I should never have assumed. I was wrong, and I am sorry."

She wanted to hold onto that flash of anger. It was so much easier to clutch at than her aching sadness, her regret. But she couldn't.

"He wants me to see him four times. And then he will take me to my sealskin."

Her father lifted his head and sat up, staring at the far horizon. "And you agreed to this?"

"Yes. But I think I'm going to go back tell him that I can't. I shouldn't have to give him anything. I shouldn't have to see him four times to get what it rightfully mine. He should take me now."

She'd expected immediate agreement from him. He continued staring at the horizon.

"You gave up eternity for this man. You sacrificed your safety, your comfort, the life you knew to be with him. You stood in front of me and told me that fate brought you to him, that your destinies were intertwined."

Jory snorted, more tears gathering, threatening to fall. "Add it to the list of things I've been wrong about."

But her father was quiet for another long moment. "I don't think you were wrong."

"But you said—"

"And I was right. He did hurt you. He did keep you from us. He did bring about your misery. But that doesn't mean that you were not also right. I think fate did bring you to him. I believe that your destinies were intertwined."

Jory gaped at him.

"We cannot become the people we are destined to be alone."

"I just want to go home," she said, her voice thick with tears, and her father gathered her close, wrapping an arm tightly around her shoulders and holding her against his side.

"You will," he said confidently. "I know you will. I feel it. You will see your mother soon and rest in the depths and find peace."

It was on the tip of her tongue to say that she would tell Callum that she had changed her mind, that she wanted the skin now, that he had no right to hold onto it. But her father spoke first. "You have been treading water for nearly a thousand years, my love. For him. Because you said loving him was worth it. Would *be* worth it."

"So?"

"So," he said, squeezing her. "What's one more month after a thousand years? Your destinies were linked. Find the point at which they go their separate ways and see it through to the end."

It had taken forever for Callum to fall asleep that morning. But eventually, sleep had found him, and he woke, groggily, a long while later. He tapped the screen on his phone to show him the time. Just past sunset. He never slept this late. Normally he was up hours before sunset, showered, dressed, and touching base with all of his managers before the business day ended. But Penny had forbidden him to work, and he had allowed her to do it.

He stood from the bed, scratching his chest while he stretched. He still wore the gray sweatpants from the night before. He climbed the steps and found Robbie sitting at the counter. The sharp smell of nail polish remover greeted him, and he saw Robbie wiping off his nail polish with a cotton ball.

"Evening, boss," he said, looking up and smiling.

"Hello," Callum said, his voice still husky from sleep.

"Time for sucky sucky?" Robbie asked with a mischievous smirk.

Callum sighed heavily and rolled his eyes to the ceiling. "Robbie, for the last time, please dinnae call it that."

Robbie snorted a laugh and returned his attention to his nails. Callum looked at the small black shadow between two flowers where he was always careful to sink his teeth. Robbie was remarkable. He offered his neck up two or three times a week and never slowed down. It was odd, really.

Normally, a feeding had the same effect on a human as losing two pints of blood. Because that's exactly what they were doing. They were normally lethargic and weakened for a few days as their bodies recovered. But Robbie never needed any time to recuperate. Rather, he seemed to have a boundless capacity for donation.

"Pardon the impertinence, but... you are... human, right, Robbie?" Callum trailed off.

"As human as can be, I'm afraid. My mama was the churchy type. She wouldn't have gotten together with a supernatural."

"Supernaturals can go to church, aye?"

"Sure they can. But not her church. Not where I grew up."

Callum nodded. It was entirely possible that way down Robbie's bloodline, someone had been something. Something that gave him enhanced healing abilities without bringing any other qualities to the surface. It was entirely possible. Likely, it seemed. Callum let it go.

"So what are you doing?" he asked, sitting on the other bar stool.

Robbie smiled brightly and held up a bottle of nail polish. "I ordered this last week, and it finally came. Today. Magda dropped it off. I think it would look dynamite on Jory, but I wanted to test it out first to show her."

He shook it rapidly before twisting off the top and dragging the little brush against the opening, removing the excess polish. He spread a long, careful stroke down his right thumbnail, and Callum realized for the first time that Robbie was left-handed.

The polish looked black in the bottle, but when Robbie twisted his hand, it was a shimmering green, and then purple from another angle. Like a raven's wing. Robbie was right. It would look stunning against the bronzed ochre of Jory's hands.

"You bought it for Jory to wear?"

Robbie looked sheepish as he continued to paint. Callum could see the blush rising up his cheeks. "Well, I bought it for both of us, actually. I thought we could share it." He looked tense, like he expected Callum to be jealous. But Callum only smiled.

"That seems verra economical."

"It ain't cheap polish," Robbie said. "And I'm not above bribing."

"Bribing?"

"Yeah. Bribing her to like me."

That made him pause. Robbie had the easy air and irresistible charm that no doubt earned him friends everywhere he went.

"Everyone likes you, Robbie."

The color heightened on Robbie's cheeks. "Believe it or not, I have a hard time making friends."

Callum arched a skeptical brow. "You have friends all over this country. Isnae that what you told me, why you're so good at finding things?"

Robbie shrugged. "I have *acquaintances* all over. But it's hard to trust people like that. Everyone's only looking out for themselves. And everything has a price. You know?"

Callum nodded. He did know. "But you trust me?"

"Well, yeah," Robbie said easily. "You're great."

Robbie switched the nail polish brush into his right hand, taking a much more careful swipe at his left thumbnail, his tongue peeking out the corner of his mouth as he concentrated. His hand shook slightly from the effort and the polish got onto his cuticle.

"Fuck. It's so hard to do my off hand."

"You do this every week," Callum teased.

"Yeah? Well, it never gets any easier," Robbie said defensively. "This hand always looks like shit."

"Here," Callum said, reaching for the bottle and brush. Robbie hesitantly handed them over and held out his hand. Callum put the brush back into the polish and grabbed the cotton swab from earlier, wiping away the errant color. He gathered more polish on the brush and took Robbie's left hand in his own left hand, painting carefully with his right.

"When I was learning to hold a sword, the weapons master made me train with both hands," he said softly.

"How did he do that?"

Callum snorted. "He belted one arm behind my back."

"Why?"

"Why what?"

"Why did he make you learn with both hands?"

"In hand-to-hand combat, the easiest way to incapacitate your enemy is to damage his sword arm. If ye sever the muscles and tendons, he cannae hold his sword, which gives ye the advantage. And if your opponent has that great an advantage—"

"You're fucked."

Callum bit back a smile as he switched to Robbie's pointer finger. "Aye. You're fucked. But if ye can take up the sword in your other hand, ye are nae fucked *quite* so badly."

"That makes sense."

"It's also a good diversion tactic. If ye charge into battle with the sword in your left hand, they think you're left-handed and that your right is weaker. Less defensible. So they go for it. And if ye can quickly switch hands, and learn to time it right, well, ye can beat nearly anyone."

"Misdirection," Robbie said as Callum painted his ring finger.

Robbie's hands were rough and callused, with dahlias tattooed on the backs and the words HOLD FAST across his knuckles.

"What do these tattoos mean?" Callum asked, blowing on Robbie's nails to dry them before going back for a second coat, as he'd watched Robbie do before.

"Oh. They're old."

"Still."

Robbie sighed. "Well, the legend goes that sailors used to tattoo their knuckles like this to help them hold onto the ship during storms or fights. So they wouldn't fall overboard."

The irony struck Callum so sharply that he shook his head. "How fortunate that wasnae a practice when I was at sea. Had I held on to the ship, I would have been killed or gone down with it and drowned. Sometimes 'tis better to jump. The trick is to know the difference, I suppose."

Robbie was quiet for a moment. "I think that you have a lot of stories, boss."

"I think you would be right on that." He chuckled and started a second coat on Robbie's thumb, the iridescent color captivating in the fluorescent kitchen lights. "But to what were ye holding fast?"

"Myself."

Callum looked up at him, at the tight set of Robbie's jaw. "And the flowers?"

"My mama always told me that dahlias represent change."

"And ye wanted a change?"

"Yeah. I guess."

"They're lovely," Callum said, sliding his hand out from under Robbie's and twisting the cap back on the nail polish.

Robbie held his hand out in front of his face, turning it

back and forth to catch different facets of the polish. He smiled.

"Not bad for a first-timer, boss."

"It's hardly rocket science, Robbie. But I think you were right. The color suits you. And I believe Jory will love it."

The wood stove crackled pleasantly, and Callum reveled in the warmth of the room. Robbie rose and began collecting the used cotton balls, tossing them in the trash before gathering up the polish and remover. Robbie hadn't known what to do when Callum offered to do his nails, to take care of him. He wondered how long Robbie had been fending for himself without anyone he could trust. It felt familiar.

"Robbie," Callum said, and Robbie turned to face him. "I think you're great too."

He beamed. "Aw, shucks, boss. Thanks."

"And I want to help ye how I can. I am sure ye have bills and—"

"Boss?" Robbie said, interrupting.

"Aye?"

"I don't need your money. I told Penny to stop sending me paychecks."

Callum reared back. She hadn't said a word to him. And neither had Robbie.

"Why would ye do such a thing, Robbie? You cannae work for free."

"I'm not doing any work for you," he said. "Or, at least, I haven't been working since we found Esther. I called Penny and told her to stop my checks right after you talked to Esther at Hank's."

"Ye arenae getting paid? Then... why are you still here?"

Robbie set the bottles down and walked over to where Callum still sat at the island. He placed a hand on Callum's shoulder. "Because, boss, I kinda felt like you could use a friend."

Robbie wasn't here because he was paying him to be. Robbie was here because he wanted to be. Robbie had bought nail polish for Jory because he thought she'd like it. He'd been a wingman—wasn't that what they called it? The *best* wingman. Robbie was...

"I dinnae think ye should call me boss anymore, then."

Robbie laughed. "Not even as a nickname?"

Callum bit back a smile. "If ye like it for a nickname, I will nae stop you."

Robbie looked thoughtful for a moment. "Magda calls you Cal. Would you hate it if I called you that too?"

Callum considered it. He thought about Jory and how she'd shed her old name like a snakeskin. He didn't feel the need to shed it entirely. He liked his name. But he liked the diminutive as well. It felt... new. Fresh.

"I dinnae mind that at all," he replied.

"Well, that's settled, then. Hungry yet?"

He must have looked famished because Robbie barked a laugh and said, "Alright then. Sit tight. I'll put this shit away, and then you can have a little Carotid Colada."

"Robbie," Callum muttered, but he fought back a laugh.

"Jugular juice it is then!" Robbie called out as he walked into the bathroom.

"Nay!" Callum shouted back.

"Arterytini!"

"You are the most ridiculous person I have ever—"

Robbie stuck his head around the door jamb. "Bloody Mary!"

"That isnae— okay. I'll give ye that one," Callum said, his laugh booming in the kitchen.

"Woo! One Bloody Mary, coming right up!"

"Wash yer neck!" Callum yelled.

Just then, there was a knock at the door. Callum was there in a flash, opening it to reveal Nat Jasper's tall, lanky body.

"Sorry to drop in like this," Nat said, bouncing a bit on his heels. He wore broken-in khaki work pants and a gray T-shirt with a National Parks logo. His hands were stuffed into his pockets.

"Hello, Nat," Callum asked, moving back toward the kitchen. "What can I do for you?"

"Good evening," Nat said, stepping into the warm cabin. "I'm headed out for a hunt and wondered if you would want to join me."

At the bonfire, Nat had told Callum more about how he lived entirely on the large animals in the national park where he worked. That he thrived on that blood, in fact, and that no animals lost their lives in the process, despite what Magda had told him. The idea was intriguing, even more so now.

He glanced at Robbie, who was now drinking milk straight from the gallon jug. Robbie put the milk down and wiped his mouth with the back of his hand. It occurred to him that much like Robbie didn't want to accept a paycheck from him anymore, he didn't want to use Robbie as a food source either.

"I'd like that verra much," Callum said. "Do I need anything?"

"Just clothes you can move in."

"I can do that. I'll be ready in just a moment."

"Great. I'll meet you outside." He turned and left with a wave, saying, "Good to see you, Robbie."

Robbie tipped his head and took another swig from the milk jug

"We have glasses, you ken," Callum said sarcastically.

"Aye," Robbie replied with an imitated Scottish brogue. "But we dinnae have a dishwasher, and this saves me many a wee dish."

"You went Irish."

"Damn," Robbie said with a laugh. "So I'm off the menu tonight?"

"Aye."

"And here I cleaned my neck and everything."

"Robbie, I—"

"Cal, stop. I'm just givin' you shit."

"I just... Are ye mad?"

"Why would I be mad? I'm your friend whether or not I'm also your food."

Callum snorted a laugh. "I'd rather you just be my friend."

Robbie smiled at him. "Well, that was a given, pal."

"But I meant what I said earlier. If ye need money until ye find something—"

"I don't need your money, Cal. This wasn't my only gig."

Callum's face pinched in confusion. "When have ye had time to do anything else?"

Robbie smiled. "Let's just say that I have a side hustle that's lucrative without taking up a lot of my time."

"Illegal, I suppose?"

Robbie snorted. "Not that you're one to talk, but no. It's legally lucrative. Now, go on and git. Those squirrels aren't going to hunt themselves, and if I'm not going to be dinner, I've got other things I can be doing."

18

Two hours later, Callum found himself laying on a huge, flat rock under a tree next to Nat. He couldn't remember the last time he'd felt so full. And while the animal blood felt different in his body, it didn't feel bad. It was fueling him just the same. More, perhaps, because he'd been able to eat his fill.

And without any death. He'd been able to eat his fill without killing anything.

Nat told him in very scientific terms that the average adult human man had one and a half gallons of blood circulating at any given time, whereas the average bull elk had six gallons. Callum guessed that he'd drunk three pints just now, which hadn't been a remotely noticeable loss for the elk. The biometric sensors at his clubs stopped a vampire from consuming more than one and a half pints at a time—more than enough to sustain a vampire for two to three days even if the vampire probably wouldn't feel completely sated. But he didn't care about satiety. He cared about survival. Survival of his patrons. Survival of innocent humans. Survival of so much.

His mind was spinning. Why hadn't he ever thought to feed this way? Or tried? Because he hadn't been around large game in a long time? Or maybe because feeding from humans was how it had always been done and he'd never questioned it?

That wasn't expressly true though, was it? He'd made his entire living making feedings safer for human blood donors. So he *had* questioned it. But while he'd sought to make the practice safer, he'd never sought an alternative altogether.

"Do you think it's a business?" Nat asked, bringing Callum back to the present.

The air was cold and clean-smelling, and the waxing moon was high overhead. Night forest sounds, so different from the forest sounds in Georgia or Scotland and yet so very similar, filled his ears as he thought about Nat's question.

"Nay," Callum said.

"Why not?"

Callum laced his fingers behind his head, supporting it as he lay on the rock. "I dinnae think it's scalable. To support bottling and manufacturing on any scale to make money, you would need a massive herd. And you wouldnae want to sacrifice quality so you would want them to range free, which means a vast piece of land. Then you'd need to hire people who could be discreet to manage the herds and the bottling, which would require every level of NDA possible. And if you managed all of that, plus bottling and distribution and inventory and lab safety testing, you would still have the public relations nightmare."

Nat sighed. "That's a damn shame. I thought I was onto something."

They were silent for a while. Callum's wheels were turning, though. Because the truth was, Nat *was* onto something.

"I dinnae think we can scale the elk operation. But what do you think about synthetics?"

"You mean blood made in a lab?"

"Aye."

"Don't you think that somebody would have done it by now if that was possible? I'm sure the humans have been trying to crack that one."

"Aye, no doubt they have. But research needs money. Perhaps synthetic blood isnae sexy enough to get the big donor money that erectile dysfunction medications have."

"And you have the money?"

"Nat, I have more money than I could spend in ten lifetimes."

"Must be nice."

"I willnae say that it isnae *nice*. But there comes a point when you have too much and you want to do something good with it. *I* want to do something good with it."

"So, what, you would fund the research? You would own the company? You'd get richer?" Nat sounded testy. Callum wasn't surprised. Nat worked as a park ranger, which paid well enough, but not enough that Nat didn't have to worry about economy.

"That isnae at all what I was imagining, actually."

Nat sat up. His eyes were bright in the moonlight.

"I would like to have you as a partner. Fifty-fifty split. I would provide the capital, but the idea was all yours."

"That's not fair, Callum."

"I think it is perfectly fair. But I have a condition, and if you dinnae agree, the deal is dead."

"Let me guess. I have to be a silent partner. Isn't that what they call it?"

Callum snorted. "Hardly. Nay. I would like to pay us a

capped salary that is tied by percentage to the lowest paid employee, who would still make a generous living wage. And I want to use the profits to fund donating additional product to human medical facilities for emergency situations."

Nat gave him an appraising look. "So the vampires purchasing would fund the aid for humans?"

"Aye."

Nat was quiet for a minute. Callum didn't mind quiet. He quite liked it. Especially when he was thinking. And right now, his mind was absolutely electric with possibility. His biometric devices were lifesavers, but with this, he had the chance to impact more lives than ever before. To *save* more lives than ever before. Not just by diverting vampire feeding away from humans, but also saving humans from car accidents and surgeries gone awry and any number of other tragedies that could befall the human body that needed blood to fix. There would be no more global blood shortages, no need to ration and triage it.

"I love it," Nat said, and Callum grinned.

"I am glad," he replied, extending his hand. Nat took it and shook vigorously.

"Cheers, partner. When do we get started?"

Callum laughed. Nat's enthusiasm was infectious, and truth be told, he was glad to have a new project, something to sink his teeth into.

"Let me make some calls. We need to find a researcher who is working on this and vet them. We need to find a manufacturing location that is easily disguised. We need to figure out a name and a logo and packaging. Distribution."

Nat cut in before he could say anything else. "I know someone who can help us with the logo and packaging."

Callum raised an eyebrow expectantly.

"Niamh's family had a whiskey distillery. It was two hundred years ago, but I can't imagine the basic principles have changed that much. And she does these amazing ink block prints. Carves them herself."

"I didnae ken she came from such a background."

"Yeah. Kilbaron."

"Niamh is a Kilbaron? I always kept Kilbaron Whiskey stocked in my homes for guests. Well, until the 1860s, anyway. They changed the recipe after that, and I'm told it was never so good as before."

A wistful look passed across Nat's face. "That sounds about right. That's when it all went to shit."

"There is a story there."

"Yeah, there is. But it's not really mine to tell."

Callum knew all about such stories.

"Well, then. Shall we?" he asked, climbing off the rock and holding a hand out for Nat, who took it, pulling himself up. They began walking, which became a run, which became the blur of movement that brought them quickly from one place to the other, racing through the dark forest and back to the A-frame cabin where Nat's truck was parked.

Nat reached into his pocket and took out his keys, manually unlocking the old truck.

"So you'll let me know when you hear something about the researcher?"

"Aye," Callum said, clapping a hand on Nat's shoulder. "I'll be in touch as soon as I have a lead. Perhaps next week we can get together to work on a business plan."

Nat beamed, bouncing on his heels. "Yes. Name the night, and I'll be sure I'm covered at work."

Callum smiled. "Be safe, Nat."

"You too," Nat said with a salute before folding his lanky body into the truck and driving away.

Callum walked into the cabin and locked the door behind him, resting his back against it for a moment. Robbie was nowhere to be seen, but he heard the muffled sound of his voice from behind the bedroom door.

He made his way down into the vault, closing the door behind him and locking it out of habit. He grabbed his laptop and climbed onto the bed, his back resting against the pillows and headboard. He sent a few messages to friends in the biotechnology field and sent a text to Robbie telling him that he was back and going to bed early and would see him the next night.

Then he stared at his laptop. Wondering what to call this new little baby of theirs. Before he quite realized it, his phone was in his hand, and he had created a new text message to Jory. There was no way she was awake. Not at this hour between the middle of the night and the wee hours of morning.

In the before, as he'd come to think of it, she'd been the last person he'd spoken to every night and the first person he greeted every morning. His heart ached to think that he'd never see her like that again, with the rising sun casting purple shadows over her sleeping face, her eyelashes fluttering as she dreamed in the hazy, morning light.

He yawned, wishing that he could lay in bed with her, their heads on pillows, talking about the day before falling asleep. As they'd done so many times. As he'd missed ever since.

I missed you.

"Fuck," he whispered to the empty room. Why had he

sent that? She didn't want him to think about her. Not like that. She'd made that perfectly clear. They were *just friends.*

But he was trying to woo her. He wanted her to stay and he'd never get there with nonchalance. Still, he could have split the difference between the two. He was typing another message when he saw the three dots that indicated her typing a reply.

> Why are you texting me at 4:30 in the morning, Callum?

Why was he texting her at four thirty in the morning? That was an excellent question. *Because I want to tell you about this new project. Because I want to hear about your day. Because I want to hear your voice and this is the next best thing.*

Instead, he typed:

> Why are you awake at 4:30 in the morning?

> I swim.

She didn't offer anything else. He bit his lip, feeling the sharp sting of his fangs.

> You always did like to swim.

A fact that made all the more sense now.

> I have to go.

Callum sighed. This would never work. He climbed out of the bed and took off the sweatshirt and joggers he'd worn to go hunting with Nat, dropping them carelessly in a dirty clothes pile in the corner. He tossed his phone onto the bed and dragged his hands down his face before raking them through his hair, pulling on the ends.

He flipped off the lights and made to crawl into bed when his phone vibrated and the screen lit up. He quickly unlocked his phone and blinked down at his messages.

I missed you too.

19

Jory had tried on fifteen different outfits. She glanced at her watch. Five twenty-three. Callum would pick her up at seven which, she assumed, really meant six forty-five. After pacing around her apartment all afternoon like a caged leopard, she had finally called Esther.

"I'm spinning, Esther. Would you mind—"

But in typical Esther fashion, Jory hadn't even gotten the full sentence out of her mouth before her friend was interrupting excitedly, "I'm on my way right now!"

Three minutes later, there was a knock at Jory's door. Esther drove like a maniac, but even for her that was fast. But when Jory opened the door, it wasn't Esther across the threshold.

"Robbie? What are you doing here?"

Robbie shifted nervously, scuffing the toe of one boot against the wood of her small landing.

"I brought you something."

Jory blinked at him for a moment before coming back to herself. "Come in."

He slipped through the door and stood in the kitchen

with the handles of a paper sack clenched in his tattooed fist. He looked around, and she watched as he took in the yarn hangings and open shelves of stoneware and pottery that she'd collected from various artists over the years.

"What can I do for you, Robbie?"

He thrust the paper sack at her. His fingernails were painted the color of a raven's wing, black sliding easily to green and then violet in the bright glow of the overhead lights.

"I like your nail polish," she said, taking the bag.

A smile stretched wide across his face, a giddy smile, as if he'd been hoping she would say that.

"What's in the bag?"

"Look for yourself."

She pulled the handles apart and saw a bottle of nail polish—expensive nail polish—that matched Robbie's along with a small, square, white box. She pulled the nail polish out of the bag and set it on the counter, noting that the plastic seal had been removed.

"I see you sampled it." Jory smirked.

Robbie shrugged, looking nervous again, which was so unlike how he'd been at the cabin. "I saw it and it reminded me of you and, well, I dunno. I wanted to make sure I was right."

Jory bit back a smile. She remembered the ravens that crowed down at her from the trees while she hiked from the parking lot to the cliffs, the forest largely silent except for their chatter. The raven sent to find land. The raven that heralded change. Death. Fortune. The ravens that saw all, that she had once courted so many years ago in Scotland, leaving out little bits of food in a special spot and being rewarded with trinkets and scraps of fabric or string.

"It's perfect," she said softly, and Robbie's shoulders

almost collapsed with how quickly they relaxed. "What else is in here?"

She pulled out the box and lifted the lid, revealing a small frosted-glass bottle with a stopper that had been made to look like antique bronze. The cream paper label said *Fanaidh* in a beautiful, looping script.

Robbie cleared his throat. "Boss—Cal is always talking about how much he misses certain smells from home. Finding a perfume that smells like heather wasn't easy. But this is made by a small perfumery in Scotland from local heather flowers, and I just thought that if he misses that smell, that you might too."

Jory pulled the stopper off with a shaky hand and pressed down to mist a single pump of the fragrance into the air. The smell of heather was almost earthy, almost herby, almost floral, and yet somehow none of those things at the same time. It was as familiar to her as the smell of rain or saltwater or dirt.

She had filled their mattress with heather, gathering armfuls and drying them in the rafters before stuffing the bedding, relishing the way that the flowers gave off their fragrance anytime either she or Callum had turned in their sleep, or moved at all. The way the scent mingled with the almost tangy, almost salty, almost earthy smells of sex.

Jory closed her eyes and breathed deeply, letting the scent fill her nostrils. When she opened her eyes again, she found Robbie looking at her with a soft smile.

"Can I pay you?" Jory croaked. Because what else could she say?

"It's a gift," he scoffed. "A gift for a friend."

Friend.

Another friend. Esther and Magda had been her only friends for quite some time. And some days, Magda was less a friend than she was the eccentric old aunt that knew entirely too much about her and had no shame in letting her know that. But Robbie looked so earnest, so hopeful, and yet so anxious in front of her just now. As if he expected her to say no. Maybe she should.

It was all so goddamn complicated, wasn't it? She was leaving. She planned to broach the subject with Esther tonight, in fact. To talk to her about taking over the store, leaving it to her entirely in every way. Esther would be devastated to hear it. Magda would be... who could say? Could she hurt yet another friend when she left?

"I wanna be your friend, Jory," Robbie said. "Not get married."

A sudden laugh burst from Jory's lips as Robbie stopped her rabbit-holing, as Callum had once called it.

"I won't be here long, Robbie."

Robbie shrugged noncommittally, as if he didn't believe her. Or maybe he just didn't care. Maybe he collected friends like utensils, setting them aside when he moved on to something else. Maybe—

"You're doing that thing again," he said.

"What thing?" Jory replied, shaking herself.

"That thing where I can almost see smoke pouring out of your ears from thinking too hard and gettin' way too far down the road. Come on," he said, toeing off his boots. "I'll paint your nails."

She nodded and followed him into the living room. He sat easily on the floor, placing the bottle of nail polish on the coffee table and patting it with his tattooed hand. Jory sank down to sit cross-legged across the table from him. He reached out without hesitation and took one of her hands in his, examining the nails.

"So," Jory said, "do you know where he's taking me tonight?"

"Yep."

"And?"

"And what?"

"Aren't you going to tell me?"

"Nope," he said, shaking the bottle vigorously before unscrewing the cap and dragging the brush against the opening.

He began painting her nails carefully. "You're not going to tell me anything?" Jory asked, somewhat annoyed.

"Not a damn thing."

"But I need to know what to wear! Taking me spelunking requires very different clothing choices than going to a movie."

"You could wear spelunking gear to a movie. Just keep the headlamp off."

"Robbie."

"Jory."

"Please. I've been in a tizzy all day. At least tell me what to wear."

"Well, what did Cal tell you to wear?"

"He said I could wear anything I wanted."

"So wear anything you want."

"*Robbie.*"

Robbie smirked over her hand, his eyes focused on his work. But then he canted his head to the side a bit. "Wear something that makes you feel... like you're the boss."

"I thought you'd tell me to wear something that he would think was sexy."

"I did."

"You said—"

"Honey," Robbie interrupted, his accent thick, with far

more twang than Esther's drawl. "If you open that door looking like you feel like the boss, he's gonna have a hard time keeping his paws to himself. Confidence is sexy as fuck."

Jory bit back her smile. Just then, the kitchen door flew open, and Esther blew in like a gale force wind.

"I am so sorry I'm late. There's like three stoplights in this damn town, and I hit every single one red. And before that, I had to help Hank hold a level because of course it couldn't wait. And—helloooo." Esther drew out the last vowel in surprise.

Robbie looked up at her with a genuine smile. "Hey, Esther."

"Hiiii," Ester drawled again, as if the vowels were moving at quarter speed. "What's going on here?"

Jory answered, "Manicure party," at the same time Robbie said, "Ritual sacrifice," and Esther's red eyebrows seemed to shoot straight through her freckles and into her hairline. Jory patted the coffee table with the hand that was drying.

"You've met Robbie, Esther."

Esther moved further into the room but made no progress toward sitting. "Yes," Esther said sarcastically. "Met."

Robbie blushed bright red, the flush rising out of the crew neck of his black sweatshirt all the way to his ears. "Esther," he said, setting Jory's hand down and capping the nail polish. "I wanna apologize for scaring you."

"You wanna apologize for scaring me?" Esther repeated.

It was funny to hear them parrot one another. Esther's accent had the smooth viscosity of Blanche Devereaux. Her vowels were long and elegant. Robbie's accent had the same shape but with sharper edges. It didn't glide around the curves as much as it sliced through them.

Esther glared suspiciously at Robbie, who, to his credit, took it. He took it all. He let Esther stare daggers at him and didn't flinch or fuss or glare back. He let himself be an open book for her to write her suspicion all over.

"So y'all are friends now?" Esther said tightly.

"As of very recently," Jory answered cautiously. "Will that be a problem?"

"I don't know," Esther said, staring directly at Robbie. "Will it be a problem for me?"

"No," Robbie replied.

"Are you sure?"

He sat up taller, meeting her gaze. "Esther MacLaren, sit your ass down and let me paint your damn nails."

And that was that. It must have been a southern thing, the no-nonsense command that broke through Esther's defenses because with a huff, she collapsed ungracefully to sit next to Jory, stretching her freckled hands on the table. Robbie unscrewed the polish and went back to Jory's second coat.

"So have you decided what you're wearing?" Esther asked.

"I think so."

"Where's he taking you? Where's he taking her?" Esther asked, bouncing her question from one to the other.

Robbie bit his lips and shook his head, a mischievous look on his face.

"Is it something you brought back from Santa Fe? Something from the store?"

"Yeah," Jory replied with a heavy sigh before taking another deep breath. "That's something I want to talk to you about, though."

"Oh, god. Did I fuck something up? Did I update the inventory wrong? I was so careful. I just—"

"No, no. Nothing like that. You're perfect. But I—" She flicked her gaze to Robbie, who was absorbed in getting her very last nail absolutely perfect. "I'm gonna be going away for a while soon. And I—"

"Away?" Esther said, and Jory's heart cracked a little at the anxiety that colored that word.

"Yes. Away."

"For how long?"

"I don't know. Maybe a long time. And I... I want to give it to you. If you want it."

"Give me what?"

"The store."

Esther's eyes looked as if they might bug out of her head.

"Jory, I don't know the first thing about running a business! Or style. Or fashion. Oh my god! Do you remember when you first met me? I had like three T-shirts, a sweater, and a black hoodie. I own exactly two pairs of shoes, and they're Docs and flip-flops. I don't know the difference between a caftan and a kimono. And did I mention that I don't know how to run a business? How am I supposed to run a business? You're the style and the brains. I don't—"

"Esther?" Jory said gently, placing a hand on top of Esther's, careful not to smudge the polish.

"Yeah?" Esther answered miserably.

"You don't have to decide tonight. Just think about it. It doesn't have to look the same seas it does now. You and Magda could do more herbals and apothecary. You could consign local handmade goods. You could rent out mascot costumes."

Robbie snorted, and Esther battled a smile.

"I own the building, and you could figure it out as you

went without that pressure. Just promise me you'll think about it."

Esther glared at her now. Jory almost laughed because Esther, normally so full of joy and humor, looked like a child who'd had her toy taken away when she glared like that.

"Your turn," Robbie chirped, breaking the tension. Esther laid her palms flat on the table, and Robbie reached for one, gathering Esther's hand carefully in his before swiping the polish brush down her thumbnail.

"I'll think about it. But I won't like it."

20

Callum had been awake long before his alarm told him the sun had set. He'd been working with one of his biotech contacts to cultivate a list of researchers and had taken a call with one of his realtors about manufacturing locations. It was quite likely that they would have to build from scratch. When his alarm rang, Callum finished the email he was typing before neatly snapping his laptop closed and climbing the steps to unlock the vault.

The cabin was dark and empty. Often, when Callum came up at night, Robbie was puttering around the kitchen or watching something on his laptop or doing something in his room that sounded an awful lot like phone sex. But a quick glance down the very short hall showed that Robbie's door was open, the lights off. The car he'd leased for Robbie, a small, hybrid SUV, was missing from the parking area.

Callum had been alone before. For months sometimes. Only casually encountering people. Or feeding from them. But he found that it had been comforting to know that

Robbie was rattling around upstairs while Callum was sleeping during the day or, at the very least, that someone else was living there. Filling the house with their scents, their sounds. He never had liked living alone.

Callum walked to the bathroom in the silent, dim cabin. He wanted to shower before going to Jory's. On the counter was Robbie's old phone that he used to play music through a waterproof speaker that he'd suction-cupped to the shower wall. He swiped the phone open and turned the music on shuffle, curious about what Robbie liked to listen to. As he stripped off his sweatpants and T-shirt, Johnny Cash's "The Highwayman" crackled through the speaker. After shucking his boxer briefs, a miraculous invention in his opinion, he stepped into the tub shower and directly under the hot water. He ducked his head and let the water cascade over his hair and down his body.

He had four chances. Four chances to get it right. That was all she'd agreed to. He might be able to convince her to see him more often than that over the next month but the only guarantee he had were those four meetings. *Definitely not dates*, she'd insisted, although she might argue that tonight's activity was a little too close to one.

He'd reserved an entire restaurant for the night, a little French restaurant two towns over that was romantic and had excellent reviews on TopTable. It was far enough away to give them time to talk on the drive to and from, to stretch the evening, but not so far as to be inconvenient.

But what was most important, the owner was a French sprite and friend of Nat's, so they would be able to talk freely. He had wanted to take Jory to a restaurant with wine and dessert and bread with compound butter and black cloth napkins and a wine list that needed its own book. He couldn't enjoy any of that, of course, but he knew that watching Jory work her way through the menu as she licked deep, red wine off her lips would be more pleasurable than any meal had ever been. He wondered if she still made happy noises when she ate something particularly good.

Once, she'd made a berry pie of sorts and had hummed and made little squeaks and moans of pleasure while she'd eaten it. And then louder sounds when he'd licked the syrup from her lips, tasted it on her tongue.

Easy, he thought, reaching down to squeeze at his groin, although he couldn't quite decide whether it was to encourage or discourage his growing erection. A bit of both, probably. But the image was now vividly playing in his brain —Jory licking sticky, sweet berry juice off of a spoon and then her fingers after she'd swiped them across the bottom of her bowl, not willing to leave a single morsel behind.

Callum groaned as he remembered snatching her hand away just before her fingers reached her mouth, sliding them one at a time into his own. Her eyes had flashed with both agitation and arousal, and what he wouldn't give to see her look at him like that again. He wrapped his fist around his cock as he pictured what had come next. He'd stripped her loose shift off, whipping it over her head, and taken the spoon she'd used to serve the pie, dragging it in a line down her torso from her sternum to her sex. He'd followed the spoon with his tongue, licking and sucking the syrup off her body while she'd writhed beneath him.

His hand shuttled faster and he braced his other hand against the wall under the steaming spray of the shower as he remembered. Laying her down on the wooden table, dropping to his knees and licking a stripe that covered the length of her cunt, tasting her sharpness overtop of the sticky sweetness of the berries lingering on his tongue. His hand was agony and ecstasy all at once as he wished it was hers.

Once he'd made her come, he'd stood, gripped her thighs in his rough hands, and pressed into her center with short, intense pumps of his hips while she had choked on a moan. But before long, he'd been thrusting into her heat so hard and with such intensity that the pie had begun sliding across the table. Just before it had careened over the side, he had scooped her into his arms and spun quickly. She hadn't missed a beat, wrapping her legs tightly around his hips and clutching her arms around his neck as he'd pressed her against the door of their cottage, fucking up into her as the wind howled outside and the fire crackled and the smell of baked pastry filled his nostrils, along with the smell of her.

With a gasp and a long groan, Callum came so hard that his vision went spotty. Long ropes of his release splashed against the wall of the shower as he stood panting and gasping beneath the spray, feeling like he had no strength left in his body but at the same time feeling as if he could lift the cabin off its very foundation with his bare hands.

As he came down from his orgasm, he remembered that night. After he'd finished, after he'd tucked his forehead into the crook of her neck, so close that he could feel the pulse in her neck against his skin. How she had traced swirls and patterns against his skin with such a light touch that it had given him shivery goosebumps. She'd whispered how much she loved him. How good he made her feel.

In the now, Callum felt a shiver wrack his body from nose to toes as he remembered that feather-light touch, those whispered words that had knocked him off his feet. *You are so good, mo ghraidh. You are my whole heart.*

He rinsed his hands and then the wall, cupping water in his palms and splashing it against his mess, letting the water carry it down the drain. He dragged his hands down his face, his chest aching from the memory.

He could not fail.

Because the truth was that she was, and had always been, his entire heart. A thousand years hadn't changed that. A thousand more wouldn't either.

And so he finished his shower. Turned off the shower speaker, which had shuffled from "The Highwayman" to "Can't You See" by the Marshall Tucker Band to a grinding, driving rap song that had a bass line Callum felt behind his ribs. He left the steamy bathroom and made his way back down to the basement.

As he put on his underwear, then shirt, then pants, shoes, cufflinks, tie, and suit jacket, he remembered the numerous, meticulous steps to putting on armor. He straightened his tie in the full-length mirror that hung on one wall before swiping his phone, keys, and wallet off the desk and climbing the stairs.

His SUV ate up the short drive to Jory's house, and before he was quite ready, he was knocking on the door, wishing like hell that he'd remembered to bring her flowers. Footsteps scuffed, and the deadbolt turned. The door opened to reveal Esther, her wild, red curls glowing in the fluorescent light of the kitchen.

Esther smiled widely before whistling. "Somebody went all out."

"Aye. Well, I figured I'd give it my best shot."

"I'd say you succeeded. And then some. Come on in. It's freezing."

Was it? Callum didn't feel a thing. But he followed her into the kitchen. Robbie was frying eggs in a skillet on the stove, and Callum smelled toast.

"Over medium, Est?" Robbie asked, and Callum couldn't

help but snort a laugh, because why wouldn't Robbie be making an egg sandwich in someone else's kitchen? It was the most Robbie thing in the world.

"Over medium!" Esther confirmed.

"Heard," Robbie called back.

"Robbie," Callum said with a dip of his chin.

"You handsome son of a bitch!" Robbie said with wide eyes and an open smile. "Give us a spin. Let's see it!"

Callum rolled his eyes but did a slow turn, his hands held out to the side. As he completed his turn, he stopped dead in his tracks. His heart, if it had been beating, would have stopped as well.

Jory stood in the doorway to the small kitchen, wearing tight jeans that hugged her curves and a gold corset that looked like something a Valkyrie would wear into battle. The jeans had holes in the thighs and a ragged hem where they were cropped just above a pair of pointy-toed, high heeled boots. Her dark hair was wavy and wild, falling around her shoulders. Her lips were stained a berry-red color. Callum's mouth went dry.

He remembered the very first time he'd seen her, opening his feverish eyes and seeing her face, shadowed by the brilliant, rare sun behind her. Her hair had blown around her like a banner, and in his delirium, he'd thought she was an angel because she had been the most beautiful thing he'd ever seen in all his life.

She was still the most beautiful thing he'd ever seen in all his life, and he stared at her from across the kitchen. Jory stared back, her eyes wide and lips parted. He took slow steps across the kitchen, stepping around Robbie, until he stood just before her. And then he smelled her. Salt and... heather.

He sucked in a deep breath. Jory's mouth opened on a tiny gasp as she stared at his mouth.

"Goddamn," Robbie muttered. "You'uns leave some sexual chemistry for the rest of us, alright?"

Jory blushed, which was charming, and Callum cleared his throat.

"Shall we?" he asked, extending his hand for Jory's. She took it and that same, bottomless feeling echoed in his chest as he felt her warm fingers slide against his palm. He squeezed her hand and led her to the back door. "Dinnae burn the house down, Robbie."

Robbie gasped, pressing a hand to his chest in mock offense.

While she slipped into her coat, Jory asked Esther to lock up when they left and stepped out the door, casting an expectant look over her shoulder at Callum.

Just before he closed the door, he poked his head through and whispered to Robbie, "Dinnae wait up."

The door shut on Esther and Robbie's laughter as Callum followed Jory down the stairs and out into the night.

21

Callum had never been on a first date. And though this was not a date, as Jory had reminded him in the car, it felt like one. Or what he imagined one might feel like.

Dating was a fairly recent invention. For much of his time on earth, a relationship was more of a business transaction than a romantic attachment. And he'd certainly never dated Jory. There had been no courtship. No chaperones. No reading of the banns in church. They'd simply walked off the beach together as soon as he'd been well enough and begun building a cottage. A few months later, they'd found a traveling priest who'd agreed to marry them, and that had been that.

Much like the measurement of time, his life had been divided into two segments: Before Jory and After Jory. And like the Jurassic period, After Jory could be segmented into three epochs: Before Losing Jory, After Losing Jory, and now, a new, volcanic era of Discovering Jory, which felt as terrifying as it did exciting.

The stakes were sky-high. Which was why Callum had

spent three evenings in a row sitting on Magda's lumpy couch next to Robbie, watching a few of the movies that Robbie had insisted were essential for understanding the nature of dates and dating. Even though it wasn't a date. Technically. But Callum was playing to win, and winning meant wooing, and wooing meant that he needed to be prepared.

"You need to get your head in the game, Cal," Robbie had insisted just before tossing a piece of popcorn into the air and catching it neatly in his mouth. "Like reviewing film before the big game."

"Did you play football?" Callum had asked.

"Nah," Robbie had answered around a mouthful of popcorn. "But I know things. Did you ever play football?"

"Nay." Callum had smirked. "But I know things."

They'd made it through seven movies before Callum had decided that he'd seen enough for his "research." From what he had gathered, the goal was to metaphorically sweep one's date off their feet with an elaborately planned evening and then literally sweep them off their feet to save them from falling into a body of water or traffic.

Callum had been entirely confident in his ability to perform the latter and not remotely confident in his ability to perform the former.

The forty-minute drive from Jory's apartment to the restaurant had been quiet, but companionable. It had felt... familiar. Not the mechanics, per se, but the tone. When he'd known her last, they'd had a horse that pulled a cart when necessary. They'd worn homespun wool. They'd grown and trapped and foraged and fished. Now, he wore a six-thousand-dollar Brioni suit and Ferragamo loafers while she— she looked so damn beautiful.

It felt more complicated now. Infinitely so as he worried

about whether she'd enjoy what he had planned or not. But she was here. With him.

She'd been surprised when they'd walked into an empty restaurant and been escorted to a table in the far back corner. The owner themselves had taken Jory's order, bringing a bottle of expensive wine for her and a bottle that Nat had dropped off earlier for him, pouring the red wine into her glass before pouring the bright blood into his.

Now, as he sat across from Jory in an empty restaurant while she sipped wine and stared at him in awkward silence, he knew his anxiety had been well-founded. If only there'd been a lake in the parking lot he could save her from toppling into.

He'd asked about the store. It was fine.

She'd asked about the clubs. They were fine.

He'd asked about her trip to New Mexico. She'd smiled and talked for a few moments about a gold mine of an estate sale she had visited at the home of a recently deceased woman who had loved fashion, jewelry, and art. Apparently, Jory had bought nearly the entire sale.

And now they were silent again. She was staring deeply into her first course, as if it might swallow her whole if she wished hard enough while he just stared at her.

Callum decided then that he hated dating. Or not-dating. Whatever this was.

He didn't want to sit across a dinner table or at a movie or wherever he was supposed to take her, and make small talk about small things, all the while wondering if it would turn into something more and being utterly petrified it wouldn't.

How did humans do this? Desperately wanting connection? And the most efficient way they had settled upon to find that connection was *dating*?

When he had met Jory, there had been no "wining and dining," as one of the movie heroes called it. There had only been a deep sense of knowing. She had stitched his wounds with her own hair.

He still knew. Deep within the marrow of his bones, threaded through the sinews of his body, was the knowledge that he belonged to her, that he would willingly follow her wherever she would go, if only she'd let him.

And yet he couldn't think of a single thing to say.

He took a sip of blood. More elk, Nat had promised. As the coppery warmth glided across his tongue, he realized he could talk about that.

Callum cleared his throat. "I have a new business venture."

"Oh?" Jory asked, not lifting her gaze from her meal.

"Aye. Nat and I are going into business together."

That got her attention. She placed her fork down on her plate and sat up straighter. A moment passed before she said, "Well, are you going to tell me about it?"

He smiled, revealing the almost-too-sharp canines that became fangs when demanded. At the sight of them, her face fell, and Callum felt as if he'd been doused in icy water from a loch.

He dropped the smile. Took another sip. And said, "Aye. Nat has nae fed from a human in hundreds of years. He's been living off the large game in the area."

She waited, never taking her eyes off of him.

"And his initial idea was to scale that into a business."

"That would never work."

"I told him that."

Jory lifted a bite of cassoulet to her mouth, and Callum felt his groin throb as her lips glided over the fork.

"But I asked him how he felt about synthetic blood."

She froze. "Synthetic blood?"

"Aye. There is some verra promising research being done in California by a scientist named Dr. Kendra Alton. She believes she's nearly there, but lacks the funding to bring the project to fruition."

"And you're going to provide the funding?"

"Aye."

"And if she succeeds?"

"Then I'll buy the patent."

"How?"

"I'll make her an offer she cannae refuse."

"You'd threaten her?" Jory hissed, dropping her fork with a clatter.

"Threaten her?" Callum reared back, horrified she'd even suggest it.

"You said you'd make her an offer she couldn't refuse to sell you the patent. Will you threaten her? Glamour her? That technology could save millions of lives, Callum. You—"

"Jory," he said softly. "I mean to offer her so much money that her great-grandchildren will be wealthy."

"Oh," she whispered, more a gust of breath than a sound.

"Aye. We mean to pay her handsomely for the patent and then manufacture it ourselves."

"But—"

"And we plan to bottle and sell it for vampire consumption and use the profits to fund manufacturing and distribution to hospitals and emergency personnel. For free."

"*Oh.*" That sound again. Shock. She was *shocked* that this was his plan.

"You believe me capable of threatening a woman to force her to give me her life's work and intellectual property? Then you believe me capable of using that technology for nothing but my own profit, that I would think nothing of everyone it could help?"

How many times had he gone away, using his body as both a weapon and a shield, to protect people who couldn't protect themselves? How many times had he turned down work because he didn't trust the motivations or care of the man who would have hired him? How many times had he joined her in rescuing lost baby creatures or bringing baskets to ailing villagers? Helping to birth the lambs and then tirelessly searching for them when they strayed? And yet he was right. She *had* believed him capable of selfishness. All because he had been capable of— he couldn't finish the thought.

"Callum, I—" She swallowed.

"Is that truly what ye think of me?"

She didn't answer. Which was answer enough. That was that, then. If she truly believed him capable of such monstrous behavior, there wasn't a damn thing he could do to change her mind. There was no point in wasting time. There was no point in getting his hopes up. There was no point in any part of this farce he'd insisted upon.

The owner of the restaurant flitted by at that moment. "Are we ready to order another course? Or perhaps look at the dessert menu?" they asked in a reedy voice.

"Nay," Callum said with a rasp, his emotions, his hurt, clogged and strangling in his throat. "Just the check, please."

Jory stared at him, her food forgotten, her wine forgotten.

He left a gratuity of one hundred percent and stood, buttoning his suit jacket. "Shall we?"

She nodded.

Callum helped Jory shrug into her wool coat, making an effort not to touch her, and then led them out of the restaurant, holding open the doors to both the building and the car, which was parked right out front. He climbed in. Suddenly, picking a restaurant an hour away felt like the most foolish decision he had ever made in his life.

He gripped the steering wheel and turned on the radio, not caring what station was on. Classical. Fine.

"Callum, I'm sorry," she said, twisting her hands in her lap.

"'Tis nae your fault," he said, his throat feeling thick.

He'd been a fool to believe that she could get over her distrust of him, her resentment. The worst part was that he couldn't blame her. He'd nearly destroyed her. *He thought he had.*

She didn't try to talk, and before long, they were pulling into one of the parking spaces behind her building. He turned off the car, and the silence was sudden.

He would get out and open her door, he would walk her up the steps to her own door because, despite what she might think of him, he was a gentleman. He would assure her that he would see the sealskin delivered to her as soon as possible. And he would say goodbye. Forever. He couldn't picture another path forward.

But long moments passed, and she didn't unbuckle her seatbelt.

"I'm sorry," she said again.

"'Tis nothing."

"It's not nothing," she protested. "I was an asshole back there. I accused you of doing something absolutely horrible. Without basis. And that is inexcusable."

"You have been wounded by me in the past," he said gruffly.

"I have been, but not because you intentionally wounded me. I said I could accept it. And yet—" He could hear the tears creeping into her voice, the words becoming thick and waterlogged. "And yet at the very first opportunity, I accuse you of being a monster."

He turned in his seat to look at her.

"I know you're not a monster. You were brave and kind and loyal and always put others before yourself. I'm just so angry. Angry at you."

"I never meant to hurt you."

"It's more than that," she said, swiping at her tears. "I'm angry at myself, too. For not telling you. You would have stayed. I know you would have. And then I wouldn't have—" She took a shuddering breath. "I wouldn't have struggled for so long."

"It hasnae been easy for me either, Jory, I—"

"But you had money! You had money to buy new identities and new situations and new circumstances! You had money to buy safety! I spent hundreds of years scraping to save just enough to escape to the next situation, hoping like hell to be able to stay for a decade or so before they ran me out. You're a man! You had money. You had connections. I had *nothing. Nothing.*" She was nearly screaming now, her tears glistening in the light from her security camera flood lamp. "And I'm *furious* with you for what you did, but I'm just as mad at myself because if I had told you, you would have stayed. I wouldn't have had to... It would have been easier."

He wanted to weep too. He wanted to reach across the center console and drag her into his lap and hold her close, to let her soak the cotton of his shirt with her tears until she felt better, as he'd done for her so many times before. But she was curled in on herself, arms crossed tightly over her chest.

"And because I'm just so angry, I assumed the worst of

your business venture, of you. But I've been thinking about it a lot, and I think it's really wonderful what you've tried to do with the nightclubs, how you tried to protect people. And I know this new business is more of the same. And I just hate myself right now for being such a goddamn—"

He didn't let her finish. In less time than a blink, less time than a heartbeat, before the next vicious word could be turned back on herself, Callum was out of the car. He threw open her door and stood in the opening.

"Dinnae be unkind to yourself, mo cridhe," he said thickly. "I cannae bear it."

She unbuckled her seatbelt and turned, burying her face in his dress shirt, gripping the sides of his jacket in her fists. He smelled the saltiness of her tears.

"It was all for you, Jory," he whispered against the top of her head.

She lifted her chin and looked at him, tears clinging to spiked eyelashes. "What?"

"Everything good I have ever done in this godforsaken eternal life, I have done for you."

22

"*Everything good I have ever done in this godforsaken eternal life, I have done for you.*"

Had Jory not been clinging to his suit jacket like a life raft, she might very well have collapsed from those words. As it was, he could have knocked her over with a feather.

Jory felt the expensive silk blend of his suit against her palms. He smelled like cologne. Or maybe it was aftershave. She let go of the suit jacket with one hand and slid it up his broad chest to his cheek, feeling the rough bristles against her chilled fingers.

He looked down at her, his jaw tight.

"I believe you," she whispered.

He blinked. She knew he didn't need to. Just like she knew he didn't need to breathe or cough or clear his throat or any of the other little affectations that he practiced in public.

She continued. "I believe you. About all of it. I believe that you didn't ever want to hurt Esther. I believe that you didn't ever mean to hurt me. I believe that you've tried your best to help humans and vampires alike. And I—"

She felt the tears falling over the precipice of her eyelashes.

"I wanted to be a man you could be proud of."

He stood just outside of the car, the door thrown open wide. She pulled on his suit jacket and he leaned in, shifting closer, one inch at a time, until his lips were a mere breath away.

"I was always proud of you, Callum," she whispered.

A sound—not a sob, not a cough—rattled his throat just before he closed the distance between them and pressed his lips to hers.

So much was familiar between them. The heat. The attraction. All of it still as bright and shocking as a lightning strike. She expected him to kiss her like he had behind the shed, to devour her one thrust of his tongue at a time.

But he didn't. He kissed her softly. Reverently.

"And I'm proud of you now," she whispered against his lips, and he groaned, pulling her closer, still. "Can we—" she began to ask, but stopped with a little shriek when he moved so quickly that before her next blink, she found herself at the top of her stairs, next to her door, the side of the building at her back and Callum at her front, cupping her cheeks in his hands.

"I'm gonna have to get used to that," Jory said with a breathless laugh, and Callum smiled before ducking his head to kiss her again. She met him, twining her arms around his neck and pressing her chest to his. She wanted to climb him, to be pressed against the wall, to cradle him with her hips.

"Let's go inside," she whispered.

He grunted and pulled back.

"Nay. Nay. We cannae—Jory, nay," he said with a groan

when she kissed his neck. "I want to do this properly. I dinnae want it to be like this."

"Like what?"

"I'm meant to bring you flowers and take you to dinner and treat you like a queen and then..." he trailed off.

"I don't need flowers," she protested, trying to kiss him again, but he would not be budged.

"You *deserve* flowers. You deserve everything."

She sighed, frustrated, but he'd made it impossible to be mad at him.

"You don't have to buy me flowers."

"I *want* to buy you flowers."

"And *I* want you to come inside."

"Jory—"

"I'm leaving soon. We don't have much time. I don't want to waste it."

He took another step back, putting enough distance between them for the cold air to chill her.

"Jory," he said hoarsely. "Please."

"Callum," she echoed. "Please."

He sighed, reaching his hands and once again cupping her cheeks in her palms. She let him, closing her eyes.

"Cannae we... enjoy the time and not put an expiration date on it? Life is long. Well, *our* lives are long. I know you mean to go, but you promised me four... *hangouts*."

She could tell how much he hated the word. She had been the one to insist that they weren't dates. That had felt like a good idea at the time. Now? It didn't seem to matter. If she only had a month with him, she didn't want to be just friends.

"Dates," she said matter-of-factly.

"I thought ye said they were nae dates." He looked suspicious, as if he was waiting for the catch.

"I changed my mind."

"Alright," he said slowly. "In any case, this was our first... date. Can we nae talk about you leaving just yet?"

"But—"

"I know. I know you mean to leave for good. But for the next month, can we just pretend you dinnae have that planned? Can we just... date?"

"Like... be your girlfriend?"

"That is what Robbie has been calling you."

"You're gonna make me wait until the third date to sleep with me, aren't you?"

"Robbie said some women find that romantic."

"I'm gonna murder Robbie."

He chuckled, pulling her abruptly in for a tight hug, squeezing her close against his chest. "Robbie said you'd say that."

"Good. So he'll see it coming."

With a laugh, he kissed her forehead gently.

"I'm leaving tomorrow," he said. "Dr. Alton has agreed to meet with us. There is a late flight from Seattle to San Francisco that will leave me time to reach a vampire hotel well before sunrise."

"Vampire hotel?"

He smiled, his fangs glinting in the glow of her porch light. "Aye. Vampire hotel."

"Why does that sound like an early 2000s band name?"

He looked puzzled.

"Vampire hotel? Vampire Weekend?"

"Of course they're open on the weekend."

She snorted a laugh. "You don't listen to modern hits radio?"

"I dinnae listen to the radio at all."

Of course he didn't.

"Is that funny?"

She laughed. "No."

He squeezed her tight against him. "I have learned that it is customary for boyfriends to call or text their girlfriends."

Her laughter died when he pressed his lips against her neck. He kissed his way up to the sensitive patch of skin behind her ear, and she shivered.

"You can text me."

"But not call?"

"No, you can call me. If you want."

Against her skin, he murmured, "I do want. I want verra much."

"Okay," she said in a breathy voice.

He dropped a soft, gentle kiss on her lips, a kiss that was dripping with longing. And then he was gone, down the stairs and looking at her over the open door of his SUV, a broad smile on his face.

"Be safe," she called out. "And bring me some of those tiny toiletries from your hotel."

"Aye," he said with a wink. "I'll talk to you soon."

Long after Callum had gone and Jory had washed her face and hung the gold corset back in the closet, his smile replayed in her mind. Her former lover. Her former husband. And now, even if only *for now*, her *boyfriend*. She laughed out loud.

23

Callum was on the road as soon as the sun set to drive to the airport for his flight from Seattle to San Francisco. A car was waiting for him at arrivals, the driver a tall, lanky werewolf named Mike. Callum had reservations at the vampire hotel, Somnus.

Somnus was a five-story hotel, but the floors were all underground instead of above. In fact, the hotel was hidden beneath a twenty-four-hour pizzeria run by an entrepreneurial, exiled fae. Getting in was simple enough if you knew how. One simply went up to the counter, ordered a pizza with extra red sauce, and then asked to use the restroom while you waited. The cashier would then direct the customer to the back hallway, where the bathrooms were. One of them was open to the public, while the other had a sign that said "OUT OF ORDER."

Of course, behind that door, the washroom was actually an elevator car, activated by turning on both taps at the same time and then pressing the button on the empty soap dispenser three times, which keyed the elevator to go down to the lobby level below.

The Somnus lobby was a lush, almost spa-like space, with neutral colors and the sounds of water features. Callum always appreciated the hotel's pared-down elegance, as well as the fact that they were nearly identical across cities. There was something nice about that sort of predictability. He'd been directed to a separate elevator, this one more traditional, which took him down to the bottommost level. The hall was carpeted in deep green. Gold sconces hung from the wall every so often, bathing the hall in soft light.

He swiped the key card for his room, and opened the door. The king-sized bed was covered in a crisp, white duvet, with a pile of pillows against the gray tufted headboard. The room had a screen on the far wall that showed the skyline in real time, the city lights shining in the night. Thick, charcoal draperies hung at the sides, to close off the screen and darken the room. Ordinarily, Callum crossed straight to the curtains and drew them over the simulcast of the sky.

But tonight, he found he didn't want to.

Callum dropped his bags by the foot of the bed and stripped off his jacket, hanging it in the closet. He toed off his shoes and nudged them into the closet as well. Then he stood in the room with his hands on his hips, feeling restless. He could go to the gym, he supposed, and work off some of his energy before sleeping. But unfortunately, it would only dull the edge. He could run for hours, lift for hours, do nearly anything for hours, without breaking a sweat.

There were some perks to being what he was.

He knew that he should sit at the mid-century desk and open his laptop to prepare for his presentation and meeting with Dr. Alton the following evening. But at the same time, he also knew that he'd prepared and planned as much as was possible. There was other work, of course, no matter how much Penny forbade him look at any of it. She'd been handling everything with the skill of a seasoned battlefield commander, leaving Callum feeling... unnecessary, which was unsettling. He wanted to feel necessary.

But what he wanted most was to talk to Jory. But he didn't know the rules. He tried to remember the movies he'd watched with Robbie. Had they called each other? Or texted? Was he supposed to reach out first? Or wait for her? He'd never felt so off-balance in all his life.

Callum's phone buzzed in his pocket, and he took it out to check the notification. It was a message from Robbie. He was surprised Robbie was still awake, or, perhaps, already awake. Though he shouldn't have been. Robbie kept weird hours, sometimes up all night, sometimes up in shifts. Callum opened the text.

> Knock knock.

Callum sighed before replying.

> Who's there?

> A little old lady.

> A little old lady who?

> I didn't know you could yodel!

Callum clicked the contact to call Robbie, who picked up on the first ring.

"Robbie, that was terrible."

Robbie snorted. "It's better if you hear it out loud! Hey! Where do vampires bathe?"

"Robbie," Callum said, pinching the bridge of his nose between his thumb and forefinger.

"In the bat tub!" Robbie said. "Get it? *Bat* tub?"

"You ken we dinnae really turn into bats, Robbie."

"Duh, Cal. Unfortunately, your party tricks aren't nearly that good."

"Alas," Callum said, smiling beside himself, as he often did around Robbie.

"So did you get checked in? How's the hotel?"

"It's nice. I've stayed at other Somnus hotels. I'm a platinum member."

"Look at you, big man. Flight went okay?"

"Aye. It was all fine."

"Good. Your meeting is tomorrow night at six?"

"Aye. I'm meeting Dr. Alton tomorrow at her lab and video-conferencing Nat in."

"So fucking exciting. I'm proud of you, buddy."

He remembered Jory whispering similar words against his chest the night before. *I've always been proud of you.* When he'd been a mortal, the memory would have made his heart pound hard and fast. Now, he just felt a swelling of pride, like carbonation in his brain. Joyous and unexpected.

He cleared his throat. "Thanks, Robbie."

They were quiet for a minute before Callum broke the silence. "Robbie? What are the rules for calling a girlfriend?"

Robbie sighed and groaned, as if he were kicking his feet up onto the couch and stretching out, getting comfortable. "You haven't called her?"

"No."

"Why not?"

"Because I dinnae ken the rules!" he said, exasperated. "That's why I'm asking!"

Robbie was quiet for a moment.

"Cal, I haven't really had a steady girlfriend since high school, but the way I see it, if they're your girlfriend, you can call them whenever you want."

"Whenever I want? What if she's busy?"

"If she can't talk, she won't answer."

"What if she doesn't want to talk?"

"Hey, Cal? Why does a vampire take cold medicine?"

Callum was silent. After a beat, Robbie answered his own joke. "To keep from coffin."

Callum did snort a laugh then.

"She'll answer, boss. But if you're worried about it, send her a text first. That's low stakes."

Callum wanted to answer that nothing was low stakes. Not when he was trying to convince Jory to stay, or to at least entertain the idea. Or to let him come with her. The stakes were immense. Every text, every interaction, every single word spoken could either brick a path to a future together, or... not.

"I dinnae ken."

Robbie groaned, as if stretching. "Cal, buddy, she'll be glad to hear from her boyfriend. Trust me. K?"

"But what if she—"

"Cal. *Text her.* Or I'll text her for you and make it really weird for both of you."

"You wouldnae."

"Are you willing to risk it?"

Callum growled softly in his throat.

"What's the most famous vampire family in Ireland?"

"Did ye buy a book of these?"

"I'll never tell. Are you gonna guess?"

"I dinnae ken. What is the most famous vampire family in Ireland?"

"The O'Positives!" Robbie answered before snorting again, the sound of his laughter contagious.

"Alright," Callum said with a smile. "That one was good."

"Yes!" Robbie crowed. "Okay, boss. I'm going to bed. I've had a long night being everyone's waking fantasy."

Callum chuckled. "Fair enough. Thank you for talking me down."

"You're welcome, Cal. What are friends for? So you're gonna call her?"

"I'm going to text her."

"Chicken."

"Perhaps. But I'm only afraid of her."

"Don't be. She's a big softy."

Callum smiled at that.

"What's a vampire's favorite ice cream flavor?" Callum asked.

"Vampires can't eat ice cream, and we both—ooooh," Robbie drawled out. "I don't know!"

"Vein-illa."

Robbie guffawed once loudly, which made Callum smile even more broadly.

"Goddamn. That's a good one. Okay. Goodnight, Cal. Call Jory."

Robbie hung up without waiting for a reply. Callum sat on the side of the bed, holding his phone in his hand and staring at the screen. He could do this. He could call her. He used to fight actual battles—wars—for gods' sake. He used to fight against three men at a time. He'd survived nearly a thousand years. He could call her. He could. He would. He—

His phone buzzed in his hand, and the notification showed a text from Jory.

> Did you get in to San Francisco okay?

Callum's grin nearly split his face.

> Aye. You're up early.

His phone buzzed again, and Jory's name flashed brightly as an incoming call. His thumb shook over the button as he swiped to answer.

"Hello, Jory," he said, his voice cracking at the end of her name.

"Hey," she said softly.

"'Tis early."

"It is," she agreed.

"I was just debating whether to call you."

"Debating?"

"I wasnae sure if you wanted me to."

She was quiet on the other end of the line. "I wanted you to."

He could hear her breathing softly through the phone and wondered how eerily silent it sounded on her end. He was tempted to sigh, just to contribute to the ambient sound.

Jory cleared her throat. "So... what does a vampire hotel room look like?"

And just like that, the tension was broken.

"One moment, please," he replied, lifting the phone away from his ear to switch the call from voice to video.

There was a beep just before the screen was filled with her face and he was lost entirely. She was laying on her side in bed, bare shoulders visible above the dark green duvet tucked under her arm. It looked like she was wearing a tank top of some kind, but the room was dim, her face lit only by the glow of her phone. Her hair was wild and wavy around her, a few tendrils curling over her shoulder. She was breathtaking.

"Well?" Jory said, pulling the comforter up to her chin.

"Aye," Callum said with a croak. "Shall I start from the door?"

"Aye," she replied, her voice teasing.

"Well," he said, rising and moving to stand in front of the door and turning to his left to flip on the bathroom light. "Here is the bathroom."

"Oh," she said. "Do you need a—"

"Nay," he said with a chuckle. "But what if I had a guest?" *What if you were with me?* He coughed. "Then there's the other usual stuff. Shower. Tub. Sink. Mirror."

Callum stepped into the bathroom, flipping the camera so it faced the mirror, where his reflection was clearly visible, with his rumpled dress shirt and even more rumpled hair, sticking on end from dragging his fingers through it.

"'Tis a myth, ye ken, about vampires and mirrors."

She nodded.

"I think that if a vampire didnae have a reflection in a mirror, we would have been discovered by humans a long time ago. At least a quarter of King Louis XIV's court were vampires. Can you imagine?"

Jory snorted a laugh and he smiled.

"Okay. So what else is there?"

He walked out of the bathroom and turned to the far wall. "Here is the view when ye first come in."

"The window is a bold choice."

"It isnae a real window. I'm five floors below ground. 'Tis a display. Here," he said, walking over and pulling the curtain away to show her the small gap behind the screen where it was mounted to the wall.

"Wow," she breathed. "Does it show the view outside?"

"Aye. A simulcast. If I wanted to, I could watch the sunrise."

"Have you ever done that?"

He thought for a minute. Usually when he checked into a Somnus, he closed the curtains over the screen immediately. Watching the sunrise, watching the sun do anything, really, felt like a cruel tease. Because what he really wanted was to feel the sun baking hot and bright on his skin as he lay on his back in a meadow somewhere, smelling the salt of the sea in the air while the wind whipped sea grass around him. With her. The thought of sitting in a hotel room and watching the sun rise on a screen had felt a bit like how Penny talked about sparkling water, like someone described a fruit to someone who'd never had one and they recreated the taste by description alone.

"Nay," he said. "I never watch it."

She was quiet again.

"Would you watch it? With me?"

Would he watch the sunrise with her? As if she even had to ask. As if he wouldn't do anything she asked. He cleared his throat and clicked so that the camera view faced him again. "I think you are about a half hour behind me for that."

"Oh," she breathed. "Well, I could watch yours."

When he was quiet, she added, "Never mind. It was a silly idea. You don't—"

"I want to."

She puffed out a loud breath. "You do?"

Callum swallowed thickly. "The last sunrise I saw was when I was away from you, before—"

"Shhhh," she said, biting her lip. "It's done."

"It may be done, but I've never forgiven myself for it."

"I have."

"You shouldn't."

"But I have, Callum. I don't want to be angry anymore. It won't help me."

He shook his head, looking at the soft carpet between his socked feet.

"Will you watch the sunrise with me, Callum?"

He looked back at his phone, the screen filled with Jory's face. Her eyes were soft, glistening with what might have been tears, but might have been a trick of the light. But she sat up, the duvet sliding down her body to reveal a white tank top. Her dark hair was a wild halo around her, the waves tangled and mussed from sleep. She'd always been a chaotic sleeper. While he'd always slept like... the dead. He clenched his jaw at the thought.

"Unless you're too tired. I know you've had a long night. And tonight is your big meeting. You need to rest. And I should get up anyway."

"Wait," he said, desperate to keep her on the phone.

Jory leaned back against the headboard, pulling the duvet up again and tucking it under her arms. She yawned, and Callum could practically hear her jaw crack.

"You are tired, mo cridhe," he murmured, daring to call her that, the words always at the tip of his tongue. "Why are you up so early? The store doesnae open 'til ten."

"How do you know that?" Jory asked with a smile.

"I looked it up. Ten to six, Monday to Friday, eleven to seven on Saturday. Closed on Sunday."

"That's right."

"So then why did you wake up so early?"

"I wanted to talk to you."

He blinked at her.

"And now I want to watch the sunrise with you."

Callum allowed himself to smile then, felt the creases at the corners of his eyes deepen. "Verra well," he said, pressing the button on his phone that turned the camera to face forward again so that Jory could see the mounted screen on the wall.

It started with the sky turning a dark blue, but sliding toward a brilliant pink at the horizon. The rising light made the clouds look like orange and yellow cotton candy, which he'd never tried, but had seen many times when the clubs did a circus night.

Then the pink turned to yellow as the sky lightened, and the blazing glow of the sun climbed slowly over the horizon, casting a bright gleam on the bay. Jory was watching the sunrise, but he was watching the little frame in the corner, the one that showed her face. Watching the way those pinks and yellows and oranges reflected on the bronze of her skin, how they made her green eyes sparkle. How she smiled from time to time, sighing just as often.

"I love a sunrise," she said.

It was on the tip of his tongue to say, "I love you." But he stopped himself.

"Can I see you?" she asked, and after wiping the melancholy off his face, he flipped the camera again.

"What did you think?" Jory asked.

"Beautiful."

"It was, wasn't it? How did it compare to what you remembered."

"My memories pale in comparison."

He remembered reading the interview where Johnny Cash was asked what paradise was for him and he had answered, "This morning, with her, having coffee." He may never drink coffee with Jory, but he'd give his last dime to spend every morning like that for the rest of his days.

"You're gonna do great today," Jory said softly.

"Aye?"

"I believe in you."

It felt like being rocketed back in time. He remembered the morning he left, the last morning he saw her before... The sun was just barely threatening to rise, the landscape bathed in deep purples and blues. His sword was strapped to his back, a sack of provisions gripped in his hand, and she'd stood in front of him, her hand pressed over his heartbeat, which had pounded against the warmth of her palm. She'd looked up at him with sleepy eyes and hair that looked much like it did in this moment.

He'd pressed a kiss to her forehead, closing his free hand over hers, pressing it closer against his skin. And just before he'd walked away, she'd said, "You're a marvel, mo cridhe. I believe in you."

He sucked in a deep breath, an unnecessary thing, and yet so instinctive that his body did it without his bidding, as the air conditioning kicked on quietly and the whirring brought him back to the present. To her.

"Callum? Are you okay?"

He couldn't speak. He felt the hot, bloody tears gathering at the corners of his eyes. He fought them back, clearing his throat and blinking quickly. "Aye. Just tired."

He didn't think she believed him, but she smiled softly and nodded.

"Good luck today. You don't need it, but good luck anyway."

"Thank you, Jory. Can I... can I call you after?"

"Sure. You can call anytime you want."

"Same for you," he said, then paused. When she didn't say anything else, he continued, "I guess I'll talk to you later then?"

She nodded again, an odd look on her face. Callum wanted to ask her about it. He had opened his mouth to do just that when she said, "Goodnight, then."

He nodded. Later. He would ask her later. "Good morning, mo cridhe," he whispered.

And then the screen went dark.

24

"Nat told Hank the meeting went well," Esther said through the Bluetooth in Jory's car.

Jory's windshield wipers swept slowly across the glass.

"Yes," Jory replied. "Dr. Alton agreed to sign over the patent. They're paying her an absurd amount of money."

"That's great!"

It was. Callum had called her the night before to tell her. In fact, he'd been so excited about the meeting that he'd called her from the car immediately afterward. Apparently Dr. Alton had been thrilled with the idea that her research would be distributed worldwide at no cost, that Callum had the funds and capacity to make it happen. And apparently, the bureaucratic end of things could be handled with a few well-placed connections.

"Nat's over the moon," Esther said before something crashed in the background. "Shit."

Jory smiled. "Callum is, too. I think they'll be good partners."

"So where's he taking you tonight?"

"He's not," Jory said, pulling to a stop at one of the three stoplights in town.

"But your date is tonight, right?"

The light turned green, and Jory pulled through the intersection. "Yes. But we're staying in."

"Ooooh, a little Netflix and chill?"

"I don't think anyone says that anymore. No, he's cooking for me."

"So, a little cooking and cun—"

"Esther!"

Esther's laugh was a bright sound over the dull whirr of the heat and defrost of Jory's car.

"Why does he want to cook? He can't eat anything he'd make. Oh! Are *you* the meal?"

Jory snorted. "Unlikely."

"It's your second date, right?"

"Yes."

"So..."

"If you're trying to ask me if I'm gonna sleep with him, the answer is no. He has it in his head that he has to wait for the third date."

"Girl, I tried to wear Hank like a weighted blanket the first night I met him. No date involved."

"I'd say it worked out for you."

Esther sighed. "Yeah. But why the third date? Weren't y'all like... married?" she asked, her Georgia accent thick and saccharine.

Now it was Jory's turn to sigh. "Yes. But that was lifetimes ago. And Callum is... stubborn. Besides, the more I think about it, the more I don't know if I even want to go down that road with him if I'm going to be leaving town."

Esther was silent. This was a sore subject, and Jory knew

it. Which is why she made it a point to bring it up at least once a day to acclimate Esther to the eventuality.

"Yeah," Esther said, her voice flat. "You're probably right."

"It's not personal, Est," Jory said.

"I know."

"And not for a few weeks."

"I know."

Jory wanted to console her friend that she would have her phone and they could text every day. Which would be true... until it wasn't. She couldn't take an iPhone to the depths. And once she went home, who knew when—or if—she would return. The loss of Esther's friendship would be near the top of the list of things she would mourn. She'd never had a friend as fiercely loyal as Esther, who supported and loved her with a dogged enthusiasm that Jory had never known before. She would miss her desperately.

But she wanted to go home. Didn't she? Wasn't it all she'd been able to think about for centuries? Leaving her human form behind and returning to the arms of her family, to the velvety darkness of the sea?

"I love you, Esther," she said, because what else could she say?

Esther sniffed. "I love you too. And don't think for a second I'm giving up on convincing you to stay."

Jory chuckled. "Fair enough. There are far more people on your team than on mine, I assure you."

Jory pulled the car onto the gravel access road that led past Magda's house and back to the little A-frame cabin where Callum was staying. The gravel rumbled under her slow-moving tires and the lights of the cabin in the distance had her heart thumping with something that straddled the divide between excitement and anxiety. "Anxietment," as Esther called it.

"Well, I'm pulling in."

"Okay," Esther said, chewing something now. "Be safe. Have fun. Don't do anything I wouldn't do."

"Is there anything you wouldn't do?"

"Don't slut-shame me, Jory."

"I wouldn't dream of it, Esther," she replied, parking the car and turning off the ignition.

There was a deep, muffled voice in the background that said something that sounded like, "Will you slut-shame me?" A smacking sound followed.

Esther shrieked and giggled. "Never! Gotta go, Jory! Have fun!" And with a high yelp, she was gone, and Jory was left in a silent car with the knowledge that her best friend was probably about to be spanked within an inch of her life before taking charge and absolutely destroying her boyfriend.

Boyfriend.

She was about to go inside her own *boyfriend*'s house. And eat food that her *boyfriend* was cooking for her. And then... she didn't know.

She got out of her car, fretting over whether she should knock. Or text him and tell him she was there? Or should she just walk in? Surely not. That would—

The door opened before she had even rounded her car, a dark shadow looming, lit from behind by the cozy light of the cabin. As she got closer, she saw him wearing a pair of athletic shorts and a T-shirt, a kitchen towel slung over one shoulder. She climbed the short stairs onto the porch and walked closer. Not close enough to touch, but... closer.

"Hi," Callum said with a smile.

"Hi," she breathed back.

"May I?" Callum asked, his gaze on her lips.

She nodded, closing her eyes, prepared to be kissed. But he didn't kiss her. He pulled her against his chest and wrapped his thick arms around her, holding her tight. He smelled like garlic and herbs, and Jory couldn't help but breathe him in deeply.

"Much better," he said against the top of her head. "I missed you."

A part of her, the part that wanted to guard her heart and feelings from running completely out of control, didn't want to hear him say that. But the other part, a much larger part if she were honest, preened. Because she had missed him too.

She felt him smile against her hair before he released her. "Come on in. Can I take your coat?"

"Sure," she said, slipping through the open door and shrugging out of her jacket. "It smells good in here."

And it did. The same smells that clung to his T-shirt permeated the air.

"I hope you like Italian food," Callum said, pulling out a barstool for her.

"I love it. How did you know?"

She wondered if Callum had asked Esther, or if he was the type of person who had learned to cook a few things, and this dish, whatever it was, happened to be one of them. She didn't have to wait long for an answer to the question.

"I had an Italian chef work for me at one of my estates in England. At the time, it was on trend to have a French chef, but I'd met Giorgio on a trip to Rome and hired him on the spot. He was a brilliant chef, and while it was unheard of for a duke to be seen in the kitchen—"

"Duke?" Jory spluttered. "A duke, Callum?"

If he'd been capable of it, Jory suspected Callum would have blushed.

"Aye. A duke," he said sheepishly, rounding the island.

He pushed her stool in and uncorked a bottle of red wine, pouring her a glass with a deft flourish, not a drop spilled, before sliding it across the counter to her.

"I would scandalize my housekeeper, Mrs. Dalrymple, by rolling up my shirtsleeves and helping Giorgio peel dozens upon dozens of cloves of garlic."

"Garlic? Isn't that supposed to—"

"Another myth," Callum interjected with a smile. "I cannae eat it, but I can peel it, touch it, and smell it with nae danger to myself."

Jory smiled, smelling wine before taking a sip. "How did you manage it? Being a duke without being discovered?"

Callum was filling a large pot with water in the sink. He carried it over to the stove and placed the lid carefully atop it before he turned to face her.

"At that time, the aristocracy kept verra conducive hours. Balls and assemblies didnae begin until nine at night. I simply avoided the supper rooms. It was an easy enough excuse to say I had eaten at my private club. Then, dancing and reveling all evening and home just before dawn. My household was staffed by a great number of creatures for whom a person of my kind wasnae such a surprise. They kept my secret, and I paid them well and gave them a safe haven."

"How did you become a duke then?"

Callum sliced a loaf of crusty, Italian bread and casually said, "I killed one particular duke's roguish heir and glamoured the duke on his deathbed so he wouldnae ken the difference."

Jory's stemless wine glass hit the counter with a sharp

thud as she set it down too quickly. "You killed him? You told me you never killed anyone."

"I never said that."

"You did! You—"

"I said I didnae kill anyone who didnae have it coming to them."

"What?" Jory shouted.

Callum rounded the island and stood before her. "Jory, Jory, mo cridhe. Listen to me. The duke's son, he... Christ, the things he did. To women. To children. To the members of his staff. He—" Callum swallowed thickly, his eyes dark and angry. "I dinnae want to speak his crimes aloud to you. But trust me when I say that I saved the lives and spirits of dozens—maybe more—by ridding the world of his lecherous carcass."

Jory heard him. She did. And while she bristled at the casual way he discussed murder, it was also so like him, so damn like him, to protect those who needed a protector. It was what he'd always done.

"Jory," he whispered, hesitant, "I didnae set out to kill him. But I came upon him—" he swallowed again, a haunted look hollowing his face. "He was careful. He only went after servants. The poor. As a member of the peerage, he'd never face punishment for that. And I—" A breath whooshed out of Callum, and his torso sagged with it. "I had been working on the estate as a night watchman. I stayed in a gamekeeper's cottage in the woods. But I heard the tales. The stories. And then I saw him. And I—"

"You stopped him" Jory repeated.

"I stopped him."

"So why take the dukedom? Was it the money?"

"Nay," he denied quickly. "I didnae need the money. I took the dukedom so that I could... make amends. I took a large sum of the money and established annuities for the victims and their families. I hired unhireable people. Gave them a place to be safe. I tried to make it right."

"Are you still a duke then? Is that even still a thing."

"Aye. That is, it is a thing. But nay, I am nae a duke. Not for a long time. When I could nae pass myself off any longer as a recluse, I faked my death and passed the title onto my predecessor, a young werewolf named George who I knew would do the title credit and live a far less suspicious life span with natural offspring and—"

He froze and looked quickly at her.

"What?" Jory asked, easing back onto the barstool and reaching for her wine, trying her best to make him feel at ease, to assure him that she wasn't leaving.

"Do you want children, Jory?"

"Why?"

"Please answer the question."

"Not particularly. Why?"

"Because I... cannae. When I was turned, it—"

"Callum?"

He shook his head, looking at the floor. "Aye?"

"If you won't fuck me until the third date, don't you think the second date is a little too soon to be talking about babies?"

He snorted and looked up at her through his long, pale lashes.

"Aye."

"Besides—" she started to say but abruptly clamped her mouth shut. She had been about to say, "Besides, I'm not going to be here long enough for that to even be a concern of yours." But he'd said that he couldn't bear to hear that. That he wanted to be her boyfriend for as long as she was here and not think about the end.

He knew what she'd been about to say, though. Of course he did. Because for all that she liked to tell herself that he didn't know her anymore, he did. Callum stood frozen in front of her, his eyes sad and his fists clenched.

"Besides," she began again, reaching for one of his hands, "there's more than one way to crack an egg."

A hint of a smile at the corner of his mouth. More of an impression of a desire to smile.

"Isnae the expression that there's more than one way to skin a cat?"

He had stepped closer, until he was nearly standing between her spread knees. She held his calloused, heavy hand in hers. She wanted to pull him closer still, until he was nestled against her. But the lid of the pot began to rattle as the water boiled, and Callum stepped away, looking remorseful.

"The water is ready."

"Sure," she replied softly.

Jory took another sip of her wine as she watched him open a box of linguine and pour the contents into the boiling water, stirring it gently with a wooden spoon. She slid off the barstool and moved to his side, wanting to be closer to him as much as she wanted to see what the sauce looked like simmering in the pot.

"It smells amazing," she said. She'd said it before, but it bore repeating. "I wish you could enjoy it too."

"I'll enjoy watching you enjoy it."

Heat flooded her body.

"Can I watch you cook?"

"I thought you already were," he said with a laugh.

"Closer," she replied, her voice barely above a whisper.

Callum had been stirring the pasta again, but his hand froze, and before she could blink—she really would never get used to that—he had abandoned the pot of pasta, picked her up, and deposited her on the counter next to the stove. His hands held her waist gently, and he stood in the empty space between her knees, his hips pressed against the counter's edge. She hadn't even had time to shriek in surprise.

"How's that?" he asked, and his gray eyes looked so bright with the stove light shining.

"Best seat in the house," she said with a smile.

"Well, I dinnae ken that it's the *best* seat."

More heat. More blush. Her core clenched and her insides tightened, and in that moment she wanted nothing more than to reach over, turn off the stove, tell him to forget about dinner, and drag him downstairs and see exactly what kind of seating he thought might be better.

"Would you like a taste?" Callum asked.

She stared blankly at him.

"Of the sauce? Would you like a taste of the sauce, Jory?"

"Oh," she answered, more a rush of breath than a word, really, and nodded.

Callum smiled and opened a drawer without looking, pulling out a teaspoon. He dipped it into the simmering sauce and held it before his lips, blowing on it. He was so close that Jory could feel the stream of air against her face, bringing with it the smell of tomato, onion, garlic. The spoon looked tiny balanced between his thumb and forefinger, and she remembered so many times being amused by all the things made to seem smaller than they were by his presence.

"Taste," he said in a husky whisper, and Jory opened her mouth, leaning forward and closing her lips around the spoon. The flavor burst across her tongue. She swallowed and then he was there, his mouth against hers, his tongue sliding against her lips.

He groaned.

"It tastes good. I havenae ever tasted it before," he said as he kissed her.

"But you can't," Jory said with a gasp.

"I cannae eat it. But oh, Jory, I can taste it. For the first time, I can taste it."

He gripped the spoon in one hand and her thigh in the other.

"Another," she said.

He obliged. Retrieving more sauce on the spoon, blowing on the contents before offering her the bite. Immediately after swallowing, he was there again, thrusting his tongue into her mouth with more intensity. He groaned again and she flung her arms around his neck, pulling him close against her body. She felt the solidness of him against her, between her legs, and arched into his chest.

"I cannae get enough," he rasped before kissing her deeply, his hand squeezing the meat of her thigh.

"More. I want more," she begged in a whimper.

"As much as ye want," he said with a rough press of his lips. "Everything. All of it. Any of it."

The next taste made him wilder. The spoon clattered to the counter and then his hands were in her hair, spearing through the thick waves and holding her head close to his. She gripped at his back, his shoulders, his neck, as he kissed her.

Callum's mouth left hers to trail hot, seeking kisses across her jaw and down her throat. He sucked gently at a spot right below her ear, another at the juncture of her neck and shoulder.

"Callum," she gasped. "I need—"

"Shhhh, mo cridhe," he murmured against her skin. "I've got you. I—"

The timer on the microwave clock began dinging a relentless, obnoxious beep. He groaned against her throat, and she let her head fall back against the cabinet with a soft thud.

"I have to deal with that," he muttered. "I—"

"It's fine," Jory said, wiping her mouth with the back of her hand.

He leaned forward and kissed her forehead before moving to the stove and scooping a cup of pasta water out with a glass measuring pitcher. He carried the heavy pot to the sink, and Jory's eyes felt glued to the sight of his flexing biceps as he tipped the pot over a colander.

She watched as he returned the drained pasta to the pot, brought it back to the still-hot burner, and ladled sauce into the pot, alternating it with drizzles of pasta water. He gently stirred the pot with a pair of tongs, and Jory's senses—all five of them—were so overstimulated she could scream. The scent of the pasta, the sight of Callum in a worn, thin cotton T-shirt, the sounds of her own panting breath, the feel of the air moving around her body after he vacated her space, the taste of—

"Hungry?" Callum asked, an eyebrow raised slightly.

"Starving."

"I ken the feeling."

She didn't answer him. What was there to say? There was more than one way to starve. To *be* starved. To *feel* starved.

"Callum," she began, but didn't know what to say. And so his name hung in the air between them along with all of the tension and want and hunger.

"Jory," he answered, setting down the tongs and the plate

he'd retrieved from another cabinet. He stepped closer to her, back toward the cradle of her body.

The hunger was a living creature. What had he said when he'd first described being turned into what he was? When she'd accused him of being a monster in Hank and Esther's kitchen. *"You dinnae understand. You cannae understand what it's like. The cravings. The never-ending cravings."*

She thought she might understand. She took a deep breath to do just that when the door banged open and she heard Robbie hiss, "Oh, fuck. I'm sorry, I'm sorry, I'm sorry, I'm sorry."

He had an arm over his face, as if to cover his eyes, as he hurried into the cabin and straight into a wall.

"Fuck," he shouted, and Jory couldn't help but smile.

Callum's eyes were closed. "Robbie," he said in the same tone someone might use to warn a child that they were nearing the end of their patience.

"Hi, Robbie," Jory said brightly, leaning around Callum's hulking shoulder to look at him.

"Hey, Jory-dory," Robbie answered sheepishly, rubbing at his elbow with a wince. "I'm sorry. I know it's the big date night, Cal, and I didn't mean to interrupt. I just... I don't really have anywhere else to go, so I'm gonna go to my room and put headphones in and watch *Fawlty Towers* and you'll never know I'm here."

He began to rush toward the little hallway that led back to the bedroom.

"Robbie, come eat with us."

"Jory," Callum said through gritted teeth.

"I can't," Robbie said. "You're on a date."

"Come eat. And then you can go lock yourself away and watch... whatever you said."

"Fawlty Towers."

"Sure. That."

"Jory," Callum said, his tone tight.

"Callum," she replied, imitating the tone.

"You dinnae get to count this as a date then if he's here. This isnae the second date."

"Oh, it most assuredly is the second date, and it absolutely counts. Because the next date is the third date, and I'll be damned if your old-fashioned ass bumps that back."

Callum's eyes flew wide, and Robbie snorted.

Jory leaned in and whispered in Callum's ear, "But fair is fair. I'll give you a bonus one."

"Get the bread, Robbie," Callum said, his eyes locked on Jory's as a thrill shivered up her spine.

"Oh my god, that was good. I'm stuffed," Jory said, leaning back in her chair.

"You outdid yourself, Cal," Robbie said and then proceeded to undo both his belt and the top button of his pants.

"What the hell are ye doing, Robbie?" Callum asked, bewildered.

"I can't wear hard pants when I'm this full," Robbie whined.

Jory snorted a laugh into her wine glass.

"Hard pants?" Callum asked. "That doesnae make any sense. All pants are soft."

Robbie was too busy petting a disgruntled-looking Walter, who had emerged from his hiding place in Robbie's pocket, eaten sugar syrup out of a saucer, and then fallen asleep on a piece of bread, much to Jory's delight.

"Hard pants are any pants with a waistband that doesn't stretch," Jory supplied helpfully.

Robbie stood with a groan. "You cooked, I'll clean."

"I'll help," Jory said, attempting to rise.

"Not a chance," Robbie said, grabbing the plate from her hand. "You just sit your gorgeous ass down and have another glass of wine and keep the boss company."

"I'm not your boss anymore," Callum reminded Robbie.

"Oh, I know," he said in his mountain twang. "But it's a cute nickname, don't you think?"

Jory smiled. "I think if anyone's the boss around here, it's Walter." She reached out and stroked a fingertip between his tiny, iridescent wings. Walter made a sound that was somewhere between a purr and a snort.

"Damn straight," Robbie said from the sink, where he was washing a plate.

Callum picked up the bottle of wine and lifted an eyebrow in silent question. Jory nodded with a smile, and Callum poured the wine into her empty glass.

"So what's the plan for the rest of the date?" Robbie asked over the sound of the faucet running.

Jory looked at Callum, an expectant look on her face. "Yes, boss. What's the plan for the rest of the date?"

"Well," Callum coughed into his fist, "I hadnae gotten that far. I thought we would eat and see what the night brought next."

Jory smiled and waggled an eyebrow. "But then the night brought Robbie."

Callum sighed and took a sip of his elk blood. "Aye. Then the night brought Robbie."

"And Walter!" Robbie said cheerfully as he poured the remaining sauce into a glass storage container. Walter glared at Callum with his tiny, bead-black eyes.

Callum turned to Robbie. "Why do you have Walter with you anyway?"

Robbie looked up. "Magda asked me to watch him for a few weeks. She said she thinks he'll be good for me."

"Good how?" Callum couldn't help but ask.

Robbie shrugged. "Who knows? But if I've learned anything, it's that when Magda tells you to do something, you do it."

Walter flitted off of the slice of bread and flew in a bumbling, bouncing pattern to land on Robbie's shoulder.

"I don't know," Robbie continued. "I've been feeling a little anxious lately? Or... not anxious, just... off? Magda thought he would be helpful."

"You didnae tell me you're feeling off," Callum said, leaning in, and Robbie shrugged a shoulder.

"You've been preoccupied."

That was true, but it didn't make Callum feel any better. That wasn't being a good friend.

"Has Esther come around to the idea of taking over the store yet?" Robbie asked, washing the big pasta pot now.

Jory sighed, twisting her napkin nervously, deliberately avoiding eye contact with Callum. He didn't like that.

"She's mad, I think. And scared. She says she doesn't know the first thing about running a business. I told her that I didn't either when I first started. Besides, the store basically runs itself at this point as long as she follows the plan."

"She'll have help too," Robbie said, leaning against the counter as he dried the pot. "I'll be here."

"You're staying?" Jory asked. "I thought you'd head for home before too long."

"Don't really have one," he said with a small shrug of his shoulder that sent Walter bouncing once.

"But I thought Savannah was—"

"I was in Savannah for a little while. Couch-surfing mostly. Met Cal and then went west. I haven't had a place that's mine in a long time."

"Why not?"

"Haven't wanted one. Didn't like being by myself in one place too long anyway."

Callum understood that all too well. How many cities had he lived in? Long enough to get clubs off the ground and profitable before moving on to the next place, never staying anywhere long enough for it to really be home. Before Savannah, it had been Chicago, and before that, Austin. He had told himself that he was lonely because he never stayed in one place long enough to make connections, but perhaps the truth was that he never stayed in one place for too long because if it kept moving, he could make himself believe that he was alone by choice. Maybe that's what had drawn him to Robbie. Maybe he'd seen something of himself in him.

But if he was really honest with himself, he'd kept moving because staying in one place too long had made him miss Jory too much. He'd never made himself at home because home was where she was and she was dead.

Except she hadn't been. She'd been alive the whole time. Maybe they'd just missed each other more than once. Either way, they'd found each other now, and that couldn't be for nothing. It couldn't be. He didn't like hearing her talk about Esther taking over the store because she would only be doing that if Jory left for good. But if he could go with her, if he could convince her to let him...

Robbie returned to the table with his water bottle. It was stainless steel and covered with stickers. He took a long sip.

"Oh!" Jory said, leaning toward him and pointing to one of the stickers. "You know Carry Out?"

"Oh my god, Jory. I love Carry Out. They're one of my favorite bands."

"Me too!"

"They're playing in Seattle this summer. Wanna go?"

Jory's smile fell, and she froze. Callum watched every single muscle ticking in her face, every twitch of her eyes.

"I won't be here then."

Robbie took another sip, rubbing his cheek against Walter's little body. "But you could fly back for it. Come visit everyone and see the show."

Jory closed her eyes, and Callum waited, frozen, for her answer.

"I won't be able to, Robbie. I won't be... I just won't be able to."

"You won't be somewhere with an airport?"

"No."

"Where are you going? The moon? The middle of the ocean?"

She flinched. A tiny, imperceptible flinch, but Callum saw it. He stood slowly. He could feel his throat tightening, the grief nearly strangling because what was the fucking point of any of this. Two dates. Three dates. A hundred dates. It didn't matter because she'd already made up her mind to leave.

"If you'll excuse me. I—I'm feeling tired. I think I'll go downstairs for a bit."

"You okay, boss?"

Callum cleared his throat. He was most definitely not okay. He would never be okay again. But that wasn't Robbie's burden. It was his. His *penance*. "Aye. Thank you for doing the dishes, Robbie."

"No problem, Cal," Robbie said quietly. He looked at Jory and then back at Callum. "I, uh, I think Walter and I are gonna get some ice cream and go watch a movie."

Callum nodded and left the table. He walked to the closet and down the stairs to the vault. He sat on the edge of the bed and listened to Robbie opening the freezer, the clatter of bowl and spoon against the countertop, Jory's quiet voice thanking Robbie for doing the dishes, asking him more about the show he was watching. Callum squeezed his eyes shut as he heard a door open and close.

He'd allowed himself the fantasy of not being alone anymore, of having a home again. Best he get used to the truth now: Jory was leaving, and nothing would change her mind.

He heard soft footsteps on the floor above, the soft creak of the closet door, and then the careful padding of socked feet on the stairs.

"Callum," she asked, her voice warm and husky, like hot whiskey mixed with tea. "Are you okay?"

That question again and, again, the same answer. No. He was decidedly not okay. He was... angry. That feeling surfaced above all the others, and he could feel it clearly now. It had been hidden beneath all the sadness and relief and goddamn hope, and now he could feel it. Righteous, scalding anger.

"Nay," he said, dragging a palm over his face and yanking at the neck of his T-shirt, which suddenly felt like it might strangle him. "I am nae okay."

"Okay," she said, and there was that fucking word again. "Can we talk about it?"

"Why?" Callum said, sharper than he intended to.

"Because we're dating? And people in relationships talk about their feelings."

"We're dating?"

Jory looked at him, confused. "Aren't we? Wasn't that the whole thing? You be my boyfriend? For real? We give it a real go?"

"That's what I thought, Jory. I thought we were to give it an honest go. But you're already halfway out of here."

"What are you talking about?"

"You've already made up your mind, Jory!" he shouted hoarsely. "You have nae intention of staying, and you never did!"

"I told you what I wanted! I told you I wanted to go home. I have never lied about that!"

"Fine. You didnae lie. But you made me believe that I had a hope of changing yer mind, of making you want to stay. To at least stay *with me*. Did I ever really even have a chance?"

She stared mulishly at him, her mouth a thin line, her green eyes bright with anger.

"I thought as much. You're going. You're leaving and you're never looking back and fuck me and my feelings. Fuck this," he said, gesturing between them.

Like a bolt of lightning bursting forth from a swollen, dark cloud, Jory's voice was sharp and fierce. "*You* left!"

He stood, moving with as much speed as he could, coming to stand before her in less time than it took for her brain to decide to breathe.

"Aye, Jory," he said quietly, clutching at restraint. "Aye. I did leave you. And I've paid for it every day since."

"Well, you seem like you're doing just fine to me," she said, and Callum stepped back as if she'd struck him.

In many ways, yes, he was fine. He had thriving businesses. He had... friends, though that was a new addition. He was fine. But in other, bigger ways, he hadn't been fine since he'd found her in the moonlight on that beach. He'd felt... dead inside. And wasn't that such an irony.

He felt as if the collar of his T-shirt was cutting off his air now. The anger and the panic were rising, and he couldn't stand another second of the shirt around his throat. He reached behind his neck and yanked the T-shirt off.

"What the hell are you doing?" Jory shrieked.

He didn't answer. He couldn't answer. He didn't have words. They were being overpowered by all of his feelings. It was like trying to shout into a hurricane.

Callum balled up the T-shirt and tossed it into the hamper in the corner. His back was to her now, his hair gripped in his fists as he closed his eyes against the torrent of those goddamn feelings. He'd done well enough for the last nine hundred years nearly numb to them. Numb was easy. It wasn't pleasant and it got monotonous, but numb didn't hurt either.

He remembered feeling this way as a human, feeling overcome by feelings. He remembered taking deep, heaving breaths. He remembered the pounding of his heart in his ears and the feeling of adrenaline coursing through his veins. How *alive* it made a person feel to be angry.

But now there was no pounding heart. There was no sawing breath. There was no adrenaline spiking through his veins like acid. There was... nothing. No heartbeat. No inhalations.

If anything, it made the feelings worse. Being able to take breaths, feeling the drumbeat of a heart, those things were the percussion, the baseline to underpin the emotion. Without them, there was just raw, unadulterated *feeling*, a chaotic dissonance that just crashed against him again and again like an angry, rising sea.

Callum rubbed the center of his chest, as if he could will his heart to start beating again. Behind him, he heard Jory. He *felt* Jory. He would feel her anywhere, his body as in tune to hers as it was to its own needs and cravings.

Jory's heart was pounding. He could hear the frenzied beat, fast like a rabbit's, echoing in her chest, sending blood rushing through her body. She was as upset as he was, her body doing what his couldn't. He wheeled around. Her eyes were wide, her cheeks full of color, her chest rising and falling with the pace of her breath.

"Jory," he said quietly. "Are *you* okay?"

"I—" She stopped abruptly, her eyes widened even more. He took a step closer. "It's not really fair to have this conversation with your shirt off."

"Why do you say that?"

"You know why," she whispered.

"I dinnae ken what ye mean at all," he said, feeling more like a hunter than he'd felt in hundreds of years.

She narrowed her eyes and crossed her arms over her chest. "You know exactly why it's hard for me to have this conversation with your shirt off. You used to take your shirt off... before. To stop an argument because you knew I..." She trailed off.

He'd forgotten, actually. But the memories came flooding back. Of a fight that wasn't going anywhere because Jory—Marjory—had needed to fight but hadn't known about what. Sometimes she got like that, itching to argue, because she was frustrated or feeling too many things that she didn't know what to do with. When Callum's brain got too full, he'd go chop something or cut something or hunt something. But Jory wasn't like that. She was... what did Penny call it? A verbal processor.

The argument would spiral like a whirlpool that kept growing and growing, dragging in old grievances long settled and petty annoyances never spoken aloud into a fight that wasn't really about any of them but more about a need to blow off steam, to vent all the feelings.

"You just liked to fight."

"I did not."

"You did, Jory. You'd pick a fight about nothing because ye liked it."

"That never happened."

"It did," he said, taking another prowling step closer.

Jory sucked in a fast breath.

"It wasn't fair then, Callum, and it isn't fair now."

"But it was effective," he said, coming close enough to feel the heat radiating off her body.

She swallowed, and in the air between them, Callum could almost taste her. He wanted to taste her. He took another step closer, her chest brushing against his as she panted.

"You like to fight."

"Sometimes," she admitted, squeezing her eyes tightly shut. "Sometimes I like to fight. *Liked* to fight."

"You liked to make up more," he said, reaching a hand up but not touching her. Only just barely.

"I'm mad at you."

"I'm mad at you too."

"It's not the third date."

"You dinnae care. The dates dinnae count. Your mind's made up to leave anyway, so what does it matter?"

"I... haven't..."

"You havenae what?"

"I haven't made up my mind."

"You're passing the business to Esther."

"Maybe it's time for something new."

"You willnae go to a concert with Robbie."

"I don't like breaking promises."

The tension between them was thick enough to be sliced like a layer cake, soft and thick and filled.

"You havenae made up your mind?" Callum asked, not

allowing hope to become one of those feelings, not again. Not yet.

She looked at him then, her eyes focusing on his for the first time since she'd come downstairs, and shook her head. He touched her cheek, skating his fingertips across her cheek, into her hair, and then down to spread his fingers wide, thumb in front of her ear, fingers wrapping behind her neck. He leaned closer, feeling her breath feather across his face. Jory closed her eyes. Callum knew that look. He knew it better than he knew his own face. Jory wanted to be kissed. She probably wanted a hell of a lot more than that, but Callum didn't make assumptions anymore.

"Jory?" he said, his lips not touching hers, but just barely.

"I don't want to fight with you," she said, green eyes peeking behind half-open lids as she gazed up at him.

"So we willnae fight," he said and took a step back, giving her space.

She reached out, grabbed the elastic waist of his athletic shorts in her fist, and pulled. And then his mouth was on hers. Ravenous. Her arms were around his neck and he reached behind her, hooking hands behind her thighs before scooping her off the floor. She gasped and wrapped her legs around his waist. He could have held her there for hours—it wouldn't have taken any strength at all—but he wanted to be as close to her as he could be. He turned and pressed her against the wall, groaning when she squirmed against his aching cock. The athletic shorts were slick and light, and he felt every bit of her heat through them as he thrust against her.

"Fuck," she hissed, biting his neck.

"Careful," he groaned.

"Why?" she asked, licking a stripe up to his earlobe, which she caught between her teeth.

With his lips against her shoulder, he said, "Because I'll bite back."

He scraped the points of his fangs, letting her feel them. He imagined biting her, tasting her—all of her—imagined biting her sex, tasting her slick and her blood on his tongue at once, married with the salt of her skin. Jory shivered, and he licked the place where his teeth had touched, pressing more firmly against her core with his hips.

"Put me down," she said sharply. "Put me down now."

He complied immediately, putting her down gently and stepping away, his athletic shorts tented awkwardly by his erection. She looked at him with... was that fear?

"I don't want you to bite me."

"Fine," he said without hesitation, his hands held up in surrender.

"I don't want you to bite me," she said with more emphasis.

"I heard you. I promise I willnae bite you."

"I don't want you to lose control and—"

"I wouldnae—"

"You did." Jory's bottom lip trembled and she gasped for breath. "I thought I.... But I— What if you— I—" She looked around, frantic, before bolting for the steps.

26

The panic had been sudden and sharp, freezing her. He had dragged his fangs up her throat behind Hank's shed and it had not caused her to spiral, but that was before. Before she knew what he had done with those teeth. It wasn't a rational response. She'd told him she had forgiven him. She *had* forgiven him. But the animal part of her, the one that needed to *survive,* had felt those teeth and screamed through the fog of her lust, *Run.*

She made it up four steps before he caught her, wrapping his arms around her thighs from behind. She froze. His face was pressed in the space between her thighs, just below her ass. They'd been here before. The night he'd told her what had happened, *everything* that had happened. She panted.

"Jory," he said, his voice a hoarse rasp. "Jory, mo cridhe, I cannae forgive myself for that night. I never will. But I was blood-mad, a new vampire. I didnae have any control. I—" He pressed his forehead against her thigh. "I would *never* hurt you again. I would *die* before I hurt you again."

She allowed herself to look between her legs and behind her. Beneath the thick bands of his arms at her knees, she saw his muscled chest, his stomach, the dusting of blond hair that led down into his shorts, which were *obscene.*

"I wouldnae bite you unless you asked me. And I wouldnae bite you unless you asked me sober, and not in the heat of the moment. I wouldnae bite you unless we talked about it," he said in a rush. "I swear to you. I would never do *anything* you didnae want, or ask for."

He pushed his forehead against the back of her thighs, his head bowed. "I wouldnae bite you, mo cridhe. You have to believe me. You *must* believe me," he begged.

For a moment, she thought about asking him to release her. She knew he would, that before the words were even out of her mouth, he would be all the way across the room. That knowledge was settling. Sobering. And within the safety of that knowledge, she felt her heart begin to beat more slowly, the clanging, screeching panic in her brain quieting. Because the truth was that she *did* trust him to keep her safe, to respect her.

And besides, she could not deny that his body wrapped around her was something she'd missed for almost a thousand years.

Jory bit her lip and, with a shuddering breath said, "Prove it."

"Jory?"

"You heard me."

He shifted back, and for the briefest second, she thought he would stop. That he would tell her no. That he would walk her to the door and say goodnight.

But then his hands skated up the front of her thighs, to the button of her jeans. He unfastened it and slid the zipper down. His big fingers hooked in the waistband of her jeans, shimmying them over her ass, her thick thighs.

"Fuck," he whispered, and she smiled. She hadn't planned on sex tonight, but she had worn a black lace thong anyway. Just in case.

Callum slid the jeans down to her ankles, and then his palms were on her calves, running up the backs of her thighs. He grabbed her hips and leaned in. She felt the scrape of his teeth against the roundness of her ass and her whole body tensed.

"Shhhh," he whispered against her skin. "I'm proving myself. Remember?"

Jory shuddered, and Callum moved to the other cheek, dragging the points of his fangs gently over her skin before his tongue followed.

"I want to rip this off of ye with my teeth, but it's too pretty."

Jory gasped. "I have more."

He hummed, and she felt the sound vibrate through his cool lips against her overly warm skin. "Someday."

A breath shuddered out of her, and he reached up once more, sliding fingers into the wide lace band of the thong and stretching it over her ass and hips and thighs. Once it had passed her knees, he dropped it, and it fell around her ankles.

She knew that he could see everything. Every slick, swollen crevice of her body, every hidden place. She squirmed, embarrassed but... not. He'd seen it before. Not like this, perhaps. Never quite like this, in fact. But he knew her. More than anyone else ever had, he knew her, and she didn't have it in her to be ashamed.

His teeth were back on the round muscle of her ass. For the briefest of moments, she wondered what it would be like if she *did* let him bite her. She wouldn't. She didn't want that... right? No. Definitely not.

...Yet.

She wanted to tell him that she trusted him, that he didn't need to prove anything, and had opened her mouth to do just that when she felt the tip of his tongue pressing against her cunt.

She sucked an inhale. It had been such a light touch. Tentative. Unexpectedly tentative, really, given how he had fairly devoured her moments before. And in the kitchen. And behind the shed. And in the cottage by the sea. She liked being devoured by him. This hesitant exploration was new. She didn't dislike it, but it wasn't enough.

She spread her feet as wide as the jeans would allow and relished the sound Callum made as more of her was revealed.

"Hold on," he said through his teeth.

"What?"

"I said, hold. On."

Jory braced her hands on the tread of the stair just as he covered her clit with his mouth and sucked. Hard. She moaned—a sharp, wild sound that only seemed to spur him on. He rubbed his tongue against her clit as he sucked, and she could feel the orgasm coming into view. She'd never come that quickly in all her life. Not even with the vibrator that she'd bought on a Black Friday deal the year before. It was pink and stimulated both her clit and her G-spot simultaneously and usually hurled her over the finish line in less than a minute.

But this? This was unbelievable. She could feel herself cresting the wave that would send her tumbling down the other side when he pulled back, dragging the flat of his tongue to her opening before thrusting it inside.

She groaned. While the denial of the orgasm hurt, his tongue felt so good. He licked into her and around, teasing. When she relaxed against the staircase, resting her head on her forearms, he moved back to her clit again and sucked as hard as the first time. She shrieked this time, and he pulled away, slapping her cunt with a short, sharp swat.

"Quiet," he said, but she could hear the amusement in his voice over the blood pounding in her ears.

Jory panted, her breath coming in short gasps as he rubbed her clit gently with his thumb, the rest of his hand splayed wide across her cunt, pressing gently.

"Please," she begged, twice denied now and becoming desperate. She wanted him to lick her into oblivion. And then she wanted him to take off those obscenely tented shorts and drive into her until she looked like a piece of notebook paper, lined, horizontal bruises down her body from the stair treads.

"I'm still proving myself, mo ghraidh," he said, and she felt the words against her cunt.

My love.

"Callum," she whined, pressing back, trying to force the contact that she so desperately needed, but he held her hips in his hands and wouldn't let her budge.

"Soon," he promised just before his tongue returned to her clit, drawing light, tight circles around it. She settled in, growing accustomed to the rhythm, letting herself become lost in the gentle waves of pleasure that lapped against her. But then she felt the sharp scrape of his fangs. They framed her clit, abrading the delicate skin as his tongue flickered gently. She couldn't help but tense at the sensation of his fangs pressing against her. She didn't dare move. One breath, one twitch, and he could—

"Shhhh," he whispered. "I promised."

"Callum," she sobbed, so turned on that it hurt, so frantic from three denied orgasms that she was nearly wild.

He sucked. Hard. So hard that, for a moment, Jory couldn't feel beyond the blinding pleasure of her sudden, knee-buckling climax to see if he'd bitten her. She shook and cried out as the orgasm seemed to go on and on in waves as he knew exactly what to do to keep her coming. He'd always known. He'd brought her to the brink like this a thousand times. Not from behind and not on a staircase, but he hadn't forgotten. How could he? She certainly would never forget the way his body worked and moved and pulsed beneath her.

"Enough," she said hoarsely, her voice gone, and his mouth grew gentler. He didn't pull away, but he pressed the flat of his tongue against her throbbing clit and held. The pressure felt good, the coolness of his mouth against the inferno of her sex felt doubly so, and she relaxed against the tenderness of his hold, his hands now rubbing up and down the sides of her legs.

And with one last, gentle kiss to her clit, Callum pulled away. He took the thong and slid it up her legs, guiding it into place with careful fingers before doing the same with her jeans.

He turned her, and she collapsed onto her ass on the step, sitting and reeling, watching as he dragged the back of his hand over his glistening mouth and then—fucking hell —licked it.

Like a siren song, she followed him, scooting down the stairs and willing her legs to support her in standing. She pressed his chest, pushing him back to sit on the bed. She grabbed the elastic waist of his athletic shorts and made to drop to her knees, but he covered her hands with his.

"Nay," he said.

"I want to take care of you," she said in a thready voice that she didn't recognize.

"Stay with me."

"I want to take care of you first."

He shook his head. "Stay."

"It's nighttime," she protested.

"And?"

"You don't sleep now."

"Aye, but you do. So stay with me. Sleep with me."

Jory looked at him. At his unusual gray eyes, his stubble, the strong lines of his throat and neck, the nose that was crooked from having been broken more than once, the blond hair that she had wrecked when he'd kissed her, standing up at odd ends. He was rumpled and vulnerable and Jory couldn't remember him ever looking more handsome.

"Won't you be bored?"

He shook his head.

"Isn't it weird to just watch me sleep?"

Another head shake.

"I'm not tired yet."

He shrugged. "We can watch a movie."

"What movie?"

"I dinnae care. Any movie ye like. But... will you stay?"

She hadn't lied to him. Because she hadn't made up her mind for sure. She reminded herself that she didn't have to decide tonight. Or even this week. She had two more weeks. And then they'd go to Scotland. Two weeks to decide if this feeling was good enough to keep her, or if she could find a way to have everything she wanted all at once.

But she had to try. She promised him she would, after all.

"Okay," she said, and climbed onto the bed. He pulled

her close and tucked her against his side as he turned on the TV and began scrolling through various streaming apps. They settled on a comedy, though Jory didn't pay much attention. She was listening to the way she could hear his laughter echo in his chest, how it reverberated without being dampened by other noises like a beating heart.

27

Callum's head shot up from the frigid ocean and into the pearlescent light of the full moon.

Behind him, he heard a squeal and a shriek before a loud splash. A bark of laughter.

He spun and saw Jory's head burst up from beneath the inky water, a brilliant smile stretching across her face.

"Lord above," Nat said from where he sat, straddling a surfboard and floating nearby. "For people with immortal strength, you two have the shittiest damn balance I've ever seen."

Callum shoved a hand through the water, sending a large splash in his direction.

"He's not wrong," Jory said. There was another squeal as Callum splashed her too. And then she was gone, dropped beneath the surface like a thrown stone.

Panic seized him. Where had she gone? In the space of a blink, he pictured something having snatched her, dragging her down. Why had he let Nat talk him into this ridiculous—

Arms wrapped around his neck from behind, squeezing

tightly. He jumped, surprised, and nearly wrenched them away. But a torso pressed against his back, long legs disturbed the water in similar rhythms as they treaded with his, kicking against the current.

"Gotcha," Jory whispered in his ear.

"You scared me half to death, Jory," he growled. "I thought something had... had... taken you."

"Like what?" she laughed.

"I dinnae ken!" Callum spluttered. "Sharks or killer whales or a giant squid!"

"They're called orcas, Callum. And there aren't any big predators here."

"How can ye be certain? I read about it before I picked you up. There are thirty shark species off the coast of Washington. *Thirty*, Jory. Thirty kinds of sharks. And kill—*Orcas*. They're everywhere. And ye just disappeared and I didnae ken what had happened and—"

"Shhhh," she said into his ear, squeezing his neck from behind. "There's nothing here."

"But *how* can ye be so sure?"

"Well, because unlike you, I can actually sense them. And there isn't a predator for miles."

"Why not?"

"Because of you and Nat. You're much more threatening predators than any shark. They know that."

Callum tipped his head back, pressing it against her shoulder, treading water with his arms and keeping them easily afloat.

"Is the big, scary vampire afraid of a little shark?" Jory teased against his neck.

He'd been a sailor. He'd seen shadows below the surface. Mangled fish on the end of a hook. He'd developed what he considered a healthy respect for the mysteries below the surface.

He'd gotten the idea for night surfing at Hank and Esther's bonfire weeks before. Nat had been raving about how much fun it was, and Jory had actually cracked a smile. Which wasn't saying much ordinarily. She'd always been quick to smile. But that night? With the fury radiating off of her like smoke? A reluctant smile had been like a beacon in the fog.

Callum had found the idea of swimming in deep, pitch-black water in the middle of the night about as appealing as removing his own appendix with Play-Doh tools. But Jory had smiled—actually, honest-to-gods smiled—when Nat had described the rush of night surfing. And because Callum would do literally anything in the world to make Jory smile, he'd asked Nat to give them a lesson.

He'd agreed on one condition.

"I'm gonna be going to these meetings with you, and I can't stand next to you in that damn five-thousand-dollar suit wearing my park ranger uniform or sweatpants."

"Ten thousand," Callum had coughed uncomfortably.

"Fine. Ten thousand. *Ten thousand*? Oh, you asshole. You fucking asshole. Ten thousand? What the hell's it made from? The hairs of vestal virgins or something? Jesus."

"You dinnae have to spend ten thousand, Nat."

"Well, that's good. Because I literally can't."

"It is a bit... ostentatious," Callum had admitted.

"You think?"

By that point, Nat had been pacing back and forth across the cabin floor. Meanwhile, Robbie had been tossing popcorn into the air and catching it in his mouth on the couch, not a care in the world.

"How about this?" Callum offered. "I'll kit you out in a

business wardrobe and promise never to tell ye how much any of it costs."

"I'll see the labels."

"I'll cut the labels out."

"No," Nat had blurted out, looking sheepish. "I... I don't want you to cut them."

Eventually, Nat had settled down enough to sit back down in the chair, to tell Callum what colors he liked, what styles he thought he might prefer. Callum had taken measurements with a tape measure that Robbie produced from his backpack. And they'd shaken on it. Callum would buy him some suits but would buy them at "normal-person stores," as Nat had put it. And in exchange, Nat would take Callum and Jory into the freezing ocean in the middle of the night and teach them to stand up on a piece of fiberglass. On top of a wave. That was moving. With living things underneath it.

He was rubbish. Nat wasn't wrong. Callum's balance on a surfboard was shit.

He had no trouble paddling out or even hoisting himself to stand. Those things required strength, of which he had superhuman plenty. But the keeping his feet under him while a wave hurtled him forward felt like trying to stand still when one's legs were made of Jell-O.

He took some smug satisfaction, however, in the fact that Jory wasn't faring much better. Unlike him, however, Jory was a good sport. She would fall off her board with flailing arms and legs, like a drunk starfish being flung into the water, but then pop up laughing, cheering herself on that she would "definitely get it next time."

Callum, on the other hand, was not used to being bad at things. Even as a mortal, he'd been one of those people who never really had to work all that hard for proficiency. Now, he had the added benefit of super strength, super speed, elevated senses. Some days he felt like more machine than man. An unbreakable shell carrying around an emptiness where a beating heart was supposed to go. He could do anything.

Except ye cannae fucking surf.

"Not as easy as it looks, is it, good buddy?" Nat said.

Callum muttered under his breath before hauling himself back onto the board, feeling the drag of his full-body wetsuit against the textured surface.

"Oh, don't mind him," Jory said, pulling herself onto her own board. "He's a sore loser. Always has been."

Callum glared at her, which only made her smile as she flicked water off her fingertips at him.

"Something you should know about your business partner here, Nat, is that if he's not good at something right away, he quits."

"I dinnae quit!" Callum protested.

"You do!" Jory said with a laugh. "You do! If you don't master something thirty seconds after starting it, you abandon it completely."

Callum scoffed. "Name one thing."

"Fishing."

"I fished!"

"No, *I* fished. And remember when you were going to start making your own weapons? You built a forge behind the house and used it exactly once."

"I didnae have the time!"

"And what about the time you decided you were going to make tallow candles?"

He would have blushed if he could have. He remembered the basket of candle wicks that he'd bartered for, the vat of tallow he'd gotten in trade. He remembered the forge, too, which he eventually put walls onto and used as a barn for the horse and chickens. The failed fishing attempts. The abandoned loaves of bread. Monuments to his failures. The artifacts of these mis-attempts, discarded almost immediately, had taken up space in corners and under furniture until Jory had finally gotten rid of them.

And then there was his home in Scotland, where the greatest monument to his greatest failure of patience of all hung on the wall in a glass case. He swallowed thickly and hung his head at the thought.

Jory paddled over, bringing her board directly next to his so that their thighs touched. She reached out and gripped his forearm.

"Hey," she said, her voice soft and warm. "I was only teasing you."

He lifted his chin and looked at her. "I havenae given up everything I'm bad at right away."

"Oh, really?" Jory said, a smile quirking one side of her mouth. "Do tell."

"I havenae given up trying to win you back."

The full moon was a silver disc in a velvet sky, casting sharp, glinting slices of light on the water's surface. The glow shone on Jory's face, her eyes bright and alive.

"Callum," she started, but he didn't want to hear what she would say next. He didn't want to hear her let him down easy or make promises she couldn't possibly keep. And so he grabbed her waist and hauled her onto his board, onto his lap, her legs wrapping around his hips as she straddled him. He kissed her, a press of lips that softened and deepened with the same rhythm as the sea.

Their bodies rocked into one another as the waves rocked against the surfboard, lifting from beneath. And as he kissed her, he appreciated that weightless moment at the crest before the board slipped down the other side of the wave, the same weightless moment when she slid her tongue against his before retreating.

"Thank you," she said, resting her forehead against his.

Somewhere between the talk about armor forging and Callum wanting to eat Jory alive, Nat had left. Callum was going to buy him more suits than he'd be able to wear in a year.

"I hope you had a good time, mo cridhe," he said, his hands resting on her thighs, feeling her muscles shift and bunch beneath his palms.

"The best time. I love the ocean."

She always had. It made even more sense now. He remembered sitting on the beach and watching her swim, his heart in his throat when she went out so far from shore that he could barely see her head. More fish than woman, he'd thought to himself as he sat and repaired nets on the sand, anxiety clawing through his body like a rabid animal until she returned to him. How she was happiest by the water, in the water. How she'd been sitting on the dark beach when he'd found her, when he'd...

He pulled her against his chest, and she went easily, wrapping her arms around his waist and holding him, letting herself be held.

"Jory," he asked, needing an answer and fearing on all the same.

"Hmmm?" she hummed against the side of his neck.

"What were you doing by the water the night I... the night you... the—"

"The night you thought you killed me?"

He gritted his teeth and squeezed his eyes shut. "Aye."

She didn't answer right away, but she didn't pull away

either. If anything, she pressed closer, molding her chest against his.

"I was waiting for my father."

"Your father?"

"Yeah," Jory breathed. "To ask for his help."

"What did you need him to do? To help?"

She sighed.

"I didn't need his help as much as I needed a favor."

He waited. Maybe she would elaborate. *Please,* he thought. *I want to know. Why were you down on the beach at midnight? Why were ye nae behind a barred door in the house? Why were ye nae safe?*

"Jory?"

Another sigh. "It doesn't really matter now, I suppose."

28

Jory clung to him, feeling the hard lines of his body beneath the neoprene. She wanted to tell him every-thing. How she'd planned to ask her father to make him immortal, to make him like her.

But he *was* immortal now. Without her father. Without her.

She didn't have an answer anymore. She didn't have an easy path. She didn't have an easy anything. Not really. Except for this, holding him, being held by him, feeling the strength of his body surrounding her, *keeping* her. That was the easiest thing in the world.

But it always had been, hadn't it?

She had shivered, more from feelings than the cold, but he had insisted they go back, removing the tether from her ankle and strapping it to his own, towing her board behind them as he paddled them to shore. He'd been quiet. Not sullen. Not angry. Just... quiet.

But that wasn't unlike him either, she was remembering. Sometimes he couldn't stop talking, his energy nearly like Esther's in its vibrance and vigor. He'd talk while he worked.

He'd talk while they fucked. He even talked in his sleep sometimes. And other times, he was quiet. Contemplative. As if he was trying to figure out how everything worked, to take it apart in his mind so he would know how to put it back together.

She could see him now, taking their situation apart bolt by bolt, trying to figure out how to fix it, how to keep her. How to convince *her* to keep *him*.

He was quiet as they strapped the boards to the top of his SUV. It was only when she was peeling her wetsuit down her body that he finally spoke again.

"Is it like this?"

The question confused her, so out of context.

"Is what like this?"

"Your skin. When you... shift? Is that the word? Is it like peeling one of these off or putting it on?"

"Oh," she said. "It's not. It's..."

What *was* it like? She'd never had to describe it for anyone. And it had been so long since she'd done it. She shivered with the longing for that feeling, of her skins melding together, of sliding beneath the waves and belonging there.

It didn't encase her like a second skin, like the thick neoprene. It *held* her.

"It's—" she tried again, pausing in the peeling to stand and look at him. The torso of his wetsuit was around his hips now, the sleeves dangling and dripping water onto the asphalt of the parking lot. Water sluiced down his abdomen, across the muscled planes, following the rest of it. Water always finds water, she remembered her father saying.

Her own wetsuit was around her ankle, one leg removed. She wore a bikini underneath it. High-waisted bottoms and a top that was more sports bra-like than anything. Her nipples were hard against the wet material, though whether from the cold or the intensity of his gaze, she really couldn't say.

"It's like slipping in and out of your favorite sweater," she said. "I put it on, and it just becomes a part of me, because even when I'm not wearing it, it's a part of me. The cells, the spirit. It's all the same. I put it on, and I just... become. And I take it off, and I become something else."

He stepped closer, close enough to touch, though neither of them did. "I'd love to see you like that. I'd love to see you... be yourself like that. That version of yourself."

She smiled. It was a soft smile, and she felt the tears gathering in her eyes, reaching for the seawater that still clung to her eyelashes. Water finding water.

"I would like that," she said.

"Really?"

"Verra much," she said, trying to imitate his burr.

Once upon a time, she'd spoken like that. With trilled r's and words that began in the soft palate, in her throat. But not for a long time. She'd left behind that voice when she'd left behind that life. Still, it felt familiar on her tongue.

He growled, took that final step closer, so close that she had to look up.

"Are you mocking me, lass?"

"Never."

"Are you teasing me, then?"

"Och, Callum," she said, the voice slipping back into her throat, the trills and rolls and burr. "Like Mr. Darcy, Callum MacLeod isnae to be teased."

"And yet Lizzy teased him anyway," he said, leaning down, his lips a mere breath from hers.

"Aye," she said, her voice more a breath than speech. "She did."

"And Mr. Darcy liked it."

She swallowed. If he was still mortal, his breath would be fanning against her lips. "He did," she said. "He liked it verra much."

There was a moment, more a hiccup in time, really, when he said, "And so do I," just before his mouth found hers in the darkness, his lips slipping over hers with the force of a hurricane.

He spun them, pressing her back against the cold side of his SUV. What a delicious contrast, Jory vaguely thought, through the haze of all the other feelings. Her body was made of heat, but she was sandwiched between the cold metal of the door and the cool marble of Callum's body. She shivered.

"Are you cold?" Callum asked, pulling back enough to speak.

"No."

"Tell the truth."

"I'm not cold," she whispered against his lips. "I'm happy."

He bit her lip. Not hard enough to draw blood. She bit his harder. He groaned into her mouth. "Why are ye so happy, Jory?"

She smiled. "Because it's the third date."

Callum went very still, as if frozen by one of those ray guns from the science fiction movies. He didn't move a muscle. Not a twitch. Not a spasm. Not a flex. He was completely still, like the tigers in the tall grass that she'd seen once. Invisible unless you knew where to look.

But she knew where to look.

She licked a stripe up his throat, sucking at the place where his pulse would have fluttered, once upon a time. She bit gently with her teeth and sucked on the spot, wondering if this would mark him the same way it would have marked her.

She could see his eyes closed now, his jaw clenched tightly. "Jory," he said. "I dinnae want to frighten you."

She sucked harder and he hissed through his teeth. The muscles of his abdomen flexing against hers, his fingers tightening on her ass. Giving himself away.

"Callum," she said between kisses over the spot she'd just wounded.

"Aye," he choked.

"Remember when I said that there were no sharks because you were the most dangerous thing in the water?"

"I—"

"Shhhh," she said with a nip to the same spot and Callum groaned, thrusting almost imperceptibly against her. "All those big scary animals are afraid of you. And they should be."

"Jory—"

"Those sharks, those orcas, those—what was it you said? Giant squid? They're terrified of you," she purred. "But do you know who isn't afraid of you?"

She had pulled back enough to look at his face, and he stared back, his gray eyes wide, brows knit tightly together.

"Do I smell afraid, Callum?"

"Nay," he said through clenched teeth.

"Is my heart racing?"

"Aye."

"But you don't smell fear. What do you smell?"

"Jory," he groaned, and she could see the veins and muscles in his neck, standing out from the effort to hold himself back.

She smirked. Because they both knew the answer to the question. And so she leaned in, her lips against the shell of his ear, and whispered, "You don't scare me at all, Callum MacLeod. Do your worst."

She felt the growl that reverberated through his chest and couldn't help but smile into the darkness as he let go of the leash.

Centered number:

29

"*You don't scare me at all, Callum MacLeod. Do your worst.*"

In an instant, the space of a human heartbeat, a thousand years hurtled through Callum's brain. Centuries of wantings and cravings, of trying to find what he was looking for in the arms of humans and vampires and one very down-on-her-luck fae countess. Those encounters hadn't been without pleasure, but they hadn't satisfied either.

He remembered vividly a summer day in his youth, when he'd been trapped in the limbo of being too big to be considered a boy but too green to be treated as a man. He'd wanted blackberries. He'd wanted them so badly that he would have overpaid. He would have worked. He would have done almost anything. But all he'd been able to get was a blackberry tart. It had tasted good, sweet and flaky, but it had lacked as much as it had possessed. He'd wanted to taste the blackberries alone, not covered by sugar and crust, but unaltered, bursting against his tongue. Dark, sticky juice sluicing across his palate to drip down his waiting throat.

It felt as if he'd wanted blackberries for centuries and been forced to settle for tarts.

But not anymore. At least, not tonight. His hands shook with the looming fulfillment of a craving nearly as old as his miserable existence.

Callum had grown accustomed to the many realities about his immortal body over the past centuries. The speed. The strength. And yet even for him, he thought that the time it took for him to open the rear door to the SUV and slam the captain's chair as far back as it could go was shockingly quick.

"Whoa," Jory breathed.

Her wetsuit was off except for one foot, still stuck on a statuesque leg, the black neoprene pooling around her like an oil slick. He had a sudden urge to take ripe blackberries and crush them gently against her body, to lick the dripping, running juices and pulp from her flesh. The way he'd once done.

He couldn't, of course, which felt somehow crueler than any denial in a long time, and he wondered if she would still be around in the summer so that he could lick the flavor of fat, swollen blackberries directly from her tongue.

She was staring at him, like a doe before a wolf. Watching. Waiting. But this doe wanted to be caught. He could smell it. She'd been right about that. She didn't smell like fear. She smelled like salt and sea and sex, the birth of everything.

"Take it off."

"Take what off?" Her voice was a whisper.

"All of it," Callum growled.

Jory looked around, as if she expected to find someone watching in the dark parking lot. As if any mere mortal would be able to see them clearly. Then, without breaking eye contact, she reached down and pulled her foot out of the wetsuit, dropping it to the pavement with a wet slap.

She tucked her thumbs into the waistband of her bikini bottoms and slid them down her legs, bending until they passed her knees and then straightening as they fell to her ankles with another wet sound.

She stood there in only the bikini top, which looked like the sports bras he saw athletes wear. It compressed her breasts, pressing them close against her chest, taunting him. He hadn't seen those breasts in a thousand years. The ochre skin with the brown tips that turned up slightly.

"All of it," he repeated hoarsely.

She smirked. But then she turned, giving him her back as she crossed her arms over her chest and lifted the top over her head, tossing in behind her. Another wet slap on the pavement. Jory had just turned her head to glance flirtatiously over her shoulder when he was there, pressing her naked body against the side of the SUV.

She gasped.

"Is it cold, mo cridhe?" he asked.

Jory shivered. The air was frigid around them, no doubt the metal of the car was just as cold against the sensitive heat of her body. Her breath was sawing in and out of her lungs now, coming in short, labored bursts. He pressed closer, feeling the rise and fall of her shoulder blades against his chest. The neoprene of his own wetsuit was tight and uncomfortable against his erection.

"You thought to turn and hide from me?" he asked, skating his lips lightly against the curved plane of her shoulder, causing another shiver to rack her body.

"Tease," she whined. "Just wanted to tease you a little."

"Tease me a little?" he asked, his teeth at her neck. Not pressing. Just... there. "Tease me a little? Dinnae you ken that you've done nothing but tease me since I saw you in Hank's kitchen weeks ago?"

She shook her head.

"Shall I tease you the way you've teased me, Jory?"

She bit her lip, and Callum groaned against her neck. He shifted his hands from their grip on her hips, sliding them up the curves of her belly, the backs of his knuckles rubbing against the cold metal of the car as his palms caressed her damp, quivering skin. When he reached her breasts, he cupped their weight in his palms. She whimpered.

"Just a wee tease, Jory," he said, his lips moving against her skin with every word.

She arched her back slightly, a subconscious gesture, that pressed her breasts more firmly into his hands. He caught the cold-hardened nipples between his forefingers and middle fingers, pinching the digits together until she squirmed. But he didn't move. He didn't roll them between his thumbs and forefingers the way he wanted to, the way he knew she liked. He only pinched. Hard enough to make her wild, but not enough to satisfy her.

"Just a wee tease," he said before scraping his teeth against her pulse.

He dropped a hand to her sex and cupped it firmly, using his hold to anchor her body tight against his but not giving her any more than that.

"Callum," she whined.

"Shhhh, mo ghraidh. 'Tis only a wee bit of teasing," he said huskily, pressing his throbbing groin against her back.

"Why do you hate me?" she sobbed, dropping her forehead to the side of the SUV with a shudder.

"I dinnae hate you, Jory."

"You do," she protested, her voice rising in both volume and tone. "You do hate me, Callum MacLeod, or you wouldn't tease me like this. And I—I—I hate you, too. You can—oh, fuck," she groaned as he pressed his middle finger hard against her clit, delving it quickly between the slick parting of her cunt.

"Do you really hate me, Jory?" Callum whispered in her ear. He made a hard, slow circle with the tip of his middle finger, circling her clit closely. She rose up onto her toes, her palms braced against the car. "Because I dinnae hate you at all. I couldnae hate you if my very life depended on it. I only want to make you feel verra, verra good. Will you let me?"

She stopped writhing. Until that point, Callum wasn't sure if she'd been trying to get closer or farther away. He wasn't sure she knew either. But she stopped, sagging against him, letting him take much of the weight of her body in his hands, holding her up with the hand at her breast and the hand cradling her cunt.

"I don't know what I'm doing," she said in a watery voice.

He gave her more of him, pressing her even more firmly against the side of the car. "Talk to me."

"I'm afraid," she said, in a voice too quiet to be a whisper.

"Of me?"

"No. I'm afraid to lose you. I'm afraid to keep you. I'm afraid of what I'll lose either way."

"You will lose nothing with me," he said, his teeth clenched tight and his lips against the shell of her ear. "Nothing, do you hear? I will give you anything. *Everything.* I'll buy the world and lay it at your feet."

"You already own the world."

"Not even close."

"It feels like you do," she said with a sniffle.

"For you. I've done it all for you," he said, feeling the hollow ache in his chest yawning and sucking at him.

Because of all the truths in his life, great and small, that was the grandest, most shimmering of them all.

She tried to turn to face him, but he held her fast, his lips still grazing the delicate rim of her ear. "There isnae a single thing you could ask for that I wouldnae scour the earth to find. To the depths of the sea. To the moon. There is no length to which I wouldnae go to make you happy."

30

"*To the depths of the sea...*"

Jory sucked in a breath, feeling the cool marble of his palms against her scorching, aching body. Because he was wrong. There was one thing he couldn't give her, one single thing that wasn't in his power to give. But if she had the courage to reach for him, to *keep* him, perhaps...

He dragged his teeth against the side of her neck once more, and she shuddered, wondering, not for the first time, what it would be like to feel them sinking deep. To feed him. But the thought was banished quickly by his tongue tracing the path his teeth had just forged, dragging up her neck to her ear. He bit gently, and her body jolted.

The car door was open just next to her. He had her pressed against the side of the SUV by the fuel tank door. The overhead light inside glowed brightly in the black interior.

"Callum?"

"Aye?"

His voice was hoarse, a whisper from the depths of his throat.

"Get in the car."

"Ladies first."

She took a fortifying breath, the intake of air bleeding into the sound of the crashing waves, of the night and all its noises. But she nodded. He loosened his hold on her naked body and she slid sideways, crawling into the back of the SUV, aware of how much of her was on display. Again.

She turned and knelt in the center, in the empty space between the two captain's seats, and rested her palms on her thighs. Waiting.

Callum's gray eyes were bright, glowing in the fluorescent light from the ceiling.

"Take it off," she said, echoing his words from before. "All of it."

A wolfish look spread over his face, hungry and ready. And then he was naked, standing in the open doorway, his arms braced on the roof of the SUV. It was gratifying to blink and see the slide deck flip from clothed Callum to naked Callum. But at the same time, she wished she'd been able to see him peel the black neoprene down his long, strong legs. To watch that slow striptease as he worked the wet, clinging material over the topography of his body.

"Get in the car."

He stood as still as a statue. Or a tiger in the undergrowth. Not even a muscle twitched to give him away.

"Please," she said before hastily adding, "but—" He paused. "But *climb* in. And *sit* down." She nodded her head at the seat. "Slowly. None of that flashy business."

He smirked as he complied, ducking his head and climbing into the vehicle, sitting on the black leather seat. Seawater dripped from his hair, sluicing down his chest.

"We're going to ruin the leather seats with this saltwater. Do you have a towel or a—"

"Fuck the seats," he said, his eyes locked on hers.

He looked like a god. An ancient deity, all muscle and hardness, finding himself in a modern car and looking both at home and completely out of place at the same time.

He reached over and pulled the door shut, and then there were no waves, no night noises. There was only the sound of her rapid breathing, her pounding heart in her ears. And there was no bright overhead light, only the dimness offered by the moon. But she didn't need either. She was a demigod herself. She could see in the darkest cave on the darkest night.

She dropped her hands to the floor and crawled closer, finding his feet with her fingers, never pulling her eyes from his. She'd always liked his feet. The high arches. How all of his toes were straight except for the one he'd broken that had mended slightly crooked. It had ached when the weather got truly bitter. She wondered if those aches followed him into immortality. She touched it.

"Does it hurt?"

"Does what hurt?"

"Your broken toe."

"Nae. Not anymore. I'd forgotten all about that."

A twinge of feeling. Not sadness. Just... grief. Grateful that he didn't hurt anymore. Sad that he *couldn't* hurt anymore. Unsure where the distinction lay.

"So nothing hurts anymore," she said, her long fingers wrapping around his ankles, feeling the bones against her palms and the shifting muscle beneath her thumbs.

"I didnae say that."

"What hurts?" Jory asked, pressing her thumbs into the long, tense line of muscle that ran down from his knee.

She'd massaged his legs for him once upon a time, starting at the ankles because he was too ticklish to start at his feet. She wondered about that too, if ticklishness was a mortal affliction. She'd never been ticklish after all. She pressed harder with her thumbs, dragging them up the tense line. He groaned.

"Does this hurt, Callum?" Her voice sounded louder in the enclosed space of the car. He felt bigger. Everything felt... more.

"Everything hurts," he said.

She paused. "Everything?"

"Not like that. I just... Holding back hurts."

"Holding back?"

"Aye," he said in a choked voice as she moved her hands up his shins, cupping the taut muscles of his calves and pressing her fingertips into the knots.

"Are you holding back?"

"If I werenae holding back, this would all be over by now."

She smiled, hearing the knuckles of his hands crack as he clenched his fists, knowing that her smiles drove him wild. They always had. It was good to see that some things didn't change.

"Well, then," she said, leaning forward and pressing her nose to the inside of his knee, rubbing it into the indent. "We can't have you hurting. Can we?"

"Jory," he said, but whatever he'd been about to say next died in his throat as she skimmed her nose up the length of his inner thigh, smelling the salt water. She darted her tongue out to lick, following the trail of soft skin, far more sparsely haired than his lower leg.

"Jory," he said again, an agonized sound.

She smiled against his leg and continued the trek of her

tongue until she reached the pinnacle. His cock was erect, arcing back towards his belly while his balls hung between his spread thighs. She leaned closer still, licking the slight divot between the twin weights, relishing his sharp hiss of pleasure. Her tongue continued on, gliding up his shaft, circling the tip. He was uncut, and she remembered how fascinated she'd been the first time by the easy slide of his foreskin beneath her hand, the way his body changed with nothing more than arousal as its guide.

Her palm circled to draw back his foreskin, and she circled the head with her tongue before spitting on it, watching the saliva trail down the rosy skin before she engulfed him with her mouth, sliding easily down his length until he pressed against the back of her throat. And then, relaxing those muscles, she took him deeper, feeling him filling her, blocking her air, swallowing against the invasion that she had invited.

He began to curse, long streams of muttered Gaelic. Love words. Praise. Gratitude. More love words. They tumbled from his lips in a semiconscious stream, as if he was unable to stop them even as he knew exactly what he was saying.

She slid off of his cock with a pop of her lips. She needed to breathe, even if he didn't, and gripped him in a loose fist, lazily sliding her hand up and down the straining, throbbing length of his sex. She stared up at him. His head was pressed back against the headrest, teeth clenched, and knees gripped in stressed fingers. Without breaking pace, she reached down with her other hand and stroked it along the arch of his foot. He jerked.

"Dinnae do that. You ken it tickles."

She smiled. Everything was different, and yet so much was the same. She hadn't expected to feel so crushed by the relief of that one small truth. It was still him. She practically dove onto him then, sliding down until her lips met her fist and began to work him, up and down in tandem, until he was writhing beneath her.

"Jory," he panted. "Jory, Jory, Jory."

He was unable to hold himself still, his hands still gripping his knees so tightly that the knuckles were white because she knew, *she knew*, that he wanted to thrust his fingers into her hair.

"Please, Jory, stop. *Please.* I dinnae want this to be the end of it."

The end of what? The encounter? The date? Their time together? All of it? She slowly slid up and off his cock, relishing the tremors that racked his body beneath her. She realized something in that moment, something that she knew as certainly as she knew her own name, her own hands.

She didn't want this to be the end of it either. The end of the encounter. The date. Any of it. All of it.

Jory released his length with care, rising to a high kneel, bracing her hands atop his knees. And then she leaned in, until the base of her ribs brushed against his sex, wet from her mouth and throbbing, and whispered, "Och, mo cridhe, we've only just begun."

31

His cock throbbed against her ribs, between her breasts, and Callum couldn't help but wonder if he felt as cool against her skin as she felt warm against his. He reached out with a shaky hand and rubbed a wet lock of Jory's hair between his thumb and forefinger.

"I want you to be certain," he said, feeling every word grating against his throat.

"What makes you think I'm not?"

"You just... I told you before. I dinnae want to do this if you only plan to leave me behind in the end. My heart cannae take it, mo cridhe."

"Callum," she said, leaning forward. She slid her hands up his thighs, and with a subtle flex of her arms, her breasts squeezed around his cock. He sucked in a breath, wholly unnecessary and yet instinctive nonetheless.

"Jory," he hissed.

She pressed closer still, the head of his cock still obscenely visible above her cleavage.

"Mo ghraidh," Callum said through gritted teeth, dropping the lock of her hair and gripping the armrests of the captain's chair once more.

Jory pressed on his thighs and lifted herself off the floor. She was moving slowly, even for a human, and Callum couldn't help but feel that it was deliberate. He also couldn't help the overwhelming gratitude that washed over him as he watched her crawl into his lap, moving in slow motion as she straddled his legs but kept her backside on his knees, far from his sex.

"You're teasing me, lass," he groaned, gripping her thighs in desperate hands.

"Turnabout is fair play," she said with a smirk.

She was beautiful in the darkness. Night vision had always been a welcome advantage since he'd been changed, but he'd never been as grateful for it as he was now, able to see Jory clearly in the dark. She was a study in contrasts, her hair inky black and spilling down her back. Her green eyes nearly glowing, otherworldly, and he wondered how he'd never seen it before, how he'd never wondered why her eyes always looked so bright.

"This is quite a car," she said, her hands braced on his shoulders. Her legs were spread wide over his thighs, her cunt glistening beneath the triangle of dark hair at the pinnacle, smelling like the ocean and the earth and the place where the two met.

"It does the job," he answered, his eyes locked on her sex.

Why the hell were they talking about the car? And why was she still so far away?

"That remains to be seen," she said, leaning to the side and reaching down. A moment later, the seat was reclining and Callum found himself looking up at the ceiling. But not for long. Because she followed him down, hands pressed to his chest.

But, maddeningly, she didn't come closer. He felt the warmth of her sex against his belly, hovering just out of reach of his straining cock.

"Put your hands on the armrests," she said.

"Jory," he warned.

"Don't move them until I say you can."

He clenched his jaw but complied, gripping the leather so hard that he worried for the stitching at the seams. She rubbed across his bottom lip with her thumb, dragging it to the side before leaning closer and nipping it with her teeth. He lunged forward to kiss her, but she was faster, removing her mouth from his reach and pushing hard against his chest.

"Behave," she said.

"Jory," he said, his voice nearly a whine. "I'm up to high doh, here. Mercy. Have mercy. I beg of you."

"Shhhh," she said, lifting herself higher so that her breasts were level with his head. He pressed his face into the soft valley between them, kissing reverently at her salty skin. She arched and threw her head back, and he took that as permission, kissing his way to one tight, brown peak, and taking it into his mouth. He sucked and nipped until she was gasping and rubbing her cunt against his flexing abdomen.

He nuzzled and kissed a trail to the other, loving how she gripped his hair tightly in her fingers when he bit gently at her breast below her nipple, regretting for a moment that the mark would be gone before they got out of the car. Her hips were tipped back, deliberately he knew, so that her cunt hovered just out of the reach of his straining cock. But she was rocking against him now, writhing against his torso, and he felt positively electrified, every single circuit in his body lit up and tuned in to hers.

He sucked harder at her breast, his cheeks hollowed, and he felt her body lowering, seeking him. She'd always been sensitive, and he'd always loved driving her wilder and wilder, watching the control shift as she released it to him bit by bit before surrendering entirely and allowing herself to be taken care of.

Because, when it came down to the barest, baldest truths, that's all he wanted. It was all he'd ever wanted. To take care of her. For her to trust him enough to let him.

He gripped the armrests hard in his fists, holding tightly, waiting for the scales to tip. It had already begun. Her hips had begun a gradual shift down towards his own until he knew he wasn't imagining gentle friction. He felt the kiss of her cunt against the head of his cock and nearly tore the armrests off the seat.

"Jory," he said against her throat, "Dinnae you dare move too fast. I've waited nearly a thousand years to have you again. I willnae let you rush it."

She leaned away enough to look in his eyes, her gaze unfocused and feverishly bright, but she slowed her descent, taking him into her one scant millimeter at a time, making him feel every single clench and flutter and breath, just like he'd asked. He wanted to touch her. He wanted to hold her close, to press his ear against her chest and listen to her heart pounding while he felt its beat with his palm between her shoulders.

Down and down she sank until he found himself enveloped entirely by her heat.

"Christ," he hissed, and she threw her head back with a little sob, digging her fingernails into the tops of his shoulders.

She rose again, lifting up until he felt the cool air of the vehicle against the damp bottom half of his shaft, before sliding slowly down once more. And then again.

A minute passed with no sound to be heard but Jory's panting and the wet slide of her body over his. And then a pained cry.

"What's the matter?" Callum asked.

"It's not enough," Jory whined.

"Tell me what you need."

"More. I need more. I need—"

"Tell me," he said, loving the way her weight felt braced against his chest.

Another whine. He knew what she needed. It was as familiar as his own face. Jory liked to be in control until the precise moment she didn't, until she wanted to let go and not think.

"Can I touch you, mo cridhe?"

"Please," she sobbed, and in an instant, his hands were on her hips, driving her down hard as he thrust up. She moaned, dropping her head to his shoulder and letting him work her over him.

"More. More, Callum."

"Hold on, Jory. Dinnae let go," he said.

And she didn't.

32

Jory blinked and found herself on her back, her ass just barely hanging off the seat. Callum had her ankles on his shoulders and knelt on the floor before her, thrusting lazily in and out of her grasping cunt. He wrapped one arm tightly around one of her thighs, and with the other hand, he thumbed gently at her clit.

Jory bit her fist to keep from screaming as the sensations rolled over and through her.

"Harder," she said, her voice hoarse.

He thrust with more force into her. But it wasn't enough.

"Goddamnit, Callum," she pleaded. "Fuck me harder. Please."

He threw his head back, and she saw the strong, corded lines of his throat in the darkness. What would it be like to watch that throat swallow? Swallow *her*?

"I cannae fuck you harder, Jory. I dinnae want to hurt you."

"You won't hurt me."

He stopped, pressing himself deep into her, grinding his pelvis against hers.

"You don't know how strong I am. I cannae hurt you. I couldnae live with myself."

She reached out with a shaking hand and placed her palm against his cheek, feeling the now familiar coolness of his skin against her own.

"I'm not mortal. You can't hurt me, Callum."

"I did," he moaned, pressing his opposite cheek against her calf and closing his eyes. "I did, Jory. I cannae do it again."

She wiggled her legs off his shoulders, wrapping them around his waist until she could press her heels into his ass. She pushed him deeper still, or rather, she pulled him closer. He fell to his hands on the seat back beside her head, his body held taut and straining over hers, his weight in his palms, unwilling to give her all of him.

But she wanted all of him. She wouldn't settle for anything less. All of his weight, his strength, his speed, his want.

All of his love.

She wrapped her arms around his neck and pulled. Like a rubber band snapped back, he collapsed onto her, letting her hold his body close, letting his weight press her into the leather seat. His hips moved of their own accord, tiny thrusts that made her wild. He buried his nose in the crook of her shoulder and inhaled, smelling her skin.

"Let go," she whispered. He shook his head, kissing her neck and thrusting with more purpose now, though without any of the intensity she craved.

But she didn't want measured pieces of him doled out in safe doses. She wanted all of him or nothing at all. She'd waited a thousand years too, and she wasn't about to settle for his restraint.

"Callum," she said, her lips pressed to his ear. "Let go or stop."

He groaned.

"You won't hurt me, Callum. And I don't want you halfway."

He froze and lifted his torso off of her in slow measures until he was staring down at her.

"You want all of me."

"Yes," she hissed.

A long pause. He studied her. And then...

"Verra well," he whispered.

She found herself upright then, her sacrum braced against the edge of the seat and one of his hands pressing against her low back, holding her close as the other gripped the hair at the back of her head and held her mouth against his own. He devoured her, kissing her like he might find the cure to a curse long forgotten within the depths of her mouth as he fucked up into her.

He fucked her fast, his hips pistoning with an inhuman speed as he drove into her body. The angle ensured that with every thrust, her clit rubbed against his pelvis. The orgasm built quickly, rising higher and higher until she felt the tingles erupt in her head and body and let loose a scream.

"Aye," he muttered through his teeth. "Aye. Give me all of you as well, Jory. I willnae have you by halves either."

Jory vaguely registered a loud bang and sudden shift in the balance of the car.

"What was that?" she panted.

"Tire," Callum said before dragging his tongue up her throat.

"What?"

"We blew a tire," he said with her earlobe between his teeth.

She gasped, clinging more tightly as he continued to fuck all of himself into all of her. Another loud pop, the other front tire bursting. Jory laughed, the sound rushing forth as another climax slammed into her without warning. He pulled out and, in another blink, flipped her over so that her knees were also on the floor now, her forearms braced on the seat. He thrust back into her heat, and she shrieked at the first drag of his perfect cock. His hands were braced over hers, their fingers interlaced, as he pounded into her from behind, grunting like an animal and just as far gone.

Another bang. Another tire, the SUV supported by one lone tire now. Jory couldn't help but wonder for how long, though, and arched her back, her ass lifting ever so slightly. He rewarded her with a groan, his hips never stopping, his pelvis slapping against her ass.

And with that, the last tire went, and Jory couldn't help but laugh again. He reached under her chest and pulled her up, holding her tightly with her back against his chest. She gripped his wrists as the friction against her G-spot intensified. He dropped one hand and rubbed her clit with two fingers, slow and hard, just the way she liked it. The sensation was too much. She saw the orgasm barreling her way like a rogue wave. It grew and grew, rising impossibly high until it crashed over her and she felt as if her entire body was made of sensation. She sobbed, tears streaming down her face as the orgasm went on and on, sending electric pulses throughout her body.

"Come. Come. Come. Come. Come. Come," she found herself chanting.

"Nay," he said, his lips against the side of her neck.

"Come!" Jory commanded.

"If this is the only chance I get to be with you, Jory, I'm going to savor it."

"It's not," she panted. "It won't be."

He groaned and she squealed as another frisson of sensation rocked her.

"Come, Callum. Please, please, *please,* come. I need you to come. I *need* it," she begged.

She felt the scrape of his fangs against her neck and shivered. They didn't frighten her. Not anymore. They were just another part of him, no more capable of violence without his bidding than his hands or his brain.

"Only just beginning," she said with a gasp, leaning to the side so that she could kiss him.

"Beginning," he said, his voice a hoarse whisper. She felt the words against her lips and smiled, kissing him.

He slowed, thrusting steadily and with force, but not as lost to desperation as he had been. And with a groan, he came. She felt his cock pulse within her and smiled.

She felt him ease away and said, "No. Not yet. Stay with me a while."

With his teeth against her neck, he said, "I'm nae going anywhere, mo ghraidh. Never again."

Later, Jory lay in Callum's arms in his bed. Callum had called Nat to pick them up, and Nat had had the good grace to not say a word as he drove them home, though Jory had seen him blush from his collar to the tips of his ears when he'd realized what had happened.

They'd showered and washed the saltwater away. Callum had shampooed her hair with firm, gentle fingers and she'd sighed, tipping her head back as the hot water ran over them both.

She lay on her side now, her head on his chest, playing lazily with his fingers.

"How are you?" Jory asked him when he'd gone quiet.

"Hungry," he said. But as soon as he had, he went tense beneath her.

She shifted, raising up to prop on her elbow, looking down at him. He stared up at her, a guarded look on his face.

She lifted her wrist and placed it against his lips.

"Jory," he said, his eyes wide.

"You're hungry," she said. "Eat."

"I can go get some elk blood from the fridge," Callum said. "You dinnae have to—"

She cut him off by pressing her wrist harder against his lips gently. "Callum, you're hungry. Eat."

"You cannae want this," he protested, holding her wrist in his hands as gently as he would a baby bird.

"Don't tell me what I want. You're hungry. I can feed you. I want to feed you."

"You are nae afraid anymore?"

She shrugged. "I'm not afraid of you."

"I willnae hurt you. I willnae take too much," he insisted. "I swear to you, Jory. I am not the man I was that night."

"Shhhh," she said. "I know. I know."

A tortured look crossed his face, like a starving man faced with a feast that he couldn't believe was set for him.

"Go on," she said, leaning down to kiss him before pulling back again and offering her wrist.

He took it, as gentle as he ever had been with her, somehow even more careful, and kissed the tender skin. Once. Twice. Three times with an open mouth before opening wider and gently, slowly, piercing his fangs into her wrist. He closed his mouth around the flesh and drank deeply. It didn't hurt as much as she'd expected once the initial bite was done. She watched his throat bob with his swallows as he drank her, so gently but with a barely restrained, almost desperate thirst.

His eyes were closed, and she smiled. A glance at the clock showed that the sun was rising above them. She lay down on the pillow next to him, watching his profile as he took what he needed, grateful that she was able to provide it. She didn't feel lightheaded or woozy. She knew that was in part due to the fact that she wasn't human. But she also knew how very careful he was being. He looked drowsy and relaxed, but she knew he was counting her heartbeats, sensing her body and its signals. She knew he'd only take so much and not a drop more. Certainly not a drop too much. Never again.

After a few long, hazy moments, he released her, swiping his tongue over the puncture marks to seal them closed. He turned his head to look at her and she smiled.

But he didn't smile back. Instead, she saw a drop of blood gathering in the corner of his eye. It dripped over the bridge of his nose and down the opposite cheek, leaving a red trail against his skin.

"Callum?" she asked.

"I'm fine," he said, wiping it away with a hasty hand. "It's fine. Fuck."

She reached out and wiped the bloody tear with her thumb before pressing it against his lips. His eyes locked on hers, he closed his lips around her thumb, sucking gently. And when another ruby tear fell, she did the same. Again and again until they stopped.

Callum kissed her knuckles, one at a time, featherlight touches of his cool lips.

"Thank you," he whispered.

"For the meal?" Jory answered lightly.

He looked at her for a moment before unfolding her fingers and speaking against the center of her palm.

"For everything," he said.

He clasped her hand in his against his chest and she scooted closer, pressing her forehead against his. She smiled, loving the way he brushed a gentle thumb over the spot where his teeth had been.

"You're welcome."

And then, like a slow sink into quicksand, Jory felt him relax into sleep and followed him there. Just before she dropped off, she thought to herself that she'd follow him anywhere.

33

Jory sat on the floor with her back against the couch in front of a roaring fire in Magda's little A-frame cabin. She was embroidering flowers onto a denim jacket for Esther. A surprise. Callum was awake and texting, but since the sun was still hovering above the horizon, he was stuck down in the vault.

Robbie was messing around in the kitchen. Jory heard cabinets opening and closing, metal banging on metal. Water running. Loud, bouncy pop music playing through his little jam box speaker. Robbie moved through the world loudly. His laugh was loud. His tattoos were loud. His energy was loud.

But Jory's life had been so very quiet for the longest time. And now? Esther and Robbie added a wild sort of technicolor to the quiet that she loved.

"What are you doing in there?" she called out.

"Science!" he called back.

"What?"

"Science!" Robbie shouted triumphantly, and then, all of

a sudden, the cabin's main area was filled with a battery of popping sounds.

Jory shot to her feet. "What the hell is that noise?"

"Science," he repeated.

"You're gonna burn the house down, Robbie!"

"Psh," he said with a casual wave of his hand. "No, I'm not. But what I am going to do is—hang on. Wait."

He turned his back to her, shaking something over the stove and then dumping the contents of a pot into the biggest mixing bowl the cabin had before returning the pot to the stove and aggressively shaking it again.

"Are—" she began, smelling deeply. "Are you making popcorn?"

He didn't answer. Instead, he repeated the dumping action once more before taking a wooden spoon and stirring the large bowl. He spun and set the big bowl on the island in front of her with a wide smile and a gleam in his eyes.

"See? Science."

"Oh my god, Robbie. This smells amazing."

"I'm starving."

"You're always starving," Jory said with a laugh.

"Lately I am, anyway." He looked immensely proud of himself. "I wish I'd known it was that easy all along. I've burned so many bags in the microwave."

Jory smiled. She could picture Robbie staring down into a bag of microwave popcorn and seeing half the kernels popped and half burned.

"Movie time!" Robbie said, snatching up the bowl and skirting the island. He flopped into the corner of the couch and brought his legs up to sit cross-legged with the big bowl cradled between his knees.

"Callum will be up soon," Jory said, coming to join him at the other end of the couch.

"Boss likes movies," Robbie said, his mouth full of popcorn.

She liked them too, but this was another small puzzle piece sliding into place, the picture of who Callum had become in the modern era coming into view. They hadn't had movies before. They hadn't had books. They'd had the land and work and the sea and play and each other. She wondered what movies he liked, what books he read.

Jory liked comedies. She avoided dramas almost entirely because, for the longest time, her life had been sad enough on its own. She hadn't needed her escapes to be sad too. But as she picked up her embroidery again and Robbie scrolled through the movie options, it struck her how *not* sad she'd been lately. How enriched her life had become with friendship and... love. Every kind of love. She didn't know what to do with it. She didn't know how to *leave* it.

Eventually, Robbie selected *Planet Earth*. As David Attenborough began describing life in the Atacama desert, Jory heard Callum's voice drifting closer.

"That's fantastic news. I knew you could do it."

The broom closet door opened and Callum stepped out, wearing a pair of joggers and a crew neck sweatshirt that had holes around the neck and looked like it had been in heavy rotation since the 1980s. It probably had been, another fact that made her smile. He might wear two-thousand-dollar shoes, but he had a favorite sweatshirt from thirty plus years ago that had probably cost twenty.

He shut the closet door behind him and raked a hand through his hair.

"I'll talk to my business partner, and we'll be in touch. Good. Aye... Congratulations, again... Alright. Bye now."

He set his smartphone carefully down on the counter

and walked with purpose to the couch before scooping Jory up and crushing her against his chest.

"Careful!" Jory shrieked. "I don't want to stab you with a needle!"

"Do your worst," Callum said against her neck, his voice muffled and lips cool and soft against her skin. She dropped her embroidery hoop onto the couch and wrapped her arms around his neck, holding tight, breathing him in.

"Hey lovebirds," Robbie called out. "You make a better door than a window."

Callum snorted and set her down, sitting on the middle cushion between Jory and Robbie.

"You're awfully chipper," she said.

"Aye," he said with a bright smile. "Dr. Alton has finished the product and its testing."

"That's fuckin' amazing!" Robbie crowed, punching Callum in the shoulder.

It was. And within forty-five minutes, Nat burst through the door. Niamh followed, closing it quietly behind her. She looked good today. She wasn't weeping and didn't seem to be in any pain, something that could not be said for every day. Before long, the three of them sat around the table, multiple notebooks open in front of them as well as Callum's laptop, as they discussed what needed to happen next.

As it turned out, Niamh was the daughter of one of Ireland's most successful whiskey distillers in the nineteenth century. And while much had changed about the business of bottling and distribution, Niamh had a sharp understanding of what made a brand successful. Jory made a pot of coffee for Niamh and herself and then went back to join Robbie on the couch.

Over the sounds of David Attenborough's narration, she

heard them setting in place the bones of the business based around Nat's idea. The plan was to sell the artificial blood in nightclubs like Callum's at first. The profits from those sales would fund the nonprofit arm of the business, which would provide free artificial blood for human emergency use.

After a while, Niamh shyly approached. "My part of the evening is done," she said quietly. "Best let them work. Can I join you?"

"Just sit right here, Nevie," Robbie said, stuffing a full handful of popcorn into his mouth. "You want some?"

Niamh reached delicately into the bowl.

"How about I go make some actual dinner for the rest of us?" Jory said. "Or are you planning to fill up on popcorn?"

"Oh, I'm gonna fill up on popcorn. And then I'm gonna fill up on dinner."

Jory rolled her eyes and stood.

"But you don't need to make dinner," Robbie said, his mouth full of more popcorn. He swallowed. "Magda's coming over."

Jory raised an eyebrow. Robbie shrugged.

"We planned it like three days ago. She said she was gonna bring dinner."

"Yeah, but will she have enough? Surely she wasn't expecting Nat and Niamh or me?"

Robbie watched as a lizard moved with alarming speed across the television screen. "Jory-dory, you know Magda."

She sat down heavily on the couch. She *did* know Magda. For almost fifty years, Magda had been Jory's only friend in town, and she loved her. But Jory didn't like secrets, and Magda was full of them.

An hour later, Jory sat at the kitchen island next to Callum. Magda had brought a casserole with chicken and mushrooms and garlic and an amount of butter that Jory didn't want to contemplate. It was delicious, which was unsurprising as Magda was a phenomenal cook. The conversation had been light. Food. Work. Robbie's latest Sweet Smash habit. Whether or not in-app purchases are a scam. Backpacking tourists Nat had rescued.

Jory sipped her wine and smiled when she felt Callum lean close and inhale deeply, smelling her.

"You smell different," he whispered.

"I'm testing one of Esther's new scent blends."

"Mmmm. What's in this one?" He grazed his nose up the side of her neck and she shivered.

"Basil, ginger, tea tree, and cinnamon. Do you like it?"

He grunted. A soft sound. Something only she would have been able to hear. "You smell like a meal."

She smiled into her wine glass and was about to say something about clearing everyone out and continuing the business meeting tomorrow when Magda cleared her throat and said, "So, Jory. When is Niamh moving into your apartment?"

The room froze, as if someone had pressed pause on the universe's remote. Callum's body went stiff next to her. She felt his gaze on the side of her face and glared daggers at Magda who, looking utterly unconcerned by the chaos she had just unleashed, reached out to stroke Walter's downy back. The Brightling Beetle had fallen asleep on top of the butter dish.

Nat slowly pivoted in his seat to look at Niamh. "You're moving out?"

Niamh looked at Jory with wide eyes.

"Goddamnit, Magda," Jory said through clenched teeth.

"What?" Magda asked with faux innocence.

"We had not discussed that yet."

"You're moving out?" Nat repeated, his voice growing

louder in the otherwise quiet room.

"That's my cue," Robbie said, placing his dish in the sink and rushing out of the room so quickly that he tripped.

"You're giving up your apartment?" Callum said, his voice tense.

But Niamh beat her to answering. "I need my own place, Nathaniel."

"You have your own place!" he sputtered.

Oh, you poor bastard. That was not the thing to say, Jory thought as Niamh focused a narrow glare on Nat's face.

"Aye. I have my own place. It's beautiful. It's also hours away from *anyone*."

"You need that!" Nat protested. "You need to be away from people during one of your... spells." Niamh and Jory both winced. But Nat pressed on. "Someone could ask too many questions! Or call the cops!"

"But I won't need to be isolated anymore because I won't be having spells anymore because you're going to follow through on your end of the bargain. Right?"

"Niamh, you—"

She crossed her arms over her chest. "Did you or did you not promise me on my mother's grave to turn me into a vampire to break my curse?"

"Ni—"

"It's a yes or no question, Nathaniel. Did you or did you not make that bargain with me?"

"It's not that simple."

"It is that simple. Yes? Or no?"

Nat looked at Callum. "Tell her, Callum. Tell her that she'd be trading one curse for another," he pleaded. "Tell her!"

But Callum shook his head and stood slowly, stepping away from the island before turning on his socked heel and disappearing into the broom closet without a word or a backwards glance. He did the same that last time there was a discussion of Jory leaving. She knew that for Callum, there were only two choices—fight or flight. He wouldn't fight her. He would fight *for* her, she knew, until the bitter end. But he would never fight *her*. If she wanted to leave, he would not stand in her way. He would serve his penance. And so he retreated.

Nat flew to his feet, knocking over his empty wine glass, a few remaining drops of elk blood splashing onto the table. He righted the glass carefully, his movements almost exaggerated in their slowness. Jory closed her eyes and sighed. When she opened them, she leveled another glare at Magda.

"Yes or no, Nat?" Niamh asked quietly.

"We'll talk about this at home, Niamh."

"No, we're talking about it now. I've waited weeks. I asked you a question. I deserve an answer."

Nat paced away from her to the door before spinning quickly and stalking back to the table.

"No, Niamh. Okay? No. I can't do it. I can't do that to you. I thought I could, but I can't. I can't watch it happen. I can't *make* it happen."

"But you're fine to watch me suffer like this."

"Niamh," Nat said, falling to his knees before her chair. He collected both of her hands in his, holding her knuckles to his lips. "You don't understand what it's like. What it can make you do at first. You... Please. Please don't ask that of me."

"Okay," Niamh replied, pulling her hands away and standing. "I won't."

She walked to the coat rack and slid into her black wool coat. "I'm so sorry to dash like this, Jory. But I've got some packing to do. Thank you for dinner, Magda. It was delicious."

Nat rushed after her, shouting her name. The door slammed behind him, leaving behind a room that was utterly silent except for Walter's gentle snoring.

"What the actual fuck was that, Magda?" Jory said wearily, her anger a snarling, lunging thing barely kept in check. "You had no right."

Magda sipped her wine. "Things needed to move forward," she answered cryptically.

"And it's your job to move them?" Jory snapped.

"You don't know that it isn't," Magda said with a raised eyebrow.

"You're just meddling! You're meddling because you're bored and using fate or whatever you're calling it this week as an excuse to justify it!"

"Tell me something, Marjory," Magda said, petting Walter with a careful finger. "If I hadn't meddled, would you be sitting in this cabin right now? Would that SUV be out in the driveway with four new tires? Would you be making the plans you are?"

Jory's mouth dropped open.

"Or would you still be hiding in your shop and apartment, leaving town when the sadness got to be too much to manage? Only now you'd know he was alive. Would you be eaten alive by that knowledge? By the sadness and the what-ifs?"

"I was fine," Jory answered mulishly.

"Sure you were. You've always been fine. You'll always *be* fine. But you deserve to be better than fine, dear heart," Magda said. "And so does Niamh. And so does Nat. And Callum. So does everyone."

"That's not your business," Jory choked out, her voice

clogged by sudden tears.

"You're right," Magda said with a shrug. "It's not. And I didn't actually do anything. Callum found his way here. I merely gave him a place to stay. You two did the rest. Sometimes things just need... coaxing. Or what's that word Jamie uses? *Facilitating*."

"And Niamh? What the hell were you facilitating tonight?"

"I told you. Things need to move forward. I know she would have gotten around to telling Nat. But time is of the essence."

"What does that even mean?" Jory shouted.

Magda leaned forward, her elbows resting on the table. "It means, my love, that things are about to happen. Things are *already* happening. And so other things need to move forward to make room."

"You're speaking in riddles."

"Am I?"

"What things are happening? Or about to happen?"

"That's not your story, Jory. It's not mine either. I'm just a facilitator, remember?"

"Magda."

"Jory," Magda said with a sigh. "You've gotten too used to being alone. You're afraid. You have insurance policies on insurance policies. When were you going to tell Callum about the apartment?"

"I was going to!"

"I'm sure you were, but when?"

Jory blinked. When was she going to tell him? On the way to Scotland? When she had her sealskin back? She wanted to believe that she would have told him sooner than that, but Magda was right. A part of her still expected this thing with Callum to fall apart.

"He left before," Jory whispered. "What's to stop him from doing it again?"

"He only left you before because there were secrets. Are there going to be secrets this time?"

Jory squeezed her eyes shut against the tears. When she opened them again, Magda was standing right in front of her. She'd always been silent as a cat.

She reached a gentle hand up and cupped Jory's cheek. "Things need to move forward. *You* need to move forward, dear heart."

Jory sniffed, and Magda produced a tissue from thin air.

"Here you go, honey," Magda crooned as Jory wiped her eyes. "I love you. You know that, right?"

Jory smiled weakly. "I love you too. Even if I don't have any idea why."

"Why do we love anyone?" Magda said, patting Jory's shoulder. "Now, I'm going to go tell Robbie that it's safe to come out and bribe him with some cookies to drive me home, and you are going to go downstairs and fix this."

"But what about Niamh and Nat? Will they be okay?"

"Are *you* okay?"

"No thanks to you," Jory said testily, but Magda smiled gently because they both knew the truth. Jory was okay almost entirely thanks to Magda. Magda who had taken her in. Magda who had been a friend. Magda who had known the truth that Jory wasn't ready to see, who had given Callum shelter, who had given them time.

"I still think you're a meddlesome old hag," Jory said, wiping her nose.

Magda laughed. "And I still think you're a delightful pain in my ass. But all will be well."

And with a swat on the backside from Magda, Jory went after Callum.

34

Callum lay on the bed in the dark, staring up at the popcorn ceiling, and feeling sadder than he'd felt in a long time. He'd had a friend once that referred to such a feeling as being "decadently depressed." It certainly felt decadent, allowing his despair to roll over him in slow, viscous waves that left behind an oily coating of despondency.

He had everything. Everything money could buy. Everything a person could *fantasize* about buying. And for what? The one thing he couldn't buy was the thing he wanted so badly he could taste it. He could taste *her,* could remember licking the flavors of seawater and wine out of her very mouth. He wanted her love. He wanted her smiles and her laughter, as freely as she'd given them to him so long ago. He wanted *her.*

Maybe he'd give it all away. Sell the houses, the cars, the businesses, the investments. Give Nat enough to run the new business for years without needing another cash infusion, even if it struggled—which it wouldn't. He'd deposit enough money in Penny's account that she'd never have to work again. She and her wife could summer in Greece and winter in Bali and drive their ridiculous RV all over the country without a care for how to pay for it. He'd give Robbie an equally large sum so that he didn't have to take the odd jobs that had led him to Callum's office and could instead do whatever the hell he wanted. Build a stilt house in Laguna Beach or move to Paris or get every single tattoo removed and redone. Whatever. And then he could give the rest to various philanthropic ventures where it could do immense good.

Maybe he'd only keep the house on the island in Scotland. The one he'd built where their little cottage had sat. He'd spend his days in the dark vault that he'd dug into the sediment with his own two hands. And he'd spend his nights sitting outside, listening to the surf pound the coast and feeling the wind whipping across his face. He'd stare out into an endless sea and wonder where in the hell she was beneath that inky surface. Whether she was happy. Whether she thought of him too. Even if only once in a while. He'd imagine her joyfully leaping above the waves and slipping through the water like a knife's blade.

And he'd be miserably, decadently sad.

Fuck.

He imagined Robbie punching him lightly on the shoulder and telling him that he missed his calling as an emo band frontman. The door to the broom closet opened overhead, and a beam of light swept over the stairs as the trap door lifted. And then it was gone.

"Callum?" Jory called out, her bare feet padding down the steps.

"Aye."

"Are you o—fuck," she cursed as something fell over.

"Let me get a light—"

"No, no! I'm fine! You want to be in the dark, we'll be in the dark."

"I dinnae want to be in the dark. It just made for the best ambiance for a pity party."

Maybe Robbie would teach him to play guitar. This album was going to write itself.

She shuffled toward the bed, touching his arm before carefully climbing in one knee at a time. Jory settled her body on the bed next to his, lying on her back and staring at the ceiling. She reached out and threaded her fingers through his, holding his hand. It felt *so goddamn good*, but only made the gaping wound in his chest feel even more cavernous than five minutes before.

"I think we should talk," she said quietly, her voice warm and resonant in the cool darkness.

"It seems we should."

She sighed.

"When were you going to tell me you're giving Niamh the apartment?"

Another long sigh.

"I don't know."

He felt a spark of anger. "Really? In all of our texts and video chats, in all the times I've seen you? You couldnae mention it? That you were even considering such a thing?"

She was quiet for a long time. Finally, she whispered, "I was afraid."

"Afraid?"

"Yes. Afraid," she said with a huff. "You've lived a thousand lives. You've been a duke, for Christ's sake. You've been everything. You've rubbed arms with royals and have businesses and houses and properties and are richer than Midas, and I have—" Her voice dropped off, like a stone hurled over a cliffside. A sudden leaving. "I have nothing but myself."

She sucked in a shaky breath. "When we were... before... I was going to beg my father to make you immortal. I was going to give you that, to give you *something* for all that you had given me. But I can't give you that anymore. You're already immortal. You already have that. You already have everything."

"Jory, I—"

"No," she said sharply. "I need to say this. My father begged me not to stay on land with you. He prophesied that it would only bring me heartbreak. But I loved you. I might have loved you from the moment you opened your eyes. And so I stayed. I stayed on land to be *with you*. And then you left."

Her voice broke on that last sentence. He began to roll toward her, but she exclaimed, "Stop!"

He froze.

She took a breath. "Please. If you hold me, I'll never get this out."

"Okay." He shifted to his back once more.

"I've been so afraid this month. What if I stayed and you left again? What if I took a chance? On you? And it just brought me more heartbreak? Because I've been heart-broken for so long, and I—I can't do it again, Callum."

"Jory," he murmured, but she didn't stop.

"What if I'm not enough? That's what I thought. That's what I worried about. And so I didn't tell you about the apartment. Because I was afraid. You have everything in the entire world. How can I possibly compete with that?"

He rolled, fast as a flash, and gathered her into his arms, burying his face in the perfectly carved space where her neck met her shoulder.

"I only want you. I dinnae care about anything else. The cars. The houses. The money. I just want you," he said, his voice mumbled but the press of his lips against her skin.

She threaded her arms up and wrapped them around his neck, holding his head close. He shifted lower, resting his ear against the center of her chest, where her heart beat a steady tattoo. He closed his eyes.

"I know," she said.

He squeezed his eyes more tightly shut, waiting for the "but."

"I'm giving Niamh the apartment because I want the space to figure out how to hold onto everything at the same time."

Again, faster than a flash of light, he was over her, pinning her to the mattress, his elbows on either side of her shoulders and his mouth hovering mere inches over hers.

"What?"

She smiled, wide and brilliant. "I want you too."

"I'll give it all up. We'll go away together," he said, frantically peppering kisses all over her cheeks, her forehead. "We'll leave it all behind."

"Don't be ridiculous," she said with a little shriek. "Callum, stop it. I mean it. Oh my god, please stop!"

He pulled back. "Stop because you dinnae like it?"

"Stop because we're still talking! And the moment you stick your tongue in my mouth, the talking will be over."

He dropped his mouth to her ear and said, "I'd like verra much to stick my tongue other places than your mouth."

She pushed against his chest and whined, "Callum. Please."

"Cannae we talk after?"

Jory snorted, the sound so familiar that he grinned. "No, *boss,* we can't."

"Mmmm," he said, burying his face in her neck again and kissing his way up to her ear. "I like it when you call me boss. How about this?" he said, nipping her ear lobe. "I'll give you anything you want. There. Now we dinnae need to talk."

"You don't even know what I want."

"You said you want me. I dinnae care about the rest. You can have it. Whatever ye want."

She slid her palms down his back.

"What if I want to move to Florida?"

He shuddered, and she laughed. "Anything, Jory."

"What if I want to buy a goat farm? With three hundred goats?"

He dropped his forehead to the pillow next to her ear with a groan.

"Aye. I'll buy you ten goat farms. I'll let you name them all. All three hundred goats. And before you ask, yes, I'd love you still even if ye make me shovel goat shite every night. I'd love you if ye were a spoon. I'd love you if ye were a squirrel. I'd love you if your nose turned green and your hands turned into pitchforks and whatever else you worry about. I'd love you in Florida. I'd love you on the moon. I'll love you until the end of days, mo ghraidh. Until this planet careens into the sun. I'll hold you and love you until we disintegrate into stardust. And even after. If only you'll let me do it again."

She brought her hands to his cheeks, guiding his head up so that she could kiss his cheek, trail her own lips to his ear.

"And what if I said I wanted to winter in Alaska and summer in Antarctica, so I never have to be without you?"

He kissed her, decadently slow, her lips warm and soft

under his, tasting garlic and lemon and wine on her tongue. Salt. *Her.*

He cradled her face in his hands. Against her mouth, he said, "My love, I'll follow you anywhere. Anywhere at all. If only you'll let me."

35

Jory's alarm rang at eight a.m.

Her eyes flew open, sticky from only a few hours of sleep, and big arms wrapped tightly around her, dragging her against a hard chest. Callum was a study in texture and temperature now, his chest and forearms still dusted with coarse hair, but cool beneath.

"Stay," he grumbled against her hair, his lips tickling the sensitive skin behind her ear.

"Callum," she said with a laugh as she turned on the lamp and winced at the sudden brightness, "I have a business to run."

"Esther is going to be running the day-to-day soon. Call in sick."

"I don't get sick."

"Call in immortal."

"That doesn't make any sense."

With lightning quick speed, he rolled, flipping her onto her back and grinding his pelvis against hers, the soft cotton of her panties the only barrier between the heat of her sex and the chilled marble of his.

He kissed her, his mouth rough and demanding against hers.

Against her lips, he said, "Call in indisposed then."

"I can't do that."

"Ten more minutes," he said, dragging his lips down her throat, scraping his teeth against her clavicle.

"Five."

"Ten," he repeated.

"I have to do a hair and body shower."

He slid his body further down, kissing his way to her breast. "Are they nae all hair and body showers?"

"No," she said. "A body shower is where you just wash your body but not your hair. A hair and body shower is where you wash both. And—" She gasped as he gently bit her nipple, his tongue flicking rapidly against the taut peak between his teeth.

"Cannae you do that later today?"

"I feel dirty, Callum."

He grunted, a low sound, coming more from his chest than his throat, and slid even further down. He kissed his way down her belly until he buried his nose against the cotton of her panties.

"Callum," she protested, pulling on his hair.

He lifted his head and looked at her across the long, ochre plane of her body.

"You promised. Five minutes."

"I didnae promise you any such thing, lass," he said, resting his chin on her pubic bone. "But if you dinnae want me to do this, I willnae do it."

"I... I never said I didn't want it."

"Well, then," he said, lowering his head back to nuzzle at her sex through her underwear, the tip of his nose pressing against her clit. Her grip tightened on his hair.

"I said five minutes. I won't be able to come in five minutes."

She felt his breath, a cool breeze against her drenched panties, and shivered. It made her think of the commercials for mint gum, with the actors' breath turning to ice in the air. He dragged his tongue up the gusset of her underwear, from back to front, and she inhaled sharply. He did it again, exhaling that cool air against her fevered body, and she jerked. His hands came around her legs and pressed her hips into the mattress.

"You dinnae think I can finish you off in five minutes?"

"It's nothing personal," she panted.

"Hmmm," he hummed, his mouth pressed close, and she felt the vibrations. "Well, shall we see what we *can* accomplish in five minutes then?"

"But—"

"I'll make you a deal," he said, looking up at her again. "If I can make you go off in five minutes, I get another five minutes."

"And—and if you can't?"

"You think about your forfeit while I work, and we can cross that bridge if we get to it."

"But—oh my god," she shrieked as he sucked her clit through her underwear, the damp fabric becoming as cold as if it had come out of a refrigerator. She bucked against him.

"Easy now," he crooned. "Easy."

It was more intense than it had been on the stairs, when he'd been behind her. Maybe she'd been so angry that she hadn't noticed how cold his mouth felt. Or maybe she was more sensitive today. Or maybe... maybe... it was different because she had spent the last few hours in a delicious sleep, with him at her back feeling like the chilled underside of a pillow and the heavy quilt on top of her, keeping her warm.

But then she felt his fangs gently scraping against the fabric of her underwear, hooking carefully into the fabric, before he quickly jerked his chin, ripping the cotton completely. She writhed and the waistband of her ruined panties immediately rode up to her belly button.

"Hey," she protested breathlessly, "I liked thoooose—"

The last word became a tormented moan because there he was. Lips and tongue, cold and consuming, in a super-human rhythm that was both gentle and firm, slow and fast in turn, his mouth moving so quickly that she couldn't follow, the result being something very like one of her toys that had suction and vibration all in one. But cool. Like he'd sucked on an ice cube a moment before. And the worst part —or perhaps the best part—was that he didn't need to breathe.

As a result, the sensation was endless.

His hair was clenched in her fists now, her thighs squeezing hard around his head. So hard that, were he a mortal man, she'd be worried about injuring him. But she couldn't hurt him. Not with her body anyway. Not when his own body was such a lethal weapon, so indestructible. No. The only thing that she could hurt was his heart. And so she let herself let go, writhing and squeezing, yanking his hair to pull him closer and, perhaps, push him away at the same time, making sounds that she didn't recognize.

And then she felt it. Like the aerial view of a controlled building implosion, the orgasm started sharp and abrupt in her core and then radiated out to her whole body until her vision went spotty and her toes curled so hard they cramped and she found herself gasping, heaving air into her lungs.

He lapped at her clit again, and the sensation was so

much—too much— that she used her grip on his hair to force his head away. He chuckled, wiping his slick mouth on her inner thigh before crawling back up her body, letting his weight rest on top of her. He looked at his watch.

"Three minutes."

Dazedly, she shook her head. "What?"

"That took three minutes."

Her eyes were wide as she panted, her chest pressing hard against his with every rise and fall. "You ken what that means, mo ghraidh."

She looked up into his gray eyes. Soft, like a rainy morning over the sea. She felt the cool, heavy, hardness of his cock against her body. It made her shiver. And it was so very easy to shift her hips, to cant them up so that the tip of him breached her. Just barely. Just enough to feel that contrast. Cold against hot.

And it was easier still to wrap her legs around his hips and urge him forward, to press her heels into the muscles of his ass and force him deeper.

And it was perhaps easiest of all to thread her fingers back into his hair and bring his face to hers, to kiss him softly as he slid forward in one slow, easy glide until he pressed his pelvis fully against hers. He made a choking sound.

"Are you well, my love?" she said against his throat, nipping him with her teeth, the coolness of his cock less noticeable now.

"I just... I am never warm. But you... you make me warm. At least part of me."

She squeezed tighter with her legs, forcing him to grind against her. He dropped his forehead to the crook of her neck and groaned.

"Well," she said, licking where she'd just nipped, "by my count, you still have six minutes. Shall we see how warm you can get?"

36

After a blur of busy days, the end of the month was upon them. Jory had never slept less, but she'd never been happier either. She and Esther had worked out a system for running the store and splitting ownership. Jory had wanted to give the store to Esther free and clear, but Esther wouldn't have it. She seemed to think that Jory needed an incentive to return to World's End. In addition, somehow Robbie had talked himself into a job. As it turned out, Robbie was an excellent salesperson, helping customers to find exactly what they were looking for and making them feel like a million bucks all the while. He and Esther had become fast friends. Jory tried very hard not to think about how much she would miss them.

She and Callum were to leave for Scotland in the morning, and she had mapped out several future estate sales she wanted to visit while she was in Europe.

The winter sky was opalescent, with sunlight making a valiant attempt at shining through the dome of clouds.

"Do you really think you're going to be able to get those corsets?" Esther asked excitedly as she tackled a stack of denim that needed refolding after a particularly enthusi-astic customer.

Jory had been chatting with a friend of hers in London, Isabeau Voland, an elf who had worked as a modiste for centuries and now ran the couture fashion house, L'Armure. They had met in New York before the Revolution, before Isabeau had fallen in love with an English vampire and followed him back to London. Recently, Isabeau had come across a large collection of richly embroidered silk and damask corsets and stays, all in impeccable condition. Jory had gasped when the pictures had come through in her text messages.

"Isabeau," she said, her tongue curling to cradle the *eau*, "tells me that she found them in an estate sale at some manor house in northern England. The owners had never fully explored the attics, and when they went to renovate the home, they found a trunk that likely hadn't been opened in more than a century. She bought them on the spot and told me she paid two hundred pounds for the lot. They're worth twenty times that much."

"We can't afford that, Jor," Esther gasped.

"No, we cannot," Jory agreed with a smile. "But Isabeau has agreed to offload them to me for two hundred and one pounds if I throw in those 1960s bottle-green Ferragamo flats."

Esther sighed. "I do love those shoes."

Jory sighed with her, thinking of the beautiful shoes, neatly packed in her carryon bag.

"I'm excited to see her. It's been decades."

She cut into a box of paper shopping bags and began arranging them by size beneath the counter.

As Jory worked, she asked, "Do you have everything you need for when I'm gone?"

"Mm-hmm," Esther answered, having moved onto a pile of soft, vintage band T-shirts.

"No worries about the store or how to handle any of it?"

"Nope. All good."

Jory broke down the shipping box in which the bags had come and moved on to replacing the receipt tape in the register. As she peeled the sticker off the end of the paper, she heard a sniff and looked up to see slow tears trickling down Esther's cheeks.

"Esther?"

Esther sniffed again.

"Is it the inventory? I know it's awful, but if you have any questions, I'm a phone call away. I'll walk you through it."

"It's not the inventory," she said, her voice watery.

"The bank drop? I promise that Timothy really is a nice man once you get to know him. He's just—"

"It's not that either," Esther said, her voice thick now.

Jory's heart sank. "Is it Hank? Is he okay? Or your cousin? Has something happened?"

"Everyone's fine." Esther flapped her hands in front of her face. "I'm just... it's just... I... I'm going to miss you," she said before releasing a sob.

"Oh, darling," Jory said, rushing around the counter and wrapping her arms around Esther. "Darling, darling Esther. It's just a few weeks. And then I'll be back."

"But what if you don't come back?" Esther cried. "What if you get your skin back and never want to come back? You've waited for so long."

"Esther," she whispered. "I'll be back. I promise."

"You shouldn't make promises you can't keep."

"I can keep this one."

Jory let Esther cry into her shoulder. She felt tears pricking the corners of her own eyes and swallowed against the lump in her throat. She had told Esther about the sealskin weeks ago. She had told her that she didn't know when she'd be back. For the longest time, she'd thought of nothing but going home. The pull of returning to the sea and her family had been so strong that she felt it on a cellular level. But that pull had quieted of late or, at least, had been lessened by a nearly equal pull in another direction, by another person. She was beginning to contemplate a life where she didn't have to choose. Where maybe, *maybe*, she could have both. She could have everything.

"Esther," she said, holding her friend's shoulders in her hands and easing her away. "I don't have to be all of one thing. I can be a bit of a lot of things. I can have my skin and be that part of myself. And I can be here, in this store I love, with the people I love, and be this part of myself, too. It might be a while, but I'll come back."

Esther sniffled and Jory reached back to pluck a tissue from the box on the counter. Esther took it and wiped her nose. "I'm sorry. I promised Hank I wouldn't cry on your last day."

Jory smiled. "And what did he say to that?"

Esther huffed a breath. "He told me that it's okay to be sad and that I could cry any damn time I wanted to. He also told me it's not your last day."

"It's not," Robbie said from the back doorway, and Jory smiled at him over Esther's shoulder.

She hadn't heard him come in. He was wearing his customary all-black and held a cardboard drink carrier with three hot to-go cups in it. But not like the Styrofoam cups from the diner. These were white cups with black lids and thin cardboard sleeves like the ones from the coffee shops in bigger towns.

"Robbie," Jory said, squeezing Esther tighter as she burst into a fresh wave of tears, "where did you get those?"

"These? The diner."

Esther turned her head to look and then wailed, "But the diner doesn't have fancy coffee."

"Right you are, sugar-butt." He slid the carrier onto the counter. "Or, I should say, right you *were*. Alright. We've got a London Fog for Esther, a quad latte for Jory, and an Americano with two raw sugars and two pumps of pumpkin for yours truly, the most basic of bitches," Robbie said, pulling cups out and scanning the sides for names before putting them on the counter in order.

"Robbie," Jory said. "When did the diner start making fancy coffee?"

"Oh. That," Robbie said, blowing directly into the sip hole in the lid of his drink, forcing a whistling sound out of the vent. "Since Boss had a new espresso machine delivered to them yesterday and told me to teach them how to use it this morning. Carol made these. She's a natural."

"Callum bought them an espresso machine?"

"Oh yeah. La Marzocco. It's a beauty. Top of the line. He told them that he wanted to have certain coffee available for you when you were in town and said he was happy to buy the machine if they'd be willing to learn how to use it. Carol might never come back down to earth after all that caffeine. And Diego made better latte art on his first try than I did after a month."

He began straightening pens in the pen cup before using the sleeve of his sweatshirt to dust the top of the counter before looking up suddenly.

"Wait. Why is Esther crying?"

"Because she's allowed herself to believe that I'll be leaving and never coming back."

"Aw, Est, you goose. Of course she'll be back."

"That's what I told her. My friends are here."

"That, and the huge piece of property Boss bought just outside of town for the bottling facility."

Jory's jaw dropped.

Robbie kept absently straightening items. "He says that there is a higher-than-average population of people like him in the area, and he wants to be able to provide safe work for them with flexible schedules."

"You mean vampires?" Esther sniffled.

"Just... not humans. Vampires, exiled fae. He told me there's a werewolf commune about forty minutes away. Did you know? I had no idea. Anyway, he's in talks with an architect now. Some orc buddy of his who's got a real knack for underground structures." He started restacking tissue paper. "He said he couldn't think of a better place to set up opera—" Robbie blanched and dropped a roll of ribbon, clapping his hands over his mouth. "Oh, fuck! I wasn't supposed to tell you! It was supposed to be a surprise."

"A surprise?"

"Yeah. Oh, fuck. I can't believe I just let it slip like that. I've been so distracted lately." He groaned. "Can you act surprised when he takes you there tonight? Please?"

"Tonight? But we're traveling to Seattle. To be ready for our flight tomorrow night."

"It's on the way out of town. He said he—nope. Nope. Nope. I'm not saying another damn word, Jory. And don't you look at me like that. It won't work. I've said way too much already," he said, grabbing his cup and disappearing into the back. "But," he said, ducking his head back around the jamb, "can you *please* act surprised? For him?"

He disappeared again, and still within the circle of Jory's

arms, a laugh burst forth from Esther's mouth with such force that Jory felt it in her chest.

"Well," Jory said, her heart pounding in her chest, her feet feeling stuck to the carpet beneath them, shocked and overjoyed and annoyed all at once.

Because who bought a luxury espresso machine for a small-town diner? Who said that they would move to the Arctic for her? And who bought secret land for secret factories because he knew that she didn't actually want to live anywhere but here?

Esther's face lit up with a smile that stretched across her face, revealing the small gap between her front teeth and causing her blue eyes to nearly disappear in the cloud of freckles that dotted every inch of her body. At least every inch Jory had seen.

Esther grabbed her coffee cup and raised it aloft. With a laugh, she said, "Cheers to you, Callum MacLeod."

37

Robbie had driven them to the Somnus hotel in Seattle to spend the day until the sun set and they could travel to the airport to catch an overnight flight to New York City. Walter accompanied them, buzzing in a drunken pattern and bumbling around the cabin of the SUV, bonking repeatedly into the side of Callum's head.

"Goddamnit, Robbie," Callum hissed. "Did ye have to bring Walter?"

Robbie sighed. "Magda asked me to keep him for a few weeks, remember? Said it was really important that I not go anywhere without him."

"Is Magda going somewhere?" Jory asked from the back seat.

"Not that I know of," Robbie shrugged. "She just said she was busy and she thought I'd be good for him. Very cryptic. Very Magda."

"Very Magda indeed," Jory said, snorting a bit as Callum made a *wfft* sound between his teeth and batted at Walter's tiny, fuzzy body.

"He really doesn't like you, boss," Robbie said with a smile, his wrist draped easily over the steering wheel.

"He more than doesnae like me, Robbie. He hates my guts."

"Well, you can't charm everyone, I suppose," Robbie drawled.

Jory watched the GPS navigate them to their destination, which turned out to be a run-of-the-mill dumpling shop called Wok and Roll Dumpling, which had a carryout counter and two high-top tables with stools. She'd hugged Robbie tightly before they stood on the sidewalk and watched him drive away into the waning darkness, Callum with a tight, concerned look on his face.

"What's wrong?" Jory asked.

"He smells different. I dinnae ken why. I just..." His voice dropped off.

"You worry about him."

"Aye."

"He'll be okay. Esther's going to keep him busy, and Hank is the most responsible person alive on this planet."

"That he is," Callum said, one side of his mouth quirking into a half smile. "You're right, mo cridhe. I willnae worry about him anymore. Now, would ye like to see the hotel?"

It turned out that the hotel was several stories underground, accessed by ordering a particular sequence of dumplings and condiments and asking to use the restroom while one waited. The bathroom contained the cleverly disguised elevator that took them down into the hotel, where they were given a quiet room at the end of a hall.

They slept off and on throughout the day. Jory was delighted to learn that she could actually order dumplings from the shop above, and she ate xiao long bao without pants on, reclining against the headboard while Callum drank one of the synthetic blood samples he'd brought.

They flew overnight to New York City and to London the next night, staying at yet another Somnus in each city during the day. The night after that, there was a flight to Kirkwall and a ferry, driven across dark waters under a cloudy sky by a water serpent shifter named Hamish, who told them stories in a cheerful, nasal voice.

Callum's assistant, Penny, had rented them a car, to be left at the dock. Jory's hands shook with anticipation as Callum put their luggage in the boot and opened her door, handing her into the black sedan.

The island was dark as they drove, and Jory couldn't get her bearings. She'd been gone for so long.

Too long, she thought.

Callum drove with an easy confidence, reaching over to squeeze her hands gently from time to time, but there was a tightness in his jaw. He was not as relaxed as he was pretending to be. As they travelled, Jory began to recognize the turn of a hill, the way the road hugged a landmark. And as Callum slowed, turning left down a long, winding lane, Jory's breath caught in her chest.

"Callum," she breathed in the warm darkness. "Is your house—" She couldn't finish.

But he knew what she was going to ask. "Aye," he said.

She felt the tears creeping as the car's headlights sliced through the darkness like a knife rending fabric, revealing the world beyond the veil. And when a low, dark structure came into view, Jory found that she could hardly breathe at all.

He parked the car, and as soon as it was stopped, Jory hurled herself out of the door, racing forward to the little crest overlooking the vastness of the sea, the exact spot where their cottage had once stood.

Distantly, she registered a car door opening, the sound of steps on the frosted ground. And then he was there, big and comforting behind her. Not warm, never warm anymore, but solid and whole and here all the same.

"How long did you live here?" she heard herself ask, her voice sounding broken. "After…"

He didn't answer right away. Instead, he wrapped both of his arms around her from behind, pressing his jaw against her temple. She leaned back.

He cleared his throat. "I left to avenge you. Right away, as ye ken. And once I'd done it, I wandered. Learned how to survive as what I am. Maybe a hundred years later, after Elspeth went, I came back. The house was nearly collapsed. But I dug out the cellar and slept in the dirt for weeks while I built the house again. I lived here alone for a time. Before moving on. But I always came back, every so often, to make repairs. To… rest."

"This is not the house you built when you came back," she said.

"Nay," he said. "This is perhaps the… sixth house? I had this one built about ten years ago by a firm specializing in sustainable architecture and design."

"When were you here last?"

He pressed his mouth against her temple, speaking into her hair. "A few months ago, just before Robbie found Esther."

"How often do you come?"

She felt like she was interviewing him, but she had too many questions to stop.

He nuzzled his nose into her hair again, his arms clutching at her more tightly. "Whenever the loneliness felt too heavy or the longing too great. That's when I would come here. Just to feel you."

The tears were welling now, spilling over her lashes. "To feel me? I wasn't here. I left as soon as I could. I—"

"But this was the place I last held you in my arms."

She sniffed, the cold wind blowing through her clothing at her front and her cold love at her back. Her heart broke all over again to realize that, while he hadn't struggled the way he had, he'd also been so very alone.

"Come," he said. "I want to show ye the house."

She nodded, taking his hand and following as he led her to the front door. He flipped a switch, and the main living area of the house was brightly illuminated. Floor-to-ceiling windows looking over the sea, warm wood floors, dark walls. And directly ahead, hanging over a buffet behind a long dining table, was a sealskin—*her* sealskin—stretched taut across a green velvet background behind clear, polished glass.

Like a moth to a lantern, she found herself drifting ever closer, tripping clumsily over her own feet as she rushed toward it. She ran a finger over the glass, feeling the pounding of her own pulse in her hands.

"I kept it," he said from behind her, and she startled. She hadn't heard him approach. "When I left ye—" Callum swallowed thickly. "I went up to the house to grab provisions and I saw the trunk where you kept it. And I didnae believe that I would ever return there again. But I—I wanted to take something of yours with me, to keep you with me somehow, when I—"

She was speechless, staring at the sealskin, which was impeccably framed.

"And the case," she asked hoarsely.

"To keep it safe. It was all I had of you. Here," he said, stepping around her.

Reluctantly, she allowed him to step in front of her. He gripped the frame in strong hands and gently lifted it off the wall, turning to lay it face down on the dining table. Her mouth felt dry.

The backing was held to the frame with dozens of metal prongs.

"'Twill take me but a moment," he whispered. "If you are ready."

She nodded and said in a voice that was ragged and hoarse, "Please."

38

Callum could have ripped the backing off with his bare hands. Or, barring that, he could have moved the hammer so fast that, within the span of a few blinks, the backing would have been gone and the sealskin in her hands. But he didn't. He couldn't.

Admittedly, part of him didn't trust her not to bolt and disappear as soon as she had it, slipping through his fingers like saltwater, leaving nothing behind but the taste of herself. She had talked to him about new beginnings. She had told him that she wanted him. But did she want him enough to give it all up? Did she want him enough to stay? And so he moved with methodical slowness, sliding the hammer's claw under each prong one at a time, prying them gently away from the particle board. He heard her ragged breathing over his shoulder.

Once, before he'd met her, he'd been impressed upon to help with the nailing of a coffin. The priest supervising the task had chanted "Mother of God, pray for us," timing the words to follow each hammer's blow. And they, the priest, Callum, and another man whose name he never learned fell into a rhythm of pounding the nails as percussion to the litany, like a timpani underscoring the symphony.

He hadn't thought of that day in centuries, but his hands shook as the claw of the hammer bent back the prongs at a steady pace, punctuated by the staccato of Jory's heartbeat, which he could hear as clearly as if it were his own.

If she ran, if she grabbed for the skin and disappeared, he may as well be nailing a coffin closed. His. Not in a literal sense, of course, but he couldn't go back to the half-life he'd been living before. Before, his life had felt every bit like penance. Missing her, wishing she was there, but knowing she wasn't. To go back to that life knowing she was in the world, somewhere, alive, and out of his reach? It would torment him until the end of time.

He slid the hammer's claw under the last prong and pried it up. Jory gasped behind him. With trembling hands, he lifted up the frame's back, setting it gently on the table next to the frame. He could feel her practically vibrating, her energy and raw desire radiating with nearly nuclear force, like she and the skin had been electrons pried apart, soon to be linked once more. The tangible chemistry made his knees go weak.

She had been caged, trapped in her human form. And regardless of what happened to him, this opportunity, this freedom? It was hers and hers alone. He had accidentally stolen it from her. So many mistakes born from one very important omission of truth. But even if she left him forever, even if he felt the agony of that leaving until the world blinked out of existence, he would not stand in her way.

With heavy steps and shaking hands, he stepped to the side, giving Jory room to approach the frame. She ran a reverent finger over the back of the skin, feeling the soft leather. And then she was gathering it into her arms, careful handfuls becoming greedy armfuls, the silky-smooth fur of the sealskin rustling as she brought it to her chest.

Her hands were shaking, her tears dry now, as she stared at him in wonder.

"At long last, mo ghraidh," he said, despair and hope coursing through him with enough force to fell a redwood.

It appeared that speech was beyond her. He watched her in the warm light of the driftwood chandelier, the sealskin clutched tightly in her arms, her eyes wide and unfocused, her breath coming in stilted gasps.

She sucked in a deep, sustained inhale, her body going very, very still.

And then she ran.

"Fuck," Callum cursed, following after her as she bolted out the door. The frosty earth was slick under the soles of his shoes as he raced after her, around the house and down the well-worn path to the shore. The sealskin trailed behind her like a cape and he chased her, the instinct to hunt, to *catch*, so very strong. He hadn't indulged those instincts in a long time.

But he slowed himself, running at a normal human pace, because he *wasn't* hunting her. He didn't want to *catch* her. He wanted to *follow* her. He wanted to go with her, wherever that might be, wherever she might lead. And so he ran, close on her heels, feeling the draft from the sealskin whipping against his face.

She didn't slow down when she reached the shore. Nor when her feet hit the water, sending splashes ricocheting back. And then, as the clouds parted, revealing a slice of bright moonlight as sharp as a sword's edge, he saw her charge deeper into the icy water before diving under the surface and disappearing from his view.

"Fuck," he cursed, his teeth clenched, arms pumping as he tried to follow.

Callum ran after her into the inky black water, until it closed over his shoulders and head, his clothes waterlogged. He swam in the direction he'd seen her go, but even with his night vision, he couldn't see more than ten feet in front of his face in the murky darkness. Panic clawed at him, old fears from years at sea, a sailor's *justified fears*, about the creatures that lived beneath the surface.

He kicked hard until his head broke the surface, wanting to follow her, knowing he'd never find her in the huge expanse of open water, terrified of what might find *him* if he tried. And so, with his fear clutching at his throat like a vice, he swam quickly back to shore, making as little splash as possible because he'd once read that sharks were attracted to splashing.

Callum crawled out of the ocean on hands and knees, saltwater pouring off of him in streams.

"Fuck," he shouted, his voice catching. "*Fuck.*"

He'd spoken around a sob, the words feeling nearly gelatinous from his tears collecting, blood mixing with the saltwater and streaming down his face, back to the ocean, back to the womb of it all.

Without a goodbye, without a backwards glance, she was gone.

He'd built this house. He'd come back here year after year after year to be close to her. Not to *her*, but to be near to where he'd once *had* her. Where he'd once held her love in his arms with the same desperate clutching that she'd held her sealskin in the dining room. As if he hadn't been able to believe she was real, that she was in his arms at all.

How many nights had he fallen asleep watching her sleep, watching the warm glow of the coals in the hearth cast shadows on the earth's clay of her skin, making her freckles dance, her breath coming easily in and out of her nose? How many nights had he wondered to himself what he'd done to deserve such a gift as her? And how many days in the aftermath had he sat alone in the dark, staring at a ceiling in a vault in any number of places, with nothing to comfort him but the memory of her sleepy smiles upon waking, her bright laugh, her mischief, her life? All gone. Just like she was now.

Callum dropped to his ass on the sand, his knees bent and forearms resting atop them, head hanging. He had always been a believer that mistakes were an integral part of success. But there were some mistakes that could not be salvaged into lessons. As the bloody tears fell steadily from his eyes, dropping into the water below him like watercolors off a soaked brush, he counted those mistakes. The calculus was agonizing, as it always ended with the sum of him sitting in this exact spot, cradling her body against his chest and cursing the fates that had brought him such a beautiful gift only to use him as the weapon of its destruction.

But he hadn't destroyed her. And that was the most painful bit of tabulation, wasn't it?

If only he'd waited. If he'd been stronger and honored her properly, letting her lie in state for a time, she would have healed, he would have *seen* her heal. He would have wept into her hair and trembled with gratitude.

But he hadn't. He'd been mad with grief and had left her as alone as he was now.

To have had her for the last few weeks, though? To have held her and loved her and *worshipped* her? To have tasted that wondrous and wondering joy again? It made the loneliness that much more bitter and painful.

Callum's misery carried him through the remainder of

the night, staring at the dark water and waiting. Before long, he distantly realized that the sky above the horizon was growing lighter. It would soon be dawn. There was a part of him that wondered if he should let the sun take him, if that would finally be penance enough. But the greater part of him would rather live in the world where he knew she was than spend the rest of eternity in the void without her.

He would wait for her. He would wait on that island for another thousand years if that's how long it took her to return. After all, what was time to him when he had endless amounts of it? What was a century? Or a millennium? Or two? Nothing, that's what. Like the spare change in a cupholder.

To do that, however, he had to be safe and get inside. He needed to reach the vault before the sun threatened to steal every possibility at happiness from him. But as he stood, he realized that in his misery, he'd misjudged the time. He would have to run.

"Fuck," he hissed, turning to hurry back the way he'd came.

There was a splash and a sharp clasp around his ankle, teeth sinking deep and pulling. Hard. The force toppled him and he found himself scrabbling, clawing with useless fingers because, as strong as he was, whatever had his ankle in its teeth was equally so. He dared to look behind him, or to try, but through the splashing, all he could see was a hulking dark shape.

It was one of his worst fears brought to life. A creature from the deep, come to claim him. A monster. A thing that could swallow him whole or tear him apart. It was easy for humans to say, "There's no such thing as monsters." But he was living proof that they were wrong.

"Nay, godsdamnit, not now," he grunted, desperately

trying to pull away, kicking his leg and gouging his fingers into the wet sand.

But the teeth bit deeper and he shouted as he was pulled farther into the water, until he was fully submerged. He shouted again, the sound muffled by the icy water. Deeper and deeper he was pulled. He'd never make it now. He'd never make it into the vault inside the house. The moment the sun rose and sent shards of light through the water, he might as well be staked. From dust he was born and to dust he would return, lost to the sea as he'd nearly been all those years before.

39

Jory had never run so fast in her life as she did when the sealskin was in her hands. It trailed behind her, whipping in the wind and her own wake like a banner. She heard Callum behind her. She heard his racing steps, moving at an almost human pace, as if he wasn't actually trying to catch her or stop her, but as if he wanted to follow her. She smiled.

She dashed into the water, and as she dove under, she felt it happening, the melding of cells, the shifting of bones and tissue, the *becoming*. In the space of a heartbeat, it was done, and she swam in tight, joyful loops, relishing the way her body cut powerfully, effortlessly through the water. As if she was born to it. Because she *was* born to it. Of it. By it.

The water was cold and clean and full of movement and intensity. She'd missed it, missed the feeling of being completely surrounded. The closest she'd come was the weighted blanket Magda had bought her for Christmas a few years before. The feeling of pressure, weighing down and around her, had been so familiar that she'd wept.

Jory popped her head above the surface and looked at

the shore. Callum sat in the sand, his forearms resting on his knees, staring after where she had gone. She waited for a long while, floating and watching him. He was so handsome, even when he looked heartbroken, and he was hers. Or at least he'd said he was. She believed him. Or she wanted to. But as she watched him, she realized that she needed one more thing from him. She needed him to stay.

In his misery, he'd flown off last time, an avenging angel, and left her. The fault wasn't his alone, she knew, and she understood her part in the tragedy. She could have told him what she was. She *should* have told him. That had been the part that wounded him most of all, she knew. Her lack of faith in him. But he'd still left her. Would he leave again? Would he assume the worst? Even after she had told him that she wanted him? Could he believe her?

They would find out.

She dove beneath the waves again, swimming in lazy curls in the dark water, scenting fish on the current, and decided to see. When she returned to shore in the morning, if he was still there, still safely tucked in the vault, she would know. She would stay. She would choose him too.

There wasn't time to go home, but for the next few hours, Jory hunted and played. She relished every moment in the body that had cradled her the longest, like reuniting with her oldest friend. As the sky began to lighten in advance of the dawn, Jory made her way back to the shore, already preparing to separate from the skin again so that she could walk up the hill to the house.

But as she popped her head above the water, she saw him sitting there. Still. His body looking defeated. She watched him lift his head and knew the moment that he registered how much time had passed, how much danger he was in. He jumped to his feet, but Jory knew he'd never make it. She'd seen ten thousand more sunrises than him, and even if he could make it up the hill to the house, he'd never get to the vault before the glint of the sun through the full wall of windows would be the end of him.

How dare he? How fucking *dare* he? She chose him, and he did something so unbelievably foolish as to be taken out by the sun. Fear and rage like she'd never known coursed through her body, and she darted as quickly as she could toward the shore, launching her body forward and closing her teeth around his ankle. He was big and superhumanly strong, but so was she. She dragged him beneath the surface, pulling with all her might against his resistance. If he was too stupid to save himself, she'd do it for him.

She'd save him a thousand times over. Again and again. He looked back at her, and she knew the moment he realized that it was her because the fight left him and his body went still. He let her tow him down into the darkness even though she knew it terrified him. She loosed the grip of her teeth around his ankle, not enough to let him go, but enough that it wasn't a vice. There was a cave nearby that she had visited many times with her father to look for crabs. He would be safe there, even if he might hate every minute of it.

Afraid, but alive. Wasn't that how she'd spent the majority of her time trapped on land? She knew his fear would be twofold. He was afraid of the creatures that lurked in the darkness of the water, but she knew that he was more afraid of her leaving without a backward glance. She had trusted him to stay; let him trust her to come back.

40

She had brought him to a cave and towed him far enough beneath the overhang that no sunlight would reach him, but not so far that he couldn't see beyond the cave's mouth. He was grateful for that small mercy. She swam down to a large rock that sat on the cave floor and circled it. He understood. Picking up the heavy rock, he held it close against his chest. It was heavy enough to weigh him down and keep him in place.

He could sense her anger. Even in her seal form, he could feel it radiating off of her. He deserved it. He'd been a fool. Losing track of time and nearly being fried to a crisp? After she'd come back? After so many promises half spoken? He was angry with himself.

She swam closer, nuzzling the side of his face with her whiskered nose before resting her head on his shoulder. He leaned his head against hers, never more grateful that he didn't need to breathe than he was right now. She was different like this and yet wholly the same. The form was different, of course. On land she was a lush woman, with curves and softness and strength, and yet he could see the mirror of those feature in this form, as well. Powerful, but soft, too. He closed his eyes and allowed his gratitude, his awe, to wash over him.

Too soon, she lifted her head and swam over his shoulder, circling him close again before moving away. She narrowed her eyes, as if she were glaring at him, and he understood that she was commanding him to stay put. He nodded, appreciating that she had kept him safe even if he loathed everything about being down here except getting to watch her. She was magnificent.

He allowed the support of his knees to go slack, lowering himself carefully to sit on the sandy floor of the cave, the rock held in his lap like a lover. She jerked her head in a way that felt like a nod before turning and swimming away, leaving him alone at the bottom of the sea, cradling a rock the way he'd cradled her in his arms before it had all gone to hell.

Callum sat on the floor of the cave, watching the sunrise lance through the water in sharp bursts, watching fish come and go, mesmerized by the dappling of light on the surface of the water, so far above his head. He hadn't seen sunlight —real sunlight—in so many years. But from the deep shadows of the cave, he was safe to enjoy, to be mesmerized. He couldn't help but remember the other time he'd watched a sunrise from the dark safety of a cave. Of another goodbye.

But this wasn't goodbye. It couldn't be. Jory hadn't said so, but she'd made him believe that she'd be back. And so he waited all day, watching the spear shafts of light shift directions as the sun traveled across the sky. The water, the world, grew darker once more, and when Callum knew the sun had set completely, he dropped the rock and began the slow swim back to shore.

He felt weak and shaky as he kicked his feet and reached

with his arms. He was tired from the journey, from the nerve-melting emotions of the past eighteen hours, and he needed to eat. There was synthetic blood in the refrigerator. He'd had it shipped to a demon friend of his who lived on the island and looked in on the house from time to time.

The water grew shallower until he was crawling, the surf rushing against his back as he rose to stand. His hands and legs trembled as he walked away from the water, making his careful way towards the house.

But there was a splash. Several, in fact. Angry stomping through shallow water.

He turned, and there she was. His Jory. Striding from the sea like a vengeful goddess, her sealskin wrapped tightly around her body like a towel, her eyes bright in the darkness.

"What the hell were you thinking?" she shouted. "You could have died! Do you understand that, Callum? You could have *died,* and then I'd have to make a deal with the underworld to revive you so I could kill you myself!"

He felt a weak smile pulling at his lips, so very tired, but she kept shouting, stalking closer until he could feel the warmth of her breath against his face.

"You're off your head, Callum MacLeod," she shouted. "What did you mean, just sitting on the damn beach like a godsdamn martyr just waiting for the sun to take you? Don't you understand that you can't leave me? Not again? Not ever again, you fucking bastard!"

A grin split his face, and he felt his eyes crinkle.

"What are you smiling for? Did you hear me, Callum? If you try something so stupid ever again, I will bring you back from the dead and murder you myself. So help me gods, I'll do it. You know I will."

The last sentence disappeared into a sob.

"Jory," he whispered, reaching out with a shaky hand.

"Because you're mine, Callum MacLeod," she said, stepping closer, touching his jaw with featherlight fingertips as the salt water dripped from his hair and down his face. "Do you hear me? You're mine. You always have been. From the moment I saw you on that beach, more than half dead from wounds and baking in the sun, I knew. I gave up everything to be with you. And I would do it a thousand times over again. You don't—"

His lips crashed against hers, and she rose onto her toes, pressing into the kiss with a desperate fury, her hands clutching at his cheeks as his arms banded around her, crushing her against him.

He kissed her with abandon, as if it was the only kiss he'd ever have again, determined to suck the very marrow out of it and nourish himself with the memory of how she felt in his arms, her mouth pressed to his, the taste of salt between them. Salt like blood. Salt like the sea.

She was strong. So much stronger than she'd been before. He felt her meeting him, matching him, pressing her body with equal force against his, pulling him closer.

He staggered, feeling his strength slowly ebbing, and she propped him up, her palms flat against his chest.

"Callum, Callum, mo cridhe, what is it? Are you well?"

"Hungry," he whispered.

She gathered him closer, wrapping her arms around him and drawing his face to the crook of her neck.

"Eat," she whispered back.

"But—"

"Eat, my love," she repeated, pressing firmly against the back of his head.

He groaned, letting his teeth sink carefully, so very carefully, into her throat. The taste of more salt burst across his tongue, and he moaned softly, drawing deeply, taking her into him. She stroked his head with gentle fingers, furrowing through the wet strands with such care that it gave him goosebumps. Something that hadn't happened in centuries. Something he'd forgotten all about.

She whispered to him, soft love words in languages he didn't know, and he drank, feeling her strength fueling his own. After a while—what was time, after all?—he carefully drew his fangs out of her neck, licking over the punctures with his tongue to close them. Then he licked the spot again just because he wanted to.

Callum raised his head and looked at her. The face of a goddess of the elements. His goddess, sculpted from the earth of clay and ebony and jade.

"Are you satisfied, my love?" she asked, her voice soft and warm.

He dropped his forehead to hers. "You came back to me," he said, closing his eyes. "How could I be anything but satisfied?"

She sighed, wrapping her arms around his neck and leaning closer. He turned his head to kiss her gently, his hands sliding carefully into the seaweed slick strands of her hair.

But then the air changed, becoming charged. He could almost feel the sparks dancing over his wet skin. The waves went still. The night noises went silent. And before Callum could look around Jory's body, it felt as if the world itself had stopped turning.

A voice, almost painful to hear for all that it was soft and low, broke the silence, slicing through the electrified stillness. "I certainly hope you are satisfied."

41

Jory spun away from Callum with a gasp, hurling herself towards a... man. And yet Callum knew he was not a man. This was an old god. The kind that Callum had heard discussed around shadowy pub tables and next to hearths on cold nights. The old gods the people had forgotten.

But memory is not required for existence. "Some things live on whether ye consider them or nay," Callum's father had once said into the suds on the deck of a ship. Callum had been on his knobby hands and knees next to him, listening as his father told tales to pass the time while they worked.

The old god was the color of deeply patinated bronze, greens and blues and golds, mottled together with a deep, midnight black. Callum was reminded of how the hull of a ship looked from underwater, the shadows broken by the movement and ungovernable lightness of water. The colors almost seemed to move across his skin in the moonlight, as if he was not just alive but *made* of life. His hair was long and dark, slick strands weaving and roping around one another. Just like Jory's.

She ran and threw her arms around his neck.

"Adda," Callum heard her say.

And this god, he held Jory tightly, one arm banding behind her back and the other cradling the back of her head with reverent care. His eyes were closed tightly, and Callum noticed that the dappled throat convulsed and a bright, glimmering tear slipped through the tight slit of his eyelids. This could only be her father. The wondering, almost worshipful way he held Jory in his arms, the way she clung to him like a child, was proof.

Callum had never been held like that. As he watched the old god's tears fall, he'd felt a sudden, sharp pang of grief for that fact. He'd never known his mother. His father had taught him to sail and use a sword, had kept him safe and fed and clothed. He'd taught him to survive. But from his moment of earliest consciousness until his father was given back to the sea wrapped in sailcloth, Callum had never once been hugged by the man.

Callum took a step back. And then another, meaning to give them space. Just then the old god opened his eyes, and Callum found himself looking into vibrant, glowing green.

Eyes he knew so well.

In perfect Gaelic, the old god asked, "How shall I speak to you? Gaelic? English? I know them all."

It almost hurt Callum's ears to listen to him. Not because his voice was loud or sharp. It was neither. But rather because it felt like it was coming from beyond some rip in the veil, with all the force of the universe rushing toward him alongside the sound of his voice.

"English," Jory answered for him, stepping back before turning a shy smile to Callum. "My Gaelic is rusty."

"Impossible," the god said.

Jory smiled again and rolled her eyes, earning an indulgent look from her father. She came to stand next to Callum, threading her fingers through his. Her skin was damp and cool, and a memory flashed through his mind, of an icy night in their cottage. They'd laid in their bed under furs and blankets, and she had wedged her toes and fingers underneath the bulk of his body. It had tickled, and he had squirmed. "I need ye, mo ghraidh," she had insisted. "I need your warmth!"

Another pang of grief. He'd never warm her again. He—

"Adda," Jory said, squeezing his hand and sidling closer. "This is Callum."

"I know who he is," the liquid voice answered.

Callum waited, feeling nearly frozen in the glinting green stare, like prey.

"Adda, please," Jory whispered. "Can he have a skin too? Can you make him like me?"

Without hesitation, the god shook his head. "I cannot."

"But Adda—"

"My treasure," he said softly, "I did not say I *would* not, or that I do not wish to, but I *cannot*."

"But... why?" she whispered. "You're a god, Adda. And you did it for Ama."

"Dear heart," he said gently, "I took a mortal woman, and I made her immortal. I cannot take an immortal and make him different."

"But—"

"He is... fixed as what he is."

"Cursed, you mean," Callum muttered.

The god cocked his head curiously. "Anything can be a curse in the right dose and from the right seat. I did not say you were cursed. But my answer does not change."

A plaintive sound bubbled from Jory's mouth, and Callum dropped her hand in favor of drawing her closer, wrapping his arms tightly around her, cradling her body against his own while she cried.

The old god was quiet, his head still cocked to the side, watching. His face was etched with concern, an eternity of concern, perhaps, and Callum realized that he had been worried after his daughter for every bit as long as Callum had been loving her, missing her.

"My treasure," he said, stepping closer, resting a hand on Jory's trembling back. "The fish cannot live among the birds. The birds cannot live within the depths. The seals can go between, but they cannot love an eagle and take it with them when they go."

"I just wanted you to make him a skin," she sobbed, her tears mingling with the clinging saltwater on Callum's chest. "I'm not a seal. I'm a demigod. And he's already immortal. He just needs a skin to come with me."

"I told you, my precious girl. I cannot remake what has already been forged. I cannot remake *him.*"

"So you're saying I have to choose."

The old god looked at Callum now, and Callum couldn't help but feel as if every thought, every deed, every desire he'd ever undertaken or experienced was being leafed through like pages and studied. But then the old god smiled. It was a small smile. A reluctant one, perhaps, but Callum felt it like sunlight, warm and comforting and complete.

"If your love cannot bear a bit of distance now and again, is it really love at all?"

She sniffled, lifting her head from Callum's chest. "What?"

The old god arched a brow at Callum.

Callum said, "You dinnae have to choose, Jory. You can

live with me when you want and go to the sea when you want. And I'll always be here when you return."

She looked up at him, her green eyes luminous and bright through the wash of moonlit tears. "But I just got you back."

"And you willnae lose me now," he said softly, pressing a gentle kiss to her forehead. "My love for you isnae fragile. I've loved you every day since I met you, even when I believed you lost. I never stopped. There's no end to how long I'll wait for you, mo ghraidh."

42

In the end, Jory went with her father, donning her sealskin and leaving Callum standing on the beach, his clothes torn and drenched. But he'd waved a strong arm high in the air as she had popped her seal head above the surface one last time to look back before he turned and walked back up the rise to the house.

She'd visited her sisters, her mother, spending her days weaving, laughing, and crying in turn, feeling as if no time had passed. She slept deeply at night in the velvety darkness of the depths, cocooned in her mother's weavings, listening to the gentle sounds of her old life surrounding her.

On the tenth day, she bid them farewell, hugging them tightly and promising to visit soon, inviting them to travel to the Washington coast. There had been more tears and laughter, more promises and thanks. And then, as the sun set, her father had left her near where the sand gradually sloped up to the shore.

She felt her bones shifting, lengthening, like being stretched and remade as she crawled from the water, her skin draped over her back like a cape. She stood, feeling the chill of the night air against her wet skin as she stood from the surf.

Her eyes adjusted to the night above water, and there he was, sitting next to the water's edge, his knees bent and forearms resting atop them, hands dangling casually.

"You're here," she breathed.

"Of course. I told you I would be."

"Yes, but why are you *here*? I thought you'd be up at the house."

He shook his head, rising with a powerful grace to his feet. "I didnae want you to walk up the hill alone. Besides, I didnae want to miss a second with you."

She moved closer, feeling as if she would trip over her own feet, unaccustomed to that feeling of clumsiness. The ground shifted under her as she walked directly into the chilled marble slab of his chest, feeling her body relax into him. His strong arms wrapped around her.

"How was home?" he asked against the top of her head.

"It was wonderful to see my family. I'd missed them."

"But?" he asked, always so damn observant. He hadn't missed the way her tone changed at the end of that sentence.

She sighed. "But it's not home anymore."

"You didnae feel welcome?"

"Of course I did."

"Well, then, of course it's your home. You ken I willnae stand in the way of you returning whenever you wish."

"It's not that," she said, turning her face so that her forehead rested against his chest. "It just... it's not my *home* anymore."

He paused, for just the barest moment, before he rested his cheek against her crown. She felt the pause in his body, the way he went very still as he asked, "And... where is your home then, my love?"

"You," she said, the word carried on breath.

His body relaxed against her.

"Jory," he whispered, pulling back to look at her, and she met his stormy gray eyes, seeing him clearly even in the darkness.

His head lowered slowly until his lips skated over her cheek, forging a path to her mouth. He paused, their lips barely apart, foreheads pressed close.

"Callum?" she asked, his name spoken against his mouth. "Take me home."

Faster than a flash, he scooped her into his arms and raced toward the house. Her giddy shriek carried on the wind because, as long as she lived, she didn't think she'd ever get used to the feeling of flying that accompanied being carried by Callum at a full, immortal run.

Through the blur of his speed, she registered the opening of a door, its slamming behind them, a short hallway with another door at the end, a deep, green room with exposed beams. And then she was on a bed, the mattress soft beneath her as Callum pressed a gentle hand to her sternum, forcing her to lay back.

She complied, her body spread and bared to the warmth of the room. Callum was above her, surrounding her, his lips and teeth and tongue everywhere, cool breath and cooler moisture following in their wake as he licked the salt from her body with worshipful attention, from her throat to her toes. He dropped to his knees next to the bed and spread her legs, bracing her heels against his shoulders before leaning in and licking the salt from the very center of her with such gentle, persistent adoration that she was writhing and begging before it was done.

She scrabbled at his shoulders with desperate hands, and he complied, standing next to the edge of the bed and sliding into her clutching, wet heat in gentle, short thrusts until she dug her heels into his rear and pulled him close, until she felt the cool shift of his flexing body against the back of her thighs. He gripped her legs and made her body ache with fullness as he leaned forward and continued his maddeningly slow pace.

"Yours," he said softly between thrusts, kissing the word against her throat, licking gently over the spot where his teeth had been before.

She sighed and sank heavily into that truth.

43

Jory and Callum stood in the alley behind the Wok and Roll Dumpling house in Seattle. Her sealskin was safely stowed in a locked steamer trunk, the key on a chain around her neck. The iron key was heavy, the bow intricately carved with filigree that had always reminded him of waves.

It was the best Callum had been able to source from his random collection of items at the house, and as he had slipped the chain over her head, he told her about using that trunk on the RMS *Celtic* on a journey from Liverpool to New York and later, back again on the same ship. He knew she liked things that had stories. She always had.

Once, at a formal dinner, he'd been seated next to a sociologist who told him that humans were acquisitional creatures. They liked to collect. Trinkets. Memories. Experiences. People. And while Jory wasn't human, she had always been like a magpie. On windowsills and shelves in their cottage long ago, there had been neat lines of shells and polished rocks, a bird skull bleached white by the sun, dried flowers, bits of glass tumbled smooth by the surf.

He knew that had led her to her business. Collecting fashion and treasures from wardrobes and days gone by. When she'd returned to their London hotel after visiting an estate sale, she'd been practically bouncing with excitement, having purchased a collection of immaculately preserved antique corsets, as well as capes, bolts of silk, and even a damask lover's chair, with two seats placed in the bows of an s-shaped frame, from the days when courting couples were forbidden to touch but wanted to be near, to speak face-to-face. She'd told him about the items, but had been more excited to tell him how they came to be, who had worn them and used them, and the lives these items had lived. Lives she was going to renew.

And wasn't that just like her? To breathe life into things that had been forgotten.

He looked over, and in the glow of the fluorescent spotlight outside the restaurant's back door, he saw her fidgeting with the key, rubbing her thumb down the shaft as she stared out into the night. A rush of affection and something that felt like longing overcame him. That key that had traveled across the ocean and back again in his pocket once upon a time and had just yesterday traveled across the ocean again around her neck, her hand in his.

A misty drizzle made the air damp, and she shivered and leaned into his side. Not for warmth, surely, because he couldn't offer her that, a fact that he didn't think he would ever truly come to terms with. But he wrapped an arm around her and drew her close anyway. Because she wanted him to. Because he could.

Headlights appeared at the end of the alley as a car turned, and she held up a hand to shield her eyes. A black SUV slowly approached, Robbie's head hanging out the driver's side window and bouncy pop music blaring.

"Knock knock," he said cheerfully, popping the trunk.

"Who's there?" Jory answered with a laugh, and Callum loaded the luggage into the trunk.

"You."

"You who?" Jory said as she climbed into the backseat.

"Yoo-hoo to you too!" Robbie said with a broad smile.

Callum shook his head, smiling as he climbed into the passenger seat and closed the door behind him.

In a thick twang, Robbie said, "My stars and garters! If it ain't Marjory Mhara and Callum MacLeod!"

"Actually..." Jory said, hesitating. "It's MacLeod. Marjory MacLeod."

Callum turned his head so quickly that he felt his vertebrae click as he looked over his shoulder and into the backseat at Jory, who was biting her lip and blushing.

"I mean... if that's okay? We haven't talked about it, I know, but—"

"Marjory MacLeod," Callum breathed, wonderstruck by the sound of it.

The beauty of that name was only eclipsed by the brilliance of her smile as she grinned at him.

Robbie drove slowly out of the alley. "Jesus Lord, you two, you've been alone and gone for three weeks. How are you still the horniest damn couple I've ever taxied? Ugh. Save some for the rest of us," he grumbled, but Callum saw him suppressing a smile all the while.

"Well? How is everyone? What did I miss?" Jory said, leaning as far forward as her seatbelt would allow.

"Well," Robbie said, "Esther is a natural at running a store. She's got the gift of gab, and I swear to god that girl could sell ketchup popsicles to people in white gloves."

"Maybe I'll convince her to work for me," Callum said dryly, only half kidding.

"Don't you dare," Jory said with a light slap on his shoulder. "You don't get to poach my business partner."

At that moment, a faint buzzing sounded from the center console, and Walter drowsily bumbled up out of a paper to-go cup, clumsily flying up to land on Robbie's shoulder.

"Somebody's awake!" Robbie crooned. "I put some honey in the bottom of that cup and he fell asleep after eating it about an hour ago."

Jory said, "That's the cutest thing I've ever heard," at the same time Callum muttered, "Jesus Christ."

Callum expected Walter to make an angry beeline directly for his face after that comment. Under ordinary circumstances, any time Callum was present, Walter was actively attacking him. He wasn't successful, of course, as he was nothing more than a yellow cotton ball with wings, but he made a valiant, incessant attempt nonetheless, flying into Callum's face like a tiny battering ram over and over.

But Walter hadn't even looked in Callum's direction. Instead, he was quietly snuggled tight against the collar of Robbie's shirt.

"Is he alright?" Callum asked.

"Who? Walter? Yeah. Why?"

"He isnae trying to murder me."

"He's been sticking pretty close to me lately. Won't let me out of his sight. But otherwise, I don't know, he seems pretty normal."

Callum narrowed his eyes but didn't argue. Jory was texting in the backseat, and Robbie tapped the console screen, switching to a new playlist. As he did, his hand shook. Callum looked at him, really looked, and thought Robbie wore a content expression, there were dark circles under his eyes and he was fidgeting. Constantly readjusting his seat, rubbing a restless hand through his short hair, scratching his neck. He drove with a casual wrist draped over the steering wheel, but Callum could see small tremors in his hand as it dangled.

"Are *you* alright?" Callum asked softly. "You look... strained."

Robbie rubbed a hand over his mouth.

"I've been... I don't know. More anxious?" he answered after a long moment. "I don't know if that's the word? But that what it feels like? I made an appointment with Hank's therapist, though. I go at the end of the week."

Callum said nothing, waiting. He knew Robbie well enough to know that if he left space, Robbie would keep talking.

"I don't know, boss. I'm just... itchy. Like something bad is going to happen? But why would it? The internet calls them 'intrusive thoughts.' I just..." he trailed off.

"Are you sleeping?"

"Not at normal times? I go to work at the store, and then I come home and pass out. And then I'm up all night. No matter what. Esther gave me a tea blend for sleep. Hank sent me a link to a sleep story app. I just can't settle down. I'm sure it's nothing. I'm anxious because I'm tired." He sighed. "Don't worry about me, Cal. I'll be good. Now that y'all are home and settled, things will go back to normal, and I'll be right as rain."

Callum wasn't convinced, but he left it alone. The rest of the drive passed easily, soft music playing as Jory told Robbie about their trip, about the estate sales, about visiting her family. As they talked, Callum closed his eyes, thinking to himself about what Robbie had said, how different he looked, how different he smelled. Like the forest and animals.

It was the animal smell that threw him. It was subtle. A human wouldn't pick up on it. But it also wasn't a human smell. Which was preposterous. Because Robbie was human.

It bothered him, and he remained bothered as they pulled up in front of the cabin. They went inside, and Callum took their luggage downstairs to the vault. When he reappeared upstairs, he found Robbie sitting at the island with a full feast spread out in front of him, leftover Chinese takeout containers littering the counter. Jory was eating cold lo mein directly out of a paper carton.

Callum leaned against the counter and watched as Robbie ate like a linebacker before clearing the empty cartons and throwing them in the trash. Walter never left his shoulder.

After washing his fork and plate, he turned and said, "Well, I'm actually feeling really tired after that. I think I'll turn in. See you tomorrow, lovebirds," before disappearing down the hall and closing the bedroom door behind him.

Callum was restless himself. How had Robbie described it? Itchy. He paced around the kitchen, his hands stuffed deep in his pockets, feeling his shoulders become boulder-like with tension.

"Hey," Jory said, still sitting at the island.

He stopped and turned to her.

"What's wrong?"

He raked a hand through his hair. "He's not okay."

"He's fine," Jory said. "He's anxious. God knows I've been there."

"It's more than that."

Jory slid off the stool and walked toward him, into him, pressing her hands against his chest and looking up into his eyes. "He's a big boy, Callum. But if you're really worried, you can talk to him tomorrow about making a doctor's appointment. Okay?"

He closed his eyes and dropped his head, resting his forehead against hers.

"Come to bed," she whispered.

"It's the middle of the night," he said, the way most people said it was the middle of the afternoon. Which, for him, it was. He had wanted to drive out to the site of the bottling plant to see what progress had been made in the three weeks they'd been gone. He needed to talk to Nat. He needed to—

"Come to bed," she whispered again, pressing her body against his, and he felt himself sag into that touch, his arms coming around her warm, solid form.

"Take me," he murmured into her hair.

She grabbed his hand and led him to the broom closet, and he followed her as docile as a lamb, letting her lead him down the stairs, letting her guide him to sit on the bed, letting her kneel on the floor and untie his shoes, slipping them off one at a time. She rose higher on her knees, unbuckling his belt then unbuttoning his pants, drawing down the zipper, and coaxing him to shift his hips so that she could slide them, along with his boxer briefs, over his knees, pulling them off slowly before folding them with care and placing them on the floor beside her.

She stood, taking the hem of his sweater in careful fingers. He lifted his arms overhead like a child as she carefully drew it up and off, repeating the action with his T-shirt underneath.

Jory stood between his knees, fully clothed, while he was entirely naked. Almost.

"Ye forgot the socks," he teased.

"No, I didn't," she breathed, leaning close. "Your feet are cold."

As he barked a laugh, she pushed him backward on the bed and straddled his pelvis, leaning down and kissing him properly.

"I'm so glad to be home," she said against his mouth, and he groaned before rolling her off and then under him, kissing her breathless.

In the aftermath, Callum lay on his back, Jory tucked close against him with her head on his shoulder. He stared up at the popcorn ceiling and relished her warmth against him, the feeling of her panting chest pressed against his.

"Do you want to stay here?"

She lifted her head to look at him, her dark waves in a wild tangle. "You've been building a factory here. I thought we—"

"Nay. Do you want to stay *here*? In this cabin? Or would you like something else?"

"Oh," she said, laying her head back down, her fingers playing delicately with the scattering of hair across his chest. "I haven't really thought about it."

He grunted.

"Do *you* want to stay here?" she asked.

He shifted, rolling onto his side so that he could look at her, her head supported on his arm, their noses close.

"I want to build you a house."

"You already built me a house," she laughed.

"Aye," he said, kissing the tip of her nose. "And I'll build a second. And a third if need be. But I want to build you a house here."

She smiled softly. "You just want a bigger vault."

"I'll admit that I've become unaccustomed to such... small quarters. It would be nice to have some space to move around if I need. I dinnae sleep twelve hours at a time after all. An office, perhaps. A sitting room."

"So a house above ground for show, and then a whole other house underground for you?" Jory teased lightly.

"Why not?"

She snorted a laugh. "That's convenient. When the climate gets so bad that we all have to live underground like moles, you'll be way ahead of the game."

It was a joke, but he caught her hand in his, closing it against his heart, his fingers tightly wrapped around it as he said, "How convenient indeed, mo cridhe. Then I'll never have to be apart from you again."

"And Robbie?" she asked, and he sobered, his smile sliding away.

"Didnae you just tell me he's a big boy?" he asked, but when she arched an eyebrow, he said, "I'll build him his own floor. Or his own house. Or he can live in the pool house. Or he can stay here. Whatever he wants. Whatever will make him happy." He kissed her softly. "Whatever makes you happy."

She wrapped her arms around his neck, and he rolled on top of her once more, knowing that he would never, ever take for granted again the way it felt when his hips settled into the cradle of her, her legs wrapping around his waist, her heart beating strong and lively against his chest.

"You make me happy."

"Then I'll build you a house, and you can be ecstatic."

"Can I design it?"

"You can have anything ye want. I'll give you anything. I'll give you the world. I'll give you my life."

A frown puckered the space between her eyebrows. "Don't give me your life."

"It's already yours. Every single day of it, from now until the very end, I'll be loving you."

She pressed her hand to his cheek, her eyes shining with tears, a smile spreading wide across her dear, lovely face. "I'll take it."

EPILOGUE

It was Friday, and Jory was meeting with the architect Callum had hired to look over potential blueprints. This particular firm had also built the Scotland house and specialized in sustainable homes for those with—how had he described them?—*unique specifications*. In other words, homes that needed vaults. Or special pools. Or any other accommodations a supernatural being might require.

The meeting had started early and run long, and it was after noon by the time Jory walked out of the conference room at the Seattle hotel where the architect and her team were staying. Esther had opened the store, and Jory planned to join her as soon as she got back to town. As she walked through the parking garage to her car, she checked her phone and noticed a missed call and voicemail from Esther. She brought the phone to her ear and listened.

"Hey, Jory," Esther's voice said through the car's speakers as her phone connected to Bluetooth. "I know you're in your meeting, but Robbie didn't show up to work this morning and I didn't know if he'd told you he was sick. I know he's got therapy this morning, but that appointment was at nine.

He was supposed to come in around ten. It's just not like him to not show up, and he's not answering his phone. Anyway, I'm sure it's fine. See you soon. Love you, bye."

Jory had left the house before six that morning to drive to Seattle, prying herself out of Callum's arms, but Robbie's car had been there. Before backing out of her parking spot, she called Robbie, groaning aloud when it went straight to voicemail. She opened her messages to send Robbie a text.

> Robbie? Are you ok?

Moments passed with no reply.

> Robbie? Esther is worried and now I'm worried too.

> Answer your goddamn phone.

She put the car in gear and called Esther, who answered on the first ring. "Did you hear from him?"

"No," Jory answered. "I'm leaving Seattle now. I'll go straight to the house and see if he's there."

"Should you call Callum?"

"He's probably asleep," she said with a groan. "And he can't do anything anyway. It's not like he can go upstairs and check."

Esther sighed heavily. "Okay. Drive safely. Call me when you get there."

Traffic was blessedly light, and Jory made excellent time, driving faster than was legal but not so fast that she was likely to be pulled over. Her heart pounded as she drove past the "Welcome to World's End" sign and still as she turned onto the gravel drive that led to the cabin; it was so loud that she could feel her pulse in her ears.

"Fuck," she said as she got far enough down the drive to see that Robbie's car was gone.

She parked the car, turned it off, and hurled herself out of the car, racing up the steps and across the porch. She threw open the door and shouted, "Robbie? Robbie, are you here?" She raced through the kitchen and down the hall, seeing that his bedroom was empty.

Her phone rang.

"Jory," Callum said sleepily when she answered. "What's the matter? I heard you shouting."

"Robbie didn't show up to work and isn't answering his phone."

Callum cursed loudly. "I'm coming up. Goddamnit. Goddamnit!" he shouted, no doubt remembering that he couldn't.

"Hang on," Jory said. "I'm going to add Esther to this call."

Again Esther answered on the first ring.

"Is he there?" she asked without preamble.

Jory sighed heavily. "No. He's not."

"I called Hank. He said he'd drive by Nadja's office and see if Robbie's car is there. If not, he said he'd ask her if she'd seen him. I'll call you when I hear from him," she said before hanging up, leaving Callum on the phone with Jory.

"I'm coming down," she said.

Callum was sitting on the side of the bed, wearing red plaid pajama pants and nothing else. His jaw was clenched, his knees gripped tightly in his hands, tension radiating off of him like heat from a flame. Robbie was his best friend.

Maybe Callum wouldn't have used those words. Maybe he didn't need to. Because the fact was that aside from herself, she'd never seen Callum so at ease with anyone. She had watched them laugh and rib one another. She'd watched them hug, chest to chest, not the way so many men hugged lately, with two forearms between them.

Jory wrapped her arms around him. He pressed his face against her chest. After an eternity of ticking seconds, Esther called.

"Fucking finally," Callum hissed and answered. "Esther? What news?"

"You've got both of us," Esther said, and Jory could hear her panic. "Hank came here after driving by the office."

It turned out that Robbie's car was not at Nadja's office. Hank had driven behind the building and found Nadja's little electric vehicle in its normal spot. But the building's lights were off, the CLOSED sign flipped.

"He's not at home?" Hank asked. "No note? Nothing out of the ordinary?

"The kitchen's a mess. Dishes piled in the sink," Jory said. "And Robbie's room looks like a laundry bomb went off, but—"

"That's normal," Callum said softly. "He likes to say that dishes are nae his spiritual gift."

Jory turned her face into Callum's shoulder.

"I figured," Hank said. "And the clothes?"

Esther sniffled. "He's a chaos goblin like me."

Hank grunted. More silence.

Callum sat up straighter.

"Esther," he said, "Can you draw cards?"

"You're shitting me," Esther shouted. "You're fucking shitting me!"

"It was just a question. Forget I—"

"The one time I actually need them, and I forget them at home!"

Esther had once confided in her that her grandmother had been one of the most well-known divinatory witches in the entire state of Georgia and that the gift seemed to be strong with her as well. Normally, she had a deck on her at all times.

"What about the deck in the glove box?" Hank asked helpfully.

"I don't have a deck in the glove box," she wailed.

"Yes, you do. I bought a spare one for the truck after you forgot them the last time we went to Seattle."

"Hank, I swear to goddess," Esther muttered in her thick, Southern drawl. "You're a prince."

Through the phone, Jory heard the bell over the door ding twice as Hank left to fetch the cards and returned. Then there was a long span of time with nothing but the sounds of shuffling cards, punctuated by the occasional tap.

"They're warming up," Esther offered helpfully. "Okay. Ready to shuffle for real, now."

Jory knew that Esther always shuffled seven times before every card draw. It was laborious and time-consuming, but Esther said that she liked to give the universe time to "get its shit together."

Seven ruffles. Seven taps. And then...

"Goddamnit," Jory heard Esther mutter through the speaker.

"What is it?" she and Callum asked in unison.

Another frustrated sound. Louder.

"She's pulling cards," Hank supplied helpfully.

Jory heard the rustling sound of cards shuffling. More slaps as Esther tapped the deck halves against the counter. She felt her anxiety rising again, felt the same tension recoiling in Callum's body.

"Ugh. I take back everything I said about this goddamn card," Esther said.

"Esther," Jory snapped. "What is it?"

There was a long pause. A longer sigh. And then Esther's whisper, "Death."

THERE WAS a brief moment where Callum felt as if time had suspended.

"Death?" Jory shrieked, and he jumped to his feet, startled.

"Now, sweetheart," Hank said. "What is it you told me? Death means new beginnings."

"Yes, but sometimes it's just death!" Esther said, her voice shrill.

"But usually it's not," Hank pushed. "Don't buy trouble."

Callum found himself feeling grateful for Hank's steadiness. He reminded Callum of a captain he'd served once upon a time a lifetime ago. Captain Marwick had been as steady as stone, and Callum had always marveled over the fact that the wilder the storm grew or the more pitched the battle became, the chaos and fury only seemed to drive the captain deeper into that reserve of calm.

Callum admired Hank immensely. He had from the very moment he'd met him. Hank's steadiness almost calmed the relentless panic spreading through Callum's body like a poison.

Almost.

But not quite.

Hank's voice drew his thoughts back as he said, "Don't you sometimes pull another card? What do you call it? A—"

"Clarifier," Esther finished.

"Yeah. That," Hank said. "Maybe draw one of those?"

Callum heard the cards shuffling again through the phone's speaker. Seven shuffles. Seven taps.

And then a long beat of silence.

"Esther?" Jory asked. "What does it say?"

"I pulled The Moon."

"What does that mean?" Callum asked, nearly beside himself, and Jory squeezed his hand.

The other end of the line was very quiet for a long moment.

"It can represent illusions. Or things not being what they seem," Esther said quietly. "Sometimes I see it representing anxiety."

"So, what?" Callum choked. "We're meant to feel anxious that he may be dead?"

Esther sighed. "I don't see them that literally. Usually. Callum, has Robbie been acting… different lately?"

Callum's mind raced as he thought of all the things that had been different, things that had worried him. Things that Robbie had shrugged off.

Just then, there was a loud knock on the trap door, and Magda's muffled voice sounded through the wood. "Are you horndogs decent?"

Callum's eyes were wide as he looked at Jory.

"Is that Magda?" Esther asked through the phone.

"Aye," Callum said. "With uncanny timing. As usual."

"Come down, Magda," Jory called up, and the trap door opened.

Callum set his phone down on the bed. Magda climbed carefully down the steps, followed by her ancient basset hound, Mr. Dick Van Dyke, who more hurled himself down the stairs than climbed.

"Esther and Hank are on speaker," Jory said as Magda cleared the last step.

"Oh, good. The gang's all here."

"To what do we owe the pleasure?" Callum muttered. He

was tired. He was sick with worry. And entertaining Magda Nutter was quite literally the last thing he wanted to do at the moment.

Magda looked at them appraisingly. "News."

"You know where Robbie is."

"No," Magda said. "Well, not technically. But I do know what happened to him."

She pulled out her own phone and pressed pay on a voicemail.

"Hey, Mags, it's Nadja. Listen. I need you to do me a favor. Robbie Cain came to my office this morning for an appointment, and shit went sideways."

The person was talking quickly, sounding out of breath, as if she was doing other things while talking.

"He's approaching his first shift. I've never heard of a wolf not shifting until the age of thirty-four, but he says that he's been a blood donor since he was seventeen, and my best guess is that the vampire venom held the change at bay? I know this is like three hundred HIPAA violations, but he told me that I needed to tell the whole story to a Callum MacLeod. He said that you knew him? He would have called himself, but he broke both his phone and his laptop this morning when the tremors began and doesn't remember any phone numbers. So I need you to pass this message onto him."

Callum's eyes were wide, and he gripped Jory's hand.

"Robbie is extremely volatile right now and needs to be around other wolves until he acclimates. He's a huge danger to both himself and others otherwise. I'm taking him to the nearest pack. They'll help him navigate his first shift. He'll be safe. The Alpha is an old friend of mine who owes me a favor. I'm gonna stay until he's settled and then I'll be back. I'm happy to talk to Mr. MacLeod about Robbie's situation when I get back, but the cell service is spotty out on the pack lands. I don't know if JJ's

gotten Wi-Fi yet and brought them into the twenty-first century or not, but I'll try my best to reach out soon."

There was a scuffling sound.

"Oh no, you don't. Don't make me strap you down, asshole. I will. Behave. Behave. Good boy."

Callum felt like he was hallucinating. What was happening?

"I gotta go, Mags. Pass it on for me? You're the best. And tell them—fucking hell. I didn't touch him! Stand down! Fucking Peep with wings! You've got to be fucking kidding me. Gah! I said—"

The line went dead.

Magda tucked the phone into her back pocket, looking at Callum with raised eyebrows. Had Callum's heart functioned the way it once had, it would have been pounding. As it was, there was a curious rushing in his ears, like he was underwater.

And then Esther's voice, crackled and hoarse through the phone's speaker, broke the silence and spoke the collective thought into the air.

"Well, fuck."

WANT TO READ MORE?

For information about this series and others, as well as bonus epilogues, new releases, and more, subscribe to Eliza's newsletter at www.ElizaMacArthur.com/newsletter.

ACKNOWLEDGMENTS

I know I say this every time, but writing acknowledgements is harder than writing books.

I would start by thanking booksellers who champion indie romance authors like myself. Special thanks to Briana, who owns Wicked Words and has been one of my greatest cheerleaders along the way, and to Jessica (owner of Swoonish Pages) and Mel (owner of Steamy Lit).

My husband is the real hero of this book. I couldn't have written, edited, or even conceived of this book without his love and support.

To my family, book nerds all, I love you.

I am once again alphabetizing my friends to thank because it makes my brain feel good. Caitlin, Danielle, Elizabeth, Em, Emily, Emma, Erin, Erin, Gloria, Jennifer, Jessica, Kels, Lara, Megan, Melissa, Nellie, [REDACTED], Rux, Sam, Sarah, Sarah, Victoria and the rest of both the MacCoven and Crane Coven, I love you to the ends of the earth.

Special thanks to Emma, for listening to me wail about this book for approximately nineteen hours worth of voice memos. I can't wait to return the favor.

As always, thanks to my editor, the unspeakably talented Sarah at Lopt & Cropt. Thank you for asking all the right questions and for your patience while I talk myself out of corners.

To my Patreon subscribers, you're fueling the dream and I couldn't do this without you.

And last but never least, to the romance readers, romance lovers, hopeless romantics, and you, dear reader.

ABOUT THE AUTHOR

Eliza MacArthur is a writer of romance and humor. She lives in the mid-south with her husband, two feral werewolf children, and dogs. She is fueled by decaf coffee and a good grumpy/sunshine trope.

She cut her teeth stealing romances from the cabinet under her mom's bathroom sink (where all good Midwestern moms kept their Julie Garwood paperbacks in the 90's.

ALSO BY ELIZA MACARTHUR

Elements of Pining

Soft Flannel Hank

'Til All the Seas Run Dry

The Laird's Holdings

Hold Fast

Visit www.ElizaMacArthur.com for more information.